MW00648068

EMBROIDERED WORLDS

EMBROIDERED WORLDS

FANTASTIC FICTION FROM UKRAINE & THE DIASPORA

Edited by
Valya Dudycz Lupescu
Olha Brylova
Iryna Pasko

Atthis Arts

УКРАЇНСЬКИЙ
ІНСТИТУТ
ЛІІКНИГИ

This book has been published with the support of the
Translate Ukraine Translation Program

EMBROIDERED WORLDS

Edited by Valya Dudycz Lupescu, Olha Brylova, and Iryna Pasko

Copyright © 2023 by Atthis Arts
Each story in this collection is copyrighted © by the story's author.

All rights reserved. Except as permitted under the US Copyright Act of 1976, no part of this publication may be reproduced, stored in a retrieval system, or transmitted in any form or by any means electronic, mechanical, photocopying, recording, or otherwise, without written permission of the copyright holders.

Cover illustration "Metahutsulka" by Taras Kopansky
Commissioned by Rhiannon Rasmussen

Cover design by Stephen H. Segal
Interior design by Chris Bell

Editorial assistance by Stewart C Baker, E.D.E. Bell, Michael Burianyk, N. R. M. Roshak, and Dimitris Tzellis

Published by Atthis Arts, LLC
Detroit, Michigan, United States
atthisarts.com

ISBN 978-1-961654-10-5

Library of Congress Control Number: 2023950483

Content notes are listed in the back of the collection.

TABLE OF CONTENTS

✦※✦

Introduction
Valya Dudycz Lupescu

What is the value of a story?

Be they myths or legends, mysteries or fairy tales, weird tales or fantasies, stories are one way people and their communities communicate who they are, where they come from, what they value, what they are afraid of, what they are willing to fight and die for.

Some of these ideas may be universal—archetypical tales reflected in similar stories around the world. Others will be specific to a time and place—capturing a moment, defining a movement, presenting the possibility of a different future.

Stories are the way we write our world into being.

So what are these fantastic stories from Ukraine and the diaspora writing into reality?

First we have to look at the context. Ukraine has long been valued for its resources, its rich, black soil, as well as its position as a "borderland" between East and West. Ukraine's history is a story of old empires and conquerors and travelers, and as a result it has a literary landscape that includes many voices: Ukrainian, Crimean Tatar, Romanian, Hungarian, Polish, and many more.

This unique position of crossroads and threshold is as rich a soil for the imagination, as is the fertile land for which Ukraine was once called "the breadbasket of Europe." If you live in a place that has often been under attack or under conquerers, a land whose people keep having to fight for their freedom and the right to exist, it is not difficult to understand the appeal of fantasy and science fiction, of mysteries and ghost stories.

Fantastic stories take the reader out of their mundane, everyday reality, and present them with an opportunity to consider the world in a new way—with wonder, with reverence, with terror . . . with hope.

You hold in your hands a collection of fantastic stories rooted in that rich Ukrainian soil. There are dead gods and time-traveling hunters, mad witches and enchanted instruments, addicted aliens and tragic scientists. Reading them in Ukrainian, shepherding them through translation, I was struck by the realization that these are stories of transformation. By luck or achievement, through wit or sacrifice, again and again the characters in these stories experience moments of rebirth, reconsideration, renewal.

Stories of transformation show us that change is possible.

In stories, we are limited only by what we can imagine: we can choose a better life among the stars, we can attain talismans that give us power over life and death, we can find heroes and justice in unlikely places. In stories, the dead may come back to visit their loved ones or to right wrongs. In stories, we can keep everyone safe from harm in an embroidered world on our baba's table.

So if stories reveal something about the people telling them, what is reflected in the mirror of these fantastic tales? Why is it important that their voices and stories are collected here and shared with an English-reading audience?

Why Ukraine? Why now?

When I was growing up in the 70s and 80s, most people outside of my family and close friends had not heard of Ukraine. *Isn't that part of Russia? Is that even a real place? That sounds like you're speaking Polish?* Not until Chornobyl did the people around me begin to recognize the reality of the country my grandparents had been forced to leave during WWII.

People heard about the breakdown of the Soviet Union, but most didn't really understand all those different Eastern European nations over there or why they were fighting each other. Even the Orange Revolution and EuroMaidan didn't make their way into mainstream awareness in America. Not until February 24, 2022, when Russia invaded Ukraine, did the world finally bear witness.

In February of 2022, Russian publishers were given the order to remove all mention of Ukraine from textbooks. Russia has been trying to erase Ukraine and her people out of existence for hundreds of years, trying to silence Ukrainian voices of the past, present, and future.

This book stands in defiance of Russia's colonial oppression. These stories give voice to the Ukrainian imagination and the Ukrainian identity.

Stories cannot bring back the dead, but they can help us to remember. Stories cannot rebuild the devastation of war, but they can paint a picture with words of what was lost and what can be rebuilt. Stories cannot conquer soldiers, but they can sometimes change people's perspectives, open their minds and hearts. Stories can show us glimpses into worlds that we have never experienced or dreamed of; and in doing so, they change the way we see the world and ourselves.

Stories are one way we keep hope alive.

Does it Exist?
Introduction by Olha Brylova, with Iryna Pasko

"Ukrainian science fiction and fantasy? Does it even exist?"
a Russian colleague asked me in September 2011.

I was stunned. We were standing in the vast hall of Karazin's Kharkiv University, in the midst of one of the biggest Ukrainian cities, surrounded by participants of the most prominent Ukrainian SF&F convention, Star Bridge. The colleague had visited that convention for 12 years in a row, since 1999. That year, like every year, several Ukrainian writers were awarded: Lyudmila Astahova from Kharkiv, Nina Tsurupa from Zhytomyr, and Natalia Shcherba from Ivano-Frankivsk. Oleksandr Zolot'ko, a writer from Kharkiv, was a chair of that convention. Oleh Ladyzhensky and Dmytro Gromov, other Kharkiv writers, were co-organizers. I was standing there, right before his eyes, a writer from Dnipro.

And still, he asked me if Ukrainian science fiction and fantasy existed.

Well, he had some reasons to ask that question. Because everyone listed, including me, was writing in Russian. And to him, a Moscovite, everyone writing in Russian was, well, Russian. That was the imperial mindset, characteristic of many people born in the USSR. And many Ukrainian authors kind of shared that sentiment. Some even emigrated to Russia, because they didn't feel like anything connected them to Ukraine.

Of course, there were Ukrainian writers who wrote in Ukrainian, and translators who translated into Ukrainian—but they did not exist in my colleague's informational bubble. He didn't read in Ukrainian (why would a man from a metropole study the language of a former colony?) and their books weren't translated into Russian, and for him, that meant they were not worth it.

Ukrainian publishers were effectively ousted from the Ukrainian market by the Russian publishing giants EKSMO, AST, and Armada. Russian books were sold in more copies, their royalties were higher, and their prices were lower. The biggest of our publishers, FOLIO and KSD, issued most of their books in Russian, just to keep up. There were some breakthroughs, like the Ukrainian translation of *Harry Potter* issued by Kyivan publisher A-ba-ba-ha-la-ma-ha, but that was a drop in the ocean. You entered the bookstore in Kyiv or Zaporizhzhia or Lutsk and saw a load of Russian books and a corner, a shelf or two, for Ukrainian literature. A publishing preserve.

And that was my fault.

Well, not all my fault, but I also wrote in Russian and published in Russia, because I didn't want to exist in a literary preserve of scarce publications and miserable royalties. I chose the wide gate and broad road. And what does the Gospel say about where those roads lead?

I had this insight while looking my colleague in the eye at that very moment. He didn't even mean to insult me, the organizers, or Ukrainians in general. He was just curious: did we really exist?

Did we?

Yes, we did. And we still do.

The main goal of this anthology is to bring Ukrainian SF&F out of the cultural cellar. We also hope to raise awareness and encourage people to help Ukrainians in need. Because of the Russian aggression, many people have lost their homes, their jobs, their health, and their relatives and friends. Everyone involved with this book has committed to putting the funds to good purpose. Thank you very much for buying this book, and please consider donating, if you can, to organizations helping the people of Ukraine.

But personally, my dear friend Iryna Pasko and I decided to join this project as editors because we wanted to help Ukraine's new authors emerge from the shadows. To reveal the unknown. To show the world that we do exist.

We have also included the works of authors of our Ukrainian diaspora. This book could not have been composed without them, and we appreciate this unity and support. Valya Dudycz Lupescu, our chief editor, did a great job bringing this book to you. But our part, as Iryna and I see it, was to bring the new authors from Ukraine, to reveal the unknown.

To speak honestly, I don't really feel like I belong here. My story, "Iron Goddess of Compassion," was a farewell gift to the Russian fandom. In 2012, when I self-published it (no Russian publisher would touch it with a stick), my Russian readers went mad, not so much about the story's premise that Russia would start a war with Ukraine, as about the statement that Ukraine would win this war. They called me a crazy Russophobe.

Two years later, "little green men" flooded Crimea, and there was nothing fantastic about them. They took Crimea, then took Donetsk and Luhansk, and made a move on Kharkiv, Dnipro, Odesa, and Kherson.

Ten years after the story was published, I woke up to explosions: Russian missiles leveled our airport. *Look, I am a freaking clairvoyant!*

My abovementioned Russian colleague totally supported what his government was doing. It didn't surprise me, for I knew he was a cunning conformist. But many Russian SF&F writers since the beginning of the 2000s fervently wrote stories and novels about a victorious Russia conquering Ukraine, Qazaqstan, Georgia, all the former USSR, then Europe, then America. I wasn't a prophet—I was but an intense reader. And I knew that the step from those wet dreams to action was just a matter of time.

The co-compiler of this collection, Iryna Pasko, is a former associate professor of Ukrainian language and literature at Oles Honchar Dnipro National University. Like most of the people we have gathered here, she has loved fiction since childhood—but for some reason, it did not even occur to her to research Ukrainian fiction professionally when she was choosing a topic for her thesis; that idea came to her later. So Iryna also cannot boast of a long-standing affiliation to the Ukrainian fantasy fandom—she started participating in its life about 5-6 years ago, with stories for contests and collections.

Her work "Rainbow Bridge" is a kind of tribute to classical Ukrainian literature of the 19th century, focused on the theme of serfdom. This literary period is often called "gloom and monotony," but this thesis is largely untrue—indeed, it is part of the imperial narrative. Serfdom in the Russian Empire was not much different from slavery, and even for those who were lucky enough to be born into this world a lord or a lady, there was always a price.

When the Hetmanate lost the last remains of its autonomy, and Zaporozhian Sich, the last guardian of Ukrainian freedom, was destroyed, Russia forced serfdom upon Ukraine. A quarter of the peasants, who weren't included in the kozak lists, were stripped of almost all human rights. Their masters couldn't sell them down the river (only with the land), but they were absolutely allowed to do everything else. And Ukrainian nobility committed that deal with the Devil. They agreed to enslave their compatriots in exchange for imperial titles and privileges—but they started losing their sons and daughters to the Empire, much like the Lady in Iryna's story, "The Rainbow Bridge."

A deal with the devil is also a motif in Myroslava Hornostayeva's story "The Stray Streetcar." Myroslava is a fantasy writer, and this particular story is taken from her urban fantasy-horror cycle "Fearful

City Z" (which means her native Zaporizhzhia—nothing to do with the nowadays Z symbol, or, maybe, another grim foreshadowing). It introduces us to the early post-Soviet Ukraine of the 1990s, a distant analogue to the Roaring Twenties in the USA, with police-mafia wars and an overall noir atmosphere. The industrial cities of Eastern and Southern Ukraine, like Zaporizhzhia, Dnipro, Donetsk, Mariupol, and Mykolayiv, create the same noir perspective. Everyone who has crossed the industrial zone after dark on a streetcar, in late autumn or winter, perfectly knows that feeling. Looking through the window at the innumerable tubes and pipes, twisted like something out of H.R. Giger's concept art and lit with the ghostly blue light of gas torches, one might expect the next stop to be "Inferno Street." And Myroslava captures that noir perspective pretty well. But the highlight of the story is the fact that the infernal tram was inspired by a poem by Nikolai Gumilev, a Russian poet shot in 1921. The hellish nightmare comes from Russian cultural space and demands its toll: your soul.

Another work which leans on a pact with infernal powers is Oleksiy Zhupansky's "Havrylovna." Oleksiy is a writer, translator, and publisher who was born and raised in the literary world—his father Oleh is also a prominent poet and translator. Together, they've founded Zhupanskyi's Publishing House, translating and publishing science fiction books by Peter Watts, Dan Simmons, Philip K. Dick, and H.P. Lovecraft for Ukrainian readers, as well as publishing modern Ukrainian writers. Gothic prose and phantasmagory are their special interests, and "Havrylovna" fits the genre perfectly. One may say that second-person narration is a cheap trick, but there is nothing cheap about "Havrylovna"—it sends shivers down your spine. Especially when you know that it's not only about a "crazy cat lady" who happens to be a witch, but also about the Soviet past and the dead hand of Imperial heritage that still demands a sacrifice.

While we're still in the territory of horror, let me introduce to you "The 'Kestrel' Travel Agency" by Tetyana Adamenko. This story

is an obvious homage to the classic story "Sound of Thunder" by Ray
Bradbury, and it also tells us about time travel. Except it is more than
that, and the main twist is not really Bradburian. And the real story
behind it is horrific by itself: "radium girls" poisoned in their work-
places, told that the paint they worked with was harmless. I don't want
to spoil the plot for you, but I think Bradbury wouldn't be ashamed of
his literary descendant.

"The Bike Shadow" by Yaryna Katorozh gives us another kind
of urban fantasy: both mystic and optimistic. It is rooted in Lviv, an
old city in the West of Ukraine, and the spirits of this city are nothing
like infernal. Rather domestic and traditional. Lviv is proud of its age,
its traditionalism and its European-ness at the same time. Those who
have never visited Lviv at Christmastime have missed a lot. And the
spirit of the Christmas miracle which resounds in this tale is what I
like the most about it.

"The Midst of Snow" by Oleksiy Gedeonov is also a miracle fantasy story, but set in the time of the Thirty Years' War, which promises
grimdark and keeps the promise. Oleksiy is a sociologist and historian, and he knows the topic well. Though he does not specify either
the country or the year of his story's events, he shows a profound
knowledge of the epoch, and that ambiguity highlights the universal
truth of the story: wars are waged by the "great people," but it is "small
people" who suffer and die. And even Mother Winter is powerless to
stop the bloodshed and protect her only child. But what she couldn't
do, a common soldier did. This is a story of hope and love amidst war
and ruin. In these times, it strikes straight home.

Max Kidruk is a rare bird in Ukrainian writing society: a
bestselling author. His recent novel, *New Dark Ages: The Colony,* is
currently at the top of the sales charts in Ukraine. He leans not so
much on the national literary tradition as on the Western genre discourse, putting acute and exciting plot above all. His story "Closest
to the Pole" is in that line: From the first pages, you root for the brave

explorers of Mars, whose stakes in a cruel race to the planet's North Pole are incredibly high. He also shows a profound knowledge of Martian geography and the environment. His story reminds me of Weir's "The Martian," albeit more pessimistic. Anyway, we hope you enjoy it.

Mykhailo Nazarenko is yet another representative of academic circles in our anthology. He is an associate professor at the Taras Shevchenko National University of Kyiv. And it shows. Not every author would make Publius Ovidius Nasō their character. In Nazarenko's telling, the ancient poet is the only one who can see the old gods of the forests and rivers, who still talks to them and writes about them. He felt the death of Great Pan in the putrid atmosphere of the Empire. Far from its fall, the Empire is rather young, and neither Caligula nor Nero are even born—but the signs of its decline are already there. Although both the poet and his friend, the young faun, could see the sign of a new hope . . .

It's difficult to say something about Olena Krasnosel'ska's "Scream." It's more a poem in prose than a tale. What's the point of talking about a poem's plot? Could you retell "Invictus" or "Acquainted with the Night?" The daughter comes to talk to her dead father at his grave, end of story. She is the pilot of a "digital ship," that's why the story is fantastic. But it is also heavily packed with images and philosophy, a real challenge for any translator, but a pure delight to read.

Ihor Silivra is renowned in Ukraine as a steampunk author. But his "Family v1.1" is closer to cyberpunk. It reminds me of Heinlein's "—All You Zombies—" except it is a philosophical dialogue by genre. In a way, it resonates with "Scream": Both stories depict a future where IT has enhanced humanity's opportunities drastically—but demanded its toll. Will humanity pay with its . . . humanity? Are those innumerable opportunities worth sacrificing what we are and who we are? Anyway, I love philosophical dialogues; I am fond of Plato, and if

xviii   *Embroidered Worlds*

you get the reference to him in the text, then you, me, and Ihor Silivra are birds of a feather.

Oleh Silin is a prominent figure in Ukrainian fandom. Not only is he a writer and a videogame scriptwriter, he is also a co-founder of the literary group *Star Fortress* and an expert for the prestigious literary contest *Coronation of the Word*. So he is not a newbie, and his story "To See Jupiter" is written with the laconic precision of a master. In a way, it raises the same questions as "Family v1.1," but from another perspective. How far are you ready to go to keep your humanity? And it's for a reason that he took an epigraph from the famous poem "You Know That You Are Human," by poet Vasyl Symonenko. And another reference one might miss: Silin's protagonist is named after another Ukrainian poet, Yevhen Malaniuk.

Ostap Ukrainets is a rising star in Ukrainian fandom. He is, actually, more of a literary scholar and a translator, and his YouTube channel "Your Underground Humanitarian" is gaining more and more popularity. But in April 2022, his fantastic story "Neptune's Day" boomed in Ukraine like no other of his works. And believe me, I wouldn't recommend it, were it *just* an acrid satire on the Russian army, written in the spur of the moment. This story has more depth to it than the place where the cruiser "Moscow" rests on the bed of the Black Sea. It is a satire, yes, and it is hilarious, but there is much more to it. This is a deep analysis of the totalitarian imperial discourse that devours its followers, and . . . read it. Just read it.

"The Last of the Beads" by Halyna Lipatova is a pure fantasy story, and it does what fantasy stories do best: studies morals and ethics under the guise of a fairy tale. And the question the author raises is the moral aspect of revenge. What I like the most in this story is the absence of that crap like "If you kill the enemy, you become the enemy" and "Revenge is futile." No, it is not. Unpunished evil goes rampant, and the heroine has no scruples about making the invaders pay. We all know the Sermon on the Mount, but sometimes revenge is the only form of justice one can have, and we learned this by heart.

With all I've written above, one might get the impression that we Ukrainians are deadly serious people who only laugh when a Russian warship goes to do you know what. But actually, we are very humorous. Even our first classic poem in the modern Ukrainian language, Kotlyarevsky's "Aeneid," is a hilarious parody of Virgil. So I am glad to present you Vira Balatska's space opera "Revenge in Pursuit" as comic relief and pure fun.

Éva Berniczky is a Hungarian-speaking author from the Transcarpathian city Uzhhorod, or Ungvár, as it's called in Hungarian. Her novels and short stories have defined the Hungarian literary canon; we are lucky to have such an author. "The Dreamers of Ungvár" looks almost realistic, balancing on the verge of "slice of life" and Kafkaesque absurdism.

Károj D. Balla, another famous Hungarian-speaking author from Uzhhorod, is married to Éva Berniczky. He is a well-known poet and a brave experimenter in prose. "In the Belly of the Dinosaur" doesn't play around the border between real life and fantasy — it kicks a reader straight across it. And don't let the title deceive you: it's not about dinosaurs.

Vasyl Dukhnovskyi is a Kyiv poet and librarian who joined the Armed Forces at the beginning of the full-scale war. He repeatedly and successfully participated in various fantastic prose contests, in particular *Star Fortress*. The short story "A Hole in the Shape of a God" is one such text written for the 2021 *Death of the Gods* competition. This ironic postmodern text begins with a picture of total, normalized regression, which is now impossible not to associate with Russians. Listen to the rustling of simulacra, the author urges. You will like it.

The text of Svitlana Taratorina included in this collection is part of the novel *House of Salt*, published in 2023, already after the invasion of Russia. Svitlana broke into Ukrainian literature with her novel "Lazarus," an urban fantasy set in an alternate Kyiv of the last century, where people coexist with whimsical mythological creatures. *House of Salt* is a multifaceted and sometimes brutal work about Crimea, the author's native land, which was occupied by the Russians in 2014. "Battle of the Gods" is the beginning of the story of the legendary Amage, the Sarmatian queen, who is one of the key characters in *House of Salt*. A girl survives where strong men die in order to start her own path and influence the destinies of many—because the salted earth does not forget anyone or anything.

Volodymyr Arenev is a veteran of the Ukrainian fandom, one of those people due to whose efforts this fandom exists. Fun fact: he has compiled another anthology of Ukrainian fantastic literature, for Poland—*The Language of Babylon*. "To the Garden" was included in that anthology, and we are glad to have it translated into English. And . . . again, while this Christmas tale carries a hint of the fantastic, it's painfully true and real.

There is so much more to say and so little space and time . . . Two years have passed since the full-scale war began. Ten years since the backstabbing annexation of Crimea. We are still here. Fighting, rebuilding, working, teaching . . . and, yes, writing.

As Askold Melniczuk, an American writer of Ukrainian origin, states: "The Russian war on Ukraine has always been a war on its language." But this time, we are going to win.

Olha Brylova, with Iryna Pasko
November 2023

A NOTE ON TRANSLATION/TRANSLITERATION

For a long time, English-speaking writers and editors would italicize foreign words. They did this to notify the reader that an unfamiliar word was in the text. Italics cast a spotlight on a particular word or phrase as being outside the norm, different, exotic for an English-speaking audience.

In recent years, there has been an increased debate about whether or not italics should be used in fiction, with the main argument being that italicizing words has the effect of "othering" the writer and their culture. In her essay "The Borderlands of Language: Using Italics for "Foreign" Words (Part I)," Jennifer De Leon writes that italics are "the borderlands of language. We let in taco, but we don't let in *pepian*. This conversation brought up ideas of access, privilege, audience, and history—specifically, colonialism."

What do colonialism and italics have to do with an anthology of fantastic fiction? It comes down to language. In a collection of stories largely written by writers from Ukraine translated into English, how we chose to translate these stories, including the choices we made about spelling and transliteration, punctuation and syntax, were thoughtfully considered. We didn't want to impose English-language preference and privilege onto a people who have already had their words and stories controlled by Russian oppressors for the better part of the last century.

Language is a critical aspect of the current war and the decades of colonial oppression that Russia has waged against Ukraine. The people of Ukraine have been subject to generations of Russification, as well as the systematic persecution of the Ukrainian culture and language. Russian propaganda has sought to delegitimize and at times criminalize the Ukrainian language.

When we started this project, we asked ourselves: How can we showcase these stories in English while still honoring the Ukrainian language? We came up with the following translation choices:

- We chose not to italicize Ukrainian words, choosing instead to normalize the Ukrainian language and culture in the context of these stories. By not italicizing, we privilege readers who are familiar with Ukrainian words, names, foods, and culture. Those who are unfamiliar can pretty easily figure out the meaning in context, or they can google for more information.

- We have chosen to opt for Ukrainian words, rather than Russian words, whenever possible and appropriate. There has been a complex mingling of the two languages in parts of Ukraine over the last several decades. While many Ukrainians were raised to speak Russian, there has been a shift by many to reject Russian as the language of the oppressor and instead reclaim the Ukrainian words of their ancestors. We choose the Ukrainian words to emphasize the fact that Ukrainian words are not the same as Russian words; they are not less cultured, less literary, less comprehensible, or less legitimate.

- When transliterating Ukrainian words, we have tried to use conventional transliteration for names and places. In some cases, the authors or translators requested a particular transliteration or word choice to help better convey the meaning of the original story.

- In translating these stories, we have tried to retain the unique stylistic and syntactical choices preferred by Ukrainian writers. You may notice a greater use of ellipses and dashes, as well as differences in traditional dialog and sentence structure from

English. Again, here we have tried to allow the readers to have an experience of the story that is closer to the original—reflecting speech patterns and conventions of Ukrainian speakers, not trying to protect the experience of the English readers but perhaps offer them something new . . . in form as well as content.

~V.D.L. 10 November 2023

EMBROIDERED WORLDS

An Embroidered World

Yuriy Vynnychuk

Вишиваний світ | Юрій Винничук
translated by Michael Naydan

In as much as I remember my grandmother, she was always sewing. At first I didn't really pay attention to her embroidering, but one time I noticed that an old cherry tree that was growing near our window had disappeared after Babusia had embroidered it. The cherry tree had completely dried up, and Dido had planned on chopping it down several times, but for some reason his hands never seemed to get to it. But now it's gone.

At that time I began to try and recall whether anything else had disappeared, and suddenly I remembered the disappearance of a wild dog that quite recently had settled in the wilderness. He wailed so awfully during the night that the entire neighborhood cursed him to the depths of hell. No one could let their children out for a walk without someone keeping an eye on them, for fear that the dog was mad. It's true that several times they tried to hunt him down, but he was either too quick or just as crafty, because all those attempts were in vain. But no one had heard him for a week already. Of course, he could have died or moved on somewhere else. I began to look through Babusia's embroidery, and on one of the pillows I saw him. Now I understood it all—everything that Babusia embroiders disappears at the very moment she embroiders it. It was not for nothing that there weren't any people on a single one of her embroideries. The sun wasn't there, there wasn't anything you'd feel sorry about losing.

I couldn't restrain myself from sharing my discovery with my grandfather. Dido just shrugged his shoulders:

"Well, what of it? I know about it."

"Then why didn't you ever tell me?"

"For some reason I always forgot. It's either this or that ... I forgot."

Then he looked at me with a warm smile and added:

"Well, good. I'll tell you about what I know. Though this was right after the war ... At that time they began arresting us. Every night they were carting off people to Siberia. The prisons were packed. They threw the young guys to the front without any preparation, without any training. They threw them right at the tanks ... Lord, how many of them were killed then! ... You know the way they looked at the Galicians ... The tiniest suspicion—and you're in the slammer. That's how they arrested me. Your grandmother couldn't find herself a place to escape from her grief. Poor thing, she walked back and forth near that prison and tried to look through everything to see if she could see me. Then once out of sorrow she was sitting down in the evening and began to embroider. She just couldn't get the prison out of her head, so she began to embroider it. She embroidered the walls around it, she embroidered the guard and the dogs. She finished her sewing late in the middle of the night ... And what kind of sleep does a prisoner get? We lie there and think about everything, we just can't sleep. When once, suddenly, it was as though everything had come tumbling down. There were no walls in the room, no stone walls of the prison—we were lying in the middle of the yard. Hey, we figured this out right away, and we made our way wherever we could ... Well, the prison disappeared, but those who put us in prison were left. We had to hide. The younger ones went to the woods, and the older ones—to the villages and farms. At that time we moved to the village. That's the way it was ... Although, we didn't figure out things with Babusia right away, that this was a result of her embroidering. We thought all different kinds of things. The people spoke about the Mother of God, that she showed pity on us and saved us from captivity with a miracle ... But after some time, I looked—and our cat was gone. 'Hannusya,' I say, 'where did our Matsko get to, why can't we see him?' When I take a look—the embroidery is lying on the table and right there is our embroidered Matsko. Then something dawned in my head. 'Well,' I says, 'Hannusya, wouldn't it be nice if you'd unstitch the embroidery?' And she answers: 'What kind of silly thoughts are these? I was going blind working so hard over it, and you want to destroy it for me?' Yoy, you think I'm gonna listen to the old bat? I took the scissors and unstitched it. Just as I plucked out the last thread I heard a meow, meow! And it's our Matsko! And he had a hungry look, because just as he saw the milk in the dish, he threw himself at it. 'Well,' I say, 'Hannusya, now you have some real tsuris! It turns out if you don't embroider something, then it doesn't disappear.' And she doesn't believe it, she laughs at me. Well, good ... Then I ask her to embroider the scarecrow that juts out in our garden. And what do you guess? She embroiders the scarecrow, looks, and it's gone in the blink of an eye! Well, now she's finally convinced of her ability. From that time on she took care not to embroider anything she'd regret losing or that might inadvertently disappear."

As it turned out later, not only Dido and I, but also the neighbors had found out about ... umm ... my grandmother's gift. Everybody began to speculate whether they'd done anything nasty to Hannusya, what if she gets angry and embroiders them? Dzunyo suddenly remembered that he once swiped a rooster from our chicken house. Gathering courage, he came to Babusia and confessed it, and like- wise brought a goose in place of that rooster. He apologized in such a manner that Babusia charitably forgave him his sin. It's true that on the next day Mrs. Buslyk ran over for that goose because it was her goose, but Dzunyo's mood didn't worsen at all because of it. It was most interesting that once again that very same goose returned to us. Mrs. Buslyk brought it and said:

"Mrs. Hannusya, take the goose, but I really beg you, if you'd be so kind as to also embroider my husband. Because that drunk will drive me to the grave."

One has to say that Babusia held that drunks were the worst, and without even thinking it over much, took to embroidering Mr. Buslyk. And what do you guess? Not a week had passed and Mrs. Buslyk ran up with another goose to ask that her husband be returned.

"Why are you bugging me?" Babusia gestured that she go away.

But my mother felt the goose and said:

"What kind of filling should I give it? Buckwheat groats or rice?"

"I'm not going to undo the embroidery," Babusia replied harshly.

"With rice and mushrooms," Dad advised.

"Good Lord," Mrs. Buslyk began to sob. "What am I now? I'm neither a widow or a maiden!"

"It seems like you're a widow," my Dido said.

"Well, who's going to wring its neck for me?" Mama asked, transferring her gaze from Dad to Dido.

"And even if a goose would kick me in the butt, I'm not going to unstitch the embroidery!" Babusia vowed.

"Ehh, I'm gonna really fuss over it—I'll chop off its head," Dad grimaced. "Here I'll take the ax—whack, whack, and it's kaput."

In the meanwhile Babusia had straightened out the embroidered cloth on the table.

"Well, take a gander—your husband turned out just like a painting. And, look, I even made his legs wobbly so it'd be obvious he's drunk. And now you want me to destroy it?"

"The ax is under the steps in the foyer," said Dido. "I had wanted to sharpen it, but I forgot."

"I'll sharpen it right now," Dad wiped his hands and started off toward the foyer.

"If you stuff that goose a la Chinese, it'll taste so good you'll swallow your fingers," Mama insisted.

"I don't like the Chinese," Dido strained through his teeth.

After Dido had been hunted down and locked up in prison again, there was a man in charge they called The Chinaman. He would amuse himself by calling in one of the political prisoners in the middle of the night and keeping him standing at attention till dawn. Because of it, Dido, after learning something new about the Mao boys, would often repeat:

"If there's going to be a war with the Chinese, then I'm going to be the first to volunteer. I have a special interest in them."

The Chinese, it turned out, were unbelievably lucky, because my Dido died before the border conflict.

"My husband wasn't so bad," Mrs. Buslyk whined. "There were times he'd go for water . . . to the store for milk . . ."

"Ehh," Babusia waved her hands, "you do the job and don't get squat for it!"

And so she undid the embroidery.

On the next day, Mr. Buslyk got drunk as a skunk, and he got under Mrs. Buslyk's skin for losing two geese for nothing.

My Babusia stretched through the window and began to shout:

"You good-for-nothing! If you don't stop, I'll embroider you again right away! And then two more geese will be gone!"

Buslyk opened his mouth to rasp out something, but, in spite of the fog in his head, he figured that it was better to keep quiet.

Then we had lunch. Momma stuffed the goose a la Chinese, and told Dido that it was according to an old-fashioned recipe. Dido was delighted and praised her:

"Eh, whatever you say, Ukrainian cuisine is the best in the world. And just for the fact that we thought up *kovbasa*, garlic ring sausage, we're worthy of eternal memory. But who knows about this now? Here, Yurko, learn so that you'll be wise and remind the world that it's in great debt to us for *kovbasa*."

Well, so I learned and now I'm reminding you.

This was the way my Babusia was, may she rest in the Heavenly Kingdom, because the last thing that she did—was to embroider herself.

Svitla
A.D. Sui

Svitla. Svitlanka. Svitlanochka. It all means the same thing—light. To Olena it means *daughter*. She squirms under the stage lights after being asked a question, a deeply personal one. "And your daughter, she had taken after you. Svitlana Vasylyk was in her own right an established ecologist. Were there signs early in her childhood that she'd be a successful scientist?"

Every interview she agrees to is always about the Garden, always about her daughter. Olena blinks slowly to carve herself some time, but a part of her is still there in the Kyiv Oblast, in a hazmat suit, the Geiger counter clicking away in the periphery. When she closes her eyes, there's only the smell of stale, recycled air, and the damn clicking. Once per second, the heartbeat of a forest becoming the Garden, becoming something else entirely.

"Dr. Vasylyk?"

But she's not there, not at the interview, not really. Olena wonders what Svitla was doing when the world around her drowned in light.

The Kyiv Oblast is a densely forested area, cut by streams and mountains too small to deserve a name. Svitla Vasylyk collects birch bark and lichen samples when the forest around her falls silent. Gone are the rock sparrows that whistle an old kolhosp song from memory alone, gone is the drone of cicadas. Svitla doesn't notice the split second when the trap shuts closed, and scientist turns captive. She's tightening a lid to a glass container when the bark around the nearest

birch unravels like a ribbon on a birthday gift. It starts at the base,
then in an even sheet it unwinds itself from the trunk, leaving behind
bare flesh. The freed bark drifts towards the sky, the pale blue sky,
higher and higher, until it disappears.

Svitla glances to her hands. The skin on her fingertips prickles
with electricity. She winces as a single sore opens on her index finger.
There's light there. There's light everywhere; harsh and unyielding. It
comes like the ninth wave, crushing everything in its path, and Svitla
is a lone schooner swept under. A drop of blood runs from the split
skin down her hand, black like her hair. She drops the glass container
and there is no sound.

витік радіації   (*radiation leak*)
негайна евакуація   (*immediate evacuation*)

It begins with those words and a missed email from the research
assistant who has been relaying Svitla's location to Olena for years
now. It begins with frantic calling and a familiar drone of dial tone
on the other end. Then comes the maddening dash to the airport, to
the offices, begging for clearances, for travel permits, for the privilege
to place herself in harm's way only to get there. Only to stand there
and bear witness. And when Olena does, a pang of scientific disappointment strikes her. She expects a shimmering light, a force field,
a membrane of some sort to separate the Garden from the rest of the
world. But it simply begins with the clicking of the Geiger counter.
The party stops and checks their wrists, all at once.

"Odd," Dr. Hryhorii Abramovych says. His brow furrows
beneath the thick sheet plastic of his visor. He's dropped his work and
graduate students over at CERN to trek through flooded plains just
to get to the zone he now calls a Garden in every form of scientific

communication. Olena has never met him before, but he acts calm enough to create at least an illusion that he knows what he's doing. None of them do, of course, but Olena appreciates the façade. Gregoriy gives a signal to stop. "Oleksii?" he calls over the general frequency. "Is your counter going off?"

"Negative."

"How odd."

Oleksii Bohdanov is ten steps behind them all, frozen in place just the same. He leads the microbiology lab over at Kyiv's International Institute and was itching to stretch out his legs in the field. He spends most of his time behind Olena, complaining of how the condensation inside his hazmat suit is fogging up his glasses and whining to Gregoriy about how the suits will probably do nothing to protect them so they should do away with them since they're at best useless and at worst a hassle.

Radiation is a stream of accelerated particles and hence cannot abruptly stop. But Olena herself is a mycologist, so she says nothing, pretends to know nothing at all about radiation and such things. Instead, she looks out into the clearing where tall grass gives way to the forest. Something scurries at the edge, bright and orange, and red—*so red*. While the men are fidgeting with their counters, she presses a pair of binoculars to her visor and squints. Instantly, she recoils in disgust.

"Dr. Vasylyk?" Oleksii's voice cuts through the rising wave of nausea. "What is it?"

Olena shakes her head frantically, trying not to puke. She claws back control from the simmering panic in her stomach. "Nothing. It's nothing. It's a fox, just a fox."

"What's so scary about a fox?"

She rolls her head back and forth, the hazmat suit too warm suddenly, too restrictive, a wave of bile rises, threatens to break free. "It's inside out. It's an inside out fox."

"You saw a dead fox?"

Oh, that would have been much simpler. "No, no, not at all, it looked at me. It's very much alive. Just inside out." Saying it out loud makes it real.

A distant memory tightens vice-like around Olena's throat. It brings up another recollection, a sequence of events that end with her summoned to Svitla's school, sitting in a cold, hard plastic chair waiting to be seen by the principal, being asked to explain why her child had chosen to draw a monstrosity instead of the assigned woodland creature.

"What did you draw?" Olena asks her daughter then, and Svitla only smiles, tracing the fox's innards on the page.

"It's a fox. It's inside out, but it doesn't mind," her six-year-old daughter sings. "Isn't it funny looking?" But there's nothing funny about the handful of psychological assessments that come next, the threats of suspension. Olena explains it's best to keep those images inside her head and curses herself instantly for shaming her daughter. If only she could tell her *yes, yes, draw and paint what you see and people will accept you for it,* but she can't because people won't, and people don't, and even she doesn't, for many years to come.

Olena tells Gregoriy, "It must be some form of radiation poisoning. It will be dead soon." By her side, Gregoriy nods along. But the fox won't be dead. Olena knows because a mother knows these things, like if her child is dead or alive. In the depths of the forest, she will find her daughter, dead, but not quite, and not quite her daughter any longer. And both relief and dread mix in the pit of her stomach.

A week later, the Garden is still too radioactive to enter. There is no cause for the radiation, no cause at all for the Garden itself. Yet, it spreads around the forest and rests there like it's the most natural thing. So, they wait.

"Come take a walk," Gregoriy says one evening and nods to the invisible divide between the familiar and the zone. Olena doesn't budge. "Just come. It's easier to show you than to explain." Gregoriy takes her by the elbow and gently nudges her through the illusive boundary. He follows closely as they take two steps, and then a few more, and all the meanwhile Olena wonders what is amiss. Only when they're fifty meters closer to the forest line does she notice the silence. No clicking. There is no radiation.

"What the—"

Gregori, hand still on her elbow, spins Olena around towards the fading sunset. "We've been monitoring the fluctuations. They do happen and they come in waves, highest peaks in the morning and rapid drops towards the evening. At night the area has no radiation, in the morning it rivals Chornobyl."

"That makes no sense, radiation doesn't have a—"

"A circadian rhythm? That's what I thought too."

Olena watches an orange disk dip below the horizon and remembers how the world used to silence itself when Svitla fell asleep, how the birds hushed, and the dog never barked, and even Olena herself wouldn't dare breathe lest she disturb her daughter. "So, then we go at night?"

Gregoriy nods and gives her elbow a squeeze. "We go tonight."

Despite the drop in temperature the hazmat suits are still sweltering and still a necessity. Even with the radiation gone there could be airborne pathogens waiting to ravage their lungs at first opportunity. "Don't touch anything," Gregoriy's steady voice comes through her earpiece. "We'll decon when we get back, but I can't be sure nothing will burrow through the suits in the moment." So many dangers lay ahead, beneath the lush greenery.

"Her last correspondence was anchored to a site not two kilometers from here," Olena says between her pants of exhaustion. "If we stop sightseeing, we might be able to get there and back in time."

Behind her, Oleksii huffs as he struggles with some roots. "I don't want us to rush. Better have a short excursion today and then push on farther in a few days. It's not like she's going—" His line is abruptly cut.

"Let's see what the trails look like first," Gregoriy says, softly, an almost apology.

Olena wants to scream at both of them for treating her with oven mitts, like she is not their senior, like she is not acutely aware of what they're all marching towards.

"When we found her, she asked me if she was made for it or if it was made for her," Olena says to the interviewer, unprompted. The blinding spotlight sends little orbs of color dancing in her eyes. For a moment she's back in her chair, a willing party to an interrogation, and then she's gone again to the oblast.

"Do you think I was made for it, or it was made for me?" Svitla asks into the night sky. A plastic visor from a hazmat suit leans over her. Oleksii touches her with gloved hands but recoils the instant rubber meets her skin.

"Pardon me?"

"Svitla wanted to know if it was—determinism, or—or *faith*?" Olena nearly swallows the word, one she's avoided her whole life.

"I don't think I understand."

Olena won't elaborate. Someone needs to understand without her having to explain every excruciating detail, prostrating herself in front of different people every other day. She understands now why the way things ended was the only way they could have been.

✥

Oleksii yells. "Do not touch her, I repeat do not touch her. She's so hot. I don't understand how she's still alive." There's clicking, maddening clicking in their headsets. They've come too close to the source, too close to death.

"It's too loud," Svitla mutters. She reaches up with her hand, up with the birch bark wrapped around her wrist, up and up, until she grabs the offending Geiger counter and silences it for good with one easy squeeze.

"The radiation is only on *her*. I don't understand," Gregoriy says. "It's like she's a small reactor of her own. It's like—Olena, no—"

Her hazmat suit comes off. Off, off goes the plastic, the zipper, the divider. It falls in one piece and on to the soft ground below, and she is bare before the onslaught of particles. Coveralls will do nothing to stop death.

"Do you think I was made for it, or it was made for me?" Svitla asks.

Olena glances to the Geiger counter in her hand, but it sleeps on. She reaches up and folds her hand over the bark. "I think you found each other, doniu."

"It talks to me, and I understand it."

✥

Olena clings to the memory, but it slips through her fingers with the grains of time, with all the lost years. Now, Svitla's tiny feet patter along the hardwood, each step accompanied by her soft sobbing. "You killed them. You killed them," she whimpers and shoves a bouquet into Olena's hands, dropping bunches of chamomiles to the floor. She wants to say she never wants to see a cut flower again, but she's five and can't articulate these things. She won't for many years to come be able to speak of the aversion she feels towards spreading flower petals or selling bouquets. She'll never find the right word for the repulsion, only that it's *wrong*. And Olena will never find words for when she holds her daughter close and feels nothing but dread.

She never gets to talk to Svitla, never gets to apologize for years of silence. Gregoriy points something, a tranquilizer gun, and pulls the trigger. A massive shudder passes through the forest, like it feels the needle puncture the same as Svitla. And Svitla's eyes, black as the black sky they stare towards, are wide open as she falls unconscious, and Olena can't help but doubt that this is good and right. There is no relief on Svitla's face and none in Olena's heart.

And then there's Svitla at five years old, round faced and grinning, climbing trees in the park, racing snails. And there's Svitla now, dying on a field hospital gurney, wires and tubes running from her pale body. Olena can't reconcile the two images in her mind, can't understand how her daughter got from point A to point B, how she ever survived or why she's resting in a lead-walled room.

Olena watches Svitla through the tiny window in the door. Her daughter is too radioactive to be near. She really is a small reactor core, like she's always been—a knot of energy and frustrations that Olena didn't know how to manage. Everything in her aches to escape. Nothing has changed. But now this energy has no internal source, rather it flows from the Garden to Svitla even now that she's dozens of kilometers away.

And the Garden itself has been withering with her departure. It's been throwing radiation plumes in violently random directions, threatening to strike a city. It's been bubbling and expanding, and shrinking, and shrieking, like an infant taken from the breast of its mother. Olena can't find a rational reason for why the two are related, but she knows they are. She's not here to decipher the origins of the Garden. She's here to keep her daughter alive. She's failing.

With the dose of radiation Svitla has received, she should have died on the spot, but her organs appear intact, better than intact, untangled and then woven back together, the doctors say—a miracle of science. But a mother cares little for scientific curiosities, for a forgotten god she's worshiped, for all of medicine and all the people. "We have to take her back," Olena whispers.

It's all a contradiction. So is Svitla. She'll call it a mother's intuition, she'll cite superstition, but deep inside forms a conclusion far more damning. Svitla is linked to the Garden, in the way an albatross senses the magnetic field of the earth, in the way a bee communicates directions in dance. She must be, to have survived its violent creation relatively unscathed. Now the Garden calls her back. "She has to go—" Olena doesn't add home. It will be home now, the only place where Svitla can exist. Olena will never hold her daughter again, never wrap her arms around Svitla's narrow shoulders. But that's no different. She hasn't in twenty-four years, she hasn't since her daughter shrugged them off for the final time with a frown on her still chubby face, and Olena drowned her exhalation of relief with maternal shame. By the time Svitla was five, Olena stopped telling herself she was a bad mother.

There is letting go and there is abandonment and Olena doesn't know which one she's doing. Who is the one being abandoned, left behind? "She has to go back," Olena says with finality. Svitla will live. She will thrive in a place that is wild and distant and strange, just like she is. Olena calls the doctors to pull all the plugs and stop all the drugs. She signs all the necessary papers with steady handwriting as they glare at her as if she is an executioner. She bears it.

She knows better. Svitla will live, even if Olena has to carry her back to the Garden in her own arms as her own skin sloughs off from radiation. She's carried her so many times, what's another? Another touch, another hug, another whisper of I love you never returned. Now it's all memories and nothing concrete, caught somewhere between the ideal of a daughter Olena thought she would raise and the child she did.

"I took her back," Olena says, and the bewildered interviewer stares at her, like she just confessed to murder. "I took her back because she couldn't survive outside. Not anymore. I don't think she ever could. She—Svitla was a difficult child, good, but difficult. We never did find a language we could both understand. The Garden—" She searches for words and the damn anger swells. She doesn't want to explain. She wants them to just *know*. Words fall short.

At first, it's all scattered. Svitla rests on the forest floor. Pale body against dark green moss. The cry of a sparrow. A squirrel sits on a rock, watches the two women with glassy eyes, and judges. Olena waits for her daughter to breathe deeply, waits for her to wake up like Sleeping Beauty from her curse. It's all random, until it's not. Olena knows that given enough observations we can make patterns in any-thing, but the pattern here is not superficial, nor organic.

Svitla makes the pattern. She doesn't open her eyes when she awakes. A small smile stretches along her cracked lips, her mouth opens. She sings a hoarse melody. Up and up rises her voice, to the treetops where the sparrows nest. She sings and sings and a moment later, the sparrows sing the melody back to her. The birds sing for her, the moss reaches for her limbs, the sky above opens up and shines like a spotlight on the very spot they are. Svitla is home and home welcomes her with open arms.

"You always let me sleep in," Svitla says, a small smile playing on her lips.

Olena watches her daughter sit up and cross her legs. A sparrow perches on her shoulder. Olena sees the bird has no eyes. "You always looked so peaceful," she says.

"I'm sorry, Dr. Vasylyk," the interviewer breaks through the memory. "You never answered my question."

"What was your question?"

"Your daughter—"

"I tried, doniu," Olena says softly, her eyes drifting to the Geiger counter, still dead in her hands.

"Don't worry, as long as we decide it's ok, it won't stir."

"We?"

Svitla nods. She reaches out with her hand and the bark from the nearest tree unwinds and floats towards her. "Again, you weren't listening. You always do that."

"I thought—"

"You thought it was a poorly worded joke, thought I was the one who didn't understand what was happening?"

Olena purses her lips. "It's me who doesn't understand."

Months later, now in the interviewer's chair, she realizes it was the moment in the clearing when she severed herself from her daughter, when the umbilical cord that held them together finally snapped. A build-up of tears threatens to break through, but she reels it back. She's a proud woman. She's a proud scientist. But she's no longer a mother.

Svitla invites her to follow through the birch trees. As they pass, bark floats around them, pulsing like veins do through the body. Such veins run along Svitla's arms and legs, black and reaching. "You don't need to understand," she says and gives the sparrow a pat on its blind head. "I never asked you to understand. That would be cruel."

Olena remembers grabbing Svitla's hand too tightly, Svitla only eight.

"I heard you all those years, you know," Svitla says. She rests her hand on a tree trunk and points towards a beautifully burgundy lake.

Olena winces at the color.

Svitla smiles and the lake turns clear. Clouds float—inside like she's taken the sky and brought it to earth. "Dear Lord in Heaven, please cure my child—"

"Enough," Olena grabs her daughter's hand, only to find that she can easily pierce it if only she used her nails. Svitla's skin is pale, fragile, like parchment paper. Olena's Geiger counter ticks exactly once. "I was young, and—"

The sparrow takes flight. In the corner of her eye, Olena sees a flash of its orange wing.

"Everything you hated me for—" Svitla raises her hand to silence Olena before she says a single word. "Everything that made me odd, the Garden wants. I don't know what it really wants, but it wants me, at least for now. And that's something—" Her lip trembles and a single black tear falls from her round eye. "I think it's time for you to go."

"I would be an awful mother to leave you here." What Olena wants to say is that she would gladly die as her daughter had, die but not quite, rather than leave this place, this Garden.

Olena's been digging her nails into her knees. She wants to tell the interviewer *and then I woke up three kilometers away from the zone and I waited for days, but the radiation never subsided, so we were made to pick up and leave. No amount of begging and threatening did anything.* She unclips her microphone, still squinting under the punishing lights.

"Dr. Vasylyk—" the interviewer calls for her, "—what became of your daughter?"

For a moment Olena pauses to explain, but the moment passes. She lets the silence linger too long. "I won't be talking about my daughter," she says at last into the empty room and pulls the microphone from her collar.

Svitla. Svitlanka. Svitlanochka. It all means *daughter.*

This time Olena comes alone, and the boundary is just as invisible as it was that first day. She holds a Geiger counter in her hand and takes a step past the threshold. One click. She takes another step and another. She doesn't understand why the counter turns dormant after the first step. She doesn't understand what the Garden is or what her

Svitla is now, or what they can be together. And she doesn't understand her role in any of it, but Olena walks towards it anyway.

Because Svitla had been right, and she doesn't need to understand—she never did. Olena tosses the Geiger counter aside. There is no sound when it hits the ground. Warm light surrounds her as she crosses the threshold to the forest. It prickles at her skin like laughter.

Svitla looks up, only two days old. She laughs and it's the most beautiful sound in Olena's world.

The Garden welcomes her.

Havrylovna

Oleksiy Zhupansky

Гавриловна | Олексій Жупанський
translated by Kateryna Darchyk

It's hard to remember when it all started. It might've begun on that gray sodden day when you were still in middle school—the holidays that you hoped would last forever had ended, and the third, longest and most depressing term that always caught you unprepared had crept up on you once again. Its end seemed putative and unreal, like a sunny May morning amid the gray winter silence.

It might've started much earlier, back when you didn't care all that much about inconspicuous signs or seemingly insignificant events that, later on, would hang around in a huge sticky bundle and sweep through your life and the lives of everyone around you with the ruthlessness of a road grader. It started slowly, almost reluctantly, rolling along the twisted road of human existence, that bundle of events, connections, causes and effects were gradually gaining speed, catching and winding other people's lives on its sticky core, and by the end of its path—which is barely discernible, if not impossible to make out, even looking backward—the bundle had turned into a giant soft orb that, slowly but relentlessly, moves through the freeways of life with a menacing chomp.

Any living person can see it even today, as long as they have eyes and know how to look. It is right there: a massive gray orb with greenish and pink flecks that glisten dimly in its translucent, murky guts. Breaking the horizon, the orb is rolling gloomily through our cities, our streets and, ultimately, our destinies and our lives—it approaches slowly, heavily and inexorably, subtly pushing out the walls of our apartments and the palisades of our ideas and worldviews. And, while perhaps not everyone can see it, there's hardly anyone who doesn't feel it, its sticky oppressive presence is hard to ignore, and almost impossible not to notice when it runs through us, seeps into us, picks us up and carries us away, turning us into yet another pink or greenish speck in its sludgy insides . . .

Although, if you think about it carefully, it probably started there and then:

You have always been a person of principle, everybody knew it and you were often praised for it. People said that in our uneasy, or even—why lie?—simply difficult times, very few people have strong moral values, such as propriety, generosity, loyalty, compassion, honesty . . . Not many knew, however, that you weren't too familiar with those latter qualities yourself. If you, in addition to having principles, were also honest, sympathetic, kind . . . then, perhaps, your life might've gone differently. Unfortunately, of all the listed virtues, the only thing you ever really had were your principles, which, in hindsight, aren't as important as they seem, especially compared to honesty or kindness.

That winter, when the adults so often talked about Havrylovna and her cats, you listened and listened to them being enraged with her, tutting over her having completely lost her mind and having made the communal hallway such a mess that it was impossible to get through—piles of bowls with dried moldy soup, containers with chunks of the cheapest, already blackened, sausages, newspapers with drying fish carcasses, even more newspapers with gnawed chicken bones and who knows what else—in brief, Havrylovna's love for homeless cats was really yanking everyone's chains. It was the middle of winter, cold and freezing, and with everything going on, even humans didn't always have something to eat. The news channels were flooded with reports of yet another person freezing to death without heating, or of lonely retirees dying of starvation quietly and unnoticed, found a month later when the stench had hit the entire floor.

And there she was, feeding street cats as if fattening those parasites. If she was able to afford it, if she had any spare food, she should've been feeding the poor pensioners, and let the cats fend for themselves.

However, Havrylovna had her own take on the situation and didn't want to hear anything about lonely, hungry retirees or their lack of heating due to arrears. Havrylovna didn't tend to like people. Unlike cats, humans didn't arouse empathy in her, and neither did they elicit any kind of trust or sympathy. What's more, the events that were to follow would prove that Havrylovna's mindset had many reasons indeed.

The woman herself didn't evoke any positive emotions in people, and no one would think to sympathize with her perpetual loneliness: she was always on her own and either didn't have children or they didn't stick around, and she had no other known relatives—all she had was cats. Even so, it was precisely the cats that made everyone dislike Havrylovna so much. What was causing particular annoyance was that none of the neighbors who lived on your floor, not to mention the entire block, could do anything about a single person and a bunch of cats who seemed to appear out of nowhere—no matter how many times you'd close the door into the building, or how tight a spring or a bungee cord Uncle Yura from the first floor would put on the doors, those wretched cats still managed to sneak in and hold their feast under Havrylovna's door. Needless to say, everybody tried to drive them away, but once they managed to reach Havrylovna's apartment, the task became a hundred times more difficult. She seemed to have surprisingly sensitive hearing since, as soon as someone tried to get the cats out from under her door, she would jump out into the hallway and start wailing hideously—so, naturally, the adults tried to steer clear.

The scumbags from the sanitary epidemiological station weren't helpful either—you were charged for the call out, plus you paid for each individual cat caught, and surprisingly enough, there were no fools willing to shell out for the entire floor, not to mention the whole block. Besides, as the adults said themselves, no one actually wanted to bear the burden of getting rid of those cats—everybody hoped it would work itself out somehow, that the cats would eventually find another spot or, even better, that Havrylovna herself would disappear together with her cats. Then the problem would be solved and they wouldn't be involved in any of it because, despite appearances, everyone did fear Havrylovna and those curses she would put on you when defending in a fit of pique her right to feed the strays.

That was when you stepped into the spotlight. Remember? Well, of course you do! You've always had a good memory—good enough for both memorizing school work and remembering incidents like this one, especially because they are so hard to forget. Tired of the endless whining of your parents and the neighbors, who all spent their evenings discussing what else Havrylovna had been up to that day and whether the cats had come again, you finally decided to take the matter into your own hands. You were genuinely surprised by the helplessness of the adults, as well as annoyed by their constant complaints about Havrylovna and her cats. It seemed to you that Havrylovna, like an evil fairy-tale witch, had cast a spell on your floor, your block, your entire building and all the adults therein, so they couldn't do anything about it—only holler and grumble all day long when they, in fact, had long ago made peace with Havrylovna and her cats. You were the only one not affected by the curse, and therefore, it was you who had to put an end to it.

Or so you thought when you decided to come in and save the day. And the day was easy enough to save unless, of course, you were under the evil spell of the witch Havrylovna. To save the day, you simply had to go to one of those weird bazaars that sold everything there was to be sold, from small white worms stored in liter jars to strange old devices that assistant scientists had, maybe out of hunger, once brought from their secret underground laboratories and were now trying to pawn for at least a few hundred hryvnias ... You were very familiar with places like that so, having invented a little tale about a rat disaster for the sympathetic old man who sold all sorts of chemical junk that was past its "best before" date, you managed to acquire some grayish powder—according to the man, it was tasteless and odorless and that was exactly the thing to go with.

You believed the old man straight away, for the sudden playful gleam in his withered eyes and the slightly inappropriate crooked smile were more of a tell than anything he could say out loud. And that weird last phrase he yelled at you—"It's good stuff, you'll see"— finally convinced you that everything should work out. And there you were, walking through the hallway and, as always, inhaling that peculiar stench that could only be a stale mixture of fish carcasses, soured milk, dried chicken and pork scraps, and other gunk you would rather never have smelled. Trying not to breathe through your nose, you followed the old timer's advice and shook the powder out onto the cats' banquet table that stretched along the walls on both sides of Havrylovna's apartment door.

And then, the day after, the news broke that all of Havrylovna's cats had died in one night and you found yourself surprised because, in the depths of your principled soul, you weren't entirely convinced that it would work and that everything would be this simple. However, that wasn't the main thing—just as the news spread, you noticed with shock that almost every adult in your apartment building, and even some children, somehow immediately flipped their attitude towards Havrylovna and her now-dead cats, and everybody was miserably shaking their heads and wondering what a soulless reprobate could've done such a thing. Then they looked at each other in their own special way, clicked their tongues and muttered, "Poor old woman."

Obviously, no one thought of blaming you, not even Havrylovna. Because when many of the apartment doors, which were all covered in the same black or burgundy leatherette, got covered in strange scribbles and inscriptions in chalk, your door was one of the few that remained untouched. Those scribbles were all very similar to each other but differed in details and never repeated themselves. They were also surprisingly difficult to wash off—the neighbors had to scrape at them with soap and bleach, which meant the pungent smell of chlorine for a while replaced the stench from the cat food in your block.

"Another hooligan gang"—the adults were awkwardly averting their gaze from each other when, in fact, they all knew, or at least guessed, that the inscriptions had been left by Havrylovna, who herself had become even weirder after the cat incident. For several days in a row, she went out into the yard, where she would wail and curse everyone around her, after which she seemed to have calmed down and became nothing more than a quiet, silent shadow that sat next to the neighborhood utility building until dark. The adults who were coming back from work would bypass the building and look away, while Havrylovna, on the contrary, stared intently at anybody who passed her by, muttering something in a low voice and spitting bitterly on the frozen dead earth.

It didn't last for long though because, within a week, Havrylovna died. To everyone's surprise, she left quietly and unnoticed, even though everybody thought she would die the same way she'd lived: slowly, loudly, with scandals and curses. But suddenly, she was gone and your building was enveloped in some inexplicable, gloomy apprehension. No one could say what exactly they were waiting for, but everybody seemed to be persecuted by a feeling of indescribable guilt that was liable to erupt into something evil. Then, the first deaths happened. And the worst thing was that those deaths were absurd accidents: someone was hit by a car, someone else fell down the stairs and drunkenly hit their head against a wall, someone was taken away in an "ambulance" after a heart attack but never brought back, someone had an old ailment that finally took its toll, and someone just disappeared mysteriously, but somehow everyone subconsciously knew they would never see them again.

All those events kept happening for nearly a month, and you, despite all your principles, got really scared. The adults were even more frightened than you but, guided by their own adult rules and rituals, pretended that everything was fine, everything was normal and that it was just a stupid coincidence, one of those things that happen in life and you just have to wait for them to pass. But nothing passed, the building was gripped by the same indescribable expectation of an upcoming disaster, which, by tacit agreement, no one talked about out loud but everyone could feel. That's when everybody recalled the scribbles Havrylovna—nobody could doubt it was her doing anymore—had left on apartment doors before she died. Now that people remembered, they were even more terrified, especially since all the deaths had some connection with the marked apartments. Many neighbors got so scared they even frantically attempted to sell or exchange their apartments, but were then told that it wouldn't help all that much, while others finally found themselves able to breathe a sigh of relief. Your parents seemed to have relaxed a bit too, considering that your apartment hadn't been marked by those deadly scribbles.

You, unlike your parents, were getting more and more afraid because no one, except for you and perhaps the old man who sold you that damned poison, knew who was really to blame for the cats' death and, although indirectly, for the death of Havrylovna herself, not to mention all the other deaths that had rolled through your apartment building in a sticky gray bundle. No one knew apart from you, the old man and Havrylovna—after all that had happened in the last month, you were almost sure that even if the witch Havrylovna couldn't see and know everything while she was still alive, in the afterworld she would definitely find out who was really to blame for it all, who stirred up all the trouble. So you started spending your days waiting for something bad to happen, for the death toll to finally reach you. Still, other neighbors kept on dying while you were safe and sound.

Later on, you convinced yourself that the devious Havrylovna, who already knew everything about you, had decided to use you as the icing on the cake and was now keeping you on your toes with this terrible expectation of the inevitable. You became gloomy and lonely, you hardly slept, and when you did manage to fall asleep, you had such nightmares that staying awake became your only option. However, the strange thing was that Havrylovna herself never appeared in your nightmares—instead, there was always a weird house that looked like an empty factory and you had to do something there, something disgusting and unpleasant, but at the same time crucial and inevitable.

Only after, when those intrusive night terrors became regular, did you finally figure it out. It wasn't enough for the cunning crone to simply kill you, as she had already done with a dozen people from your building—no, she had prepared something way nastier. She had her own plans for you that she hinted at repeatedly in your nightmares, which had already turned into a routine, but a routine that strained you harder and harder with each passing day, and eventually you started fearing that she would put you to the sword with nightmares alone. But no, she didn't want you to crash and burn, she'd prefer to have you servile instead—you somehow knew it after yet another nightmare that had finally shown you exactly what was required of you.

Following that last dream, the nightmares suddenly stopped, and you then knew what to do to atone for your guilt and to appease the terrible Havrylovna. You realized that the ominous building from your dreams was none other than the unfinished apartment building that stuck out like a dingy gray box in the middle of a field on the outskirts of town. It was believed that something bad had happened there, more than once even, so the place was securely cloaked in a shroud of infamy and even the homeless and the drug addicts would always keep clear. Guided by the hint from your dream, you picked the abandoned building to set up a secret place, a hidden sanctuary— an altar for Havrylovna. It is still there, at a dead-end in the tangled labyrinth of a basement, in that strange room with a bright green fleshy nettle bush in the corner and a rusty piece of rebar dug into the center of the clay floor: a cardboard box with a rough portrait of Havrylovna that you drew from memory with a black sharpie. And although everybody knows that you are a piss-poor artist, the portrait did turn out a bit too scary for your liking, so you tend to avoid looking at it altogether.

Frankly, Havrylovna appeared much more frightening in your drawing than she ever was in real life, but you rightly believed that the portrait was of her in the *underworld* and therefore, the ominous black hollows of her eyes and mouth, along with *all the other features*, were appropriate. You placed four candles on the four sides of the portrait, because you couldn't imagine an altar without candles. Then, to appease the all-seeing Havrylovna and not end up like your dead neighbors, you started making sacrifices to her. Small at first, just trivial gifts—a few beetles, a ball of worms that wiggled out after a warm spring rain, a chicken from the neighboring yard that had gotten tangled in thick lilac bushes and that you found by accident and immediately dragged to Havrylovna's sanctuary. You were taking a long time with the offerings and the nightmares had started bothering you again, with Havrylovna's shadow now present in them, and that terrified you more than anything.

Bringing a new offering while turning your gaze away from the hideous portrait in the square of lighted candles, you always mumble the same thing, "This is for you, Havrylovna," and spit on the compacted clay floor, just like Havrylovna always did. Then you blow out the candles and leave. You secretly have a naive hope that when the time comes again and you show up with another sacrifice, you won't find the altar there—stray dogs, vagrants, junkies, or even some young underfuckers, doesn't matter who—someone will have just destroyed the temple to the irksome witch and then, you can feel it in your gut, the evil spell will be broken and you will be freed from your terrible duty. Despite your hopes, the blasted altar is always there, and so you keep coming every month and bringing new victims with you.

But that's not even the worst of it, is it? Havrylovna's hunger is growing, just as your fear of her is, and she rarely wants chicks and hatchlings anymore, she is no longer satisfied with the kittens and puppies that you sought out for her with great difficulty—she needs something more. She follows you in your nightmares again, an obsessive shadow that arrives with a demand—she threatens, whines, blames you for ending up in the other world and complains about how horrible it is, repeats that, to comfort her a little, you have to try and bring better offerings to the altar.

To be completely honest, you have almost given in to her last command which she's been pestering you for several months with, seeing it as the only way you will be able to get rid of her spirit and of those inextricable nightmares that had become your perpetual companions after Havrylovna's death. You've already decided that you won't go to school tomorrow, instead you will go . . . No, you hate to admit it even to yourself, for it's so repulsive and inconceivable that you forbid yourself to think about it just yet. Not now. Tomorrow is tomorrow. Today, you need to rest properly and get good sleep. And somehow you feel, even know, that there will be no nightmares tonight and that you'll sleep peacefully and see dreams you haven't had since when you were a baby, dreams in which Havrylovna does not exist, and nor do her dead cats—instead, there is a strange, magical place that you once knew but have forgotten all about. Having once again seen that place in your dream, you'll start weeping, and then turn over to the other side and sleep even more soundly, right until a gray January morning crawls into your room and the alarm clock rattles on your desk, buzzing repulsively.

Geddarien
R.B. Lemberg

Zelig's grandfather liked to smoke with his window half open, even though winter's breath melted on the old parquet. When the snow on the streets turned as porous and yellow as a matzo ball, a pigeon flew into the room. It hid under the chaise, there to await compliments or perhaps breadcrumbs.

Zelig asked, "Do you think the pigeon would like some cake?"

Grandfather examined the offering from the lofty height of his chaise: a piece of honey cake on Zelig's outstretched palm. "A good one like that, he will want."

The boy clambered onto the chaise and wormed his way under the blanket, close to the old man's legs. Grandfather smelled comfortably of chicken soup, hand-rolled papirosn, violin rosin. Outside the window the abandoned cathedral still sputtered pigeons into the darkening square, and a neighboring house obstructed the rest of the view.

Grandfather said, "Do you know what Geddarien is?"

Zelig flattened a piece of cake and dropped it into a crack between the chaise and the wall. Moments later, he heard hesitant crooning from below. "No, grandfather. What's Geddarien?"

The old man closed his heavy eyelids. "These cities like ours, my boy, they have a life of their own. And sometimes, you should know," he whispered, "the city dances." Grandfather's eyes opened again: watery gray with a thin grid of red, like railroad tracks across a thawing country. "Could you bring it to me? My fiddele?"

"Grandmother says it will only make you upset." But he threw the rest of his cake under the chaise and jumped off. In the small polished wardrobe, the battered black case was buried under an avalanche of hats. Not so long ago Grandfather used to go out, dandy like a pigeon in his gray pinstriped suit and a fedora; but these days he could not even properly hold the instrument. His grumpy nephew Yankel now came to give Zelig music lessons.

Grandfather opened the creaky case, and inside it the old violin glowed, waiting for touch. "Your fiddele, now," the old man said, "is only a quarter-fiddle, and newly made. But soon you will graduate to one-half, and then to full." He stroked the large fiddle's neck with his fingers. "To this one. My father played it, and his grandfather, too." He took up the cake of rosin from the case, moved it slowly along the horse-hairs in the bow. Zelig felt the sounds this movement created, a music of honey sap upon wind, melting the heart into his bones. "Grandfather, what of Geddarien?"

"Ah. Geddarien, there's a story." The old man smiled sadly. "The houses in this city, they do not meet. They are fixed in their places. But once in a hundred years they come all together, the living houses, and they dance." He put the bow back into the case and took up the violin; his fingers shook. "And they need music then, so they call us, the musicians. My father played at Geddarien once, and I was there as well, you see, with my quarter-fiddle, and my big sister Bronya with her trombone. And my father had this violin in its case and I held onto the handle right here," Grandfather put Zelig's hand on the worn leather, "and he took Bronya's hand, and off we went. Oh, Zelig, the music was nothing I have ever heard. The houses, my yingele ... I have seen Sankta Maria spread her gray marble hands and dance, and the old Blackstone house, and this little library I used to go to, and the Town Hall—very fond of waltzing, they all seemed."

Grandmother entered the room from the kitchen, carrying a steaming cup of cocoa on a tray. "You are not telling that old tale again, are you, grandfather?" She shook her head and placed the tray in the old man's lap.

"And what's the harm in it, grandmother?" The old man blew the thin film of milk off the top of his cocoa, closed one eye and took a cautious sip.

"There are things going on in the world more important than old stories. The war will come here ... Yankel's wife says they are going to move away."

"Oh, the war," Grandfather said, not impressed. "It's going to be just like the last time. They won't harm us. Our languages, they are almost the same, yes?" The old man took another gulp, and boasted, "I played my fiddele to the generals of three different armies!" He paused, contemplative. A soft crooning voice came from under the bed, and grandmother tilted her head in suspicion. "Yankel isn't going to leave this city if you paid him. He too is waiting for Geddarien. Missed the last one ... What are you doing? No, no ... "

Grandmother bent laboriously, and looked under the chaise. "Oy vey 'z mir! An airborne rat in my house! Are you out of your mind?" She brought the broom from the kitchen and waged war on the poor bird.

A cube of sugar sat upon the kitchen table, a small shining king adored by three musicians, two old and one young. This summer the war had reached the city of Luriberg. "This war's nothing at all like the last time," Yankel grumbled; but grandfather shook his head and smiled, sipping his unsweetened tea. "You see, Zeligel, war is like this, that you drink your tea looking at the tsuker. It feels as sweet, melting in your mouth, but it doesn't go anywhere." He winked, and Zelig smiled back, his hands busy sewing a blue star onto the old man's second-best jacket.

Yankel fidgeted in his chair. "You're a mishige, old man. Haven't you seen the loons marching in their uniforms and their eyes all steely, not caring, not seeing . . . ”

"What are they, not people?" Grandfather shrugged. "They'll take off their uniforms and they will have parties. They'll want music. Just like the last time. I don't remember his name, that big guy who married. And a groiser bandit he was . . . remember?"

"They all were banditn." Yankel stared at his hands.

Grandfather turned to Zelig. "Yankel and I had played them the wedding music, the freilakhs, so jolly they gave us a big piece of lard to eat." The old man fingered the sugar cube and looked plaintively at Grandmother, busy at the stove.

"Stolen from some peasants, no doubt." Yankel murmured.

"You weren't supposed to eat it, old man." Grandmother peered into a bubbling blue pot. Potato steam rose above it, reminding Zelig of the times when he had a stuffy nose and she made him lean over this very pot, and covered his head with a towel, and told him to breathe in, deep, deep, my Zeligel, neshumele, my little soul.

"What did you want, for us to starve? We were hungry. We ate it all night."

"It was good lard," Yankel sighed, "with plenty of garlic."

Grandmother fished out a potato and banged the plate down onto the table in front of her husband. "Well, here. No lard. No butter. We're lucky to have the kartof'l."

The potato broke on the plate, yellow and mealy, puffing out sweet healing steam. Grandfather dug into the salt-cellar. He rubbed the salt between his fingers, and it made a secret sound, like a door opening in the night, like the smallest movement of bow against strings. Zelig looked up, and his grandfather said, "Do you hear it?"

"Yes," Zelig whispered.

Yankel said, "Hear what?"

"How can anyone be upset," Grandfather said, "when the whole world makes music?"

Grandmother slammed the lid and sat down heavily. Before the war, her blue pot was magic; it cooked 'pigeon rolls', cabbage with filling of meat and rice; and twice a year, gefilte fish . . .

Yankel said, "I will tell you how. Yesterday they made some yidn kneel by the Opera theatre, in the street, just like that, and the passers-by pointed fingers and laughed. That's what those blue stars mean. Now I am asking you, is that right?"

"What did the Opera theatre have to say?" Grandfather's eyes sparkled in the dim light.

"Nothing. What could she say?"

"That's not right," said Grandfather.

When the snow curdled again on the ledge of Grandfather's window, they came to make all the yidn move to the ghetto. Grandmother did not want to go. She did not want to leave her blue pot. You can take the pot, they said. She said in the other room there was a big cardboard box of her old theatre dresses, smelling of must and love letters and music sheets. You cannot take the box, they said. You don't understand, she said, I played the oldest daughter of Tevye the Milkman . . .

They shot her in the belly.

In the ghetto they lived in a single room: Zelig and Grandfather, Yankel and his wife. The windows had no curtains. Steely wind wailed outside, and the horse-chestnut scraped its frozen fingers on the glass. The neighbors came to whisper of all the old people who had disappeared; a woman with bruises for eyes said they had all the grandparents shot on Peltewna street because they couldn't work, and please hide your grandpa, it's a miracle he's still alive. She brought them a blanket that smelled of heart medicine and cinnamon, an old woman's smell.

There were only two beds; Zelig and grandfather huddled in one, and sometimes in the night they'd pretend not to hear each other cry. In the evenings grandfather made Zelig take out the old violin and play doinas. The fiddele wept in his hands, in an old man's voice, in a boy's voice, in its own voice; it sang of a shtetl, the girl with the loud voice betrothed to a rich man, that girl who fell for a fiddler, and how one night they ran away on a bumpy road in an old cart drawn by a horse that loved to eat sugar. Some evenings Yankel would play second fiddle, his fingers stiff from working in the construction sites in the cold.

When snow started turning to sleet on its way to the ground, Zelig's doinas became livelier. Yankel listened, frowning. "Soon you will want to play wedding freilakhs, boy, shame on my gray hairs. Have you been to any weddings of late?" No, even funerals now were haphazard affairs, and hushed.

The winter exhaled the last snowy breath and died. The horse chestnut plastered its newly hatched leaves on the window outside, and the neighboring house sent pigeons to clap their wings when the fiddling was done. Yankel's wife brought out her stash of tea to celebrate the spring, but there was no table to sit around, and the magical sugar cube was lost.

One late afternoon Yankel's wife did not come home. There was a party at one of the uniformed big shots' place and you can play waltzes, they said to Yankel. They turned to Zelig too, but Yankel said, quickly, "This boy is my student. He's good for nothing, something horrible."

The door closed.

"Grandfather," Zelig asked, "Why didn't he want me to go?"

The old man spoke with eyes closed. "Some things, my Zeligel, your eyes are too young to see."

Darkness fell, but neither Yankel nor his wife returned, and the neighbors came by to whisper, whisper, whisper, until it was past time for bed.

"Wake up!" Grandfather was shaking him.

Zelig murmured, "Is Yankel back yet?" Thin music waved in the air, an outmoded waltz melody that made his feet want to move. "Is it Yankel?"

"No, give a look!" The old man pointed. Lights flickered through the dark chestnut leaves outside the window. He put his feet down. The floor shook slightly, as if invisible dancers were whirling on the unpolished parquet. "Another bombing . . ."

"No, silly. It is Geddarien!" Joy melted in Grandfather's voice like raspberry syrup in tea. "Now, quick, you must help me dress." Grandfather looked alive, for the first time in months, as if miracles bubbled right under the surface of his wrinkled face. Zelig swallowed a lump in his throat. They would have to brave the dark streets, chasing . . . looking for something that wasn't quite there. He grimaced when he thought of returning, and Grandfather's face parched and empty like the bruised-eye woman's. Better not to think about it.

He helped the old man pull the pants over his white kaltsones, and then the shirt, the suspenders, the jacket . . . "Hurry, Zeligel, please, take the violin." Grandfather slid from the bed into Zelig's waiting arms; "how good that you've grown so tall," but in truth it was Grandfather who had become little, little and white like the sugar. They were almost to the door when grandfather slapped his forehead. "My hat! The city will not approve otherwise." Zelig topped the old man's white head with the fedora, and arm in arm they made slow progress down the stairs. Nobody was awake. Outside the front door, the drain pipe dripped with the memory of rain, and an echo of music beckoned them further into the empty streets. There was no electricity in the ghetto at night, and yet the lanterns gave off flickering blue warmth. "Gas," the old man said, "Just like in the old days. We must find us a living house . . ."

Zelig soon understood what this meant when a three-storied gray building stepped out of the street's row. It stomped and pranced on the cobblestones, as if impatient to be gone. Zelig rubbed his eyes with the back of the hand that held the case; it swung awkwardly in front of his nose. Grandfather took off his hat and bowed.

"Good evening, Mendel's house!"

The dark double doors swung open, and Zelig, still disbelieving, helped grandfather in. The hallway was covered with murals, and the boy's young eyes made out pale figures, a bride with a rooster for a crown and two leaping sheep. The stairway shook and danced. Grandfather urged Zelig up to the roof, where parasite maples grew through rain-painted tiles.

"Play, Zeligel," grandfather said, and the boy took the warm fiddle out of its case. He adjusted the pegs and lowered his chin to the chinrest. The polished blackness of it creaked gently under his face, and with his ear so close, he heard the sound of the still strings waiting for music. Mendel's house moved, and the bow flew up in his hands, and lured the melody out of the night into the polished planes of the fiddle. The house jumped over the ghetto's border, broke into a gallop on the sleeping streets, leaving behind it a trail of plaster.

They found the city's Geddarien in the Market square. The arrangement of streets had been discarded, and houses large and small whirled round, embracing their dancing partners with hands of stone and glass. And there, by the dried-up fountain, two human musicians sent silver and feathered honey into the night: a young cellist whom Zelig did not recognize, and grandfather's friend Velvl with his clarinet. "Finally!" Velvl cried, "We need violins ..." Zelig sat Grandfather down on the fountain's edge. He smiled and swung his bow, and the waltz poured from under his fingers.

All round them the bright Market Square kept unfolding, a dance-floor for hundreds of houses, for churches and bakeries, palaces, libraries, humble graystones with their windows a-flapping, revealing inside sleeping figures tucked into their beds. The stone dancers moved *one two three, one two three, one two three,* and they whirled and they turned, swinging trees from the rooftops, and pigeons kept balance pretending to sleep, but they secretly flapped *one two three, one two three,* and in Zelig's hands music was magic.

The golden spiral of the waltz died down, and through the wild thumping of blood in his ears Zelig heard Grandfather speaking to someone. "It is too soon, my city, my Luriberg. I know. I counted. I wasn't supposed to live long enough to see another Geddarien."

"I am afraid ..." someone said, making words into old-fashioned shapes, "that soon there won't be any musicians left, and what kind of Geddarien is it without music?" The speaker was a warm glow wrapped around the Council Tower, and its face was the shining face of an ancient clock. "When Zbigniew rode up this hill to lay my first stone, Reb Lurie was riding behind him with a fiddle in his hands." The city itself was speaking through the tower, Zelig felt; Luriberg's face wavered, as if concealing tears. "I wanted a dance, one last dance from my yidn musicians before they're all gone."

Other houses came closer now. Good riddance, one said, and another one added, these yidn people are pigeons, thieving and dirty, and the Opera theatre said no, the music is too fine to die, but a sharp-roofed one said, there'll be music without them. Other houses wanted more waltzing and why did you stop, we don't care what kind of people they are for as long as the dancing continues.

Grandfather said, "Where is my Yankel?"

"He is not well enough to play here," said the city, "but if you want, I can invite him."

Grandfather said. "Please . . . He waited all of his life."

A black building approached, its stones finely chiseled; it was crowned by a lion that stepped on a book. Zelig inclined his head to the famous Blackstone house, and he thought that it nodded back at him, but the building did not speak. The Council Tower that was the city swung its doors wide, and the musicians waited in silence. The houses shuffled their feet.

Then a voice cried out on the tower's doorstep. Yankel's face was a doina that stopped in mid-wail. He could not walk properly. His left hand that used to hug the fiddle's neck so tenderly now hung useless at his side, and his good right hand was empty.

"Yankele, what's with you?" Grandfather pushed Zelig gently in the ribs, and the boy ran up to Yankel and helped him wobble over and sit by the old man.

"You want to know? Then I will tell you. They took all these people to kill . . ." He took a gurgling breath and leaned over, put his face in his hands. "They made me play Hava Nagila."

Grandfather pulled him close. "Your wife?"

It was some time before Yankel whispered, "Yes."

The cellist crouched and took Yankel's good hand. "Have you seen my girl there? My Gita?" No, the fiddler whispered. She might still be all right.

Luriberg's light dimmed. "Can we please have the last of the music?"

"Everything's gone." Yankel said. "We need to run. There's nowhere to run."

The Blackstone House edged closer; its lion spoke. "I can guide you to a place of safety."

"I know what you have in mind," the city said, "But they must not go yet. I have waited for eighty years."

The cellist said, "Well, I am not going, not without my libe. Later we'll try to escape together."

The clarinet-Velvl said, "I also will stay. Whatever happens, happens."

Grandfather said, "I will stay if you let my Zelig go."

"You're too old to play," the city replied, "and what kind of dancing is it without the fiddle?"

"You'll see."

The boy knelt by the old man and put his hands on grandfather's cheeks. "How can I ever leave you?" It seemed that the old man was melting under his hands, his wrinkled warm skin insubstantial like a memory.

"You must go," Grandfather said. "This fiddele wants to meet your grandchildren."

"Come with us then. Yankel's going, and you . . ."

"I cannot."

"Please. I will help you . . ." But Zelig wasn't sure he knew how. Grandfather seemed translucent, and his shadow merged with the fountain's water that spilled over to become a modest river that ran through the Market Square. Strange, Zelig thought that the fountain was dry before.

Grandfather's eyes crinkled. "It's all right. I want to play again, here in my shining gray city."

The doors of the Blackstone house wavered. Yankel hauled himself up somehow and grabbed Zelig by the hand. "Come on, come on, come on."

Zelig got up, then leaned over and kissed grandfather's wet cheek. "But how will you play without an instrument?"

The old man's lips turned up. "Oh, like this." He brought his palms sharply together, and announced, "Patsch Tants!"

The doors of the Blackstone House swung gently behind them. Outside, the clarinet swirled into the lantern-lit night, and the houses stomped their stones in tune with the music of grandfather's soft white hands.

Blackstone house was a respectable building once, a palace of commerce; he had traveled wide between Luriberg and other free living cities. In his rooms he kept shells and dark wooden commodes inlaid with mother-of-pearl; mermaids looked coquettishly out of aged oil paintings. Blackstone opened all doors wide, and swung his stairs down. "Underneath me," he said, "there are roadways of old wood and brick that lead south and west to the land by the sea. Always take right turns until a living city speaks to you from above. If you do not hear her voice, do not go up."

"Thank you, Blackstone," Zelig bowed, but Yankel was strangely docile, not complaining, not even frowning. Slowly they descended the stairs. The catacombs under Blackstone were dry and warm, and the brick floor felt reassuring beneath their feet; the walls sported a dark-red paint splashed with little gold dots. After three right turns the brick began to lose shape and the paint on the walls to chip; there were other hours and turns, and clean water that seeped through the ancient floor-slabs and pooled in the cracks as they walked. "Enough of this," Yankel suddenly said, and Zelig made him sit on the drier stones by the wall. The fiddler was out of breath, if not out of words.

"I was wrong to drag us down here. There's no point in walking further. There's nothing here. We're as good as dead. Everybody's dead."

Zelig sighed. "Well, Grandfather is still in Geddarien . . . "

Yankel looked at him strangely. "He is gone, my boy. There never was a Geddarien. I came back to the room and found you both . . . He died of starvation. White and empty."

"No, Geddarien really happened." Grandmother had died, but grandfather was still there, where the houses whirled in the last waltz; Zelig could hear them inside his violin case if he brought it close to his ear. Like a shell that caught the whole ocean inside it the violin caught the city, and if he were to play it again, the houses would spill from under his fingers and dance. "Geddarien is here, Yankel. All here inside."

The fiddler petted him on the head. "You are delirious with hunger. Perhaps tomorrow we'll have some mazl and find us a bisele to eat." He bent his legs awkwardly, as if they were soft and filled with rags. "I don't know where this tunnel leads," he whispered, "I do not remember how we got here . . ."

"I do," Zelig said. He put a hand on Yankel's forehead. It felt furnace-red, but still real. "You should try to sleep."

He curled on the cold tiles himself, but rest did not come. He cradled the violin case and listened to Yankel's kettle-thin snores, and after a while it seemed to him that he heard music come from inside the black case, a slow and sweet melody that covered his back in grandfather's gray pinstriped jacket, and grandmother's face leaned over and whispered to him, shluf, mayn kind, and he sank into the goose-down of sleep.

In the morning Yankel was cold to the touch and did not wake, no matter how much Zelig shook him. He just sat there with his face all sharp and his mouth open, revealing teeth. Zelig put both hands on the wet wall just above Yankel's head, and brought himself up somehow, fearful to touch the cold flesh. Zelig's feet came to life then and carried him away, away, further down the tunnel.

A rat darted between his legs and tripped him, and he fell face first into the dirt. He lay there for a while, empty of feelings, empty of himself. "*He died of starvation. White and empty.*" He should have at least covered Yankel's face and said shma. But he could not go back. Yankel was . . . no longer human. And what if he lost his way? No, no ... but he hugged the black fiddle-case tightly and backed out into a crawl, then clambered to his feet. The water still seeped on the floor, and he traced it back, hoping that back was back, hoping that he had not taken turns.

A tiny drumming sound grew alongside him, like chubby old fingers on glass, like rain on a coffin. He would here die, too, somewhere underneath living cities too large and important to bow down and take a look. He heard tiny squeaks now; and suddenly Yankel swam back into view, still propped against the wall, but now his half-solid form was surrounded by diners. Rats. Dozens of them, hundreds, with naked pink tails and shifting, beady eyes. Zelig could not even muster a scream; the horrors boiled over in his heart. He opened his case. The fiddle was cold under his cheek. It played nameless dances, the music of might-have-beens. It licked sounds from the semi-transparent red candy of childhood, it scraped on the residue of loss; it vibrated along the frosted windows of winters, tip-toed over rooftops to glide the bow over the moon.

The rats were gone. Zelig's soul poured viscous and heavy, back into his hollow clothes. The boy put the fiddle back home and said shma for Yankel, but his voice rang inhuman after the fiddle's.

The corridor stretched before the boy again; endless, lightless. He put his right hand on the damp wall and walked where it guided.

Days later—or was it weeks? months?—he heard a voice, a gentle voice from above. *Caro mio, não percas a esperança.* A woman was speaking. Was that the city? Her voice of stone mingled with salt water in his eyes, and Zelig walked on blinded, trailing fingers over the wall. Light blinked uncertainly; he dragged his eyelids open. A square of sunlight spread its promise on the floor by his feet.

"Here you are!"

Zelig tilted his head up. The movement made him suddenly dizzy. A girl's face peered through the grating. "The city sent me to look for you." Zelig sheltered his eyes against the unfamiliar sun, but he could not make out her features. The girl shouted to someone, "Boruch! Borya! Come here quick!" He heard the long scrape of the grate being moved. He wanted to say something, anything, but could not draw a breath. The world tilted.

When he came to, he was sitting on a small piece of cloth under a white awning, overlooking the ocean. Everything was full of sound; in the harbor, ships spoke to each other in a language of metal and rope, and the breeze played a lazy melody tilting small boats in the water. Gulls and pigeons strutted on the pier, waiting for pieces of bread, pieces such as he held in his hand. He bit into his bread hastily, afraid that the world was unstable yet; but it was real enough.

"And a good day to you." The girl that had found him now sat by his side. She was older, maybe sixteen, seventeen; she had a nose like a potato, and laughing brown eyes. The most beautiful girl in the world, he thought, but said nothing, his mouth full of bread. "I am Reyzl, and this is my brother Borya." The youth beside her had the same face, only sadder and thinner somehow. "Is that your fiddle?"

"Yes," he said. "I am Zelig. From Luriberg. Where are you from?"

"Oh. Malin." Into Zelig's confused eyes she added, "It's a small town near the border. We've never been to Luriberg, but we heard . . . "

"How did you escape?" Zelig asked, a bit more harshly than he intended.

"Malin's kosciol sheltered us. Her name is Sankta Elzbeta."

Zelig gulped. "A church saved you?"

"Yes, us and some others. We hid in the basement. Malin is a small town, you see. Only four living buildings. Luriberg, now, Luriberg must be so big. I heard that once every hundred years there is a thing called Geddarien . . ."

Zelig interrupted, his mouth dry. "How many yidn survived in Malin?"

"More than half, I think. Two hundred are here now, waiting to sail to America."

The serious boy spoke up for the first time. "How many survived in Luriberg?"

"I . . . I don't know about anyone else."

Reyzl frowned fiercely, and said, "Well, you're coming with us, of course. I play the clarinet, by the way, and my brother is a fiddler like you."

Borya said. "I lost my fiddle . . ."

"Maybe it's for the best," Reyzl said, "It's not good for you to play. He gets too excited, you see, and he has a bad heart," she explained to Zelig.

". . . but I can sew pants."

"Our grandfather went to America once," Reyzl said, "he came back, said it was a poor country. He brought back a sewing machine and he taught us."

"I will work hard and buy me a new fiddle."

Reyzl sighed. "But who knows if they even need musicians there . . ."

"What are they, not people?" Zelig shrugged. "Everybody wants music." Even the people who kill do, he thought, yes, even the stone-clad cities.

"Everybody wants pants," Borya said. "That's for sure."

"Would you like to play a bit now?"

Zelig nodded. "Of course! Anything but Hava Nagila." When he saw Borya's haunted expression he added quickly, "I can show you this melody. Patsch Tants for clarinet and hands."

He took Borya's palms between his own to teach him his grandfather's music.

Neptune's Day
Ostap Ukrainets

День Нептуна | Остап Українець
translated by Oksana Katsanivska

1.0

Twenty-year-old conscript Vanka Vanyukhin died at midnight, the very moment when April 13th turned into April 14th. He was heading to the main deck to get some cold night air and clear his head from the oily machinery fumes that permeated the holds of the decrepit cruiser. In his thoughts, he was already savoring the salty breeze, casually shifting his legs on the stairs that had shed dozens of layers of equally gray paint when suddenly, a fire erupted from all sides, consuming him and taking him away. Vanka Vanyukhin transformed into fine dust in the gusts of the salty breeze and woke up in his bunk.

He took a few minutes to recover from the shock and let his cold sweat become just regular sweat in the resuscitating atmosphere of the iron hold. Then he swung his bare feet onto the familiar rough rusted floor and sat up. The voices of his fellow servicemen, Vanka and Vanka, who had just two days left until their demobilization, echoed behind the bulkhead. Of course, they were discussing the upcoming Immortal Regiment parade and joyfully sharing their plans.

"Damn, neither of my grandfathers served in the army," Vanka complained. "One had flat feet, the other had some fucking sinusitis. So, I thought about it and decided to carry Yakob Millerov's portrait."

"Who the hell is that?" asked Vanka with grave surprise. It was obvious that he had never ever heard of that Yakob Millerov guy before.

"Are you fucking kidding me?!" Vanka barked. "He was a

legendary Soviet captain! They even made a damn movie about him. He got wounded in the midst of an operation in the enemy's rear. And then, damn it, a brand-new 'Tiger' targeted him. All Millerov had was one TT pistol and five rounds. So, he fucking destroyed two SS armored divisions with that TT pistol, and accidentally killed a sniper in the neighboring village with a ricochet."

"Holy shit! That's insane . . ." astonished Vanka uttered.

Stunned silence, saturated with gossip about Yakov Millerov's act of bravery, hung in the air. But deep down, Vanka understood that something was off. Poorly oiled wheels slowly turned inside his head. Thoughts—like cockroaches—scurried through his mind, trying to find the forgotten word.

Déjà vu.

A déjà vu ("a glitch in the Matrix when they change something") was clenching Vanka's heart with its icy fingers. He had already heard this dialogue. In that very dream where he died. Right after waking up. But was it really a dream?

Vanka touched his face, feeling the soft, youthful stubble. He hugged himself by the shoulders and opened and closed his mouth several times. Then, with his usual gesture, he slid his hand between his buttocks to check if the bottle of vodka was stashed where he had left it. The bottle served as his totem (he had picked up this technique from Nolan's "Inception") and was firmly in place, just as he had fixed it. So, it wasn't a dream. But what had happened before this?

The conversation behind the bulkhead continued.

"Imagine if they make a fucking movie about our cruiser!" Vanka mused dreamily. "Just like that *Crimea* movie."

"I bet they will," Vanka replied. "We're the flagship, damn it. The fucking pride of the fleet!"

"Damn, I want to be played by Kozlovsky. Or Bezrukov . . ."

"No fucking hope! Bezrukov is a fucking Actor! With a capital 'A,' damn it! Bezrukov should only play a cruiser . . ." Vanka chimed in.

"Damn, Vanka, you scared the shit out of me!" Vanka clutched his chest. "But I swear, that's exactly what I was going to say! Word for word, damn it! Who are we to be played by Bezrukov? You gotta be a damn hero for that."

"I knew you were going to say these exact words," Vanka whispered conspiratorially.

"What the fuck do you mean?"

"I fucking mean that all this has already happened," Vanka replied in an even more mysterious voice, raising his finger meaningfully. "Déjà vu!"

"Vanka, what déjà vu are you fucking talking about?" Vanka waved him off. "Damn, why are you even bothering us with this nonsense? Isn't it time for your fucking shift?"

"Not yet," Vanka snarled, looking at his grandpa's watch.

Vanka's grandfather—unlike Vanka's and Vanka's—had actually fought and left his grandson five real trophy watches, both men's and women's. So Vanka had every reason to consider himself superior to his two neighbors. And that's why their disrespect hurt him so much. After all, he did everything right—as soon as he suspected the time loop, he immediately tried to convince others that he knew what would happen next. And what did they say to him? Fucking grandpa-less assholes.

Offended, Vanka forgot that he had wanted to go to the upper deck to breathe in some cool night air, and wandered through the dark hold instead. After pacing the length of the ship several times, he finally understood why he was drawn to the stern, where the artillery ammunition was stored. There, in the corridors, he could sense a faint scent of tobacco smoke. It was a nearly forgotten smell for Vanka as his cigarettes had run out several weeks ago. As far as he knew, everyone else's were all gone, too. This was the first whiff of tobacco smoke he had sensed in many days.

He tried opening all the doors and even a wall that looked like a cracked door because of the separated welding seam. Nobody. Nowhere.

Vanka was already beginning to convince himself that the scent of cigarette smoke was his imagination and that he was losing his mind because of the déjà vu and several weeks without smoking. Then, finally, one of the doors yielded. Inside, sitting on a tall box of naval artillery shells was the cruiser's Captain, His Majesty's Anton Kuprin. Spotting Vanka, he instinctively threw the cigarette butt over his shoulder, jumped to his feet, and stood at attention—old army reflexes never die. But after realizing that it was just an ordinary seaman Vanka, he angrily narrowed his eyes and began to hiss, "Listen, you, bastard . . ."

He never finished though. The fire that suddenly flared up behind him instantly consumed both Captain Kuprin and Vanka, and took them away.

2.0

Twenty-year-old conscript Vanka Vanyukhin died at midnight, the very moment when April 13th turned into April 14th. And then he woke up in his bunk. The ship was swaying differently than the last time, but now Vanka had no doubt that it wasn't déjà vu. It was a new twist of the time loop.

He needed to act smarter. He had to catch the two Vankas even more off guard and say something that would make them believe him immediately. Because what he had done last time, jumping out of nowhere with his Bezrukov, was really stupid.

"Damn, neither of my grandfathers served in the army," Vanka complained. "One had flat feet, the other had some fucking sinusitis. So, I thought about it and decided to carry . . ."

"Yakov Miller's portrait!" Vanka barked at them.

"Yeah..." stammered Vanka in astonishment. "But how the fuck do YOU know?"

"Because all this has already happened!" Vanka yelled. "Millerov destroyed two SS armored divisions and killed a sniper with one TT pistol. You want Bezrukov to play you, and you, Vanya, think Bezrukov should play a cruiser. Am I fucking right?

"Holy shit, you are..." Vankas murmured, like Bobchinsky and Dobchinsky[1].

"Bezrukov only plays heroes. So, if you want to be fucking heroes, follow me!"

"Where and why, fuck it?"

"Our jerk of a captain is smoking in the hold near the ammo. Time's running out, if we don't stop him, he'll blow up the whole damn ship!

"Smoking?!" Vankas exclaimed in unison. "What a dickhead! Lead the way!"

So, the three Vankas rushed through the corridors. They nearly bumped into the political officer, but he just grunted and kept walking, without asking anything. It was hard to run—much harder than the previous time—as the cruiser was rocking heavily. But they didn't waste a minute. When Vankas burst into the compartment, there was no one there yet.

"Where's your Captain, damn it?"

"Our Captain," Vanka replied indignantly. "Wait a few seconds. Last time I came here later."

"What do you mean, last time?"

"Oh, just fucking forget about it. Let's hide behind the boxes."

So, all three Vankas squeezed behind the boxes and fell silent, waiting. Vanka looked at his grandfather's watch. 23:30 ... 23:35 ... This meant that not much time had passed since his awakening, at

---

1   Characters of Nikolai Gogol's "The Government Inspector".

best half an hour—definitely less than in most time loop movies. At
23:36:02, the doors opened, and the cruiser's Captain, Anton Kuprin,
entered the compartment. At 23:36:30, he sat on a box and pulled out
a crumpled pack of "Belomorkanal." At 23:36:32, the cigarette was in
his mouth, and his hand reached for a lighter. At that very moment,
Vanka ordered: "Get him, damn it!"

Vanka and Vanka jumped out from behind the crates and
grabbed their captain by the arms. Vanka opened the door and led
their way yelling: "Hey, guys! Come here; we've caught the Captain!
This motherfucker was sneaking a smoke!"

Hearing the news, sailors left their posts and rushed towards
them. Everyone considered it their duty to slap Captain on the face
or spit in it. The political officer watched the execution from the corridor but didn't intervene—after all, it was an old marine tradition.

They dragged Captain Anton Kuprin onto the deck, gave him a
good shake, and threw him into the ruffled sea. Some random Vanka
lost his balance and fell overboard, too, but by then, nobody cared
anymore. Vanka triumphantly stood on the deck, holding a half-
empty pack of "Belomorkanal." Sacrificing one or two Vankas for a
pack of cigarettes was a good deal. It was a moment of triumph.

For a few minutes, Vankas stood on the deck sharing several
"Belomors" under the stormy wind. The lucky ones were eagerly pulling at trophy cigarettes. The less fortunate made do with the secondary
smoke blown into their faces by the cold sea wind. Then the executive
officer, who took control of the trophy cigarettes by law, gave them all
a stern look and yelled: "Listen up, fuckers! The celebration is over!
Get back to your posts NOW! Vanka, you're on duty in five minutes."

"But I . . ."

"YOU are going to take your damn ass to the post and watch out
for the missiles from the Ukrainians! NOW, damn it!"

"Why the hell would we need to do that?" Vanka protested,
still feeling like a hero. "Why would we give a shit about some

missiles from khokhols if we are protected by the True Cross, for God's sake?!"

"Shut the fuck up and go to your post, or I'll find some cigs on you, too!"

Clearly pleased with himself, the executive officer turned around and walked away. With bitter tears streaming down his cheeks, deeply offended Vanka headed to his observation post on the stern. Suspended by two yards, a cage swayed directly over the sea, sullenly rocking to the rhythm of the ship's rolling. Vanka took a seat on two crossed reinforcement bars, welded together, GOST 8732-78, "Military Super-Durable Chair," and stared in the direction of potential Ukrainian missiles.

He immediately felt a bitter knot rise in his throat. Tired from barely edible cabbage soup and porridge, his stomach revolted against two puffs of a cigarette. His guts completely wrenched, Vanka was staring not at an invisible skyline somewhere in the north, but at the bottom of an old bucket (GOST 20558-82), that was filling up with sticky, starchy, tobacco-scented vomit.

He took a break from his favorite on-duty activity—a mere moment to breathe in some air. That moment was just enough for him to spot two missiles rapidly approaching the stern. And then a fire erupted from all sides, consuming him and taking him away.

3.0

Twenty-year-old conscript Vanka Vanyukhin died at midnight, the very moment when April 13th turned into April 14th. And then he woke up in his bunk. There was no rocking this time—not even the slightest. Behind the bulkhead, Vankas were about to start their conversation, but this time Vanka decided to stay out of it. The missiles had struck anyway. So, it wasn't the Captain. After all, it would be crazy if state-of-the-art naval artillery shells detonated from a mere "Belomorkanal" cigarette butt!

Vanka sat up, attempting to ponder his situation seriously—for the first time in his life.

However, his attempt failed. No matter how hard he tried, his thoughts kept circling back to this surreal cycle, a loop that had trapped him. Just him, out of the entire crew. But why?

Feeling desperate, Vanka started praying but quickly bit his tongue. Prayer! He had uttered this very prayer to the miraculous True Cross yesterday, begging to make him a hero. Except, he had been smart enough not to tell anyone about it—unlike those imbecilic Vankas. Perhaps God was answering his prayers? Perhaps God was granting him the chance to become a hero, all on his own, without the help of the other Vankas. Now that he knew precisely when and from where to expect the missiles, he could avert disaster. Everyone would see, everyone would know it was him. Surely, there would be a medal waiting for him on the shore. If luck was on his side, the Captain might even share his 'Belomor,' with Vanka—perhaps he would get two whole cigarettes, not just two measly drags! "The Chosen One!" echoed in Vanka's mind as he sprinted to the upper deck to watch for the dreadful missiles. His joyful thoughts were abruptly interrupted by the iron grip of the political officer's hand, clamped around his forearm.

"Where are you going, so damn happy?" the political officer asked with disdain and suspicion.

"Damn, I was just, you know, thinking ..." Vanka began confidently.

"You are not meant for thinking, Vanka," the political officer warned and then disappeared in the ship's shadows. His eyes gleamed suspiciously after Vanka.

Vanka realized that the political officer suspected him of something, but he couldn't quite grasp what exactly. Maybe the political officer sensed his chosen status? After all, it was the political officer's task to ensure that everything on board went according to the Plan, devised by God and approved by Putin. Perhaps he could sense the chosen ones. In any case, soon all of this wouldn't matter. Soon he would divert the missile strike on the cruiser, and then nothing else would matter.

That's what Vanka thought while gazing at the calm Black Sea—having forgotten that he wasn't meant for thinking. He kept shifting his gaze from the sea's surface to his watch and back. The missiles were about to come any moment now. He just had to notice them in time. But instead of missiles, a tiny dark speck appeared on the horizon. Then it grew into a black spot. It was quiet and slow, nothing like an approaching missile. Vanka, as if spellbound, stared at the dark spot, terrified to move. Only when a sail with taut camouflage canvas emerged from the night, Vanka realized what was coming at them. He crossed himself, and, as it seemed to him, instantly turned gray. NATO's kamikaze brig. Completely silent and absolutely deadly.

Vanka attempted to shout, to warn the crew, to finally become a hero. But now, in the most critical moment, his lungs ran out of air. In his head, he knew that everything was pointless, that it was too late, but he kept opening and shutting his mouth trying to utter at least one word. At that moment, the brig kamikaze rammed the cruiser's side, and water rushed into the hole, choking candles and gas lamps in the round-the-clock political information room, dampening the fuses of shells and missiles. Then the hollow charge of antimatter, placed in the brig's bow and Moskva's stern, exploded, tearing them apart in an instant. The shockwave threw him overboard into the cold, dark Black Sea. The fire that engulfed the cruiser caught up to Vanka even before he touched the water. It consumed him and took him away. Of course, all of this didn't escape the watchful gaze of the political officer.

4.0

Twenty-year-old conscript Vanka Vanyukhin died at midnight, the very moment when April 13th turned into April 14th. And then he woke up in his bunk. This time he knew exactly what to do. Relishing in his chosen status, Vanka darted out of the compartment and raced through the corridors, trying to avoid the political officer, who had a well-known habit of appearing in the most unexpected places. Vanka headed straight to the political officer's office.

He spent a couple of minutes reading the sign "Vanyukhin V.V." on the cabin door to make sure that it indeed belonged to the political officer, one of the few initiated members of the crew. Vanka thought that he had done quite well. The cabin was cramped, with barely enough room to move, but Vanka wasn't interested in numerous Psalters, Navy Regulations, and Criminal Codes of the Russian Federation. He went straight to the writing desk, in the top drawer of which the political officer kept a cellphone with internet access. If anyone knew something, Vanka thought, it would be the Ukrainians. They were the ones sending missiles, brig kamikazes, and God knows what else.

Luckily, the phone was unlocked. Vanka started surfing the net searching for Ukrainian news. The political officer was always saying that khokhly were pretty dumb, so Vanka figured that they would probably publish something about the attack on the cruiser a few minutes before the actual hit. The political officer was supposed to monitor their most critical communication channels. However, there was nothing in the news. Most of the words contained unfamiliar letters that Vanka couldn't read, and looking at some of them gave him a headache. Only one headline in the "Top Secret" folder made sense to him: "Russians, you are trapped in your own propaganda loop!"

Vanka understood all the words but for some reason, he felt that it would be better not to read any further because there could be some terrible secrets not meant for his poor intellect. Nothing. No answers. And then, as he was sliding the phone into his pocket, Vanka noticed a plain paper folder in the drawer. No, not plain. The Folder. Capitalized, just like Bezrukov, who was destined to play their cruiser one day. "Planned measures for optimizing oxygen usage by the crew of the cruiser 'Moskva' under conditions of negative surfacing. Report by chronic political officer Vanyukhin V.V."

As if mesmerized, Vanka turned the first page:

Iteration 0.0, 04/14, 00:00—destruction by subsonic low-altitude anti-ship missiles;

Iteration 1.0, 04/14, 00:00—destruction due to the explosion of ammunition caused by the cruiser's Captain, Anton Kuprin;

Iteration 2.0, 04/14, 00:00—destruction by supersonic low-altitude anti-ship missiles;

Iteration 3.0, 04/14, 00:00—destruction by a NATO brig kamikaze with a charge of antimatter;

Iteration 4.0, 04/14, 00:00—destruction by plastic explosives planted by "Azov's" underwater assault brigade.

Current report: changes in the media narrative do not lead to significant changes in the observed results of optimizing oxygen usage by the crew of the cruiser "Moskva" under conditions of negative surfacing; observations are hindered by high sea state, apparently influenced by the narrative within the iteration. Further research with changes in the initial causes of planned submersion is still required for more reliable results. See individual results below.

Vanka could feel his heart pounding loudly in his chest. Suddenly, the headline of the Ukrainian article started making much more sense. "Trapped in your own propaganda loop!" ... "planned measures for optimizing oxygen usage" ... "narrative within the iteration" ... It all fell into place. The political officer, in his immense concern for the crew, was trying to optimize the disaster and minimize losses. To do this, the General Staff repeatedly launched a scenario that would explain everything to the public. So far, judging from the report, all scenarios caused the same result.

Vanka understood that he had to do something. But looking at the watch, he realized that such an opportunity wouldn't arise in this iteration. Only a few seconds remained before the explosion of the plastic explosives planted by the underwater assault brigade of the "Azov" regiment. If he had just a little more time, Vanka might have realized that his discovery put an end to his chosen status. And then, naturally, the fire that engulfed the cruiser consumed Vanka and took him away.

5.0

Vanka was finishing the last iteration with a clear understanding of what to do in the next one. He needed to make his way to the political officer's cabin, find out the cause of the cruiser's destruction, and prevent it from happening. However, this time, he was woken up by a piercing alarm signal.

"Moskva" was in turmoil, everyone was rushing to the upper deck, and Vanka, raised in the spirit of Russian brotherhood, followed their lead. The air was charged with panic and agitation. Everyone, with mouths agape, stared in the northern direction. From there, from the Ukrainian side, a squadron of NATO's long-range strategic bombers was approaching. They formed a sharp arc over "Moskva" and began to dive down. Now everyone could discern their riders— Polish winged hussars clad in tactical armor. Their wings flapped in the wind, striking fear into the hearts of the sailors. Each hussar held a Javelin in each hand, aiming them straight at the deck.

The lead hussar took a deep breath and astonished Vanka realized that he was about to hear the legendary battle cry of the hussars. The very cry that on multiple occasions had caused Kadyrovtsi to flee the battlefield, abandoning their Kalashnikovs and iPhones.

"Geese, geese!" shouted the lead hussar flying at the front of the squadron.

"Go-go-go?" echoed the rest, launching rockets onto the cruiser's deck.

Vanka cowered from the repeated dreadful Ukrainian sound, which his indoctrinated Russian ears couldn't decipher.

The deck burst into flame. In response, the ship's anti-aircraft systems roared to life, but it seemed like they missed all their aims. Long-range strategic bombers formed another wide circle, giving the hussars time to reload their Javelins. Taking advantage of this brief respite, Vanka dove into the hold once again.

This was beyond belief. Unthinkable! Vanka didn't mind dying as many times as necessary if it helped the General Staff find the right narrative. But this scenario seemed like the last straw. Vanka didn't mind dying, but fighting? Doing something? He ran through the empty corridors of the cruiser, driven by the sole thought of reaching the communication room and telling the General Staff exactly what he thought of them. The ship quivered violently but Vanka was unstoppable.

Luckily for him, the communication room was unlocked. The unit for communication with the General Staff was prominently placed between the "Seven Arrows" icon of the Mother of God and Putin's portrait. Red bakelite dimly shimmered in the light of an old forty-watt bulb, hanging from the low ceiling, sizzling and singeing the hair of anyone who entered the room. Vanka grabbed the receiver and shouted, "Are you fucking nuts over there?!" Then sharp pain pierced his body.

Dropping the receiver, Vanka collapsed onto the floor. The door to the communication room was blocked by the imposing shadow of the political officer. Or, to use his proper title, the chronic political officer.

"Damn it, another Vanka down the drain. One piece of crap

in the personnel, neither fish, flesh, nor good red herring! Did you really have to do it, Vanya?" the chronic political officer asked, almost sympathetically, as the regulations dictated.

"To do what?" Vanka wheezed out.

"Desert, damn it."

"Desert the ship?! Are you fucking shitting me?" Vanka said with resentment, bloody foam at his mouth.

"The loop, you piece of shit. You were supposed to trust your command. Or are you so damn stupid that our twenty-minute sessions didn't make it clear to you?"

"They did . . . " Vanka mumbled, feeling his cheeks burning with shame.

"You dumbass, if the command ordered you to die, you should have asked 'how many times,' damn it. While you're dying, the General Staff is calculating the optimal explanation for all this shit!"

"But I wanted to . . . "

"I don't give a damn about what you wanted!" the chronic political officer continued to respond by the book, but each subsequent line sounded more natural. "You are not meant for wanting anything, damn it!"

Vanka understood that he wouldn't survive in this room. The merciless voice of the chronic political officer, the dark iron of the pistol in his hand, and the two bullets in Vanka's vital organs all hinted at that. Vanka's life experience told him that this was the climax, so there was only one thing left to do: "Tell my mom . . . "

"You're a complete idiot, I swear. There's nothing to tell. Officially, no one died on the cruiser. You'll just shift to another iteration. It's beyond our control, so we're dumping all defective Vankas there. You'll disappear from here," the chronic political officer's face suddenly became incredibly serious, as if he was announcing Vanka's new rank—"Heroically Missing in Action."

6.0

As the sound of the last shot rang out, Vanka closed his eyes and reopened them in a new world. Somewhere far in the steppe, a timid lark was singing his song. The night dew covered Vanka's uniform with big, round droplets. On his left, smoke was rising from shell-pierced concrete. Around the crater, technical wreckage that used to be a tank or a helicopter was piled up. Vanka couldn't tell the difference, nor did he care.

Bullet holes were still burning. And he woke up not in his bed but on duty, as if he had suddenly become someone else in the middle of a scene. Vanka remembered everything. Everything that had happened more than an hour ago was already blurred, of course, but what had happened a second ago—he remembered. He remembered that he was still in the loop, and so, with a habitual motion, he pushed up his sleeve from his wrist and looked at his watch.

In thirty seconds, the first Verba (MRLS) rockets began striking Vanka's post in the middle of the military air station in Chornobaivka[2].

---

2   A town in the Kherson Oblast, Chornobaivka airbase was one of Russia's military targets. However, it became a symbol of Russian defeat as Ukrainian forces picked off targets sometimes on a daily basis. On April 14, 2022, an attack by the Ukrainian army destroyed the ammunition depots of Russia's 22nd Army Corps stationed at Chornobaivka. Russian forces continued to fly into the base again and again, taking on ever-increasing losses. The name Chornobaivka became a war meme for Ukrainians, synonymous with Ukrainian glory and Russian defeat.

Closest to the Pole

Max Kidruk

Ближче Всіх до Полюса | Макс Кідрук
translated by Tetiana Savchynska

1

The undulating stretch was almost over when the ice crust under the front wheel split, and the rover jerked to a halt.

Vlad Bortko, who had been watching for cracks up to fifty paces ahead, looked back. Despite the rarefied atmosphere and his helmet glass, he heard the titanium cleat on the rim crack with a dry screech.

Linda was behind the wheel in the pressurized cockpit. The sun hung low, and Vlad saw her hastily pull her hair into a ponytail and put on her helmet. The next moment, the helmets of Mervin, Vlad's sixteen-year-old son, and Vega Leniero, the expedition leader, poked out over the side of the unsealed stern.

"A spoke?" Mervin asked.

"A cleat."

The second one today.

"It sounded like a spoke."

Vega didn't respond.

Linda Wojczynska climbed out of the cockpit and slid down the ladder onto the sand. A specialist in the ionosphere, she had joined Leniero's group as a doctor and driver of one of the two expedition rovers, a six-wheeled Toyota ATV[1], Type 44.

All four of them gathered around the damaged wheel. Six of the thirty-two cleats were missing, and the wide titanium rim reminded Vlad of a gouged-out mouth. Vlad was a mechanic and could replace

---

1   All-terrain vehicle.

the cleats, but that would require stopping for at least a day, and Vega Leniero, worried that Hartry would beat them, had been pushing her group northward for three weeks.

"Enough," Linda said, glaring at Vega. "We won't get our reward if we have to be evacuated on the way back."

Her words made no sense. They had crossed the 80th parallel the day before yesterday. They were too far. It would take them ten sols[2] to reach the Duster, which was abandoned in an unnamed crater in the middle of the northern lowlands, and from there, it was another 1,500 kilometers in a beeline to the nearest field station on the Acidalia Planitia. And if the last ATV broke down, no one would evacuate them. No one would even try. It would be simply impossible. Regardless of whether Leniero's group managed to reach the North Pole, they would have to get back on their own.

Vlad shuffled his feet. Sand mixed with water ice crunched underneath.

"We can keep moving," Leniero said stubbornly.

"We can keep moving only as long as the 44 keeps moving," Linda said, kicking the wheel with her shoe.

Vega turned to Vlad.

"What do you think?"

"Well, either way, we are not going to reach the Pole in it," the mechanic said, glancing at the Type 44.

Mars has a significant surface asymmetry. The northern hemisphere is represented by plains, while in the south, there are cratered plateaus.

The road north of the Colonies ran mostly through flat plains: first the Chryse Planitia, then the Acidalia Planitia, and then the Vastitas Borealis, or the northern lowlands. In some places, the road was punctuated with shallow furrows or rocky areas, but in general,

---

2   A sol is a solar day on Mars.

the plains could be crossed on rovers. But at the 80th parallel north, the plains gave way to the Planum Boreum—an ice-covered elevation with canyons, and no vehicles could tame its slopes.

Yesterday, Leniero's group had entered one of the canyons that ran to the northwest and arced toward the Pole. Its walls were already visible in the distance, but Vlad Bortko knew that in a day or two, the group would run into steep escarpments that their Type 44 could never cross, and they would have to continue on foot.

"I don't need you to tell me that we're not going to make it," Vega snapped. "I'm asking if we should stop now."

Vlad raised his hand palm side up and waved it up and down, a gesture borrowed from astronauts that corresponded to a nod.

"We need to change the oil. And check the filters. And then have a look at the suspension. We also need oxygen, after all . . ."

"Okay. Over there," Vega said, pointing at a small elevation to the east, "it's a good place to camp."

In fact, that place was no different from where they had stopped now. A sea of undulating dunes stretched around them. Their smooth surface was deceptive, hiding myriads of rocks of varying sizes and treacherous ice covered with a thin layer of reddish soil. But Bortko didn't argue. Linda climbed back into the cockpit, Mervin hopped into the back, and the team headed for the hill Vega had chosen to set up the inflatable shelters.

2

Linda was the last to go to the "bathroom" to take a shower.

The shelter consisted of two polypropylene domes connected by an airlock, and the "bathroom" was one of them, which was designated for spending some time alone and wiping the body with wet towels. Linda Wojczynska was always the last to go to the "bathroom" and stayed there the longest, rubbing herself as if she were trying to tear off her skin. She couldn't stand the dirt; it seemed to bother her more than fatigue. And lately, there had been more and more dirt. Setting up and disassembling the inflatable shelters, setting up camp, and inspecting the rovers required time that Leniero didn't think they had, so the team had been pressing forward without stopping for weeks. They took off their spacesuits in the rover only to change diapers. They ate liquid food, squeezing it into their helmets through food tubes built into the PLSS[3] units. They slept out in the open because it was more efficient to heat and supply oxygen to four space-suits than to heat a poorly insulated cockpit.

Vlad sat on a folding chair, with his hands clasping and his elbow resting on his knees. He had been in the "bathroom" for less than five minutes. What's the point of "washing up" if your clothes stink and you can't do anything about it? The coveralls under the spacesuits were made of dirt-repellent fabric, but no dirt-repellent technology will help if you don't change your clothes for weeks. They had run out of clean clothes back on the Acidalia Planitia, and they didn't have enough water to wash them.

"Is there anything you want to say, dear mechanic?" Leniero asked. She was lying on the cot with her hands behind her head, and her tone suggested she was looking for a fight.

"I didn't say a word."

"But you wanted to say something, didn't you?"

Vega was wrong: he didn't want to complain. Even in his mind. In fact, at exactly the same moment when Leniero tried to tease him, Vlad was thinking about how good it would be to just stretch out on a normal bed and finally eat normal food because it seemed that he would soon not be able to distinguish the mush he was sucking through the tube from the watery substance that soaked his diaper during the day.

---

3   Portable Life Support System.

Mervin looked up from his tablet.

"We are at the 81st parallel!"

It took a moment for Vlad to realize what this meant.

"What?"

"We've beaten Wolford and Jalali," the boy reeled off. "Eighty degrees, fifty-nine minutes, and nine seconds of northern latitude!"

The Martian Council of the Nineteen established the North Pole Prize back in 2114 to encourage colonists to conquer the North Pole of Mars. However, it was impossible to reach it by conventional means. The flight range of jet convertibles didn't exceed 400 kilometers. Ballistic hoppers could reach any point on the planet, but they needed a launchpad for takeoff and landing. Launching an orbiter to the Pole was possible, but getting it back into orbit required a launch vehicle and a spaceport because, without them, the polar explorers that landed from space would have remained at the Pole forever.

The idea behind the North Pole Prize was simple: instead of organizing the expedition themselves, they promised a reward and thus encouraged others. This would relieve the Council of responsibility in case of failure and, more importantly, would allow them to achieve the goal at a lower cost: only one team would receive money if they succeeded, while many daredevils would rush to the Pole, and all of them would have to secure their own funding.

And yet, the Council underestimated the complexity of the task. Initially, the cash prize was only three million euros. A year later, it was already five million, and then fifteen million euros. But even a decade after the reward promised by the Council had increased to thirty million euros, only two expeditions had managed to cross the 80th parallel: the al-Jalali group in 2129 and John Wolford in 2133. Unlike the polar expeditions of the early twentieth century on Earth, led by Amundsen, Nansen, or Robert Peary, Martian polar explorers had to carry not only food, fuel, and equipment but also the oxygen they breathed. That's a hell of a lot of oxygen. Of course, O2 could be extracted from water ice, which was plentiful in the north, or from carbon dioxide in the atmosphere, but both processes required bulky equipment and considerable energy. The production of this energy required even more equipment and even more fuel. The situation was complicated by the fact that the surface of the Vastitas Borealis was rocky and fragile, which made rovers get stuck and break down, so at some point, the explorers had to abandon the vehicles and carry all their equipment, food, fuel, and oxygen on their own. Al-Jalali and Wolford's expeditions reached 80°01'37" and 80°45'24" of north latitude, respectively, and then turned back.

"We are closest to the Pole," Mervin said and then, after a brief pause, added, "Well, at least among the living."

There was one other expedition organized by Carson Fleming in the summer of 2136. Fleming's group reached the Tenius Cavus, the area within the polar cap where the underlying surface is visible through the glacier. This area is located at 84 degrees of north latitude, and it is about 300 kilometers away from the Pole. This is much further than Wolford and Jalali had gone, but the problem was that after reaching the Tenius Cavus, all communication with Fleming's group was lost, and none of the expedition members returned. Mervin realized that it wasn't enough to go as far north as possible, the main thing was to get back to the Colonies alive, so . . .

"So what?" Vega Laniero asked. The boy hesitated.

"Well, except for Fleming, Donlon, and Rutherford, no one else has ever gotten this far, and I thought . . . "

"Is there a medal for reaching the 81st parallel?"

"No."

"Then I want to hear none of this bullshit," Laniero snapped and turned to Bortko. "You have twenty-four hours. The sol after tomorrow, we start moving again."

Vlad bit his lip. He would barely have enough time, even if he found no damage in the suspension. And if there was damage—and given the speed with which they had been moving for the past three weeks, he would be surprised if there wasn't any—twenty-four hours would not be enough. And they also needed to replenish their oxygen supply.

"This isn't enough," he said.

"I wasn't asking whether it was enough. I said that you have twenty-four hours, and then we start moving again."

"We haven't stopped for three weeks." Vega didn't respond, and Bortko raised his voice: "We need oxygen."

Over the last four weeks, they had crossed one thousand seven hundred kilometers from the Ortigia hills, past the Kumanovsky and Lomonosov craters, to the first spurs of the Vastitas Borealis. Leniero was the first one to cross this area so fast. They had crossed the entire Vastitas Borealis on a rover, and no one before Leniero had managed to do that either. Most expeditions didn't dare to take the risk and abandoned their vehicles as early as the 75th degree of northern latitude. Vega was afraid that Dexter Hartry, whose expedition had left Dawson City six sols later, would get ahead of her, and that's why she was in such a hurry. But they had a price to pay for their haste.

"We need oxygen," Vlad repeated.

The expeditions that stormed the North Pole set out on several ATVs and, as the fuel ran out, abandoned them one by one in the desert. In the meantime, these ATVs were extracting oxygen from the atmosphere, and the polar explorers retrieved it on their way back. When the group was left with one last vehicle, they had to watch their stocks of liquid oxygen. They had to have enough to be able to walk to the last abandoned rover in case of an accident. Bortko knew that they had extremely little oxygen left. If the zirconium filters that extracted O_2 from the carbon dioxide in the atmosphere were to break down, or if the hydrazine that powered the water electrolysis machines were to run out, their current reserves would not be enough for the four of them to reach the Duster abandoned ten sols ago. Actually, there would barely be enough gas for three of them, which meant that in case of emergency, one of them would definitely stay on Vastitas Borealis. Forever.

"Damn it," Leniero barked. "Am I the only one who needs this? Don't you need the money, Vlad? Or you just don't understand? If we don't make it, I'll become just one more loser who failed. And I'll be telling stories in the pubs of Rockville that I made it a few fucking kilometers further than Wolford and Jalali. But you . . . you will fly off Mars like a cork from a bottle of champagne."

Vlad's wife died eleven years ago after inhaling carbonyl fumes in a foundry. Vlad raised Mervin on his own. Bortko had worked as a mechanic at the Planetary Solutions railroad depot and lost his job six months ago when the workshop was automated. He hadn't found a new job, nor did he have enough money to start his own business, and the Council of the Nineteen was preparing to revoke his residence permit. He wouldn't get his share of the North Pole Prize if they didn't reach the Pole, and the Council would soon deport him to Earth. And then Mervin would have to live on his own. The boy was born and raised on Mars, in the low Martian gravity, so he physically could not return with his father.

Bortko didn't say anything.

"We'll replenish the reserves as much as we can," Leniero said. Her voice sounded more calm now. "You have the whole day tomorrow to patch up the 44, and then we will get moving," she added before turning to the wall.

The silence was so deep that Vlad could hear Linda Wojczynska sniffing in the neighboring module as she rubbed herself with a towel.

3

Vega was quickly asleep. Vlad sat down next to his son. Mervin looked up from his tablet and said:

"What do you think happened to them?"

Vlad glanced at the screen. The boy was reading about Fleming's expedition. The screen showed the pictures of all three polar explorers: Carson, Ella, and Medard.

"I don't know. And it's unlikely that we will ever find out. Carson abandoned the last ATV further south than we did. About two days' walk away. He decided not to risk it. But he continued on foot. The last signal from his navigator came from the Tenius Cavus."

"Is it far from here?"

"About two hundred kilometers north in a beeline," Vlad said after a pause.

"That's not far at all."

"Yes and no. Crossing these two hundred kilometers is very hard. You will soon see yourself. In some places, we will have to climb more than walk."

"Do you think they fell off the cliffs?"

Vlad shrugged.

"Maybe they did. Or maybe they fell through a crack in the ice. Maybe the fuel cell exploded. Or perhaps the MPS transmitter simply stopped working, but Carson kept walking."

Although that was unlikely, Bortko thought. Fleming was a smart fellow and probably wouldn't have continued the expedition if he realized he didn't have a working navigator.

"Do you think we can run into them on our way?" Mervin asked.

"Who?"

"Someone from Carson's expedition."

"No," Vlad said, shuddering at the thought.

"Why?"

"Because . . . they could be anywhere."

No one knew how long Fleming's group had been out there after the connection was lost.

"Even at the Pole?"

"Yes."

"It would be so disappointing if we got to the Pole and found Fleming there," the boy said, frowning. "I mean, their bodies. Well, you understand."

Vlad sighed.

"I think they no longer care whether we would be disappointed or not."

"But if they did make it all the way there, it wouldn't mean they were there first, would it? Conquering the Pole means not just sticking an MPS marker but also successfully coming back, right?"

"I don't think they are there," Vlad said. He didn't like where the conversation was headed. "They had gone further than us, that's for sure, but they had to come back. They didn't have a choice. They may be already behind us. And we passed them."

What's the point of trudging to the Pole to stick a marker into the ice and die proudly? No matter what happened to Fleming, they had to head south after the navigator failed. It was their only chance to survive. And if something happens, we will head south too, Bortko thought.

He caught a strange smell.

"Do you detect that?"

"What?" Mervin asked, alarmed.

"The smell."

Vlad looked around. The scent of burning rubber tickled his nostrils. Somewhere, the isolation was melting.

"I didn't . . ." Mervin began and then screamed, pointing toward the front airlock. "SMOKE!"

Vlad jumped to his feet. The climate control unit was propping up the polypropylene fabric to the left of the entrance to the shelter, and thin wisps of smoke were rising from its back wall.

"MASK!" the man yelled.

Fire was the second biggest disaster on Mars after explosive depressurization.

Mervin dashed to the emergency box, threw open the lid, took out two oxygen masks, and hurled one at his father. Vlad didn't put it on, he just threw it around his neck and knelt near the climate control unit. Mervin took a fire extinguisher out of a drawer, put the mask under his armpit, and froze behind his father, ready to use it. Vlad pushed the dome's fabric aside with his elbow and leaned against the fabric. The bundle of wires that ran from the batteries to the carbon dioxide absorber twisted into a knot, the insulation melted, and the bare copper-clad aluminum wires cut into the polypropylene. Right before Bortko's eyes, they melted and stretched the fabric. They cut through it like a hot knife.

"PUT YOUR MASK ON!" He barked at his son.

The threat of fire instantly became the slightest of the worries. If the conductive wires burned through the polypropylene, they would all die.

"WAKE UP LENIERO!" Vlad yelled, turning off the climate control unit. He wanted to add something else but didn't say a word. It was too late.

The wires burned a hole in the polypropylene. The air was escaping with a hiss. Bortko felt his ears pop as if someone was pushing his eardrums from the inside of his head. In a macroscopic fraction of a second, the crack at the place of contact opened as if someone was cutting through the polypropylene with a knife, and the dome burst like a soap bubble. Puff! Just a moment ago, the inflatable shelter was above them, and now it was gone. Just a moment ago, they were in a hemispherical rubberized bag, with the climate unit maintaining half the atmospheric pressure, and now, the grey Martian sky hung low over their heads, the rocky wasteland stretched as far as the eye could see, interrupted only by the hulk of the rover a few steps away.

And there were no spacesuits on their bodies.

When Vlad saw the polypropylene coming apart at the seams, he managed to open his mouth. It didn't save him from gas embolism, but at least it mitigated the barotrauma. The next moment, the air rushed out of his lungs and anus—with all its contents—and his ears popped as if a balloon inflated inside his head. The man pulled the oxygen mask over his face, opened the valve, and took a deep breath. Pure oxygen filled his lungs. Pain pierced his sinuses, and Vlad felt saliva boiling on his tongue, but he didn't lose consciousness.

He stood up and looked at his son. Mervin had dropped the fire extinguisher and was pressing an oxygen mask to his face with both hands. The boy was shaking from the cold.

"Airlock!" Bortko shouted, waving his hand. "Module two! Hurry!"

Out of the corner of his eye, the man saw Vega Leniero jump up from her cot, but she dropped down as soon as she took the first step.

Mervin was shaking. Vlad rushed to the neighboring dome. If the airlock wasn't damaged, they could hide inside. He yanked the emergency release handle. The relief valves responded, air gushed out of the holes around the entrance in clouds, and the hatch opened. Vlad opened the lid, looked around, and stepped back, gesturing to his son to get in. Mervin mumbled something through the oxygen mask nozzle clamped in his teeth and pointed at Leniero, lying unconscious. Vlad grabbed his son by the arm and shoved him into the airlock. The airlock could fit only one person, and the boy thought he had decided to stay outside and began to cling to him, trying to drag him inside.

"Let me go!" Bortko shouted. "I'll try to drag Leniero in!"

Oxygen masks didn't solve their problems. Without them, in case of explosive depressurization, a person had no more than twelve seconds before the oxygen-deprived blood rushed to the brain, triggering a loss of consciousness. So the masks allowed them to buy some time—sixty, or maybe ninety seconds—but no more than that. After that, the caisson disease took its toll, causing nosebleeds, unbearable muscle pain, convulsions, and even cardiac arrest.

Vlad felt his limbs go numb from the cold, and all he saw were flickering dots. He pulled himself together, dragged Vega into the hatch, crawled into the airlock feet first, and tried to pull her inside. It didn't work. Her neck and torso already started swelling, and gasses and blood mixed with bodily fluid were gushing out of her gaping mouth. All of this quickly evaporated, freezing her flesh before his eyes. It seemed as if Leniero had just fallen asleep, but Bortko knew that nitrogen bubbles were forming in her eyes, arteries, and organ cavities, gradually stopping her blood flow. Just one more minute and the damage caused by the caisson disease would be irreversible, and Vega would die.

Vlad turned the woman around and tried to drag her into the airlock feet first but failed again. There was barely enough room inside for him and Merlin.

"Scoot! Squeeze yourself against the wall!" Vlad said, pushing his son with his hip. "I have to get her in!"

Suddenly, the leg that was touching Vlad's lower back twitched. The man glanced at his son and saw that Mervin's nose was bleeding. The next moment, the boy started coughing, pulled back his mask, and lost consciousness.

Bortko looked around. The blood drummed in his ears. Through the inner hatch window, he saw Linda's terrified face. The woman was yelling something, but Vlad couldn't hear a word. There was no choice. The man pushed Vega's body out and slammed the outer hatch shut.

The compressor hissed, pumping air into the airlock.

4

Linda was ready. She pulled the spacesuit over her naked body and dove into the airlock as soon as Bortko carried his unconscious son to the housing module. Mervin regained consciousness after receiving pure oxygen for two minutes. In the meantime, Linda got outside and dragged Vega in through the hatch, but when the pressure in the airlock became equal to the pressure in the module, the expedition leader was already dead.

For half an hour, Bortko and Wojczynska took turns performing CPR on Leniero, but they couldn't bring her back to life.

Linda was the first to give up. She went outside again and dragged Mervin's and Vlad's spacesuits into the remaining module. Meanwhile, Bortko continued pressing frantically on Leniero's chest until Linda put her hand on his shoulder.

"That's enough, Vlad," the woman said. "Vega is dead."

Bortko stopped. He sat in front of the body for a while with his hands on his hips.

"What now?" Linda finally asked.

"We will bury her," Vlad said.

"Why?"

The man didn't respond. The next moment, Mervin's shrieking voice pierced the silence.

"Look!" The boy leaned against the dusty window. "The rover is on fire!"

There was no oxygen in the atmosphere of Mars, so, strictly speaking, their Type 44 could not be on fire, but the fact that the boy perceived whatever was happening to the rover as fire was not a good sign.

Linda and Vlad dashed to the window. Clouds of whitish steam were coming out from under the bottom of the rover.

"What's that?" The girl asked in disbelief.

"The fuel tank," Bortko said, already putting on his spacesuit.

"What?" Linda couldn't understand.

"Hydrazine."

"Fuck."

Linda put on her helmet, pressed the rim against the neck ring on the spacesuit's cuirass, snapped magnetic locks, and was the first to slip through the airlock.

5

The steam had already dissipated when all three of them gathered near their Type 44. Bortko, crouching, stared at the hydrazine tank. Mervin and Linda froze behind him. A hole as long as Vlad's forearm gaped in the top of the tank. The jagged edges were bent inward. After searching under the middle wheel, Bortko pulled a fiberglass rod out of the sand and handed it to Linda.

"What's this?" she asked.

"A segment of the inflatable dome arc."

For better durability, the inflatable shelters were laced with fiberglass-reinforced arcs.

"What the hell," the girl whispered. "How did it get here?"

"There was an explosion."

The dome had been torn apart with such force that one of the fragments of the frame arc flew aside as if hurled from a sling. It hit the hydrazine tank and ripped through it.

"How bad is it?" Mervin asked.

"Well, we are out of fuel," Bortko said, tapping on the tank.

"All our hydrazine was in there?"

"Yes."

"So we no longer . . ." the boy frowned. "We are not going any further?"

"I wish that was our biggest problem," Bortko whispered.

And then it hit Linda. She scrambled aboard and jumped into the back.

"How much oxygen do we have left?" she yelled. "Bortko, can you hear me?" Linda threw open the box with liquefied O2 tanks.

Vlad climbed into the back of the truck after her. "Oxygen is your fucking responsibility, so you should know!"

There were ten tanks in the first row. The tiny digital gauges on the valves were inactive. They weren't even at zero, but completely off. The gauges on the valves in the second row were also dark. She grabbed one of the tanks and weighed it in her hand. It was empty.

"How many of them are full?" she asked. There was a note of panic in her voice.

Bortko glanced over his shoulder, making sure Mervin couldn't see them and held out his index and middle fingers. Linda's face grew pale. Two. Only two tanks. Leniero was the one to plan the expedition, but it wasn't the first time Linda had participated in long trips across the Mars surface. In a frenzy, she began to count. Two six-liter tanks . . . Twelve liters of liquid oxygen . . . The coefficient of thermal expansion when a substance changes from liquid state to gaseous state is 860:1 . . . That gave them ten thousand liters of available oxygen . . . A person needs five hundred and fifty liters of gaseous O2 per sol, so . . . A deep furrow appeared between her brow. Two tanks would be enough for nineteen sols at most. For one person. This meant that only two of them would be able to reach the Duster. And only if they were lucky.

"Gosh, but this means that we . . ." She was gripped by an intense, sickening fear.

Vlad grabbed the woman by the arms, turned her to him, and put a finger to his mouth. Be quiet.

Mervin's helmet popped up over the side.

"How many do we have?" the boy asked anxiously.

Bortko put the tanks back one by one.

"Eight tanks," he lied. "Forty-eight liters. Maybe a little less because one is not full."

Linda gasped when she heard him, but Vlad immediately dug his elbow into her spacesuit: shut up!

"So this is ..." Mervin jumped into the back and poked his finger into the helmet glass. He wanted to scratch his nose. He still hadn't gotten used to his spacesuit. "So this is good, right?"

"We don't have as much as we would like," his father said. His voice sounded very tense. "But it will be all right."

"We don't have enough ..." Linda trailed off, catching Bortko's eye.

There was barely enough oxygen for seven sols for the three of them. She began to shake. The tremors seemed to have come all the way from her bones. Mervin noticed it and frowned.

"Let's go to the module," Vlad said, slamming the box with the oxygen tanks shut. "We need to think this through."

They dismounted from the rover, let Mervin through the airlock, and when he closed the hatch behind him, Bortko and Wojczynska were finally alone. Vlad took Linda's hand, opened the cover on her forearm communicator, and deactivated the push-to-talk switch, turning off the microphone inside her helmet. He then did the same with his own communicator. After making sure that Mervin wouldn't be able to hear them on the radio, he put his hands on both sides of Linda's helmet as if he was going to kiss her and pressed his face shield against hers. The atmosphere on Mars was too thin for them to hear each other's voices through the spacesuits, but if they pressed their helmets together well, voice vibrations were quite clearly transmitted through the glass.

"What the fuck are you doing?" Linda yelled, not so much out of a need to be heard as out of despair. "What eight tanks are you fucking talking about?"

"Just trust me," Vlad yelled back.

"We need to get in touch with Dexter! It's our only chance!"

"No!"

"Dexter should be ..."

"No!" Vlad shook Linda so hard her teeth snapped.

Usually, when working on the surface of Mars, the tinted helmet shields hid facial expressions, but now Bortko was too close and could see Linda's eyes. He saw them widen slightly, and then something seemed to swell deep in her eyes—a different shade of fear gripped her. It wasn't hard for Vlad to guess what Linda was thinking. He and Mervin were family. Considering that there was enough oxygen left in the tanks only for two people to get to the Duster, he could finish her off, dump her body in an icy ravine at the foot of the Vastitas Borealis, and head south with his son. He could save himself and his son and later tell everyone that Linda died together with Leniero as a result of an explosive depressurization, or that she had a heart attack, or . . . He could come up with a gazillion versions of what happened. No one would ever know. No one would ever find her body, and even if they did, they wouldn't bring it to Newborn, where the Special Service could determine the cause of her death. Linda was afraid of suffocating from lack of oxygen but she was even more afraid that Bortko would throw her down on the sand and start smashing her helmet glass with a rock or try to pull out the pipeline that supplied oxygen from the PLSS unit inside her spacesuit. This realization was so heartbreaking that it made Vlad want to shake Linda even harder.

"Dexter won't help us," he said.

"Why?"

"He left Dawson City a week later than we did. He isn't as crazy as Leniero was, so he's almost certainly a week behind, or maybe even more. But it doesn't matter because even if Dexter is only one sol behind our schedule, he can't save us because we have enough oxygen only for six days."

"But what if he . . . "

Bortko didn't let Linda finish.

"If Dexter raced across the plain as we did, he might make it here on the sixth sol, but he definitely won't have enough oxygen for three extra pairs of lungs. Do you understand?"

Linda only blinked in response, but Vlad felt her body soften.

"But why did you lie?" The woman was no longer screaming, and her voice had dropped, so Vlad didn't hear her as much as he read her lips.

"Because if I told Mervin the truth, he wouldn't go to the Duster with you," Bortko felt her body grow tense again. "Tomorrow morning, you and Mervin will take two oxygen tanks and head to the Duster."

"And what about you?"

"I will take the other six and . . . try to get to the Pole."

"What other six?" Linda asked, raising her brows. "What Pole? Are you out of your mind? What the fuck are you . . ."

She fell quiet without finishing her sentence. She looked dejected, and her eyes welled up. Bortko let go of her helmet and turned on the radio.

"Let's go talk," he said, pointing to the airlock.

6

"So here's the situation," Vlad began, contorting his lips into an eerie semblance of a smile, his sunken cheeks creasing. "We are a little low on oxygen because we've been racing like crazy for the last three weeks and didn't replenish our supplies. We also lost all our hydrazine. This means we can't heat the zirconium filters and pump carbon dioxide through them to get oxygen. The rover's battery is also at zero. Therefore, we can't chip ice from the ground and extract oxygen by electrolysis. That's the bad news," Vlad took a breath. "The good news is that there is still some oxygen left. And it's even enough to get to the Pole," he looked away, his eyes darkening. Linda was biting her lower lip as if she wanted to tear it into pieces. "For one person," Bortko added.

"Really?" Mervin didn't believe him.

Vlad opened the MPS map on the tablet.

"The Pole is six hundred kilometers away in a beeline. Two oxygen tanks will be enough for you two to reach the Duster. Actually, it will be enough for a nine-day crossing, but you can save oxygen at night and . . . I think you'll make it."

Vlad glanced at his son. Mervin nodded approvingly: yes, we will make it.

"There are six tanks left. I'll leave one here with the Type 44 so I can pick it up on the way back and get to the Duster. I'll take the other five tanks with me. Thirty liters of liquid oxygen. This will be enough for forty-seven sols if I don't conserve. And this means that I will have to walk only twenty-five kilometers per sol. I'll take a sled, load up the oxygen and food, and try to reach the Pole."

Mervin still couldn't believe it. He glanced at Linda. She knew Bortko was lying, there were no six oxygen tanks, but she forced herself to nod, and the boy seemed to calm down.

"Can you really walk twenty kilometers a day?" he asked.

"I just need to climb up the plateau, and then . . . it will get easier. If I realize I'm not going to make it, I will . . . I will just come back here. Or I'll go straight to the Duster if I have enough oxygen.

"We can wait for you near the Duster. There's plenty of food there. And we still have plenty of time until the dust storms start."

"No. You will replenish your oxygen supply, leave the oxygenator for me, and then continue south. If I'm lucky, I'll catch up with you. And if not, I'll see you in Dawson City. Or in Newborn."

Linda kept her eyes on the mechanic. It seemed to her that even a baby would have guessed what he was really thinking just by looking at the shadows on his face. Blackness seemed to ooze out of Vlad's eyes. And Mervin felt it, too. He couldn't help but feel it.

"I don't like this plan," the boy said. "I don't want you to go."

"I don't have a choice. We don't have a choice."

"Let's go back together."

Bortko shook his head slowly.

"You know perfectly well that is not an option."

Mervin was quiet for a moment.

"What do you think?" he asked Linda after a pause.

"He'll be able to make it," she said, almost managing to keep her voice from trembling. "Your father will be fine. And we have to go."

7

The grave ended up being quite shallow. Under a thin layer of reddish dust, the ground was hard like concrete. Vlad Bortko didn't so much dig as hollow out a half-meter-deep pit, drag Vega Leniero's body into it, and cover the grave with sand and stones.

When he was done, he sank down next to the grave and sat there for a while, staring at the cargo sled. Vlad had loaded all the necessary equipment to make his son believe that he was indeed headed to the Pole, and now he looked at the empty oxygen tanks with a strange feeling. It wasn't even devastation. No. It was rather complete emotional anesthesia. But, come to think of it, there was something else. He felt comforted by the fact that Mervin hadn't mentioned Dexter Hartry. It wouldn't have changed anything. But if Mervin had mentioned him, Vlad would have had to tell his son the truth, and then . . . Who knew what would have happened then?

After he had rested, he climbed on the roof of the Type 44 and looked around. The plain gradually sloped down to the south. He stared for a long time in the direction where Linda and Mervin had gone, but no matter how hard he strained his eyes, he could no longer spot them. And that was a good thing. Turning around, Vlad looked north. In the distance, there was an icy wall—escarpments, steep cliffs—surrounded by mesas. Vlad hadn't thought this through far enough to plan what he would do after Mervin and Linda left, and for a moment, he just stood there, hesitating, but then he realized how much he had grown tired of the monotony of the Martian lowlands over the recent weeks. He didn't want to die amidst this dreadful grayness. And definitely not next to Leniero's grave. Vlad dismounted from the rover and started walking northward to the highlands, laced with canyons.

He chose one of the mesas to the west of the ice wall, and it took him four long hours to reach it. When he reached its foot, the Range Awareness System[4] gave the first warning. A yellow light flashed in the upper left corner of the face shield, and the text below it read:

> › WALKBACK CONSTRAINTS: APPR CRITICAL RANGE
> › OXYGEN SUPPLY: 03 hours 57 minutes
> › STAY ALERT

The RAS system was warning him that he had gone too far from the ATV. Vlad ignored it. He spotted a ledge at the top of the mesa, thought it offered a good view and scrambled up the cliffs.

The climb took another two hours. Vlad had almost reached the flat top when a warning signal went off in his helmet. The indicator on the face shield turned red, and the warning below it read:

> › WALKBACK CONSTRAINTS: CRITICAL RANGE
> › OXYGEN SUPPLY: 02 hours 06 minutes
> › RETURN TO YOUR ROVER ASAP

Vlad scrolled through the menu on his forearm controller but couldn't find the option to disable the warnings. Ignoring them, he started walking northward along a winding slope but stopped before he could take even a hundred steps.

About two hundred meters ahead of him, he saw three figures

---

4   Range Awareness System is a range control system in a spacesuit. Based on the parameters of the life support unit, it determines the maximum safe distance away from the rover or housing module.

in spacesuits sitting on the very edge of the cliff. Two of them leaned their helmets against each other while the third, hunched over, sat a little to the side. Vlad was so taken aback that he stumbled and almost fell. When he got up, he shook his head, thinking that the lack of oxygen was making his brain foggy, but the figures were still on the cliff.

After standing there for a minute, Vlad headed toward the group. He walked carefully, watching where he was stepping so as not to slip into the abyss that opened up on his right, but it looked as if he was deliberately tiptoeing, trying to get close to the figures on the cliff unnoticed.

When he got closer, Vlad stood still for a moment, studying the spacesuits. Up close, they looked more like statues. The neoprene inserts in the places where the moving parts joined were cracked, the fabric faded, and the cuirasses were caked with dust.

Eventually, Vlad knelt next to the two figures with their heads bowed together and leaned forward, trying to get a good look at them. The helmet glass had darkened so much that it was impossible to see the face behind it. Although there was probably no longer any face inside, Bortko thought. Perhaps only skulls with paper-dry skin. Dried out, shriveled mummies.

Vlad looked down. The patches were also faded, but the letters were still legible. Bortko leaned as far out as he could without touching the spacesuit closest to him and read the names. Medard Rutherford. Ella Donlon. He decided not to lean out and read the third patch. It wasn't worth the effort. He already knew that it was Carson Fleming.

Who would have thought . . .

Vlad got up. After some time, he finally worked up the courage to touch Ella's back with his fingers. The fabric gave way, but the body underneath was hard as a rock.

They really do look like statues, he thought. A museum of ice sculptures.

He crossed them from behind and sat on the edge with his feet dangling into the abyss. He put his hands on his knees and exhaled. To the south, on the ice-free surface, the spiky patterns of countless impact craters and dunes pierced the landscape. To the north, as far as the eye could see, stretched a glacier.

It was a good spot.

> **WALKBACK CONSTRAINTS: CRITICAL RANGE**
> **OXYGEN SUPPLY: 01 hour 43 minutes**
> **RETURN TO YOUR ROVER ASAP**

Vlad sat there, almost touching Carson's shoulder. Half a meter closer than Carson to the Pole. The sun hung right before him, filling his eyes with a cold blue glow.

Big Nose and the Faun

Mykhailo Nazarenko

Носатый и фавн | Михайло Назаренко
translated by Claire Haffner

Everything we know for certain about this, we learned thanks to the inquisitive mind and generous pen of Plutarch. In one paragraph of his essay titled "The Obsolescence of Oracles" (the seventeenth, to be exact), he says that a trireme sailed from Pylos to Rome and stopped near the mountainous coast of the island of Paxos.

December is a dangerous time of year for sea travel—it's not worth disturbing Neptune in the winter. But imperial orders know no seasons, and here a ship heading for the metropolis is loaded with a special kind of cargo: everything that had yet to be taken from an impoverished, semi-barbaric country to the well-groomed, well-fed, bravely marching capital. Stones. Chunks of marble. The arms, legs, and heads of forgotten gods. With peeling paint, gouged-out eyes, and an alabaster flute clenched in the stumps of stone fingers ... Shattered, trampled, humiliated—it was impossible to distinguish Apollo from a satyr. From all over Hellas, enterprising merchants came to dig through the ruins of sanctuaries, perhaps destroyed during the Persian Wars. Augustus paid generously for their findings from state funds. Gossips, still at large, called the emperor a "potter": for he, the honorary patron of the temperance society at the altar of the Good Goddess, had an inexplicable fondness for old amphorae, which caused them to double in price. Olympus remained indifferent, and if sometimes the mountain hid itself behind gloomy storm clouds, people would say: it's an atmospheric phenomenon—and archaeological activity would continue.

This time Fortune turned away from the grave robbers. Due to the general ecumenical census, the ship's departure was delayed, and the entire crew was made to endure a long line at the local demographic office. The delayed departure was a bad omen, even though the ship frolicked beneath its sails that whole first day at sea. But the next day, when the clock crept towards noon, and Notus the south wind stirred and subsided, the water thickened like honey beneath the oars, and the slave driver couldn't get the slaves to make the trireme move. Neither prayers nor sacrifices helped.

The ship came to a standstill in the strait between densely wooded shores. In the brisk air, the invisible wings of angels rustled as they flew east. Silence hung beneath the dim sky. The silence thickened like the water, absorbing all sounds and voices, and when the world was already trembling from the tension, the quiet was torn asunder by a cry:

"The Great Pan is dead!"

These are the established facts.

We don't know for certain, but can rightly assume that a few hours before the events just described, on the morning of the same day, a creature was wandering the streets of Rome, who from a distance could have been mistaken for a child. A passerby, able to see him by the grace of the gods, wouldn't have been as surprised by the nakedness of the boy (although you'll agree that one can't walk around without clothes on a piercingly cold December day) so much as by the fact that his legs were covered in thick fur and ended in hooves, and neat little horns protruded from his mop of curls. Having taken all of this in, the passerby would surmise that before him was a young faun, and he would have been correct.

"These people don't see anything," the faun boy thought, not for the first time. "They're like small children. What can you do about it, these mortals . . . Rocks—they're like rocks." He came to a stop and squinted, looking up at the pale sky. The chariot emerged from a band of clouds and the charioteer drove it confidently towards the zenith.

"They're deprived of even this!" he said aloud, snorting with contempt. "They think the sun is a ball of fire! What nonsense."

The putrid stench of decay blew through the streets. The wind picked up and drove pieces of papyrus, densely covered in writing, through the frozen mud—gods only know from which ruined libraries they came.

The sound of sandals slapping the ground grew louder. With an impudent movement, the little faun lifted the hem of a passing matron's wide palla, and ignoring her cries, he continued onwards. "If someone doesn't see me, they only have themselves to blame ... Yes, but how to pass the time today?" he wondered, kicking a bench out from under a dozing watchman. "Should I set the lions upon the gladiators? Go to a brothel? Even I, a faun, can't think of anything better ..." Suddenly a wide, childlike grin spread across his face, because he realized where he could go right that minute. To his best friend—the only person who could see him, and whom he hadn't visited for two whole days—the big-nosed poet.

He turned around and set off at a run for the northern reaches of the city—a city of half-dead houses and crumbling frescoes, of new temples and endless galleries adorned with statues of Augustus; a city that required a permit to cross from one side of it to the other, and only weightless fauns could jump over the demarcation lines. From time to time, stones freed themselves from the walls built during Romulus's rule and tumbled into the gentle embrace of the ivy below. The freshly dug ditches were overgrown with weeds—Augustus had taken Rome as a city of brick and intended to leave it a city of marble, but he continued to destroy more than he built. The immortals tried to avoid visiting the city boastfully called Eternal, but the smell of decay reached even Olympus.

In the distance, the swampy loop of the Tiber and the flat roofs of snow-white villas came into view.

The faun's first encounter with Big Nose occurred under rather scandalous circumstances. The little guy, exhausted from the summer heat, sought refuge in a shade-dappled park in one of the northern gardens, climbed over a low fence, and in a single leap found himself in a tree, where he lay down to rest, cradled in a tangle of branches. Something stirred in the grass nearby, and lifting himself up on his elbows and poking his head out between the leaves, he saw a couple caressing each other in accordance with the art of love as described in the elegies of Big Nose. There was a cold sparkle in the faun's eyes. He already knew what he would do, and after sounding a drumroll upon his knees, he prepared for action. Suddenly, the man looked in his direction, squinted, and shouted:

"Hey! Get out of here, boy!"

The little faun looked around and wondered, "Who else here is so curious?" when a heavy sandal hit him on the back of his head. He cried out and fell headfirst into the prickly bushes below. He didn't feel any pain—he had fallen from much greater heights—but he was seized by a mix of astonishment, confusion and, it would even seem, shame. Who had ever heard of a man noticing a faun, and not only noticing him, but daring to do such a thing?

And the man—huge, and stark naked!—was now standing over him, his eyes blazing with madness and his nostrils flared with fury— Pan save us, what a nose he had! He gripped the other sandal in his hand and was clearly getting ready to give him a good thrashing.

"You're bluffing, I won't go down that easily," hissed the faun, assuming a fighting stance (he barely came up to Big Nose's chest) and lowered his horns.

Time stopped. They stood without stirring, and Big Nose's face slowly turned to stone, his mouth slightly open. A grasshopper chirped, and the wind swept the faun away like a breeze while the man stood still, not heeding Corinna's calls.

The faun squeezed through a gap in the fence, skirted a thicket of nettles, and climbed the well-trodden path up to the house. Crossing the worn mosaic floor of the veranda, he peeked into one room, greeted the Penates, glanced into another, then a third, before finally laying eyes on the master of the house. Big Nose was sitting at his desk and writing something, quickly and in a sweeping manner. Even the momentary delay of moving from one line to the next clearly irritated him. At first it seemed to the faun that they were alone, and only once he peered at the dusky figure in the far corner did he see the young woman in old-fashioned Greek clothing. He didn't immediately understand who she was, but once he did, he nodded in greeting.

He walked over to Big Nose and tugged at his toga.

"Oh, it's you," he said without looking up from his writing. "Hello … Don't bother me right now, all right?"

The faun stood on his tiptoes and looked at the papyrus. The page was so densely covered in crossed-out scribblings that only a few words had managed to make their way through the thicket of his corrections. The faun snorted loudly and walked over to the window.

This is how it always goes, he thought, pouting. *You drop every-thing to go see someone, and he's busy writing . . .*

On the shelves, adorned with parchment cases, stood a number of scrolls. One of them was half open, and the faun, feigning a yawn, glanced at it.

> *Once more the circling centuries begin—*
> *The Virgin reappears and Saturn reigns:*
> *From heav'n descends a novel progeny;*
> *Now to this child in whom the iron race*
> *Throughout the world shall cease and turn to gold . . .*

"What nonsense!" exclaimed the faun. "A new generation descends ... Who's the Virgin? What's with this novel progeny? Ah, forgive me, it's a touchy subject ... Is this your writing?" he nodded at the shelf.

Big Nose, with visible reluctance, tore himself away from his writing and smiled. "You don't like mysticism?"

"I don't," retorted the faun, proudly throwing his head back. "We Olympians ..."

"Olympians!"

"Alright, fine. We Parnassians don't need mysticism. We are our own mystics ... So are the verses yours or not?"

"You flatter me," replied Big Nose. "That's Virgil."

"Who?"

"Virgil. He's dead now, he wrote that eclogue some forty years ago."

"Aha," the faun said sarcastically. "He was a good prophet, I see. It all came to pass. During the rule ..."

"During the rule of Emperor Caesar Augustus," Big Nose finished dryly. "We don't need to get into it. You already know that I ..."

"That you are a loyal quirite," the faun interrupted him. "Just as well. It's your business. Go on, keep writing. I see inspiration has struck."

"Yes, you could say that ..." Big Nose again smiled sheepishly. "I've been visited by my muse, in a sense." With the conversation now focused on his verse, the poet found himself at a rare loss for words.

"Why 'in a sense'?" the faun asked, surprised. "She's standing right over there!"

"Where?" Big Nose asked quietly, and then slowly, afraid of startling her, turned around in his chair.

He did not see Calliope, of course. The muse turned, and with a rustle of her skirts, disappeared through the wall.

"Was that a joke?" Big Nose asked, disappointed.

"Muses are nothing to joke about," the faun snapped. "You keep working, I won't bother you."

"If only," Big Nose sighed and moved his chair closer to the desk. The faun watched him with interest. The poet chewed the end of his reed pen, then moved on to his nails, then crumpled up the page and threw it to the floor.

"Forget it," he said. "Today isn't for working anyway, and I have friends coming this evening... Only here's what I don't understand. Every time you want to have these... anti-government conversations. What don't you like? What has Rome ever done to you?"

"No no," the faun sat down, crossed his legs, and began to scratch himself unrestrainedly. "You humans are blind. You don't even see us, but we see everything. The city is falling apart, rotting away. You can't walk through the streets, and wherever you look, there's a bust of your..."

"Watch it," Big Nose said in a threatening tone.

"As you wish," the faun shrugged. "I'll be quiet. But if you ask me, it would be better to make sacrifices to the gods, and not to..."

"No no, don't even say it," the man interrupted him. "You don't know what it was like before order was restored. Devastation, riots, civil wars! And what about the slave uprising? And..."

"What do you mean I don't know?" the faun threw up his hands. "That was a wonderful time. I remember it like it was yesterday. And the city wasn't what it is now."

"I always forget..."

"That I'm five hundred years older than you. Of course! Who am I to remember that!" His voice cracked, he coughed, and muttered hoarsely, "Puberty. Don't mind me."

"Come now, don't get upset," Big Nose rumbled in a soothing tone. "You have certainly seen more than me..."

"You can only imagine." The faun was growing more insolent by the second.

"And you must understand that the Iron Age is ending, and the Golden Age will come . . . sooner or later . . ."

The guest looked at the poet with clear eyes and said quietly, "Let's change the subject."

"Don't be evasive!" Big Nose jumped to his feet and began pacing back and forth. "Yes, not everything is perfect yet . . . But overall . . ."

"Twelve hundred years ago," the faun chimed in, "humans had multiplied to such a degree that Gaia could no longer bear their weight, and you know how that ended."

"How?"

"The gods exterminated them in the Trojan War. That's how."

"Hang on," Big Nose squatted down and studied the faun's face. "You mean to say . . ."

"I don't mean anything. I'm just telling you—let's change the subject."

Big Nose shook his head—the little faun could be very stubborn!—and deferentially said, "So persistent . . . Let's change it, then. What shall we talk about?"

"You," suggested the faun. "You've been so quiet and you've dragged your Virgil into this. What are you writing about, other than the ladies?"

The poet grunted, straightened up, and went over to the desk, where he began to rummage through the papyrus pages.

"Well, how can I put it . . ." At last, very slowly, as if he was squeezing out each word, he said, "About life. About people. About the gods. About the world."

"Oh, I see," the faun pursed his lips. "Homer's laurels don't give you any rest, huh? And yet here I see that Calliope pays you regular visits."

Big Nose cast a glance towards the dark corner of the room.

"But that's only natural," he said in a guilty voice. The poet for some reason turned his face away, so the faun had to get up and move closer. "Our lives, generally speaking, aren't that long . . ."

"*Your* lives aren't that long," the faun corrected him, hopping up onto the desk. "Yes. And I'd . . . Well, I'd like to show humans everything, the things they don't see and the things they will never see. Remind them, perhaps, of something. Humans notice very little, and if I'm able to . . ."

The earth shuddered, and a crack snaked across the ceiling. Big Nose fell silent.

"*You* don't see that your house is falling apart," the faun said, seeming not to notice the omen. "And you haven't seen much in life, to be honest. If I didn't tell you what's going on in the world . . . Are you at least going to write this down, or am I shouting into Tartarus?"

"What's this?" the poet asked, indignant. "You constantly inspire me. With your mere presence! A bucolic eclogue right at home, just sitting and scratching himself. Very charming."

"Oh, how witty we are . . ." the faun replied, trying to appear indifferent, though he stopped scratching himself. "What's the poem about? Can you tell me? Only for Jupiter's sake, keep it simple! No philosophy."

"It's about change," Big Nose answered, thinking. "It's a topic that calls for some philosophy, but I'm trying to write it in simpler terms."

"Then explain it in those terms to this uneducated faun."

The sky, meanwhile, had darkened and filled with low, swollen storm clouds. "Could it really be about to snow?" the young faun thought, and suddenly his heart caught, which almost never happens to fauns. The garden cowered in fear, and the river grew dark.

"You see," Big Nose said, "nothing is permanent. If you only talk about what's enduring and immutable, you won't get anywhere. Life seeps in like water through sand. Take Daphne—she isn't a river nymph or a laurel tree! Daphne is a moment of transformation. That's what it's all about!"

"First of all," the faun turned away from the window, "the gods are immutable. You don't need me to tell you that . . ."

"What about Jupiter?" the man countered. "The bull, the golden rain . . ."

"But his essence is the same—he's still divine!"

"That's what I'm talking about," agreed Big Nose. "That's why life is possible, because there exists . . . Well, how to put it . . . Unity. Something that binds everything together, holds everything in place."

The faun looked at him with interest.

"I just don't know what to call it," the poet said in a faltering voice.

"But you already said it!" the faun exclaimed and jumped to the floor. "I don't know how, but you understood and named it!"

"What did I understand?" Big Nose asked, surprised.

The faun smiled and shook his head. "You're a genius, a genius, but so clueless sometimes . . . 'Everything' in Greek is . . ."

And before he could speak the name, the man remembered it himself.

Pan.

How to describe it? What words to use?

His fingers—not old at all, despite being callused and blackened from the sun, with blue-black nails. His voice was like a panpipe, the modulations of Syrinx's breath—His one, unforgettable love.

Straw got tangled in His fur, and when He sits on the slope of Pelion, watching the luminous Selene, horned, like He is—it's so nice, so cozy to lean against His fluffy side, to close your eyes and listen as He sings an ancient shepherd's song. And all that exists in the world exists in you, and in Him, and in everyone.

You remember how, without His knowledge, you once cut a stalk of reed—and horror, aptly named panic, rolled through the grass like a wave, bent the cypresses to the ground, sent flocks of frightened birds into the cold sky and drove them all away, away from the furious ancient eyes, the primordial wrath.

The most ancient. Not the son of Hermes, not the son of anyone. He is the immutable Father.

"Strange," muttered Big Nose, "I didn't think . . . I've written about Syrinx, sure, but as for Him . . ." The man suddenly felt a pang of jealousy. For so long he had tried, not only with his heart, but also with his mind to learn, and find out . . . And yet this young faun—dirty, disheveled, ignorant—knew more, and felt things more vividly. He saw that which Big Nose would never see.

"Tell me more," he said. "Go on."

The faun sat silently. His eyes were closed, and his face, tanned though it was by another sun, went pale, and his fur seemed to fade.

The man immediately forgot about his own thoughts, gently took the faun by the hand, and asked quietly, "What's wrong?"

He didn't answer. Spots swam before his eyes, and below . . .

"Boy!"

. . . the earth shook, spun under his feet, and pulled him in.

He fell through Big Nose's outstretched hands into the abyss.

The goat-legged old man, clutching the panpipe in his hands, sat on the side of the mountain.

He was dying, and the cosmos was collapsing. He knew this and accepted it calmly, as all mortals accept that the universe dies with them—forever. The firmament was tearing into pieces, burning ribbons falling into the ocean. In the space around the stars, where once harmonious spheres had revolved, he now saw only emptiness.

I'm not Atlas, I cannot hold the world forever, he thought, already slipping into non-existence when again he saw her—Syrinx, the one and only—and just as on that day, he ran.

He ran, gasping for breath, he couldn't see anything else but her, and she was always ahead of him—just a few steps ahead, he would catch up with her in a moment, he reached out, but, like in a bad dream, she was always ahead of him, forever unattainable, running without stopping, and he already knew how this chase would end, and, knowing, he ran slower and slower, trying to delay the moment even like this, even in a dream, when he would see her for the last time ... *Connections are breaking, meaning is slipping away, could it really be that I can't hold onto anything, could it really be that no one can* ... He struggled to return to the present, to the world where nothing lasts, where only chaos and decay prevailed. Olympus was crumbling, falling apart like stale bread, and the palaces were disappearing in the midday haze. *We deserve this,* he understood, *deserve this for our selfishness, our divine obliviousness. Everything has turned into rubble and dust, everything we nurtured and abandoned, created and cast aside. Apollo and the satyr, Prometheus and Zeus—who will distinguish you now? Fragments of legends, pieces of pitchers, at best—a song.*

The wind disappeared, the water thickened like honey, and he again found himself on the bank of that strangely named river, Ladon. Time slowed and he stopped running, still hoping to change the inevitable, drinking it all in, committing to memory forever her every movement, her every line, because there is nothing left for us but memory—only a reed, only a departing voice. *The gods don't get a choice. No one gets a choice. We haven't asked the question yet, but we know there won't be an answer.*

He was again on Pelion. He sat, leaning against a mossy boulder, and looked out into the darkness—there was nothing else. *How long ago,* he said. *The world was so young. It's too late now, there's no point in remembering.*

He glanced down at the earth. It seemed as if the mortals hadn't noticed anything, bustling around as usual. *Humans,* he said quietly. *I bid you farewell, humans. But now at least lift up your heads, look at me, I don't have much longer.*

They don't see me.

Nothing and no one will save them.

Just like Syrinx. When he ran out on the loamy cliff, she was already down below, and came close to falling in the shallows—which is how he made up a few paces, he was already close to her, so close, and he saw fear in her eyes, mixed with revulsion—and slowed down, stopped for a second, and then it was too late.

Nobody will be saved. No one has such a fate.

His heart beat faster and then stopped. To the east shone a rising star, and at the last minute he understood why he could depart and who allowed him to do so.

He was there, he had time to embrace her before she turned into a reed. He made it.

The earth shuddered and shook him off like a speck of dust.

Khaîre, Charon!

He hit the frozen ground and pain shot through his leg. The faun had learned how to manipulate space back in the days of Pericles, but he had never traveled this far. He lay there writhing, curled in a ball, waiting for the spots he was seeing to disappear, leaving only darkness behind. Then he stood and, with a slight limp, set off up the mountain. He felt nauseous.

There was no sky. Above him swirled a gray mist unlike any clouds he had ever seen, unlike anything else. It breathed steadily, occasionally expelling a sticky drizzle. The darkness deepened, and if the faun hadn't known Pelion like his own two hooves, he surely would have tripped over the oaks' gnarled roots, once strong and thick, now withered and lifeless, covered in rotting leaves.

He walked out onto the cliff. His legs disappeared in the thick fog blanketing the earth as far as the eye could see. He could only see a few paces in front of him, and then nothing. He could make out some blurry figures, meaningless shapes in the gloom, but didn't understand who they were—dryads, usually sunning themselves on the banks, or satyrs, his cousins, or Dionysus himself, the last of the gods.

The fog was illuminated for a moment by a golden flash. The broken chariot fell into the sea, and Helios followed the path of his son—into nothingness. Nobody noticed him—there wasn't even a splash.

The gloom became so dense that the faun had to feel his way forward with outstretched hands. *I'm the last*, he repeated to himself, *I should see this for myself, I should hang on . . .* The path rose sharply and the faun stumbled, almost falling off the cliff, but managed to hang on, ordering his knees to stop shaking, and forged ahead.

He touched cold stone and came to a stop. Holding on to the lichen-covered boulder, he slowly made his way around it. There was less fog here at the top, and the faun could make out the dim outlines of nearby bushes. Suddenly his fingers brushed something soft and covered in fur. He pulled back his hand and turned away.

The survivors gathered around the boulder. Someone began to sing an ancient funeral dirge, but their voice broke off. He could feel the damp in his bones. The faun trembled and the pain in his leg grew sharper. To his right stood a dryad. Her hair was stuck together and she trembled slightly, unable to look away from the dead Pan. A tiny satyr clung to her, bawling and crying out for his mother.

Priapus approached from the other side of the boulder. The faun had known him since childhood and couldn't stand him. He was a sorry sight—Priapus had never been very tall, but now he had gotten even smaller. He combed his remaining hair over his bald spot, pulled his head into his shoulders and barely dragged his legs.

"Ah," he rasped, seeing the faun. "The young generation . . ." He started coughing and spat on the grass. "The damp . . . Well, how do you feel before the end? Lousy?"

"Is this really the end?" the young faun asked loudly. The dryad looked at him fearfully and stroked the little satyr's head.

"There, there," she murmured. "Such a big boy, and you're crying. Come here then, let me hold you . . ."

"This is the end!" Priapus proclaimed. "What are you doing here? What are you hoping for? *Deus ex machina*? No god is coming! They're all dead, we're the only ones left!"

"Don't yell," the faun said. "Look, the little one is sleeping."

The dryad clutched the little satyr to her, covering him with her hair, and began to sing in a hushed voice. They didn't pay attention to the others.

Priapus began again, quieter this time. "Listen, boy, what is there to hope for now? Huh? What do you have to say? We lived, never knowing sorrow, never thinking about tomorrow—and now here it is, tomorrow has come. And what is there to do? Go down to Hades with Him? No, he has plenty of company down there now without me . . . Stay here? In this sleet?"

"There are other places aside from Pelion . . ." the faun replied listlessly. "But all in all you're right, there's nowhere for us to go . . . I'd like to live out my days in some backwater, where they haven't forgotten how to make sacrifices to the gods, and from there to

Hades . . . I'm cold. Why don't any of us wear clothes, except perhaps on Olympus . . . ?"

"There is no Olympus," the old man answered darkly. "And maybe there never was . . . Do you at least know where to look for this backwater?"

The faun shrugged.

"We'll see."

"I feel better," Priapus wheezed and bent over in another coughing fit. "I've seen a lot in this life. Somewhere outside Miletus I'll find myself some young shepherdesses and stay there forever . . . " Priapus buried his face in his hands. He was breathing heavily, and something whistled in his chest. "What nonsense . . . " he said after a long silence. "We make plans, we have hope . . . But all in vain. There's no creating the future. We don't have anything left, it's all over. We'll walk around in the fog like this until we fall into the abyss. This is the end for us."

"Go," urged the faun. "Look for your . . . shepherdesses. And I'll . . . I don't know." He turned to the dryad and said firmly, "You don't need to stay here. Let's go. Do you hear me? Let's go."

"Boy," she spoke quietly and with a note of pity. "Where would I go? And what for? What should I do, abandon the little satyr? Don't be ridiculous . . . " The dryad bowed her head and whispered, "We'll just close our eyes for a little bit, and then we'll look for something to eat, and everything will be all right . . . "

Fool, the faun thought angrily and began to walk downhill. *She's lost it. She found herself a distraction.* It occurred to him that Pan needed to be buried in accordance with the old customs. He stopped, then waved the thought away and continued onwards. *It's useless. There's no sense in doing it. We won't survive the night anyway.*

Ovid sat at the window, beyond which hung a dense, motionless darkness. The clouds dissipated towards midnight and the river glistened with reflected light. The vast world stretched around it, and the whole city was visible, from the nearest gate to the Greek altar of the Unknown God on the other side. Before the poet's eyes, things, trees, houses were strangely transformed, and the sky trembled.

The world has always been fragile, Ovid wrote. He didn't know how much time was left before the End and was hurrying to write down what he saw. The need to speak—it didn't matter whom with, even with himself—had always been in him. And now, realizing that no one would ever read these pages, and even if they did, they wouldn't understand— now, in solitude and desperation—he did what he was born to do: write. *Now … I'm still afraid to say it … In the end, I don't know for sure … Quit equivocating, Big Nose, you see and know it all: the world is broken, shattered to pieces like an old pitcher: the last metamorphosis: the last thing that awaits us. Like in the paintings of fashionable artists,* Ovid wrote. His pen broke, he flung it away and seized another. *The universe has disintegrated into planes, into geometric shapes. The world bristles with unimaginable angles. A giant abscess protrudes from the middle of the earth into the sky — the Capitolium. I look at things without comprehending their meaning. I haven't lost my mind. I'm still here, still thinking. I'll repeat what matters most: here, in this terrible new world, I can't forget how things were before. What's left? Just naming things, repeating names. Come on now! You wrote about transformations, you talked about everything you had seen in this world. So get started! Window. Night. House. Don't stop. Stack up the wreckage. Write, while you still have something to write with. Pen. Desk. Papyrus.*

He put his head down on the desk and rubbed his temples. He whispered something, but slower and slower. They called him, but he didn't answer.

Useless, he thought. *There's no point. I've forgotten it all. I don't remember anything.*

The wind found its way in through the cracks in the room, rustling the sheets of papyrus and scattering them around the room, glancing back at the threshold and slamming the door, leaving to walk through the house. Ovid had been shivering all morning, but now the cold became unbearable. Opening his eyes with great effort, he pushed back his chair and stretched his hands out over the stove. The flames didn't warm him, and he didn't see a fire—only faded stripes of red and yellow trembled before him.

That's when he decided. He bent down, scooped up an armful of the pages and put them in the fire.

If this can change anything at all, he said, and only a moment later did he realize that this had been a prayer.

He was busy for the rest of the night. Ashes flew around the room and filled all the cracks. The sheets of papyrus, without adding any heat, turned to dust. The mocking flame, taking ahold of the last page, illuminated the words:

> *My task is now complete. Here I end my work,*
> *which neither Jupiter's rage, nor fire, nor sword,*
> *nor gnawing time can ever wipe away.*

The door creaked open and in walked the faun. He approached Ovid silently and sat down at his feet.

"That cursed fog is here too," the faun said in a mournful tone, and then suddenly asked, "When did you understand?"

"When ..." Ovid repeated, and reluctantly answered, "When you disappeared. Everything started swimming before my eyes, and I saw ... I don't know what, exactly, but it was ... abominable. Were you there?"

"Can't you tell just by looking at me?" snarled the faun.

"And you know what the strangest thing was?" Ovid continued, not hearing him. "Or the scariest ... That no one—no human, other than myself—noticed, no one even felt it. Are you listening?" He nodded in the direction of the drunken hubbub. "They're having fun. And not one of them ... Not even Corinna. 'What's wrong, dear? Take a break, dear! You're working too hard, dear! We have an audience tomorrow . . . ' So tell me, since you know more than I do—what did I do to deserve this? Why do I alone see this chaos?"

"You're a poet, after all," the faun responded after a pause. "It would be better to answer what *we* did to deserve this."

"Mysterious ways . . ." Ovid began, smiling wryly.

"Stop!" the faun cried. "Forget your beloved quotations! There is no Jupiter! He doesn't move in mysterious ways! And there's no point in any of this! Get it?" He suddenly buried his face in Ovid's knees and burst into tears. He had never allowed himself to behave in such a way, not in front of the Olympians and especially not in front of mortals, and now here he was sobbing, unable to stop no matter how hard he tried. He bawled like the little satyr. The man hugged him, wanting to say something, but couldn't.

"It smells like burning," the faun said.

They sat by the window again, just like in the morning.

"Ah . . ." Ovid waved his hand. "It's me . . ." He suddenly realized that it would be difficult for him to confess. No, he didn't feel regret, but rather something like shame, unfounded and incomprehensible.

"Yes?"

"I burned my book," he said quickly.

The faun stared at him uncomprehendingly, looking at the stove and back to Ovid.

"How could . . ."

"How could I do it?" the poet became angry and jumped to his feet. "You said it yourself—there's no point. Where's the world I wrote about? What was I writing for? So many years, so many years!" His voice shook. "And everything was destroyed in a day. What's left of my book? A collection of fables? Fairy tales that no one will believe? Then why is it needed? Answer me!"

The faun jumped onto the chair to look Big Nose in the eye, and shouted, "You didn't have the right to destroy it, that's why! The Book is all that's left . . ." He swallowed. "All that was left of the previous world! They . . ." he waved his hand. "They'll forget in an hour. Only you saw and understood how it was! Ah, what is there to say . . . There are no copies?" he asked hopelessly.

Ovid shook his head.

"Maybe your friends have some excerpts . . . ?" The faun sighed and climbed down from the chair.

Dawn was approaching. The darkness grew thicker. The moon sank below the horizon, and stars appeared in the sky. It was as if they had surfaced out of nothingness: there was one, and another, and another; they kept appearing, already whole constellations, bunches, clusters; unchanged on their celestial paths, as it should be.

"You know . . ." the faun began slowly, "everything is pretty much over, and yet I feel . . . I don't know what to say. But you understand?"

"Yes," Ovid nodded. *My soul feels calm,* he thought. *And it's not acceptance of the inevitable, it's something entirely different. And I, who spent twenty years choosing words, can't give it a name. Maybe it's hope . . .*

And then on the eastern edge of the sky a star appeared. It shone so brightly that both the man and the faun took it for a ray of sunlight at first. But it was a star, and as it rose higher, its light intensified; now the star looked like a glass sphere filled with fire. It moved smoothly and confidently until it reached its zenith and froze, pulling all the other stars and rays towards itself, and the sun hesitated to show itself in the sky for a long time.

The man and the faun looked at the star. They saw more than others, but even they didn't know that the census had reached the eastern borders of the empire. They didn't know, and never would know, that there wasn't room for two travelers at an inn in Bethlehem.

There, in the east, the light-winged angels of Giotto, forgetting to sing hosannas in their excitement, crowded around the cave over which the star shone.

SHORT GLOSSARY

> *As all stars shrivel in the single sun,*
> *The words are many, but The Word is one.*
> G. K. Chesterton

Calliope—the muse of epic poetry and mother of Orpheus. She has appeared to poets on multiple occasions, and some have even been fortunate enough to see her.

Charon is mentioned erroneously. He only transported the souls of those who had been buried, which is why the unburied Pan could not possibly have seen him.

Faun—it is unknown whether Ovid was actually acquainted with fauns, but Horace was and dedicated an ode to one of them (3.18).

Khaîre—("rejoice") an Ancient Greek greeting.

Quiris, plural **Quirites**—what a full-fledged Roman citizen would call himself in a civil capacity, while, in regard to his military and political capacity, he would use Romanus.

Ovid, born **Publius Ovidius Naso** (43–17/18 BCE)—poet. He consigned the central work of his life, the poem *The Metamorphoses*, to the flames. It was reconstructed by the poet's friends, but the final authoritative text remains unknown.

Palla—a long, elegant cloak.

Pan—god of flocks, forests, and fields. His name comes from the Indo-European *p(a)us* meaning "to make fertile." Due to the homonymy of the Greek *pan* meaning "everything" it was interpreted initially as "liked by everyone", and later (in the mythology of the Orphics) as "the Almighty," and on this basis Pan was associated with Jupiter.

Paxos—a Greek island in the Ionian Sea located north of Ithaca (glorified by Homer) and south of Corfu (glorified by Durrell).

Penates—household deities, similar to the Ukrainian *domovyk* or house spirit. These deities can be both domestic and state-related. They were brought from Troy by Aeneas.

Plutarch (approx. 46 – 126)—encyclopedist. For an account of the essay "The Obsolescence of Oracles," see *The Greek Myths* by Robert Graves, 26g. According to Plutarch, Pan died during the rule of Tiberius, not Augustus. Nineteen centuries later, a certain Basel professor, walking along the shore of a lake, heard a voice say: "God is dead."

Trireme—an ancient warship named after its three banks of oars per side. The author admits he's not at all certain that triremes were ever used to transport cargo, but he likes the word.

Virgil, born Publius Vergilius Maro (70–19 BCE)—a poet and imperial classic. The text quotes his eclogue IV, thanks to which he enjoyed the reputation of a prophet and magician in the Middle Ages.

Quoted Sources:
Eclogue IV by Virgil, translated by John William Mackail
Metamorphoses by Ovid, translated by Ian Johnston
Four Faultless Felons by G. K. Chesterston

A Bitter Thing
N. R. M. Roshak

"But O, how bitter a thing it is to look into happiness through another man's eyes." —Shakespeare, As You Like It (V.ii.20)

I should have known that something was wrong when I found Teese in the backyard, staring at the sky. It was sunset and the horizon was a particular shade of pale teal. At first I thought Teese was just admiring the sunset, but then I realized he was trembling all over. His eyes were wide, and irregular patterns swept over his skin, his chromatophores opening and closing at random, static snow sprinkling his skin.

I touched his shoulder. "Are you all right?"

Above us, the sky darkened toward night. Teese shook himself like a dog, blinked, looked at me. "That sunset," he said. "We don't— these colors—This doesn't happen on our world."

"You don't have sunsets?" As I understood it, sunsets should happen anywhere there was dust in the air.

"No, no," he said. "Of course we have sunsets, Ami, but they tend more toward the red side of the spectrum. Your planet is so rich in blues. These colors, they're not very common on my world. I suppose I was surprised by my reaction to seeing that particular shade of blue spread across the sky." He smiled down at me. "Anyway, it's all changed now. Fleeting as a sunset, isn't that the expression?"

Teese was back to his usual smooth articulateness, so I wrote it off as his being momentarily overcome by the Earth's breathtaking beauty. In retrospect, that was pretty arrogant and anthropocentric of me. But at the time, I thought: who wouldn't be struck dumb by my amazing planet?

That night, Teese stared deep into my eyes as we made love, and trembled, just a bit. Static flared across his cheeks as he came. His heart-shaped pupils flared wide, drinking me in, and he murmured "I could stare into your eyes forever."

So, of course, I thought we were all right. We were all right. However unlikely, however improbable, what could it be but love?

The next warning sign came weeks later, when Teese painted the linen closet blue. He moved out all the towels and sheets, took out the shelves, painted the walls (and the ceiling, and the back of the door) greenish-blue, and perched on a stool in the middle of the closet. He called it his "meditation closet", jokingly, and said that he went in there to relax. At first it was for minutes at a time, then slowly his "meditation time" grew to hours.

"The things your people do with color are amazing to me," he said. "So many colors, and you put them everywhere."

"What, you don't have paint where you come from?"

"Of course we have paint," he said. "But we use it for art. No one would think to put gallons of blue and green in cans for people to take home and spread all over their house. It would cost—" He paused. Interstellar currency conversions were impossible, finding correspondences of value almost as difficult. "Many years of my salary, I think, to paint just this closet."

"Well, that makes sense. If you went to an art supply store here and got your paint in little tiny tubes, it would cost a lot more here too."

"And the colors," he continued. "I think I have told you that most of our colors are in reds and browns and oranges. Even in paintings, we don't have so many shades of blue."

"That's weird," I said. "I mean, you can see just as many shades of blue, right?"

"Yes, but—" He considered. "Ami, I think that you have so much blue that you don't see how it surrounds you. You can make a painting with a blue sky and blue water, and use one hundred different shades of blue, and everyone sees it as normal and right. But think of another color that you don't have in such abundance, like purple. Imagine a painting with nothing but one hundred shades of purple."

His words triggered a memory. "I actually had a painting like that once," I admitted. "I found it in the trash in college. It had a purple sky and a purple-black sea and two really badly painted white seagulls. It was so awful that I had to keep it."

Amusement fluttered across his skin. "Tacky, right? Well, that's what most of my people would think of your sea and sky paintings. But I love it. I love to be surrounded by blue."

"Meditating?"

He waved an arm noncommittally. "Ommmm," he said, brown fractals of laughter flashing across his skin.

Then Teese bought one of those fancy multi-color LED lightbulbs, tuned it to the exact shade of the walls, and didn't come out for a day.

He was in the closet when I left for work, and still there when I got home. I tapped on the door—no answer. I told myself to give him his space and went about fixing dinner, even though it was his turn to cook. Teese's diet was similar enough to ours that we could cook for each other, though there was a long list of vegetables he was better off without. I knocked on the door when dinner was ready and called his name. No answer. I ate without him.

Later, I pressed my ear against the door but heard only my own heartbeat against the wood. It was dark by then, and blue light seeped out from under the door.

Finally, I eased the door open a crack and peeked in. Teese was sprawled on the floor next to the upturned stool, eyes vacant, skin utterly blank.

I yelled his name, shook him, even slapped his face. My fingers shook as I pressed them urgently into his skin. I remembered that Teese had two hearts but I couldn't remember where they were, or how to find his pulse. There was no one I could call, no doctor or ambulance who could help him. I was alone with Teese and Teese was gone, sick, maybe dying.

I dragged him out into the hallway, slowly. Teese doesn't have any bones to speak of. He's all head and muscled limbs. Normally he holds himself upright on four powerfully muscled limbs and uses the other two like arms. Passed out, he was a tangle of heavy rubber hoses filled with wet cement. I had to pull the blanket off the bed, roll him onto the blanket and drag the blanket out of the closet with Teese on it.

I stood over him in the hallway and felt terribly alone.

I had met Teese at a party I hadn't planned to go to. At the last minute I'd let myself be swayed by the rumors that one of them would be there. A so-called hexie. Their ship had landed months ago, and while the VIPs on board were busy hammering out intergalactic trade deals, most of the ship's crew were just sailors who wanted to get off the ship, get drunk, and maybe get to know some locals. They'd been showing up by ones and twos at bars and clubs and parties all over town. I'd seen the hexies in the news, heard about their appearances at bars and parties, but never met one in person. And like everyone else, I was curious.

I saw him the moment I stepped in the door: big head held up above the crowd, two long and flexible arms gesticulating, one of them holding a drink. His eyes swept the room, scanned over me, and snapped back. From there, it was like a romance novel, of the kind I'd always found tedious and unrealistic. Our gazes locked. He stopped mid-sentence, handed his drink to someone without looking, and started pushing his way across the room to me. My heart hammered in my chest. Of course I couldn't take my eyes off him, but why was he staring at me?

He stopped in front of me and took my hand, coiling his powerful armtip around my fingers as gently as I'd cradle a moth.

"I am Teese," he said. "Forgive me for being so direct, but I have never seen eyes as beautiful as yours before."

Hackneyed words, but they sounded fresh coming from his lipless mouth.

"I'm Ami," I stammered. "And I've never seen anything like you either."

Orange and brown checks rippled across his face. Later I would learn that this meant interest, arousal, excitement. I let him lead me to a quiet corner.

We talked. He told me about his ship, the long watches tending to the cryo boxes, the vastness of interstellar space. I told him about my job at the Citgo station and my apartment and the time my cat died.

"When I look at you," he said, "I feel things that I've never felt before."

What else could I do? I took him home, and he stayed.

Now I was alone in my hallway with Teese unconscious. I stepped around his arms and closed the linen closet, and sat down on the ground next to him. Soft blue light leaked out from under the closet door. I turned on the hall light and turned off the closet light, for lack of anything more constructive to do. Then I sat down on the ground next to him and wondered what to do. Smelling salts probably wouldn't help an alien from another planet, had I even had any to hand.

I could sprinkle water on his face, but I had no idea if that would work on him. I could pinch him.

I could sit next to him and stare at his open, blank eyes and wish I'd thought to ask him for a way to contact his ship.

I could search his things for a way to contact his ship, but I didn't want to go there if I could avoid it. Teese had been living with me for two months, which is both a long time and not long at all, and as far as I could tell he'd never gone through my closet or papers while I was at work. I owed him the same respect.

Teese stirred sluggishly on the floor next to me.

I leaned over him. "Teese?"

His eyes focused on me. "Ohhh, Ami," he said, half moaning. And then his skin was suddenly, completely covered in violently red spots. Across his face, all up and down his arms, from the dome of his head to his armtips, he was covered with hexagonal measles that shifted and spun.

Teese's emotions showed on his skin, but I had never seen this one before, never seen such a violent and complete display.

I laid a gentle finger on his cheek, trying to pin one of the spots under my fingertip. "Teese," I said. "I don't know this one."

Teese looked at me for a long moment before replying.

"Shame, Ami," he said. "It is shame."

Teese's people feel emotions the moment they see them. If I'd been one of Teese's people, I would've been flooded with shame the moment I saw the red blotches on his skin, and a paler echo would have bloomed on my own skin. It's beyond empathy: it's instant and direct and irresistible. If I'd been a hexie, I would have said: "Why are we ashamed?", while my skin and emotions thrummed in synchrony with his.

But I wasn't, and so I could only ask, "What are you ashamed of?"

Teese sighed, a sound I had taught him to make. "I spent too long meditating," he finally said.

"Did you forget to eat?"

"Hm. I suppose I did, but I don't think that's why—You shouldn't have had to drag me out of the closet."

"I think we're doing something a little beyond gay here," I quipped, then wished I hadn't as gray puzzlement dusted itself over the shame blotching his skin. "Never mind, bad joke. But if it wasn't hunger, why did you pass out, or whatever that was? Teese, are you sick?"

"No, no," he said. "You don't need to worry, Ami. I'm fine." He sighed again. "It was—I was—I just don't know how to explain it."

"Try," I urged him. Partly because I was worried and scared, and partly because, as we talked, the shame was slowly fading from his skin, supplanted by the dark-orange fractal trees Teese sported whenever he was thinking hard.

"Well," he said. "I was . . . I was looking at the walls and I got . . . too much blue."

"Too much blue," I said.

"Yes," he said. "I thought, I am meditating, I am going deeper and deeper into the blue. And then it was too much."

That was unusually inarticulate, for Teese. He was usually better at expressing himself in English than I was. His skin was clearing and dulling to a muddy grey.

This one I knew well. "You look tired," I said. "Let's get you into bed."

"Yes," he said. He started to haul himself down the hallway toward the bedroom, not even bothering to stand.

I covered my mouth with my hand. Teese usually stood himself up on four of his six limbs. The velvety undersides of his limbs gripped together along most of their length and the tips acted like feet, scooting him along the floor. It made him about as tall as a person, a head above the average man, and left him two limbs free to act like arms. Of course I'd known that the posture was for our benefit, that Teese's people didn't spend all their time standing like that on their own ship. But he'd always kept it up, even in our apartment, with just the two of us. And now—now he was just hauling himself along the floor, one tired limb at a time.

"I'll get you some water," I said, and fled to the kitchen.

When I came into the bedroom, Teese was in bed, head on the pillow, eyes almost closed. I fumbled for a limb-tip, pressed the damp glass into it.

"Thank you," he said. "Ami, will you stay?"

His skin was still gray with exhaustion. "Yes," I said. "Teese—"

He opened one eye fully, fixed its heart-shaped pupil on me. "Ami?"

I'd been about to scold him, to tell him I had had no one to call, no way of knowing whether he was near death and no one to ask. But even in the dimness of our bedroom, I could see the gray mottling his skin. If I'd been a hexie, I would have felt exhausted just looking at him.

"I was worried," I said instead. I slid into bed with him and curled up against his arm. I think he was asleep before I'd pulled the covers up. But I lay awake a long time, watching the light from car headlights slide across the ceiling, mottling it bright and dark.

✣✣✣

Teese was my first live-in boyfriend, although that feels strange and wrong to say. Teese was a friend, more than a friend, but there was no way to think of him as a boy or a man. I can't say that he was my first love. He didn't move in because I loved him. He moved in because the sex was great and because he couldn't rent an apartment to save his life. The morning after our first night together, I learned that Teese had been couch-surfing his way up the Atlantic seaboard. Then I went to work at the gas station, and when I came home we had fantastic sex, then ordered pizza and ate it together messily on the couch and fell into bed, and the next day was pretty much the same, and slowly it dawned on both of us that Teese was staying.

I couldn't really afford the rent on the apartment by myself. I needed a roommate, someone willing to pay me to sleep in the living room of my one-bedroom hole-in-the-wall slice of crumbling neo-Gothic shitpile. Instead I got Teese.

"I can pay you," Teese said. "I receive high pay and long leaves in exchange for my long watches. The trouble is that local landlords do not want a hexie and I have not found a hotel that will take my currency."

From somewhere he produced a thin, shiny rectangle. "Here," he said. "This is rhodium. I haven't checked the price for a while, but it should be worth at least a month's rent."

I took it gingerly. It was about the size of half a Thin Mint, maybe a little thicker. There were odd markings on it, presumably spelling out "YES THIS IS REALLY RHODIUM" in Teese's language.

"Teese," I said, "I have no idea what to do with this."

"You could sell it?"

"Who could I sell it to? Do you seriously think I can go to

Downtown Crossing with this and find some guy in Jewelers Exchange who'll say 'Oh yeah, this is alien rhodium, we get this all the time' and give me a stack of cash?"

Teese waved a tentacle that was freckling olive-green with exasperation. "Well, at least you believe me. All the hotels I tried just pushed it back at me and said they couldn't take it."

"All the hotels—wait, did you try taking it to a bank?"

The olive-green freckles spread. "Of course I did. They told me they required a jewelers' assay. The jewelers told me they required payment in advance for the assay. And of course they cannot take payment in this possibly worthless metal."

I sighed. "Well, maybe you should try again next month. Sooner or later one of your shipmates is going to get a paycheck cashed, and then all the rich people will be buzzing about the dank alien rhodium and scheming to get it out of you as fast as they can." I pushed the rhodium tablet back into Teese's tentacle.

He made the tablet disappear again. "Maybe you're right," he said. "But in the meantime, Ami, how will you pay for the rent? Shall we get a roommate?"

"Um," I said. "I don't know if that's a good idea with you already staying here."

"It would be crowded," he said, stippling with agreement.

"Right," I said. "Crowded. I'll see if I can pick up any extra shifts at work, and if I can't, I'll short my student loan payment this month." Again.

I had to take two buses and a train to get to the Citgo where I worked. Metro Boston, where none of the workers at the gas stations can actually afford to keep a car. But, unlike driving, the bus gives plenty of time to watch the scenery. A sign in a restaurant window caught my eye. "WE SERVE OCTOPUS!!!!" Not calamari, octopus. I didn't know octopus had a culinary following, I thought. And then, Wait, are they trying to say they'd serve Teese? Hexies can eat there? But then another sign flashed by. Tiny baby octopus marinated in a thick brown gravy, with thickly markered letters shouting "THIS IS HOW WE LIKE 'EM!" "This" was underlined six times. And another: "I LIKE MINE CHOPPED AND FRIED". And another: "OCTOPUS IS BEST DEADED AND BREADED $16.95!!!" I shifted in my seat. I was starting to feel uneasy. Were people really eating octopus to express their resentment at the hexies' presence? It was stupid, a stupid thing to wonder and an even stupider thing to do; so stupid that I could just about see people doing it.

I shifted in my seat again. How many people on the bus with me felt the same way as the sign-writers? How many were chopping up octopus at home and calling it Hexie Surprise?

And what would they do to me if they knew I was fucking one every night?

✦❋✦❋✦

"Ami," Teese asked, "what are you feeling?"

I opened my eyes. "Umm," I said. "Sleepy?"

He shifted in bed beside me, propped himself up on one limb so he could look down at me in the dimness. "Besides that. Are you happy? Are you sad? Are you annoyed? It is difficult for me to tell."

I shifted too. "Well, now I'm feeling awkward," I said. "I think everyone has trouble telling how someone else is feeling sometimes, Teese. Especially in the dark, you know?"

"For my people," Teese said—he never called them 'hexies'—"it's harder to see feelings in the dark too. But it's not that dark. You can see my skin, and I can see your body and your face."

"It's probably just harder for you than for, you know, other humans," I said. "Like, I had to learn that when you go a certain kind of pattern of olive green, you're getting really annoyed. And it doesn't hit me in the gut the way it does when I see a person with a mad face. It's like I have a—a secret decoder ring in my head that I have to check. I turn the dial to 'olive green squigglies' and I see Oh, Teese is feeling frustrated or annoyed. And then I can start to have my own emotions about that."

"Hit you in the gut," Teese said thoughtfully. "When you see someone angry, Ami, you feel their anger too?"

"Not exactly," I said. "I might feel scared, actually, especially if they're mad at me and they're bigger and stronger."

Teese lay back down. "That is very different," he said. "In my people, if I see someone who is angry, I feel their anger immediately. And they know I feel it because they see it reflected on my skin."

"Yeah, I know," I said. "Do you ever get a surprise that way? Like, you didn't realize you were angry until you look at the guy next to you and see that he's mad too?"

I felt Teese shift to look at me with both eyes. "Why wouldn't I know I was angry?"

"Or sad, or whatever."

"But why wouldn't I know I was sad? Ami, all my life I have seen my feelings on myself and on everyone around me. I would have to be—damaged not to know my own feelings by now." He paused. "Probably there are people who are damaged like this, children who are born blind and have to be told their feelings and everyone else's. But you won't meet them on a starship's crew."

I said, "Jeez, Teese, we don't call blind people *damaged*." But what I thought was: *Is that how you think of me—damaged?* I held in the words. But I felt my body moving away from Teese slightly.

After a pause, Teese spoke again. "I will try to remember that. But I feel blind with you, Ami," he said. "I see your face change and I don't know what it means. Or your voice, or your body. I am like that blind child who can't read skins, when I'm with you."

"Welcome to the human race," I said.

After he moved the towels back into the closet, Teese asked if he could use my computer while I was at work. I told him I was shocked that he hadn't been using it already, and showed him how to log in and how to connect to the wi-fi and how to google. He tapped the keyboard delicately with the very tips of two tentacles, like a two-fingered typist, while I got ready for work. When I left, he was browsing Reddit at the kitchen table.

When I got home after work, Teese was still in the kitchen. "I found a way for us to make money," he called.

I stuffed my coat in the closet and headed into the kitchen. "Really? Whatcha got?"

"Look at this," he said, pushing my laptop toward me.

"Oh, ewww," I said. A naked woman rubbed a dead octopus over her genitals. "Are you kidding me?"

"I know, I know, just look," he said, pulling up another page. A woman was having sex, improbably, with a horse. And then another: a man and a—pile of balloons?

I was getting a nasty feeling about Teese's idea. "What the hell?" I asked.

"I know! There are all kinds of pictures of people putting their genitals in things and on things. All kinds of things! Animals, people, food, machines! And they get money for this! Is this news to you? It was news to me."

I made a face. "Teese, I am not going to put an octopus on my twat for money. That's . . . ." Words failed me.

"No no, of course not," he said quickly. "I would not ask you to do that, Ami. But there is one thing I did not see in all my searches. I found all kinds of people having sex with every kind of thing, but never with . . ." he paused dramatically ". . . one of my people!"

His big eyes focused on me expectantly. Yes, my boyfriend was suggesting that we camwhore ourselves for rent.

"Oh, Teese," I said helplessly. "Setting aside the fact that I'd probably be lynched, that's . . . that's . . ." I sighed. How was I going to explain porn to someone from another world? "Let's get delivery. That's a long conversation."

I got home the next night to find him swiping tentacles broadly across the keyboard and staring at a text editor. "I installed Python," he said. "I hope that is all right."

I stood staring at his keyboard technique. "Sure," I said, "just ask first next time, and . . . how are you doing that?"

"Doing what?" he asked, covering the keyboard with two arms. Lines of text appeared on the screen as if by magic.

"Typing?" I said. "You are typing, right?" If I looked very closely, I could just see the top of his arms twitch.

"Oh! I found that this is the easiest way to operate your keyboard, Ami. A little focused pressure on each key works just as well as striking. It took a bit of practice, but it's not too different from the interfaces on our ship."

"It just looks like you're hugging the computer and it's writing text for you," I said. "What're you writing, anyway?" I peered over his shoulder. It looked like free verse in English-laced gibberish.

"Python!" said Teese enthusiastically. "I told you, I installed one of your programming languages. It is not terribly different from your spoken language. I am writing a program in Python. Do you know this language too?"

"Um," I said. My nearest approach to programming had been customizing my Facebook settings. "No, can't say I do."

Teese lifted his arms off the keyboard and started telling me about his program. I tuned out and watched his skin. Watery gray patterns rippled enchantingly across his arms as he gestured. It wasn't quite like anything I'd seen before, but it was familiar, reminiscent of his skin when we were having a particularly intense conversation.

"And then —" Teese interrupted himself abruptly. "But you are not interested in this, Ami?" He peered up at me.

"I'm not a programmer, Teese," I said. "But go on. I can tell you really had fun working on this."

Teese's skin pinked and dimpled, his way of smiling. "I did indeed. Here, look at this."

He hugged the keyboard again. The screen blanked, then broke out in cheesy red hearts. "I LOVE YOU AMI" scrolled over the pulsing hearts.

I burst out laughing. "Is this what you spent the day on, you nutball?" It was awful. I loved it.

Teese's skin rippled with pinkish-brown giggles. "Anything for you!"

Teese kept up with his programming hobby. After the love note came bouncing hearts that filled the screen, blanked, and repeated. Then it was fractals, lacy whorls that spiraled chromatically across the small screen. Then seascapes where the shifting lines of ocean blended into deep blue sky.

I thought Teese was programming to kill time. I had no idea he had a goal in mind. Day after day, I came home to find that he'd built another seeming frivolity. His electronic compositions were getting bluer, though, tending toward the same pale teal he'd painted the closet.

I suppose that should've been the third warning sign; or maybe it was the fourth. I've lost count.

But I ignored it, like I'd ignored all the others, because every night when we made love Teese looked deep into my eyes and told me he couldn't imagine life without me.

✦✦✦

When I got home the next night, Teese was back at the kitchen table. "I found another way to make money!" he called to me.

I couldn't help grimacing. "I think I liked it better when you met me at the door with sex," I said.

"This is better, I promise," said Teese. "I'm going to surprise you with it. Some of my crewmates have figured out the banking system and they are the ones who will pay me."

"In rhodium?"

His skin rippled with brown giggles. "No Ami, no more rhodium! Cash! Wire transfers!"

I came to stand next to him. The screen really was filled with gibberish, as though someone had transliterated a foreign language into English and sprinkled it liberally with varicolored emoticons, often mid-word.

"This isn't a program, right?" I asked. "Just checking."

"Chatroom," Teese said happily. "It is a non-sanctioned

communication between members of my ship. There is a metals exchange in California where my crewmates have been able to exchange their pay at a reasonable rate. I have known about this, but I have no desire to go to California, actually —" he peeked up at me almost shyly "—I would much rather stay in Boston."

"I'd kinda rather you stay here, too," I said. "So are they going to exchange some of your rhodium for you? Like, you have a ship bank you can transfer it to them with, and then they transfer you back the US currency?"

He waved a tentacle. "Actually, shipboard regulations would make that complicated," he said. "Private crew currency exchanges are not very encouraged. Otherwise I could already have done that. But now I have something to sell."

"You do?" I said. "What is it?"

Teese pinked with pride. "I have created a program that my crewmates desire!"

"Really? What does it do?" I was really curious. I couldn't imagine what Teese had cooked up on my old laptop that sophisticated space-faring hexies would pay cash for.

Teese stroked the keyboard. The screen went black, then slowly faded into a shifting, pale aquamarine. It was a seascape, an abstract, a fractal, all of these and none of these at once. Barely felt lines radiated from the center, branched, shifted, dissolved. Dozens of fractal forms shimmered and danced in the background, shifting and changing. It reminded me of waves rippling the ocean, of sand grains roiled by wind, of the patterns on hexie skin.

It was mesmerizing. It was beautiful, it was somehow alien, and something about it was hauntingly, naggingly familiar.

After a few minutes, the screen blanked. "It has a timeout," Teese said quietly. "So that I do not become—lost."

I sat back. "It's gorgeous, Teese," I said quietly. "Are you an artist? Back home, I mean."

"No, no," he said. "I never had any interest in this. But now I have inspiration, Ami."

"I can see why your people would pay for this, especially if they're all as into blue-green as you are," I said. "But wait, didn't you tell me that your people would find so much blue tacky? Like that all-purple painting I had once?"

Thoughtful orange fractals rippled Teese's skin. "Actually, it is kind of tacky," he said. "But it is more than that. Ami, you can have no idea how interesting, how appealing and stimulating this is for one of us. When I look at this, I feel—things I cannot feel without it. That's why I put in the timeout," he added pragmatically.

Art has always prompted strong feelings in people, so I assumed that's what Teese was talking about. I thought it was a little weird for Teese to talk about his own art like that. But Teese clearly hadn't been exaggerating, because the money started rolling in. He'd never managed to get a US bank account, so the money went into my account. Suddenly, rent was no problem. I paid the rent, made up all the student loan payments I'd shorted, and still we had more money coming in each week than I made in a month at the Citgo. I thought about quitting my job, but didn't.

Teese wanted to take me out to dinner, to shows, to operas that neither of us had the slightest interest in. I demurred. We hadn't been out together since he'd come home with me. At first there had been a steady flow of invites to parties, ostensibly for me but always appended with "Oh, and be sure to bring that hexie who's staying with you." But we'd been too wrapped up in each other to go out, and the invitations had slowly dried up. Now we had piles of money and nowhere to go. I wouldn't have minded taking Teese to a few house parties, but Teese wasn't interested. "I've met lots of humans," he told me. "Now I have met you. Meeting more humans will just be—disappointing, I think. But I want to take you out, Ami."

"I don't really need to be taken out," I told him. "I'm pretty low maintenance." *And I don't want to be lynched,* I added silently. Teese might have met lots of humans, but they'd mostly been liberal, east-coast, college-educated twentysomethings at house parties. As far as I know, he'd never even seen the "WE SERVE OCTOPUS" signs I passed on my way to the Citgo. And I wanted to keep it that way.

We compromised on a museum date in the afternoon. Boston is dripping with museums. We went to the ICA and looked at all the blue things.

"I think your computer art is better," I murmured to him, just to see him pink.

He rippled brown with laughter instead. "I did have unique inspiration," he said cryptically.

"Being inspired to pay the rent is far from unique," I shot back. He just laughed in return.

That might have been the fifth warning sign; or maybe I'm just paranoid in retrospect.

+✳+✳+

The next day, I had a double shift at the gas station. I came home to a dark, silent apartment.

"Teese?" I called out, groping for the light switch. Maybe he'd gone out?

Something moved in the darkness. Startled, I dropped my coat and hit my head on the door frame. "Ow! Shit!" My hand finally found the light and I snapped it on.

Teese was hunched in the corner of the room, skin soot-black. He'd been nearly invisible in the dark.

"Teese, what's going on? Are you okay?" As I spoke, I noticed that the little duffle bag he'd brought with him when he moved in was sitting beside him.

"Ami," he said quietly. "No. I am not okay. I have been recalled to my ship."

I came in and closed the door behind me. "Why? What's going on? Are the hex—are your people leaving?" I hadn't heard anything on the news.

"No," he said. "Not as far as I am aware. No, this is personal. My commander is displeased with my actions and has terminated my leave."

"Your actions—Teese, what did you do?"

"It's about my program," he said. "And about selling my program to my shipmates. This has been ruled, ah, trafficking I believe is the word."

"Trafficking? Like your program is a drug?"

"Exactly like that," he said. "I told you that it has a strong effect on my people. It has been deemed an intoxicant."

"Your art is a drug?" I slid down to the floor, back against the door. "Are you in trouble?"

He waved a tentacle. "Yes and no," he said quietly. "If I report to the ship immediately, it will not be so bad for me. I should have left a few hours ago, I think. But I had to speak with you first."

"I had a double shift," I said inanely. "Wait. Wait. Are you coming back?"

"No," he said softly. "I will not be allowed to come back. And I have more bad news to tell you." He was still coal-black, but now his skin blotched red with shame as well. "The money has to go back. Everything my shipmates have paid for the program must be returned. Even though I made a gift of it to you. The ship's bank will take it back, right out of your account." His voice had faded to a whisper on the last.

"But we spent some of it," I said. I'd go into overdraft.

"I know," he said. "I—I will leave you the rhodium. Perhaps you will be able to exchange it soon."

I stared at Teese. The red hexagons spun and spun on his coal-black skin. He focused his heart-shaped pupils on the floor.

"I know the red," I said, "But what's the black?"

He murmured, so softly I could barely hear him, "I am afraid."

"You're scared of what they're going to do to you?"

"No. I'm afraid of how I will feel, not seeing you. I am afraid of how it will hurt me."

"I could come with you," I said suddenly. "It's an interstellar ship, right? And you have years-long shifts watching over your frozen shipmates? You must have some provision for bringing your partners on there or you'd go crazy."

Violent brown lightning flashed across his black-red skin. A bitter laugh, I realized. "Take you with me!" he said. "Ami, don't you realize? How don't you realize? You are the problem, Ami, you are the last human they would ever allow on the ship!"

I felt like he'd slapped me. "What? Why? How am I the problem?"

The shame-red bled away from black skin that crackled with jagged, bitter laughter. "How are you the problem!" he repeated. "You'd be a walking riot. My shipmates would fight each other to look into your eyes. They'd beat each other to death to be the one to make you come."

"Make me come," I said slowly. An awful light was dawning inside me. All the times Teese had said he loved to look into my eyes. My greenish-blue eyes. The strange familiarity of his program, as though I'd seen it somewhere before. His greenish-blue program that was, I realized now, the exact shade of my eyes. Just like the sunset that had so captivated him, and just like his "meditation closet."

"The way your eyes change," he said, "Ami, the way your eyes change when you come. The blood vessels, the tiny capillaries, they dilate."

I saw it now. "Fractal patterns moving through them, like hexie skin," I said. "And what you see, you feel."

"And what I see in your eyes, I have never seen anywhere else."

Teese's romantic-sounding words came back to me. *I have never felt before what I feel with you.* He had meant it literally. His limbic system responded to something in my changing eyes with a new emotion, one that none of Teese's people had ever felt before, while his skin struggled and failed to keep up, lapsing into static.

I sat with my back against the door and thought back over the past months. Teese had only said he loved me once, in a cheesy e-valentine. But he'd told me that he loved to stare into my eyes at least a dozen times. I'd naively thought that that meant the same thing.

"I was never your girlfriend," I realized out loud, "I was your drug."

"Please don't say that," he said. But I was pettily satisfied to see red shame-spots creeping back onto his black skin.

I stood up. "You'd better get back to your ship," I said, moving away from the door. "Just tell me one thing. What did it feel like? What did you feel when you looked into my eyes?"

He was silent for a long moment. "What is the word," he said finally, "for a color no one has ever seen? How could there be a word for it?"

"Was it a good feeling, at least?"

He closed his eyes. "It was like nothing I'll ever feel again."

He paused at the door, as if wondering whether to kiss me goodbye. I stared him down. He looked into my eyes one last time, and left.

After Teese left, I pocketed his rhodium and went for a walk. I wanted to hate Teese, but I couldn't. He'd never lied to me. He'd been telling me exactly what he saw in me from the moment he'd first seen me. I just hadn't heard.

And what if I'd been the one given the chance to feel a brand-new emotion, one never felt by anyone before? I probably would've taken it. Hell, I'd let an alien move in with me mostly for the orgasms. And if I'd loved that alien later—well, that wasn't his fault either, not really.

I fingered the rhodium. Teese couldn't get anyone to exchange it, but that might've had more to do with his tentacles than with the metal's value. I still couldn't see myself haggling over it at Jewelers Exchange, but I could probably pawn it for a few hundred to tide me over, and buy it back when I had the money to pay for an assay.

Because I did plan to have more money. Teese might be a terrific programmer, but he'd never learned to clear his browser history. It'd be easy to find the hexie message boards where Teese had sold his now-banned software. I didn't need the software. I'd just aim a webcam at my eyes and the money would come flooding in.

I'd have dozens of hexies staring into my eyes, chromatophores fluttering. Maybe hundreds of hexies—who knew how many Teese had hooked on his program? Enough to worry his bosses. Enough, I realized, to enforce a ban on Teese if I made it a condition of my show.

It wouldn't be porn, not in any human sense. Not as long as Teese wasn't watching.

I couldn't truly hate Teese. But I'm only human. And I couldn't help thinking of Teese, sitting alone in his quarters, skin rippling with regret, while his shipmates watched my eyes as I came. And I felt —

Well. If I had been a hexie, my skin would have pinked and dimpled at the thought. But I'm human, so I had to make do with a smile.

The Dreamers of Ungvár
Éva Berniczky

Ungvári álmodozók | Berniczky Éva
translated by Bogi Takács

Mr. Bekk is "... one of those twisted dream-builders who could only be produced by a positivist era."—Miklós Szentkuthy

We'll take it across the roof of the garage, my friend, Mr. Bekk yelled back over his shoulder to his mate. He gave orders to the person wheezing behind him, with such conviction as if the two of them had only had to lift an entirely weightless object. The small, thin man holding up the other end of the blue sofa bed followed him blindly. The small taxi driver from Kharkiv had believed his helper that the two of them could easily lift this massive piece of furniture up to the slightly angled metal roof of the garage. Why would he have doubted, when for months at that point, he had been haunted by the impossible. The huge oaf carrying the sofa in front of him kept on smiling back at him, it's going to work out, druzhe. They had been carrying that weight down all the way from the second floor already in this altered state of consciousness—even though it had not been easy to descend in the narrow stairwell. On the walls: painting canvases, framed drawings, swing arm lights jutting out. It had been like skiing downhill among porcelain vases, carrying this monstrosity; yet they hadn't broken anything. In their upside-down world, caution had become superfluous, the china shop moved around inside the elephant. No handrails or physical dimensions presented a barrier, nor did gravity. The two of them had only realized on the first floor that the sofa bed couldn't fit through the entryway. Regardless of how they rotated it, turning it at one angle after another, the piece of furniture always proved about a centimeter wider than the opening. Finally they tilted the sofa up on its shorter end and took a breather. Mr. Bekk seemed determined, like someone who could only accept one possible solution. Now that he'd already driven the company truck up the hill, he'd either leave with the donated furniture, or not at all.

You can't sleep on the ground, druzhe, the endless fall rains are coming. You have no idea how nasty the mountains are here, whatever or whoever they grab ahold of, they won't let go—neither drought nor a flood. The wife will be happy with the free sofa bed, believe me, druzhe. It's a bit worn down, but it will help chase away the nightmares, help you forget the hells of insanity, the smell of the basement. He imagined the puny little man's tall wife, with her model's physique, how she'd embrace the startled, boy-faced Misha in gratitude. The truck driver didn't quite understand how it was possible for someone to have such a gentle blue-eyed gaze in the middle of the war like his refugee friend had. It had to have been the jittery Karina shining her husband's irises every night until they gleamed so innocent. She had an easy job, she sold topaz stones set in silver in a small jeweler's shop. The two of them had started working almost immediately upon arriving, on the very next day. Misha now takes the shopkeeper Karina to her brand-new workplace every day. They sit in their car, the shop-taxi, and in that moment, the taxi driver from Kharkiv becomes a driver from Ungvár. His passengers are the happy unhappy folk.

Mr. Bekk is one of the happy happy folk. He doesn't have to insist in any of the three languages he speaks, neither separately, nor simultaneously (as he usually does), that women have always valued him. Even though they keep on leaving him for other people, but before they leave, they do give him the respect that's his due. István Vilmos Bekk has a lifetime membership. The aristocratic "Vilmos" might have an appeal to women, this is why they address him as *Mister* Bekk. If that scammy-sounding "István" weren't there to disturb his game, he would be all set.

Alas, there had been no women in the military enlistment office; the commander bit off his "Vilmos" in pure charity, as if it had never been printed onto his paper file. Well, what should we do with you, Styopa, he asked, using the Ukrainian for "István." There you go, trained rifleman. Again hiding behind your momma's skirts.

His mother had had a stroke over a decade ago, and since then she hadn't been able to get out of bed. There was only one sentence that remained stuck in Manci Bekk's head: Eventually we're going to leave this place, my son, she would declare every morning. And go where, Mom, where? Mr. Bekk washed her body with care; but she didn't allow her desires to be washed away. Find a place like that, my little Vili, on your all-knowing telephone, where we'll have a river and we'll have mountains, or at least a hill with a castle, with crumbling steps leading up to the top. We'll settle for nothing less, Mom, Mr. Bekk always answered once he was done with his procedures. His ever-active mother who knew no limits even in dying deserved at least this much hope. She would pedal her bike even while lying in bed. There are two memories connecting the two of them inseparably, and they wobble and bike ahead on those for decades now. His mother is sitting in her puffy chair covered with red faux fur, and is planning how they'd move to a better world, and he's already in this imagined place, squeezing his fingers tight. The neighboring kids are trying to pry his fingers apart, what's in your hand, little Vili? It's a star. They laugh at him, they call him names, uncomprehending; how could you have one, you're crazy. But yes, he insists with his three-year-old's vehemence, yes really, a star. You surely got it from the soldiers on top of the mountain. No, no, he's shaking his head desperately. Mom went all the way up to the sky on her bike and she brought it from there. Oh wow, they're envious now, show me. Manci Bekk rolls past them on their street every day, you can't make up someone like Auntie Manci, or the bike, so then the pilfered star has to be real too.

The commander is frowning, he doesn't believe him that Mr. Bekk has been taking care of his mother alone for over ten years. He places the documents on the officer's desk. The officer glares at them suspiciously. Bring Mom into the office, show her, and then we'll issue an exemption, he slams his palm down on the desk in frustration. Together with the bed? Mr. Bekk asks. The bed can stay, get her out of it, get her dressed and bring her somehow. She doesn't even have street clothing or shoes, how could I afford to buy her some, even her underwear has vanished. All six pieces. Yes, Commander, I report she has a sleeping gown. Are there no women around you who would undress so that your Mom could wear their rags? There are only women around me, Commander.

Just yesterday three women held him by his legs so that he wouldn't fall into the sewer pipe while fixing it. They lowered him into the narrow sewer opening, upside-down, like a bat, to fix a mains break. That was the only way he could get to the pipe, the way he could cut out the piece that had rusted away, screw everything back together, swap out a valve down below. They lowered him-raised him, lowered-raised . . . He hung in the dark hole wearing a miner's head lamp, and the entire morning, all that people could see of him were his two legs. I reached it, he kicked out so that they wouldn't lower him further. They held onto his pants' legs like they'd won a prize. Kick twice, Mr. Bekk, when you're done, and we'll pull you up.

He'd left the despondent Misha alone only for three minutes or so, not more. Mr. Bekk had a talent to guesstimate. He determined without measuring anything that the sofa bed could fit through the doorway that led to the interior courtyard. He went out to the porch, ran down the steps all the way to the courtyard a whole level below. He found the street exit. The sidewalk between the building and the steel-frame garage looked hopelessly narrow. And then he had his indisputably great idea—they would take out the sofa bed through the roof of the garage. They had taken it all the way down, then dragged it up to street level in the direction of the garage. Once they got to the final obstacle, they put it down vertically again, took a breather. Then Mr. Bekk jumped up to the roof and bent down to pull the sofa bed up, yanked at the side of it he could reach, while from the other side the tiny taxi driver lifted it up and pushed it skyward; as much as he could due to his height. In just a moment they were both sliding across the roof holding onto it. People in the first floor living room could watch a live broadcast of the blue sofa bed flying over the garage with a devastating metallic roar, soaring toward the street.

The rest is child's play, druzhe, he patted the shoulder of the delighted new owner of the sofa bed. Once the hard-to-ship piece of furniture was finally set to be on its way to his friend's temporary dwelling, Mr. Bekk stepped out to the porch for a moment of rest. He lifted his head proudly up high. From the third floor of the apartment building right across, a young woman was waving to him. She yelled, are you furniture delivery people? Well, not really, shrugged the truck driver. Come on up, the neighbor called out to him, I'll show you something, if you like it, you can take it.

In a few minutes, he was welcomed into the foyer. The living room opened directly from it. No, I can't go inside, he apologetically brushed dust off the front of his pants. I'll just glance inside from here, he tried to fend off the homeowner's aggressive attempts to foist some furniture on him. He had a bad feeling. He knew he would see exactly what he had imagined he would. Even though they'd passed the trial by fire with the taxi driver from Kharkiv. This would never end. The dual-pane door opened wide, showing an easily recognizable, run-down living room. The woman lifted her arm and pointed at the offered piece of furniture with merciless, murderous determination. Mr. Bekk immediately closed his eyes, but he was too late. The familiar worn-out blue sofa bed was there, spread out mockingly before him.

Three Forest Tales

David Demchuk

Krisztina

I am the girl in the water. I am the rusalka.

One day when I was thirteen, I woke up very ill, so tired that I could not get out of my bed to go to school. Mama felt my head, listened to my chest. I had no fever, no cough, my heart was strong. I was a good student and rarely unwell, so she kept me home, but I could see she was concerned. At lunch I could eat very little, the smell of everything was overpowering to me. I was sick all over myself and again in the sink. Finally she warmed some clear broth for me and brought it to my bed.

"Mama," I said. "I have a fish in me."

It was as if she didn't hear me, so I said it again, and louder. "Mama. I have a fish in me. The fish is making me sick." And I took her hand and pressed it to my belly. The little fish quivered and curled under her hand, and she pulled it away as if she had burned herself.

"How did this happen?" she asked, frightened and furious. "Who has done this to you?"

I was confused, I didn't know what she meant. "I don't know, I don't know," I insisted, now as afraid as she was.

She slapped me across the face. "Have you let any boys touch you or kiss you?"

My cheek was stinging, my eyes were wincing with tears. I didn't like boys, never played with them at school or after, ran and hid and waited for them to pass whenever I could. And then I had a thought, not knowing it was the worst thought of all.

"Mama," I said. "Could a woman have put the fish in me?"

She became very still. "What do you mean?" she whispered.

"When Papa was out in the field," I said, "and you were at the church with Mrs. Derhak, a woman I didn't know came to the door, an old woman, and she wanted to play a game with me, and she said I shouldn't tell you or we would all get into trouble. She said it would be a game but—all I remember was she held my hands up with one hand and tickled my belly with the other, and I laughed and I laughed until I fell asleep, and then when I woke up she was gone."

After a long moment, with her face turned away from me, she said "I see."

I waited and waited. The little fish was whirling around inside me, as fearful as I was. But she sat and sat on the edge of my bed and then finally asked, "Have you ever seen this woman before? In the village? On someone's farm?"

"No," I said.

"Only this once?" she asked.

"Yes," I said.

She turned to me, and somehow her face was so dark that I could barely see it, even though the sun had yet to slip down and out of the sky. "Come then," she said, "you must get dressed. I know how we will make you feel better."

She bundled me out of the house while I was still wrapping my cloth coat around me. The fish was frantic now, swimming in tight wild circles, and the sickness and weakness were like heavy hands pulling at my shoulders, my legs, my hair.

"Please, can we go tomorrow?" I asked, but it was like shouting into the wind. She led me through the field to the path into the woods, which I knew eventually would lead to the lake. I knew there were plants you could eat, herbs and flowers and mushrooms that could take your sickness away. I had heard many stories of Baba Yaga, and the children at school often said that such witches still lived among us. Perhaps that was where she was taking me. Or perhaps she was a witch herself.

I struggled to keep up with my mother, whose stride had become broader and more purposeful as we emerged from the woods. The large cold lake stretched out before us. Soon we were at the water's edge. She pulled the coat from me, pushed me towards the water and said, "Go in."

"But it's so cold," I cried, and it was true—I could see my breath between us and knew the lake would be liquid ice.

"Good," she said. "The cold water will tighten around you and the fish will swim out, and you will feel much better. Go in."

Sick and cold and tired and sore, I obeyed her and stepped into the water. "Come over here where it's deeper," she said, "and put your hands up here on this edge." Soon the cold clear water was up to my chest, my neck, I held on to the edge and looked up at her.

"How long?" I asked. "How long?" I was shivering so hard I could barely hold on, my teeth were chattering.

"Not long," she said, kneeling down to me; then she reached out and grabbed a fistful of my hair and pushed me under the water. I tried to fight, I tried to struggle, but I could not. My final breath bubbled out of me, and soon even the little fish was quiet and still. Mama gently let go of my hair, and I sank to the lake's dark floor.

Then she screamed.

"Noooooo!" she screamed. "Noooooo!" And soon some men ran from the church, which was not far away.

"Mrs. Malyk!" they shouted. "What is it?"

"My baby, my Krizstina—she ran in the water and threw herself in—she was too fast, I tried to catch her!"

I looked up and saw the men peering over the edge, but I was too deep for them to see me. Suddenly, I felt the little fish quiver and curl inside me again, felt it flicker and warm me like a tiny red flame. The heat spread through me to the tips of my fingers and the ends of my toes. My body grew long and lithe, my breasts full and rounded. My hair, now long and lush and red like oxblood, eddied and swirled around me.

I swam out into the centre of the lake, then spiralled up to the surface—looked across to where the cluster of men now poked at the water with long sticks and hooks. Even though it was impossibly far, I saw Mama, saw her face, and I fancied she saw me.

And then I turned and I dove down
down and

down

Luisa

This was many years ago, back in the first land, when my grandmother was still alive and I was a small child. I would be sent to visit her in the woods, and while she was cooking she would tell me stories of the Bone Mother. *The little girl came up to the Bone Mother's house and knocked on the heavy wooden door. It opened all by itself and the little girl, who was very much like you, saw the Bone Mother at her giant wood stove. There she stood, throwing handfuls of vegetables in a big black pot made of iron, just like her teeth.* And then my grandmother would smile with her teeth made of iron, and I would giggle and shiver.

The Bone Mother lived in a little house deep in the woods, just like my grandmother's house, where she received visits from lonely young women, children cast out by their heartless parents, and handsome but treacherous men. The Bone Mother could be very wicked or very kind, and sometimes both. *Do all I ask and I will reward you. If not, I will eat you up.*

Once, as she was telling these stories, a whimpering came from one of the cages in the darkest corner of the kitchen—from one of her little kurchas, or chicks as she called them. Over she flew like a big black crow, pulled a little hand out of the cage and bit off one of its fingers. As the little kurcha screamed and screamed, my grandmother sat back on her stool, a thin trickle of blood dribbling down to her chin. "There," she said. "Now you have something to cry about."

I never looked too closely at the cages.

I would visit every Saturday, and always for lunch, and lunch was always a boiled egg, a bit of cheese, a bowl of potato soup, fresh-baked bread and some cold salted meat left over from the night before. She would watch me carefully as I ate, and in particular when I ate the meat, to make sure I finished everything she fed me. Once I eyed my plate suspiciously—the meat was so much like a tiny leg, with a tiny foot at the end and tiny little toes—and I asked her "Are you the Bone Mother, Babcia?"

"I might be and I might not," she answered. "But I will tell you this: I am the oldest of our mother's daughters and, of all my children's children, you are one who will one day take my place. You will live in my house, you will have all my jewels and gold. My cooking pots. My iron teeth. My many visitors. Some will come to you for wisdom, some for strength. Some will come with cakes and wine, asking for help to find true love or to seek revenge. Others will come to cheat and trick you, and even try to kill you. You must protect this house, and our families, and you must protect yourself."

"Why are you telling me this?" I asked. "Is something going to happen? Are you going to die?"

"Everything dies," she said simply, "and I am no different. One cannot be afraid. As you become a woman, my time will come to an end. And then, when you are very old, another in our line will take her turn."

"But the Bone Mother is a wicked witch who eats naughty

children," I cried. Babcia smiled and pushed my plate closer to me, the little leg glistening in a sauce of butter and herbs. Nervously, I picked it up with my fingers and tore at the meat with my teeth. It was, admittedly, delicious.

"Good children do taste better," she said wistfully, "but there are so few of them. If you can be satisfied with naughty children, you will always have food on the table. They are never in short supply."

"But I don't want to be wicked, I don't want people to be afraid of me. I want to make them happy. I want them to love me."

She seemed hurt by this, and became very still, and the whole house grew quiet around her. "I wanted that too," she said softly. "We all want that at the start. You will see how the world changes you. Your kindness will be met with hate. Your wisdom will be met with fear."

I set the bones back down on the plate, stripped of all their flesh. I took a piece of thick white bread and wiped the juice from my plate, and from my chin. My grandmother's long thick tail, pink and hairless like that of a rat, unfurled from behind her and swept the bones into a bowl to be set aside for roasting.

"I cannot tell you how to be," she said, taking my hand. "You can only be who you are. But to be the Bone Mother is to always be hungry. What you eat, and why, depends on you."

Two full centuries have passed. I am the now the oldest one. The little house is gone, as are the jewels and gold. I have outlived my own children and their children. Few from our families have survived, and those who did so fled to escape the enveloping darkness.

Yet among those few there is a child, one who will succeed me. She feels the gnawing in her belly and it draws her to my hiding place. For a time, we will dine together. I will tell her my stories, and teach her what she needs to know. Through her, our kind will live anew. I will not be the last.

✦❋✦

Nicolai

I do not remember this. I cannot say what is true. A year after she and my father married, my mother lost her first child and was told there would be no other. This was hard, as you can imagine, and my mother told my father to go and find another wife who could bear him a boy. My father loved my mother and remained. But their dead son was a shadow between them that even strangers could see.

The story she tells: One day, just as winter was turning to spring, my father was helping a neighbour repair his barn while my mother stayed at home sewing. She heard a cry from the forest behind the farmhouse and, rather than wait for him to return, she went out to see what it was. Just beyond the line of the trees, still in sight of the house, she found me lying in the fresh-fallen snow, a baby, naked and shivering and close to death. No footprints anywhere. I had white hair and pale eyes. She thought I was her first son's ghost. She named me after him, nursed me as if she had borne me and, when no one came to claim me, she and my father made me their own.

But there were wolves in those woods, sometimes heard but seldom seen. They howled, but did not come near. One evening, my father was out back with me, near the berry bushes. He looked up and saw a pack of dark hunched figures, with glittering eyes, watching from within the trees. He bundled me up, startling me into tears, and he hurried me into the house. He had a gun, his father's hunting rifle, but he had never killed with it, and my mother had never touched it. He took it down from the back closet shelf, stepped out the door and raised it. The dark figures and their shining eyes were already gone.

A few mornings later, my mother awoke to feel a cool breeze curling around her toes, the scent of fresh grasses filling the bedroom. She looked out into the hall to see the back door into the kitchen was open, sunlight bursting into the house. She gasped, jumped from the bed, checked my crib. I was gone. She screamed, waking my father, and pulling her clothes around herself she ran into the sunshine, blinded, shouting and crying, into the forest. She stopped just where the leaves cast their shade on the ground, and she stood and she looked and she listened. And my father stopped and stood beside her, holding the rifle.

It was quiet and still. Quiet as no forest should be.

"We will need help to search," he whispered. "We will need ten, maybe fifteen men."

"No," she hissed. "I will not leave. We must find him now."

She looked to the right, where a small rise was crowned with a trio of beech trees. She moved slowly towards it while my father watched—then stopped, listened again. A high light whine, and then gentle panting. She motioned for my father to come in closer; then she carefully crept to the source of the sound. In a den on the other side of the rise, a white wolf was nestled on a pile of rags, nursing her young: three tiny white pups, and me—the warm wolf milk smeared around my hungry mouth.

My father raised the gun—and my mother stopped him. "No," she said. And as the word spilled from her mouth, three other wolves emerged from among the trees. He lowered the barrel, and he and she moved backward slowly as the animals stared intently. Once out of the forest, my father turned and asked "What will we do?"

"We will wait," my mother said. "I will wait. They will not harm him, or they would have done so." Then she turned to my father and said, "She saw my face, and I saw hers."

"They are animals," he spat. "Our son, is he also an animal?"

"We are all animals," she answered. "I will wait."

The next evening, my mother was in the kitchen making supper, talking to my father in the other room when she realized she was alone. He had slipped out the door behind her. Suddenly she heard one shot, and then another. She rushed out to see him stagger out of the woods, and fall to the ground. She screamed and ran to him—his face and neck had been mauled, and he shuddered furiously, the blood coursing out of him and then slowing to a trickle. The convulsions slowed and stopped. He was dead.

A howl tore through the forest behind her. She turned and ran to the den to find a woman who was not a woman, a woman with long white hair and eight teats, shot in the shoulder, her pups bewildered and mewling around her, and around me. She saw my mother and pulled the rags over herself, which my mother saw were her blouse and skirt.

My mother went to her, knelt with her, tore her own skirt to clean and dress the wound. She fed the pups warmed goat milk. She went and fetched water and food as the three wolves watched and wailed. She stayed through the night with the woman, came back with me day after day, until one day the den was empty. The wolves had moved on.

I do not remember. I cannot say what is true. But I do know this: when my mother died many years later, I knelt beside her bed and cried, and the wolves in the woods, they cried along with me.

The Bike Shadow
Yaryna Katorozh

Велосипедник | Ярина Каторож
translated by Kateryna Darchyk

I've always appreciated a tale with a good beginning, although my own birth could hardly be deemed special. One very unremarkable day, I appeared from the flashes and the everlasting motion of a bike spoke. When the movement had suddenly ceased and the cycle had been parked in the driveway of an unknown neighborhood, I, still nothing more than a spoke, crashed onto the pavement. That was when I witnessed my own transformation for the first time. Someone had discarded an old mirror, and its smooth surface clearly reflected how the unmoving spoke that lay on the ground suddenly started quivering, glowing—and then transformed into a silverlike creature with four slim legs, a long tail and oblong features. I was about half a meter tall and had long, sleek fur. From that very day, I already had a few instinctual skills: I was good at watching people and good at hiding from them, and I had a perpetual affinity with bicycles. This latter fondness would eventually earn me my name.

I didn't know who I was yet, and neither did I give it much thought. When I craved adventure, I changed into a bike spoke and traveled around the city, hopping in on a random wheel and watching hundreds of different feet pedal away: some wore sneakers, others sandals; some dressed in casual jeans or classic pants, while others ignored pants altogether, their tanned and slim shapes adorned in colorful dresses with flowing hemlines. I loved spending hours in bike wheels and, whenever I got bored, I could always transform back into my four-legged self, sneaking into the shadows of nearby buildings and windowsills, or hiding under the tables on summer terraces, watching humans. Always going unnoticed. Grasping their language, habits, and appearances. Learning how to love them. I was curious to find out how they ate and slept because I myself never did. I never stopped moving around and watching them for a single second—not during the day, not at night. I wanted to know why humans changed their clothes every day. And I could never figure out why they kissed either.

Most people around me called themselves Leopolitans. As far as I understood, the city we'd all been born in was called Lviv. The word was like music to my ears.

One day I realized that not all the townspeople deserved admiration. I was about four months old and already very aware that every bicycle had an owner. I had been spending the last few days in the wheel of a strange girl who cycled to a little shop where she worked in the morning, then rode around with her friends or went back to her apartment on the outskirts of the city. There she left her "iron horse"—her words, not mine—in the driveway of her apartment building, chaining it to a little fence. One ordinary evening like that, after the daytime warmth had been replaced with heavy dusk, *he* appeared. I was right there, my bigger form sitting on a tree and watching the birds feed their squealing nestlings, when I felt uneasy all of a sudden. The feeling I got in my gut made my fur curl—I turned my head to look at the small fence and saw at once a man, in a black hoodie that covered his whole face, approach the bicycle I'd been traveling in. Having retrieved an unknown device, he got rid of the protection lock. Carefully, I took a few steps on the tree branch . . .

The man got on the bike—and took off! But the "iron horse" was not his!

Instantly leaping off the branch, which flustered the sleepy birds, I sprinted after the burglar. I had no time to worry about humans seeing me, especially since I could be easily mistaken for a huge slim cat in the dark. My strong paws pushed off the ground, and I dashed onto the road with cars driving past me. I looked around, for a moment losing the target from my sight—when my instincts pulled me to the left. I ran in that direction, jumping along the pavement, and saw a familiar back in front of me. The thief was fast, but not as fast as . . .

I hopped on one of the nearby parked cars and jumped from there, aiming at the back in black . . . *One more moment, and I will bring him down!*

I wasn't thinking about what would come next. But as I was flying through the air, I suddenly realized my rear limbs felt weirdly numb. I felt cramps going through my body—but before I could even get scared, or comprehend what was happening, a swift, winged something bumped into me and both of us went straight into the lilac bushes on the side of the road.

"Idiot!"

The offensive word came from behind. I roused myself but groaned at once—my rear paws were burning. I opened my eyes and saw a winged silhouette among the dark leaves, lamppost light shining down on it. I blinked a few times and, to my own amazement, realized that the blurred blob was a creature similar to myself, except it had longer fur, colored in black and red, a fiery red nape and two sets of wings that got darker closer to the tips. The creature swung its tail, and I could see then that it was forked and had a small tassel on each end.

The tassels trembled nervously when the flying cat blinked at me with her bright green eyes. I figured she was female straight away—from the dissatisfied look on her sweet face and the way she insulted me straight away. Sometimes human females did that when talking to males. I never understood that behavior, even though I did find it funny.

"Are you out of your mind?" the redfur asked me again and, unable to contain myself, I snorted.

"Why are you insulting me?"

"Because I haven't seen such stupidity in a while … a spirit attacking a human. We can't do that, don't you know?" she asked, standing up and moving to a different spot, where she sat down again. Then she got up and moved back again. I watched her walk, enchanted, and then noticed I could feel my rear limbs again. I sat down too.

"I didn't mean to harm him," I offered quietly. "He stole a bicycle and someone had to stop him."

"That's not what this is about! We can't interfere with people's fate, got it? I knew you were a novice!" The creature blinked again. "You felt your paws go numb, didn't you? I could see you were hurting. The reason for that is, we turn into stone when we mess with people's business. We can't let humans see us, and we mustn't touch them. If you ever break the rule, you might turn into stone one day and never wake up again!"

Suddenly, she turned away and left.

"Wait!" I yelled. The winged one stopped and looked at me expectantly. "Who are you?"

"Others call me Roof Shadow. I am a spirit of this city. Just like you," she responded hesitantly. She took another step away from me, then added, "We have long been calling you Bike Shadow. You are far too fascinated with your wheely stuff."

I wanted to ask something else, but the Roof Shadow exited the lilac bushes and, pushing herself off the ground, flapped her strong wings and flew up into the darkness.

She was so close to the sky. I had never even looked at the thing properly. But the next few days I couldn't take my eyes off it, so much so that they started getting watery. I was looking for her, the Roof Shadow, for I wished to see her again. For having met someone like myself, I instantly felt even more lonely in this city where I had to hide from those who elicited such warm feelings in me.

A few times I thought I'd seen the wave of the familiar wings—but it always turned out to be a fat pigeon moving swiftly between cornices, cobbles, and monuments. When I was in a good mood, I loved chasing pigeons: the funny thing was that, when scared, those birds were too lazy to fly off and so they just ran down the street, waddling on their short, thin feet.

Once, one such fat, winged sluggard crashed right into the head of my cyclist companion at the time. What a relief the guy was wearing a helmet! We face planted so hard that the road was closed off for the next five minutes.

The pigeon, clearly, was safe and sound.

Others have long been calling you Bike Shadow...

Does it mean that the Roof Shadow and I are not the only spirits in Lviv? But why is no one reaching out to me? Why am I always alone?

You'd have to be alive for longer than four months to answer that question. And to figure out why people hurt each other. Even when traveling in other bike wheels, I sometimes went to visit the girl who'd lost her "iron horse" so unexpectedly and unpleasantly. When she left her apartment the next day and noticed that her bike was gone, she started crying! But she made peace with the loss soon enough. In the meantime, I was spending hours in the same spot, the dark alley between the apartment buildings that both overlooked the shop my dear human worked at and enabled me to discreetly lift my eyes up to the sky. After it had been a few weeks, then months, my hope of once again seeing the Roof Shadow started fading away.

The summer passed, and the rainy season started. One day the ground got covered in ice and the world snowed—everything around me was so thick and white that I almost thought I was in a different land. But no, the houses in Lviv were the same as before. The people, however, were dressed so warmly you could barely see their noses behind layers and layers of scarves and collars. And you couldn't spot a single bicycle around.

Sadness took over me. If spirits can be depressed, I suppose that was exactly what hit me. Like a stray, I wandered the city aimlessly, spending nights in garages next to the bicycles stored there. As naive as I was, I was convinced it would last forever, convinced that no one would ever get on their "iron horse" again, and that I would freeze lying next to them in a shed . . .

One day before dawn, my head in the clouds, I wandered to the place that used to be dear to me. To the alley where the sky could no longer be seen behind all the snow. Darkness had long fallen over the city, which meant most humans would be in their beds. The shop lights, however, were still on and I could see a familiar stranger through the windows—the girl who had once upon a time had her bike stolen. She was decorating the shop windows with lights and, from what I could see, singing. Her red hair and pink cheeks, along with the warmth radiating from the shop and the light flowing out into the street, suddenly made me see the world differently. That girl there, among the shelves full of presents, was singing. The girl who'd lost her bicycle. The only bicycle she'd had. I had a whole city of them, and she'd only had one.

Still, she was singing.

That night I decided to walk her home.

The redhead left work very late. She locked the shop and strolled along the street. I went after her, listening to her soft steps and hearing music in them. Her good mood was contagious.

Then suddenly . . . The girl slipped and fell!

Silently, right on her back.

I was expecting her to stand up, let out an annoyed groan—like humans usually did—and walk away, shaking the snow off her clothes. But the girl lay still. On her own, with no one around to help. I carefully approached her and picked up on her quiet breathing.

It seemed she had fallen asleep from the slip. I couldn't find another explanation for what I saw.

For a moment I stood still, not knowing what to do, then came up closer and nuzzled her nose with mine. She moaned quietly and painfully. The girl was hurting!

I need to wake her up! As soon as the thought came to my mind, the top of my nose went numb and I felt painful cramps running from my snout to the end of my tail. I jumped back.

My body was turning into stone from touching a human.

But how could I wake up my stranger if I could not touch her? If I could not interfere with her destiny? How would I . . .

There was no one else around.

And I realized—there wasn't another way.

I couldn't wake her up without harming myself. And so I had to choose: become a stone-hearted spirit and keep on living my eternal life, or save the fleeting life of a human. Perhaps, the impermanence of their lives was what made them so valuable.

I approached my friend again, feeling the numbness spread into my paws. But I willed myself not to stop. I pounced on her and nudged her pallid face with my snout again. The girl started grunting, and her face twisted. I pressed my paw against her cheek, then the other one. *Don't freeze, my friend . . .* I was pawing at her cheeks, her lips, her forehead, like a cat trying to wake up its human—I saw them doing it through house windows. With each movement the cold was piercing my muscles deeper and deeper. I did not stop. The girl twitched her hand slowly and moaned again, but I didn't achieve any further response. Her eyelids didn't tremble once ... It seemed she had hit her head too hard.

Everything was going black before my eyes. I gave the last of my strength to nose her face, stomp on her jacket, even growl. All was in vain. Breathing was becoming difficult.

"You're doing it wrong, Bike Shadow! It's wrong!" I heard someone's desperate scream. Suddenly, a winged cocoon hit me—once again!—and we rolled over into a snowdrift next to my human friend. I snarled, trying my best to go back, pushing the Roof Shadow away. But my body wasn't listening to me anymore. I was barely breathing. And I was so afraid! I was scared to die and afraid that the unconscious girl would freeze to death and never wake up again. And all of it would be pointless!

White snow was settling on her red hair—it looked like an icy blanket enveloping the cold cobblestones underneath.

"Don't you ... dare ... I must ... I must save her," I mumbled, feeling my muscles tighten under a layer of stone, unable to fight it. Breathing became even harder, but I kept muttering dreadfully and desperately, hoping that the Roof Shadow would hear me, "You don't care ... You come and go as you please ... Go ... Go away ... "

I wished to express all the hurt I'd been holding inside for weeks.

Her green eyes regarded me ... not with anger. No. With compassion and fear. And then the Roof Shadow ascended and disappeared from sight again. Just a moment later, I heard the clanking of broken glass, followed by the sound of a spirit crashing into the snow on the other side of the street.

The last thing that reached my ears was the angry—and then terrified—screams of the house inhabitants whose window the Roof Shadow had just broken. It sounded like they'd looked out the window and saw an unconscious girl in the middle of a dark street.

The Roof Shadow did what I hadn't thought of. She harmed

people by having woken them and caught their attention. They were going to save the redhead.

It all made sense then. People were always meant to be saved by people.

And the spirits could give in to the stone.

The pain was bringing back my senses. I assumed that was how humans felt when their hands got frozen and they revived them in warm water.

The pain didn't scare me though. I was surprised that I felt warm and soft.

"I'm alive?" I muttered, opening my eyes.

"Very much so," replied someone's husky voice. "Roof Shadow saved you in time."

The room around me was dark, yet the smell was lovely. Pastries. Could it have been a storage room in some bakery, closed for the night? It certainly looked like one. I could even make out the shelves for the bread and buns.

Slowly, I could discern a few silhouettes around me. Their bodies all looked similar to mine and that of the Roof Shadow, although some were bigger than others. One of them had four long ears and narrow turquoise eyes that glowed in the dark; another one was covered in scales.

They were the spirits of Lviv. Each one of them was bound to something, like I was to cycles and the Roof Shadow was to roofs, where the sky met the built world. There were about ten of them in the room.

"Why didn't I die?" I asked quietly. The pain was passing, and I was starting to think more clearly. The memories of the latest events came back. "Is the girl okay?"

"I already told you: you are alive because Roof Shadow took you away from the human in time. The girl is okay, the neighbors with the broken window saw her and called an ambulance."

"What about Roof Shadow? She fell . . . "

The spirits stepped aside and behind them, in the corner, I saw a familiar figure—the Roof Shadow was curled up in a ball and using her wings as a blanket. Her eyes were closed. The stone layer was slowly receding from her paws.

I felt burning shame for everything I'd said to the Roof Shadow. She fell from the sky because she started turning into stone. Her wings hadn't been listening to her anymore.

Because she chose to help me.

"Roof Shadow is fine. Those of us who are close to the sky don't take falls well. She'll be asleep for a few more hours," the same spirit prompted. White, with silky fur.

"There are so many of you," I said, getting up. "Why have I never met any of you?"

"Every spirit is different. Some choose to live forever with a heart of stone rather than doing a good deed and ending up in a stone shell. We've always been here, watching you and making sure you weren't in trouble. Roof Shadow is extremely preoccupied with naive novices. As you can see, she came to your aid when you needed her."

"What do they call you?"

"Doc Shadow. It's probably my white fur, looks like a doctor's coat. Plus I love living in hospitals."

The Doc Shadow smiled at me, which looked astounding on his animal-like visage, and I couldn't help but smile back. He turned his gaze to the Roof Shadow once again.

I never understood why people kissed. But I was lucky to find out why they love and save each other.

Approaching the Roof Shadow, I lay down next to her and hugged her from the back. She stretched herself slightly, barely opening her eyes, then turned to the other side and blanketed my body with two of her four wings. For the second time in my life, I felt myself drifting off. Perhaps we only ever get to sleep after a great challenge.

This tale of mine had a good beginning.

Iron Goddess of Compassion

Olha Brylova

Залізна богиня милосердя | Ольга Брильова
translated by Anatoly Belilovsky

In my dream, rockets screech and fall, their warheads explode, part of my sleeping brain screams, "*Grad!* Down on the ground!" while another whispers, "Serves you right for sleeping on the job," then the next concussion is close, really close, even the floor shakes beneath me, and Zhang is yelling, swearing a blue streak, but it's all in Russian so my dream logic tells me not to worry, and then at the end of a string of well-chosen epithets Zhang says, "Who dropped wet scrap in furnace, she full of *xuě*" and it's the Chinese word for "snow" that alerts me that things have gotten out of control and I dive, trying to fall flat on my face, and finally come wide awake. I'm lucky I don't react as fast to dream emergencies as I did in real life—instead of sprawling on the floor of the control room amid total confusion I manage to catch myself before my forehead hits the control panel.

The explosion was real. Fire licks the ceiling of the doghouse, sparks dash themselves against the safety glass a meter from my face, and in three seconds the flames abate and the white-hot drops of molten iron fade and extinguish, and all is well again. Scrap mixed with snow and ice got dumped into the furnace, blew up on contact with molten steel. This happens all the time. All in a day's work, except that it's the middle of the night.

"Why xuě? What for xuě in scrap?" Zhang yells at Pasha, the shift foreman.

"Snow," I say, but Pasha understands.

"Because Siberia," Pasha says. "Because it's winter. Xuě is everywhere. These old tank turrets are full of it."

It's standard procedure to preheat and dry the scrap before

dumping it in the furnace. It should have been done. It should have been done the dozen other times this has happened. No harm done, this time. Unlike the time the electrode tore off its mount and fell into the melt—now *that* was a show to remember.

"Sì jiǎo dì yù," Zhang says and sits down in his chair.

Hell of four corners.

"Want me to translate that?" I say.

He shrugs. "*Ad v kvadrate,*" he mutters.

Hell Squared.

I like his translation better.

Working night shift with Zhang is a crashing bore, for the most part. He hardly ever lets me do any translating. Zhang's wife is Russian, and he thinks he speaks the language. Which he does, sort of; he certainly has no trouble understanding it. Most of the time, when the furnace roar sounds like the purr of a titanic pussycat and Zhang yells at the workers in idiosyncratic but comprehensible Russian, I fall asleep the moment I sit down.

I do not dream at all when the furnace is quiet.

"Sasha, tea?"

Zhang says it in Chinese so I wake up immediately. My sleep brain has developed a knack for waking me when Zhang needs help. When he runs out of Russian he peppers his speech with Mandarin, or worse, switches to English and handwaving, thinking it makes him easier to understand.

"With pleasure," I reply.

Zhang avoids the free teabags we get at work. As a matter of principle he only drinks *Tieguanyin*[1] tea, and only from a teapot. I'm not too crazy about *Tieguanyin*, preferring like most Russians

---

1 Tieguanyin is a variety of Chinese oolong tea named after Guanyin, the Chinese Goddess of Compassion. Other names for the tea include "Iron Goddess Oolong" and "Tea of the Iron Bodhisattva".

the highly fermented black teas. When Zhang heard about that, he told me I know nothing of tea because the best white and green tea never reaches us, only the rejects, hardly better than garbage. What they sell in Russian stores under the name *Tieguanyin* is like a bald man attempting to pass for a Buddhist monk. Having tried the tea he brought from home I have to admit he's right.

"Why you always sleep?"

I stretch, knead my numbing wrists. "You don't need me to translate. What else do I have to do?"

"I do need you. I always tell you to correct me if I say wrong."

"You know what Ni said when I asked him to take Russian electricians into the crane's main distribution board and show them what's wrong? He said that he's not paid to train them!"

"But that's Ni!" Zhang says in a mildly insulted tone. "Working with him is like plucking an iron rooster. This is me. Do you want me to pay you?"

"For translation, I am paid, thank you. You think Bering Tunnel is going to wait for its vault rings while we concentrate on your language lessons?"

"Of course not. Just correct me—"

"Zhang, you make so many little mistakes, if I start correcting each of them we'll never get anything done."

"What kind of little mistakes?"

"Well, first of all, pronunciation. Your consonants are hopeless. I don't blame you, Mandarin doesn't have many closed syllables, or any multiple consonants in a row, or for that matter soft and hard consonants. And because you tend to tack on a vowel at the end of a word, and because Russian feminine words usually end in -a, you automatically say *she* for everything. Like, you just called the metal *she*. But it is *he* in Russian".

"But you call steel *she*, and it ends in -l."

"Soft -l, palatalized, is usually feminine. Steel, furnace, casting machine are *she*. Metal, scrap, carbon are *he*. Lance, iron, blade—*it*. The pronunciation difference is like how you say *wan*, 'ten thousand,' compared to *wang*, 'king.'"

"What about names? Why Pasha if he is a man?"

"You just have to memorize it. Pasha for Pavel, always male. Masha for Maria, always female."

"And Sasha can be—"

"Exactly."

"Ah," Zhang says. "What a difficult language. So much to memorize."

"It's true; in Chinese, gender never rears its ugly head: not in nouns, not in verbs, not in prepositions. But the tones, and the ideographs! Do you know what we call something incomprehensible? 'Chinese Scroll!'"

As we drink our tea, white-hot electrodes rise like infernal lights. A fiery maw gapes, and an assistant steelmaker driving a device made from a converted Hyundai frontloader starts to clean the threshold. Slag pours across the threshold in a solid stream. Zhang watches it, head tilted.

A steelmaker approaches the furnace, his sample probe like a lance in his hands.

"Why not automatic?" Zhang says in Chinese, too startled to think in Russian.

"Why are you checking the temps by hand again?" I ask.

"Day shift burned the autosensor again," Pasha says. "Forgot to replace the headpiece."

Zhang understands without my help; his brow wrinkles. "Sun Wukong rules under the heaven, though his limbs be hairy," he mutters under his breath, and then: "Don't translate that."

"Why not? It's very much worth translating," I say, and to Pasha: "Comrade Zhang expresses his dissatisfaction with the lack of competence on the part of Russian personnel."

"All these boys they hired," Pasha says and shrugs. "What can they do? Monkeys have better hands."

"You are sure he doesn't speak Chinese?" Zhang asks anxiously.

I stifle a chuckle. Pasha caught the denotation of Zhang's proverb about the Monkey King after I only translated the connotation. "Calm down, of course he doesn't. And don't worry so much about insulting him; he's too smart to take offense easily."

Comrade Zhang sighs with relief. He had been warned how difficult Russians are to work with—how different their traditions are and how important it is to treat those traditions with respect. Chinese and Japanese workers balk at these customs; they struggle to respect Russian indifference and irresponsibility, when both are frowned upon at home. That is, they can feign indifference and behave irresponsibly, but respect such things—never. But the instructions say: Russians are quick to take offense, and God forbid you should call them ham-handed monkeys if they, for example, burn out the automatic temperature probe.

"Temperature 1570. More heat?"

"Just little," Zhang says and shows with his fingers. "Sample done, we pour."

The lab hasn't sent us a sample test result yet but Zhang and Pasha have an understanding: as soon as they have a result, the ladle will pass to the vacuum degasifier.

"Tea?" I ask.

Pasha thanks Zhang: "Xièxie!" He places a plastic cup under the spout of the teapot. Zhang squints at me: am I sure Pasha does not speak Chinese?

The fiery maw closes, and the electrodes descend.

"I'll go to jīngliànlú and liánzhùjī, see how they are doing there," I say, noting to myself that, while speaking Russian, I called the Ladle Refining Furnace and the Continuous Casting Machine by more or less Chinese names. Tower of Babel, well and truly.

Zip my jacket to the neck, cinch my balaclava over my face, cover it all with a helmet. The temperature in the plant was 28 degrees below zero earlier today, probably more like 40 below now. It's called "hot shop" but it's only hot close to the melt; walk three meters away and you freeze your arse off. If you work near the preheating ladles, your face burns while your butt gets frostbite.

Steelworkers pass, sweat shining on their unlined faces where they aren't covered with soot and coal dust. Children, nearly. Can't skimp on equipment, but people are a different matter. All the hardware is the ultimate—well, penultimate—in modern technology, and management decided it's easier to train youngsters straight out of vocational school than retrain old farts. On the other hand, you still need experienced people, so each shift has at least one senior steelmaker over thirty with at least a decade on the job. Such as Pasha.

It's clear as daylight I'd be useless at the ladle or at the CCM and if they needed me they could call me in over the phone. But everyone understands I need to stretch my legs. It's eight minutes to six AM, and it's the next-to-last tap of the shift. I get back right as the melt is being released, and Zhang and I marvel, for the sixth time this night, as the bottom of the furnace drops away like a gigantic arse sitting down, and a tight stream of liquid metal pours into a red-hot fireproof bowl.

"What number ladle?" Zhang asks.

"Fourteen."

"Footing must replace yesterday, why no replace?" he yells at Nikita, the apprentice steelmaker.

"Why is he screaming?" Nikita asks, uncomprehending.

"He is screaming because we can lose the ladle!"

"It's not his ladle," the young steelmaker says and shrugs; his expression makes my hands itch with the desire to grab his shovel and whack him over the head with it. Zhang clearly feels the same, but only walks away to the railing, pulls off his balaclava, and lights a cigarette before reaching for the lance. This isn't where the autoprobe got burned; it was never used here in the first place.

The stream of fire drops to a trickle, the damper closes, cutting off the still-hot "icicles", Zhang puts down the lance and pulls off the headpiece. I still can't believe a headpiece made of compressed card-board survives immersion in molten metal. I understand the physics of the process, but I'm awestruck every time.

"Not enough slag," Zhang says, frowning, and throws the useless carton into the melt and the cigarette butt after it. I don't ask why that's bad, as I did a month ago. I can trace the logic of the statement: worn footing and not enough slag mean that the melt will cool faster than intended; this means in turn that it might overcool in the vac-uum extractor degasifier and need to be reheated, and every extra minute the furnace is engaged means greater chance for the ladle to burn through.

"If we lose this ladle, too, what then?" Zhang says.

"Roll it into the parking lot, fill it with topsoil, and grow tea like Master Wei," I answer.

Zhang smiles. He never smiles just to be polite, only when a joke comes off. Can't work without jokes, not in our business, where equipment and people work 'till they wear out.

Zhang and I climb the bridge over the pit, waiting for the ladle to pass Position 1. Directly above us is the prominent Pironelli logo. I often think of utterly irrelevant things, such as: that "sparks" are called "fire flowers" in Chinese; and that, when Mao Xie or Mo Ye threw herself into the furnace, she actually added carbon to the mix, and a sack of coal would have solved Gan the blacksmith's metal-lurgic problem just as well. Right now I am thinking of the future that science fiction promised us, of the world united in friendship and in scientific curiosity. Now I see the practical embodiment of this ideal: steel for the Greater Silk Road smelted in a plant built by an Italian company in the Siberian Republic, with workers from all over the world but under the management of the Chinese branch of Pironelli, closest geographically to Kurgan. So here we are with mainly Chinese and Vietnamese staff, some Japanese, Korean, Chilean, Filipino, and occasionally the west wind blows in a few Austrians, Croats and Brits.

We recycle what's left of the Soviet military.

We melt old tanks, BMPs and BRDMs and portable pontoon bridges and rails and rolling stock and old rebar from crumbling bunkers. We cast tunnel vault rings and rails and more rebar for concrete foundations for a railroad to run high speed electric trains feeding off low cost solar panels. On the map, dotted lines show planned extensions: the Sunda causeway via Singapore to Australia, the Bering tunnel via Alaska to Vancouver.

We Soviet children (yes, I am that old) were taught our country will always be in the vanguard of progress, assisted by fraternal Socialist allies. Being part of something great is a potent drug; my generation went through a nasty withdrawal when the Union ended along with our childhood. I don't recommend any of the substitute drugs we got into; not even the one I'm on right now, capitalism. Not even with the K2Pult, the Himalayan Orbital Mass Driver, on the drawing board somewhere in Beijing, its projected budget a significant but not impossible fraction of China's GDP.

And just like the stories hoped, there is a multinational crew building that enormous structure, but the old Soviet writers never imagined that the force that brought the workers together would be money and that the dreams that went through their heads would revolve around going home to bed at the end of a long day, not to space or to other planets.

At the end of the day it's not matters sublime but base materialism and mutual profit that both bind and separate us. Even at the management level no one is thinking about the global trade and transport network right now. Pironelli's priority for the moment is to be done, as soon as possible, with what they call "hot testing" or "test-launch," and the interest of "Kurgan International Tube" is to manufacture the most product on Pironelli's time and on Pironelli's equipment, before "hot testing" is finished and Kurgan assumes responsibility. The international Pironelli staff is completely freaked out by this approach; under the guise of "testing," the plant is running in full-capacity production mode and the entire personnel of KIT from director to the last steelmaker's apprentice does their job according to the time-honored Russian tradition: not my property, not my problem. What can I say? Weren't you all warned about Russia being a riddle wrapped in a mystery inside something incomprehensible? Well, there you are.

And suddenly as if by evil eye—mine, perhaps—there is an automatic signal that the ladle car is stuck before Position 1. Trying to reroute it from the control panel via bypass gets us nowhere, and Zhang, swearing, goes over to look for an obstruction.

One of the reasons my services as an interpreter are so highly valued (considering my knowledge of Chinese and Japanese is mediocre at best) is that I never refuse. If I have to climb a crane on the heel of a foreign specialist, up I go. If I have to enter the collector, I'm there. Now I crawl under the ladle car with Zhang. As usual, at least a half dozen people are loitering by the pit—electricians, mechanics, part of the ladle furnace brigade—and not one of them even attempts to figure out the problem, while even my nonprofessional eye can see the long furrow on the rail.

"Shield stuck against the rail," Pasha says and knocks against the steel plate that protects the wheels of the steel carrier against splattering melt. Zhang lifts his head and swears in Chinese. Pasha screams at the gathered multitudes: "What is this, a circus? You, ox-fucking mechanics, what are you doing standing around clacking your beaks? Can't you see the shield is stuck? Bring the torch, now!"

The multitudes fade away. Senior mechanic arrives, swears up and down at his charges—that's the signal to start work. Half of them know what needs to be done, anyway—the mechanics at least.

"We're never getting out of this shithole," Pasha says and sighs, looking up where reflections of fire dance on the ceiling. "Never."

I know what he means, but this is none of my business. I am an interpreter, not a crisis manager. And it's not like Zhang and Pasha even need an interpreter: curses have become the universal language that science fiction writers dreamed of for so long. Yes, Sir Arthur C., some dreams come true, though not quite the way we imagined.

A winch lowers the acetylene torch. One of the mechanics crawls under the ladle car, but Pasha curses him roundly and cuts off an edge of the shield himself. I understand why he does it: he is ashamed on behalf of the dozen or more young, fit, and far from stupid men who watched the steel carrier rattle in place for fifteen minutes without doing anything constructive about it. Pathological lack of initiative. Everyone complains how difficult it is to work with Russians; everyone knows that Russian traditions must be respected, but no one knows how to get any work done while doing so.

Having cut off part of the shield, Pasha returns the torch, we climb out of the pit, and Zhang gives the signal to start the ladle car. The car rolls smoothly to Position 1, the crane operator reaches for the lever to pick up the ladle, and the ladle picks that very moment to burn through.

During the war I discovered that under fire I lose all fear, entirely. It's odd: I vacillate and waste time in online hack-and-slashes, but in a real battle I act rationally, and quickly. Quicker than anybody else, except for that last time death stared me in the face, when a Russian boy moved quicker. The boy who died all the way while I only died partially.

This time Zhang and I act faster—we pull Pasha beneath the

protective cover literally from under the stream of fire. A thought flashes in my head: *with luck, the score is even.*

Twenty-six long and unpleasant seconds follow.

The awning isn't there to protect people. It covers the electric cables that power the ladle car. Vietnamese workers built it, completely to spec, of reinforced concrete covered by fireproof brick, and it held under the river of molten steel, but it was not deep enough for the humans underneath it to be entirely safe and comfortable. We push our backs into the concrete wall behind us while melted steel drips down in front of our noses, turning solid the second it hits the floor but still red-hot at a good 700 degrees. The wall behind us grows hot as well, two hundred or so degrees, and everything flammable around us catches fire, even the dust suspended in the air. We do not inhale fire—we are not even all that badly burned—but for a time we disappear from the world at large behind a wall of flame.

And then the world bursts in behind a hissing stream of fire extinguisher foam.

We jump out from under the steel-encrusted cover and spend the next minute getting our breath back while the ladle brigade puts out the fire on the car. The melt no longer gushes from the hole—it trickles and cools in sags like candle wax.

We are very, very lucky that the ladle burned through near the top and only a small part of its load poured out.

The ladle car looks like it survived a nuclear attack. I don't remember taking off my helmet, but suddenly it's in my hand, dented where my fingers clutched it.

Of course we all wear fire-resistant jackets, but hot as the wall was, it feels like I had my jacket ironed while still wearing it on my back.

They drag the three of us to the infirmary, cut our clothes off, and slather our backs in panthenol before we even realize how much we hurt. We each get a shot of anesthetic, and we lay on the infirmary beds facedown under sheets, waiting for ambulances.

Some time later the moment comes when awkwardness is possible.

"I don't know how I didn't piss myself," Zhang says, rolling a bit under his sheet to scratch his itching back.

"What's wrong with that?" Pasha says after I translate.

"I need to go now but they took all my clothes," Zhang says.

"There's an empty Coke bottle in the trash bin," I say. Zhang raises his eyebrows. "I'll keep my eyes closed," I add.

"Ah," says Zhang and pulls the sheet over himself before getting up. I close my eyes, as promised.

Pasha can think of nothing better to do as Zhang's urine trickles into the bottle than to start apologizing.

"Why?" I interrupt him.

He grows silent, sweat rolls down his brow, and he averts his eyes. And quite belatedly it dawns on me why he had never bothered me with stupid questions.

He thought I was a man.

A maimed man, or one born not quite complete. A pseudohermaphrodite, perhaps.

Back *then*, the boy who had been quicker was called Sasha. That's a convenient name. Especially if sex isn't marked on the passport. Which it is not, if the passport is of the European standard.

"Did that happen . . . in the Ukraine?" he asks. And, tired, I cut him off, forever:

"In Ukraine, Pasha. In Ukraine. It's a country, not a desert."

Everything is complicated, Zhang. Everything is more complicated than you think.

We're very much alike, Russians and us. We're probably more alike than people from Guangzhou are to northerners. Almost the same people. Some think we *are* the same people. Russians think so, mostly. But when they came ... You may not believe this, but in three months they earned the hatred of all—including those who had greeted them with flowers.

What you see now is eight years later, after the war and after the defeat. I will say something that might insult a son of the Celestial Realm such as yourself, but all imperial ideologies are egocentric. All. Look at Americans—each individually is a remarkable person, each wants only good for others, but how much trouble begins when they are asked to see things from someone else's viewpoint? Take an American; take from him his wealth, his power, and the magnanimity that comes of never knowing weakness or want. What is left? Exactly—that's what came to us. Russians didn't want to bring us evil—I mean the tank drivers themselves, not the cadaver in the Kremlin. They really, sincerely, thought we had been ruled by Neo-Nazis, that we'd been forbidden to speak Russian, that we'd be happy to forget twenty-five years of independence and rush back into their embrace. It began with arrests of all those in any way involved with our government, except, of course, for those who'd run away. Who hadn't run away? Small fry, of course. Odious personages, most of them, corrupt and mendacious, but hardly guilty of the charges against them—oppressing the Russian minority. In the old days we wouldn't have bothered defending them, but the very lawlessness inflamed us. We protested. Things went downhill from there: monuments leveled, memorial plaques removed, holiday parades banned. We pushed back—threw empty bottles at patrols, wrote "Moskali go home" on walls ... "Moskali" is perjorative for Muscovites, I wonder how to write that in ideographs—Mosike is Mandarin for Moscow;

"Li"—is that with lì for "strength" or lì for "profit." Or lǐ for "plum?" Never had to write "Moskali Go Home" in Chinese.

Anyway, it started small, then someone blew up an urn, killed a sentry. Scapegoats were needed. Scapegoats were found, six students caught leafleting. Six boys and girls, shot summarily. Tortured to confession and executed.

You are from Nanjing, originally; you must understand. There comes a time when things can no longer be tolerated. Somehow, at that moment, many people started looking to me. Where did we find weapons? Not everyone turned them in when ordered. Buried in gardens or orchards. Some bought guns from the occupiers themselves, who were not averse to a little trafficking on the side when the upper ranks weren't looking. And the rest we captured.

How do you manage guerrilla warfare in urbanized, deforested Eastern Ukraine? You'll laugh; our biggest trump was our shared Soviet past. Same weapons, same vehicles, similar uniforms, standard ammo. We freed some POWs, wore clothes taken from defeated enemies. IFF codes were not just easy to get, but very easy. Once we camped in a small town, across the square from a Russian unit. They didn't know who we were until we destroyed their armored vehicles. Attacked warehouses, blew up rail lines and trains carrying reinforcements, preferably those with supplies and ammo rather than personnel. I don't like killing people, it's true, not as a matter of kindness but because building new tanks and guns and armored cars is more expensive than herding in new soldiers. You may find it laughable, coming as you do from China, but by European standards Russia was a very populous country. Then, too, there was the PR factor. We didn't have a snowball's chance of success, Zhang. We knew we could not defeat Russia; the most we could accomplish was to sabotage their plan for "peaceful reunification of historically Russian lands." To show the world that there was a war on. Last six months, a year at the most.

It was awful to watch the deaths of boys who joined us in those early days, when success came on the heels of success. They started dying . . . desperately. As if they sought the bullets that killed them.

We each took a nom de guerre, to save our families from retaliations. Just to the north of us was a squad led by a man who styled himself Porthos, after the strongest Musketeer. An ex-Soviet military man, that's all I knew about him. To the south, Owl, a funny-looking fellow with huge glasses. They died in autumn, and in the winter came our turn.

We held a council, and decided to lay down our arms. Surrender. The mission was accomplished, the world seethed with disapproval of the Russian actions, UN and NATO rattled sabers at Russia, and it looked like they'd be forced to withdraw from the Left Bank of the Dnipro. We chose captivity over death.

All but one of us. He wanted to fight on to the last. He was my friend; none of us could make the tough decision, I least of all. No one expected him to bring us a surprise on the day of our surrender: a suicide vest he'd built the night before.

A piddling little vest: it's time-consuming work, to make necklace after necklace of hex nuts and washers and wind them around the plastique core. He ran out of time. And plastique. And washers and nuts.

He had only brought enough for me and Sasha, the Russian boy who, at the same time as I, saw the trigger in my friend's hand. Sasha was quicker. He was the first to knock my friend down and jump on top of him. I ended up on top of both of them. My friend kept hold of the trigger.

Don't think I did this out of bravery. It's just that, as the squad commander, I had the bleakest future to look forward to if I lived. A death sentence, or a very long prison term. And no place to come back to: my children were in Europe with my ex-husband, emigrated long before the war; my parents did not survive the occupation. Simply put, I leapt on top of him, in certainty that the lethal outcome was the best thing that could happen to me.

Sasha was the real hero. Half my age, strong, handsome. He had a reason to live, and a chance to survive. His bones extruded from my body for months. My friend's bones, too. And the nails he had stuck in the bomb.

These aren't torture scars, as you had thought. These are the scars of my survival. Not a bit of skin left intact, neck to knee. Field surgery is save what you can, amputate the rest. Radical mastectomy, the hard way. The doctor said, if I had been a man, I would have died. Women are tougher.

There was a Russian writer named Shklovsky who managed to blow himself up with homemade explosives, also near the Dnipro. He wrote that when the bomb fragments extrude, they squeak and scrape against the underclothes. It's true.

Now that I think about it, my kamikaze friend probably saved my life. Had I surrendered whole, I would have ended up in Solonoye, the special camp for "disarmed terrorists," and died of quiet strangulation there. But lying near death at the hospital gave them hope that I'd die unassisted. And then you know what happened: the famous "ten-hour war."

Fifteen years ago, before the war, books about a nuclear war with the US were very popular in Russia. Russia lost all these wars, but lost them heroically: a submarine would strike at America with MIRVs, and a nuclear holocaust would ensue. In reality, apparently there had been an idiot like that, but he was shot by his own crew. No one wanted to incinerate his family with American assistance. No one.

His Majesty the Tsar of All Russias (including ours) shot himself in the Kremlin, and the Provisional Governing Committee sued for peace. Russia fell apart: Siberian Republic, National Republic of Cossacks, Ingria, and what remained of the Russian Federation, the central part. For that, they blamed us, of course. And Americans, but then it's convenient to blame Americans for everything. After that they released all the surviving members of the resistance from prisons and camps. I never saw the inside of either, spent the entire time in a hospital; they just transferred me to a different hospital, one of ours. Then Ukraine, being the victim of aggression, joined all the unions and pacts, speculating all the while on our reputations as heroes of the war. Our President sat out the war in Poland, came back scattering medals everywhere, called me to get mine. I refused. Some of our boys went upwardly mobile on it. I don't disapprove of them, we all lost much in the war, some wanted back a little bit of lost happiness. I didn't. In truth, I didn't really want to live. Got up in the mornings, forced myself to go somewhere and do something ... It wasn't because of the injuries, I was only "pretty" at my best, which was long ago. I lost friends, I lost my family, I lost the man I began to love—missing my tits seemed stupid after all that. Hands—I would mourn. Two bags of fat—barely.

Later the Resistance fighters were declared military veterans, eligible for pensions and medical insurance including reconstructive surgery. And I thought, I lived as a woman for 40 years—how about trying to live as a nonbinary person? And I never went for reconstruction. In truth, I had grown sick of surgeries, and that might have played a role; I had had more than enough of cutting and stitching. And there's the story of a frontiersman who lost a horse and found a herd—if there hadn't been advantages to my situation I would not have remained in it.

Yes, I acquired my tattoos in China. Shanghai.

I changed my name. I changed it to "Sasha"—short for Alexander or Alexandra, take your pick. Passport office personnel were so busy, they didn't argue. Sasha didn't even faze them; someone else in our neighborhood called himself Darth Vader.

So I went to work for Pironelli, and asked for the Eastern division. That's all. This is my story.

There was nothing to keep me from going to any part of former Russia. I do not hate Russians, and though the war has thinned their ranks, I still have Russian friends. They didn't die, of course, they're all my age, well past the cutoff for conscription. None fought. Those who questioned the propaganda reels about how we crucified Russian boys on gates and fences are still my friends, and those who believed the lies—why mourn the lost affection of idiots? Some, though they didn't believe the propaganda, still turned away from me: how could you shoot at a Russian soldier? We have a joke in Ukraine: "I'll go shoot some *Moskali*."—"What happens if *they* shoot *you*?"—"Shoot *me*? Whatever have I done to deserve it?"

You want the real reason? I hope that here there is something to save. These boys—could I succeed in pounding into their heads that slapdash, slipshod work is a bug and not a Russian national feature? That humans must be treated like humans and ladle footings must be replaced on time? That neither people nor ladles should be used until they break?

Why are you laughing, Zhang? You think I can't? But you like Pasha. Where Pasha is, is hope.

Why don't I ask you out loud what you think, instead of arguing with this Zhang I built in effigy in my mind?

Because I know what you'll say. You'll say that empires are built by people who do their jobs today while thinking about tomorrow, and fall under the weight of people who want to have their empire and eat it, too. That you like Pasha, too, but as the shift foreman he is responsible for the incident, and will likely be fired. Never mind the choice he had, or rather didn't: go on as he did, or stop the process. He'd have been fired then, too.

We need to talk, Zhang. We need to find a way to save his face. Pasha's face. The face he'll likely turn away from me when he finds out I'm not only nonbinary, but also the ex-commander of the Huliaypole guerrillas to boot.

Will I regret it?

Yes.

"You could have killed me," Pasha says to me in the manager's office.

How odd. None of the Russians at the other end of a rifle from me has ever said: "I could have killed you." I'm used to that.

"Pasha, strife is antagonistic to virtue. We didn't kill each other; that's cause enough to celebrate."

"But you haven't stopped fighting, have you? You brought your war here, to the plant?"

My eyebrows leap, startled.

"Pasha, what are you on about?"

"You know."

I do know. Pasha is the senior worker on the shift, the burnthrough was his responsibility. It was his duty to see to the replacement of the footings. True, there was no other ladle. True, if he refused to work with a defective ladle it would have meant a stoppage of production, and he would have been assessed a staggering fine. Or they would have fired him, a father of two children. Hobson's choice: stop production and be fined; go on, cause a disaster, and then be fined and fired.

We made a deal: I take part of the blame myself. Pretend I hadn't translated Zhang's warning of worn footings, that I left Pasha in ignorance. Of course everyone on the shop floor knows Zhang and Pasha understand each other just fine without me, but the head office doesn't so they won't question the report. I lose my job; Pasha gets fined but keeps his. I get fired from the Kurgan division and quietly transferred to the Sichuan plant.

The deal was between me, Zhang, and Signor Caruzzo, head of the Kurgan office of Pironelli. Pasha wasn't in on it.

What I had not expected is that Pasha would believe it, too.

"You should have said something about the footings. You should have told me."

I rub my hand over my face to hide my look of astonishment. Of course; the Russian national trait is the ability to believe. They did believe that we were the Nazis and—at the same time—Russians, brothers and sisters oppressed by Nazis. They opened fire on us believing they were defending us. Why shouldn't he believe I should have done his job?

"You are right," I say. "You are never getting out of this shithole. Never."

His fist strikes me in the solar plexus; I slide down the wall to the floor.

"I don't hit women, usually," he says. "But you are not a woman. I don't know what the fuck you are."

We are alone in the corridor, and I do not call for help. In truth, the whole thing is overwhelmingly funny, and I laugh even as I'm writhing in pain.

Pasha leaves. I don't find it regrettable, Zhang.

Not a bit.

I find it very, very funny.

Three Love Stories

Anatoly Belilovsky

Ghost Nutrients

Lipids

1970s

"Can I have some ice cream, Mom?" I ask. Mom's gaze flicks at my waist and back to my eyes. "Sure, if you want to," she says. "But think of your weight" rings in my ears . . . something she had said yesterday.

And now I don't feel like having ice cream.

2020s

I pass the ice cream aisle without a second glance. Let her ghost enjoy it fully. Bon appetit, Mom's ghost.

Proteins

1970s

The bread is like nothing I've seen. Salami, ham—the kind you don't find in regular stores. At home we only ever put a single layer of cold cuts on our bread, and I've never seen anything like this. The other guests are piling their sandwiches as high as they can open their mouths, but I hesitate. I meet my mother's eyes and she whispers, "don't get used to this."

I put two layers on my sandwich: one transparent slice of ham and one of wine-colored salami.

2020s

I make my sandwich to take to work with me, with just a few slices of ham, one of low calorie cheese, and a pickle. You can have the rest, Mom's ghost.

Carbohydrates

1970's

There's an open box of chocolate on the table as I come home from school.

"Hi Mom!" I say. "What's the occasion?"

"Your report card is due, isn't it?"

"Yes," I say, dreading what is to follow.

"Do you have it?"

"Yes." I reach for it to show Mom.

"I don't need to see it. Just tell me if you think you earned this chocolate."

There is a B in my report. "I don't know," I whisper. It's mostly A's, but I see the A's like the cloth and the B like that hole in my pants I ripped in first grade, that Mom patched, that other kids teased me about all semester.

"At least you're honest about it."

The chocolate goes back untouched.

2020s

My wife leans in against my back.

"What have I done to earn—"

She shakes her head. "You looked like you needed a hug."

I twist in her embrace and put my arms around her.

Mom's ghost will have to go hungry for now.

Virror, Virror

She blinked three times to boot her contacts, and braced herself for her double vision to clear, the real and the virtual images to coalesce, but the lag was a fraction of a second this time, much less disorienting than before.

"Oh, I love this new upgrade!" she said, and watched him stagger momentarily as he booted his own. He looked like a sailor on a ship in a storm, she thought, and playfully willed him a pirate hat and an eye patch and a beard, erected a virror, and chuckled as he did a double take at their reflections.

"Arrgh," he said. "Shiver me lumbers!"

She laughed out loud then, still unfiltered and in street clothes. He loved her laugh, and her face when she laughed. The memory warmed her, as did his answering smile. The beard, she thought, creased very realistically, and rakishly. Perhaps he'd keep it in the mask he'd wear shortly.

"I can't wait to see what you have in mind," she said. "You must have spent a fortune on my rig. Perfect real time masks, wow. Who are we, this time?"

Last masks and chill they had been Anthony and Cleopatra in Tutankhamen's burial chamber; the time before, Jane and Tarzan in Hagia Sofia.

"I've something different in mind," he said. "Shall we undress?"

"I can't wait," she said, her blush deepening. She willed the room to darken, in meatspace as well as in virtual, and shed her clothes in the privacy that gave her, trusting him not to switch to low-light vision. She heard his belt clink against the floor, and softer noises he made; she smelled his shampoo on a tiny gust of wind, most probably as he took off his shirt. She smiled, again, in the darkness.

She willed the lights to brighten slowly. "I'm ready," she said, turned to the mirror, and gasped.

In twilight, two naked people stood in front of the virror. Part of her mind admired the detail of the seamless, hi-res masks they wore, that moved without a perceptible lag, that were both unmistakably them and unmistakably old, sagging in all the places she was afraid she'd sag, wrinkling along her smile lines and frown lines and lines she did not know she had but that were clearly hers, her mask's hair gray and sparse; his own unsparing masks, potbelly and jowls and all—

"Oh my," she said.

The brightening light revealed in ever-sharpening detail their imperfect bodies: age spots, stretch marks, hair they had always taken care to remove. She moved, instinctively, to cover herself, and her mask's breasts swung in pendulous arcs. The room around them appeared faded too. Literally faded; wallpaper yellowed, printed flowers wilted, stains appeared on upholstery, cobwebs on the ceiling. She looked down, and the clothes on the floor appeared patched and wrinkled, too.

She looked at him, and met his gaze. Neither looked away. Not for a long time.

"Marry me?" he said.

She willed the masks to drop, showing him what she wanted him to see: not her real, younger, prettier face; not her real, athletic body; but her real, flowing, tears.

Bottled Up

"You won't like it," said the corkscrew. "A most disappointing product, not what I expect from a Grand Cru winery at all. Hardly any nose to speak of, and the tannins are totally unbalanced. You really should pull me out of this cork, lay the bottle down for a few more years, and make yourself a nice cup of tea."

He made it for her once and she pretended he got it right but he knew he didn't; the tea she made herself was so much better, its aroma suffused the whole house, and she would sit in that enormous old chair in her comfy old sweater two sizes too big, feet tucked under her, nose in the teacup, eyes half shut behind steamed-over glasses, her smile would light up the room more than the fireplace ever did, and he would just sit and look at her for hours on end.

He might be looking at her still if she weren't dead.

"Just pop it," he said through his teeth, eyes blurring, hands beginning to shake.

"Are you going to chug the wine?" said the corkscrew.

He looked around, opened a cabinet, selected a glass.

"That's a white wine glass," said the corkscrew.

"So?" he said.

"The volatile scents won't be properly concentrated," said the corkscrew. "It will interfere with the proper enjoyment of the wine."

"What are you, my mother?" he said.

"No," said the corkscrew. "I am not your mother. I am Smorkscrew, a beverage management solution equipped with artificial intelligence. Now, what food were you considering to accompany this wine?"

He looked around again, pointed at a dish. "This?" he said.

"*Peanuts?*" said the corkscrew. "That would be an insult even to this inferior excuse for a Valpolicella. Haven't you got any cheese?

Fresh mozzarella would be perfect. Or turkey prosciutto and melon. Be sure to slice the prosciutto very thin—"

"She's dead!" he shouted. "Can't you get that through your—" he waved his hands "—whatever you use instead of head!"

"I know she's dead," said the corkscrew. "It was my honor to open many a bottle for you and your guests as you sat *shiva*. Many people came."

"Everyone loved her," he said.

"She wasn't there," said the corkscrew. "She was dead, remember?"

"What's your point?" he said. "Get it? Point?" He tried to laugh, but only a sob came out.

"They came for you," said the corkscrew. "Many people. They all love you."

"And now?" he said. "Where are they now?"

"A phone call away," said the corkscrew.

"Screw you," he said. "Get it? Screw you?" He turned away, covered his face with his hands. "I want to be alone," he whispered. "Just open the damn bottle."

"She wouldn't like it," said the corkscrew.

"She is not *here* to not like it," he bit off. "She is not in this room. She is not in this house. She isn't anywhere on this Earth, anywhere under the sun, anywhere except..." He clenched his fists. "Open the bottle, please. Just ... I'll get a proper glass, I'll make some sandwiches, I'll sit in her chair and cuddle her sweater, it won't be like I'm drinking alone, I'll drink to her and I'll drink to me, just open it."

"She's not in that bottle, either," said the corkscrew.

"What makes you such a damn expert on her?" he screamed.

"I *am* an expert system, you know," said the corkscrew. "Able to access the totality of information about the two of you throughout the World Wide Web, and correlate its implications upon the problem at hand."

"Would my medical history be part of that totality?" he said quietly.

"I must regretfully decline to divulge trade secrets of Smorkscrew, LLC," said the corkscrew. "However, consider this: I am—was—her present to you. The process of gift selection gave me an opportunity to perform a thorough assessment of her character and motivations."

"What you mean is, she loved me, and she didn't want me to drink myself to death," he said. "In case ..."

He trailed off. An old clock ticked off the seconds in the silence. The cherry tree shook in the wind beyond the window, shedding the last of its dry brown leaves *(it had been white with bloom the day they packed to go on their second honeymoon, the sun had shone so bright, the shadows so crisp—)*

"She knew, then, didn't she?" he said.

"Yes," said the corkscrew.

"She found out about the cancer, and then we went on the anniversary cruise, the best vacation ever, and she bought you for me as a present, and I thought it was cute and thanked her, but I had gotten her a pair of diamond earrings so it kind of irked me for a while that all she got me was a stupid corkscrew and all I said was, 'Cute,' and then a week after we got back she told me she was going to die, and then she died and I never said I was sorry ..."

"Apology accepted," said the corkscrew.

It wound itself from the cork and rolled toward its drawer, pausing at the counter's edge as he shook with sobs too long in coming.

A Hole In The Shape Of God
Vasyl Dukhnovskyi

Діра у формі бога | Василь Духновський
translated by Tetiana Savchynska

> "Ma'am, you have a hole in the shape of God in your soul."
> "No worries, it's for sex."
> —Jeoke-Paul Sartre, *Anecdotes of the Broken World*

They were getting on a trolley bus. Two young men who, judging from the color of their eyes, started playing with drugs too early. The taller one, dressed in a red parka, was Denys Tsinesh, nicknamed Denchyk. He worked as a waiter in an often deserted cafe. The other young man, wearing a neat coat and shades, was Yaroslav Bodrin, also known as Capiton. He worked for a small bureau, or rather, an institute, that had spent decades on only one research, or rather, investigation, depending on how you look at it.

Once on the trolley bus, the men started searching frantically for small change, and Capiton was the first to find some coins. With great care, he put them on the conductor's open palm.

"Two tickets," he said.

The conductor stared at the coins in disbelief.

"You gave me sixteen hryvnias, but the ticket costs only four. Boys, you gave me twice as much money," she said.

"When did everything become so cheap," Denchyk wondered out loud.

"What can I say," Capiton replied, "God is dead."

They took two vacant seats and rode through the Lisovyi Masyv neighborhood, barely speaking, only staring out of the window. An old lady anywhere between eighty and a thousand years old, by Capiton's estimates, got on the trolley bus at a bus stop near a nursing home for the vision impaired. When the conductor came to her, she only shook her head:

"I'll pay with a card."

Suddenly, Denchyk stopped looking out the window and noticed the old lady's existence.

"Gosh, there are still people who pay with a card. Crazy."

"Yeah, crazy."

"It makes me want to look her in the eyes and say, 'Hello, Auntie, the invention of cash has been a thing since like forever, throw away your card and forget about it.'"

"Go ahead, look her in the eyes," Capiton said enthusiastically. "Just be careful, or you might catch the retrograde bug and start paying with a card yourself."

"Screw you, idiot, don't joke like that."

"I'm not joking," Yaroslav said. He was clearly enjoying himself and didn't want to stop. "And then you'll switch to a smartphone or, even worse, will start using wireless earbuds."

"Ugh, quit it. I don't want to talk."

They rode for about five minutes without saying a word, but then Denchyk broke the self-imposed silence.

"You know, I keep thinking about it: people often don't understand how important it is to have opposites. I mean, the opposites are valuable only together, and once we divide them, we'll have two totally senseless things. Pacifists, for instance, are worthless if there are no militarists, and the other way around. The left and the right are also inextricably linked."

"Why did you even start talking about this, Den?"

Judging from his tone, Capiton was not happy, which wasn't surprising—he was almost dozing off when Denchyk started talking.

"Well . . . I don't know; it's just something that crossed my mind."

"Sorry, buddy," Capiton said with a laugh, "but the things you say out of the blue are so weird that I don't even want to imagine what's happening in your head."

"All right, all right. I'll stay quiet."

And they did sit quietly for some time. But not for long. This time, it was Capiton who broke the silence.

"And what about men and women?"

"What about them?"

"Do you also consider them a pair of opposites who are worthless without each other?"

"Of course, I'm not queer, you know."

Capiton took off his sunglasses and started wiping them with care.

"I read the other day," he said, "that in Sweden, queer men can still walk around the streets freely."

"Why are you surprised, it's Sweden," Denchyk replied nonchalantly, "progress has always been slow there. Remember how long they kept using electric cars even after the entire civilized world switched to gas-powered cars?"

"Yeah, Sweden is damned."

Sharing this profound observation, Capiton put on his shades once again. The trolley bus moved slowly, but it was for the best. The young men hadn't slept all night; they'd worked on their laptops for twelve hours straight, typing up a short story for a writing competition. They stopped only when they ran out of amphetamines.

If you asked Capiton which phenomenon in the world he found the most horrifying, his answer would be straightforward: an amphetamine hangover. There's no other substance, no other illness or stress capable of turning a human into such a vegetable.

That's how both of them felt today: they felt like vegetables. And this trolleybus was their chance to catch a break.

The Auntie got off at the Marshal Zhukov Street.

"I still remember the old name of this street—"Kuban Ukraine," Den said. "It takes me a while to get used to new names."

"Well, it's hard to get used to communization, but you have to understand that it's absolutely necessary."

"Listen, Yaroslav, when did you turn into such an ass?"

"Well, God is dead, didn't I tell you?"

"I thought it was me who told you . . . guess we need a new God now."

"Nah, we're better off without him. And only the killer of our previous God can become our new God anyways."

Den closed his eyes, and when he opened them again a moment later, he screamed with horror. The interior of the trolleybus disappeared and instead turned into a pitch-dark room lit only by a couple of ultraviolet lamps. The worst part was Den's hands, covered with blood almost up to his elbows.

"Where am I?"

No response.

"Are you happy, killer of killers?" Den asked, surprising even himself.

There was no response, only dead silence. Dead? Silence can't be dead, can it?

"And who can be dead? Only God. God can be dead if we kill him. You smeared your knife with the blood of the holiest and most powerful being in the world, who will now wash it off?"

"Who are you? Who is talking?" Den yelled, looking at his blood-covered hands.

And then he realized that no one was saying anything, and it was time to get off the trolley bus. "The Institute of God bus stop," the most unpleasant, monotonous voice announced from the worst speaker in the world. Capiton also got up, and together, they got off near a building next to a big pine forest.

From the outside, the building looked just like any other

Soviet-era research office, if it wasn't for a huge inscription above the entrance that read:

THE INSTITUTE OF GOD

"You dozed off on the bus, you must have had a nightmare," Capiton said quietly as the men approached the institute.

"I remember having a nightmare, but I can't remember what exactly it was about ... " Den started thinking so hard that he even stopped walking. "Did you say 'on the bus'? But we got here on a trolley bus?"

"Buses, trolley buses ... none of this matters anyways. Technically speaking, we weren't going anywhere at all. Or, we were going everywhere at once."

"Because God is dead?"

"Den, you're starting to get my point," Capiton said with a laugh. "I'm glad you're starting to get my point."

Den kept trying to remember his dream as they entered the lobby. He dreamt of a room. Yes, a room filled with ultraviolet light, so dim that he could barely see his hands. That's right, hands. With blood on them.

"Den, are you here?" Capiton asked, going up the stairs.

"Yeah, sorry, I was just lost in thought. Do you think we can buy some tabs on the way home?"

"I don't know," Capiton said without a pause. "The way home will be very weird."

Den checked his pockets for some cash but found only a dozen metro tokens. He was trying to figure out what he did with all his money when suddenly he remembered buying a knife. It was a decent, beautiful butterfly knife, sharp and comfortable. But where did the knife go? Where did the butterfly go?

They went up to the fourth floor and walked down a long corridor lined with small offices. Four hundred and seventeen, four hundred and eighteen, four hundred and nineteen ... Reaching the next door, Capiton stopped abruptly, and Den crashed into his back.

"Here it is, my office. Make yourself at home."

Yaroslav unlocked the door with a small key without any trinkets. Capiton's office looked like a paranoid person's room rather than an office of a research institution: maps hung on the walls with colorful threads stretching between them, the desk was covered with folders filled with large photographs, and there was a gun on a low shelf of the bookcase.

"Are you sure you work as a researcher at an institute?" Den asked seriously.

"Are you sure you work as a waiter?"

"No ... Yes ... I don't know."

"You don't know," Capiton repeated with a smile, "because your memories are contradictory. God is dead, the world is falling apart, and the integrity of the world is slowly degrading. I think you can still remember what the world was like before God died."

Den clutched his head. He really wanted to remember something and finally understand what his friend meant. An imaginary butterfly knife was stuck into an imaginary table, surrounded only by pure will. No, this wasn't a memory, it was a delusion.

"It's a dream!" Den exclaimed suddenly.

"No, it isn't a dream, try to remember!" Capiton said, putting his hands on Den's shoulders. "I was the one who brought you here, but you have to remember everything yourself."

Den pressed his temples even harder, and something in his chest began to tremble.

"Can I go out for a smoke?" he asked quietly.

"No, goddamn it!" Yaroslav yelled, holding his friend by the shoulders. "No, you have to remember. I can tell that you notice how everything's upside down: the world is moving in the opposite direction on a bizarre trajectory. Technical progress turned into a regression, and soon, everyone will switch to cash, having forgotten about the existence of bank cards. Who knows how long we have until people switch from cars to horse carriages? And communization? It's so absurd it's grotesque. It's like Philip Dick meets Alzheimer's disease! And you notice all this, my friend, you remember everything. Other people can't remember because they have nothing to do with it, but you remember everything, you just can't admit it. Just accept that."

Den's legs gave out, and he almost fell, but Capiton grabbed him by the arm and threw it over his shoulder.

"Let's sit down."

"Yeah, let's sit down," Den said in a faint voice.

"Now, remember. This world is broken, just admit it, and you know who is to blame!"

"Who is to blame? God!" Den yelled. "God is to blame because he died and left us to fend for ourselves."

"But how did he die, Den? Try to remember how God died. What happened to your butterfly knife? Only one person is to blame for breaking the world."

Denys covered his ears, screaming and crying.

"Don't tell me who is to blame," he yelled, "don't tell me, please!"

"You," Yaroslav said anyway.

The crying, the screaming, and the trembling stopped. Den did everything to block this memory, but it was too late, the reality was poisoning him, hitting him where it hurt the most.

Denys remembered the knife stuck in the table. He remembered God, a majestic and terrifying being that looked not like a human but rather like the angels of the Old Testament, covered with multiple eyes, teeth, and inexplicable openings. Den pulled out the knife from the table and looked at his reflection in the blade. God was trembling and shuddering, he was shaken. He was pulsating and saying something, but Den couldn't remember the words.

"Den, I've been looking for you for a long time because you are the only one who can help me," Capiton continued. "But first, you need to remember, why did you kill God?"

"I can't, I don't remember the words. Everything is too blurry," Den said, looking up, tired and teary-eyed. "Can I take a smoke break?"

"No, Den, you can't."

"Wait," Den shuddered as he realized what he just heard. "What do you mean you've been looking for me for a long time? We've known each other since childhood!"

"Yes, but no. I made sure that we've known each other since childhood when I found you. The world is broken, and sometimes, if you have certain knowledge and talents, you can do amazing things with them."

"You mean that all the memories we share are fake?"

Den's voice no longer sounded desperate as his despair gave way to resentment.

"Fake? No, I don't know how to create fake memories. I changed reality so that we could spend our childhood together. I needed us to be good friends on this day, and I have lived twenty-five years in this messed-up world to achieve this goal."

Den got up and walked toward the window.

"You've been friends with me all my life to punish me for killing God?"

Capiton started laughing, and Den found this laughter calming. He remembered now how the knife entered the Lord's flesh, how it wrenched God's guts and released the stream of his blood. Meanwhile, Capiton kept laughing, yet it wasn't an evil laugh but rather the opposite.

"I'm not going to punish you for anything, friend. I just want to fix everything."

Den took a deep breath and then slowly exhaled. Maps, folders with photographs, the Institute of God—all these absurd images fell into place of a perfectly logical puzzle. But the gun . . .

"If you weren't planning to take revenge for killing God, why do you need a gun?"

"To shoot myself," Capiton said with a shrug. "If it doesn't work out, I don't want to live in this broken world forever. So, I've thought of a backup plan. Nine grams of peace."

"All right."

Den stared at the maps, recognizing familiar places.

"Can I ask you one more question?"

Capiton nodded.

"How come you know all this? All these things about 'changed reality . . .' Why do you, unlike all of us, realize that you live in a broken world?"

"I can't quite understand this myself, friend. I have a few theories, and most of them boil down to the fact that the reason is you."

Den began to understand how the broken universe worked. Distorted causality, the effect is ahead of the cause. Cause: Denys, the killer of God, and Yaroslav are best friends; effect: Yaroslav has the ability to change reality. It doesn't matter that the effect came before the cause.

"So what do we do?" Den asked.

"First, you need to remember why you killed God. I have something that might help."

Capiton walked over to his desk, opened the bottom drawer, and took out a paper envelope. After opening the envelope, he took out a small bag and then a couple of small pieces of paper.

"Put them under your tongue and keep them there for twenty minutes. And try to remember. Think about God. What did he do to you to deserve being killed?"

"I don't remember that. I remember cutting the flesh with the knife. I remember all the colors of his eyes, but I don't know what he said to me or why I killed him."

But after thirty minutes, Den could recall everything much better. The light was now not just flooding the room, it was dancing to some strange rhythms. The boundaries between reality and memories were getting more and more blurry.

Den was in a tunnel. In a tunnel?

No, Den was at the Institute of God, in the office of his best friend.

And yet, he was in a tunnel where hundreds of colors shimmered on the walls, the floor was pulsating, and the patches kept moving. He was walking. He was walking because he was remembering this place, this tunnel. He was remembering where the tunnel led. To walk along the thin matter of reality right up to its edge, that's what he had to do. And Den was walking.

Den and Capiton were lying on the office floor in the Institute of God.

The Institute of God? Ha, that's absurd.

Den was in the tunnel, the edge of reality was very close. And here it is, the long-awaited memory. Den was standing with a knife in his hand, and right beside him, God was flying, looking like everything living and everything dead at once, like a predator and a victim. The majesty that filled the room became so overwhelming that it almost took Den's breath away.

"Kill me," God said in all the voices of the world.

Den hesitated. He was supposed to kill the same God to whom he had been walking for so long? The God with whom he had talked for hours and hours on end every day? But could he refuse the request of such a majestic being?

"I'm sorry," God said in a looming voice. "Kill me. Kill me."

And then it struck Den that he really didn't have a choice. He had a butterfly knife, and God had a desire to die. So the man showed

God the blade, and he nodded without saying a word. For another minute, they both just stood there, and finally God said:

"Kill me."

That's when the slaughter began. The memory became complete, and anxiety subsided. God was dying from the stabbing, Den's hands were covered with blood, but he continued to stab, blow after blow, cut after cut, wound after wound. And only when God turned into a bloody mess did Den lay down on the floor next to him, looked at his bloodstained hands, and let out a terrified scream.

But Den wasn't with God, he was at the Institute of God. He woke up, got up from the floor, and helped Capiton to his feet.

"Well?" Capiton asked. "Did you remember why you killed God? Was it because he was one creepy dude?"

"Yes, I remembered. I killed God because he asked me to do it."

Den had never heard his voice sound so calm.

"Damn it," Capiton said, slapping his forehead. "Damn it, damn it, damn it. This ruins everything. The whole plan has gone down the drain." He started pacing the office, muttering something under his breath.

"Why does this ruin your plan?" Den asked, confused.

"The whole point was to get compensation, to exploit your feeling of guilt for killing God."

"And?"

"And God himself asked you to do it. This means that you are not guilty. You have no fatal divine guilt that I can exploit to fix the world."

Den sat down on the floor.

"Fuck, I even calculated your best age for this and figured out the exact day," Capiton said, walking over to the bookcase. "I had waited for twenty-five years for this moment, and everything just fell through."

"Now you see," Den sighed, hiding his face in his hands, "all this agony was for nothing. And it turns out that the world cannot be saved. In such a case, perhaps we'd better go and buy lots of crack and die of getting high?"

Den suddenly heard the click of a jerked gun.

"Actually, my friend, there is another way out."

Den looked up and immediately saw the gun pointed at him. Capiton's face was trembling, he was almost crying but kept aiming the weapon at Den.

"Is this your way out? Killing me?" Den asked, rubbing his eyes.

"Not quite, Den. To fix the world, we need a new God. But only the killer of God can become our new God, remember? I have told you this before. That's the way we do things around here."

"You want to kill me so that I can become God? Have you lost your mind? Do you realize that you want to shoot me? Kill me! How do you even know it's going to work out? What if I don't become a God and only become a corpse, huh? I'm pretty sure it will be the latter."

"It has to work."

Den was still sitting on the floor, afraid to move.

"Don't do this," he said, looking Yaroslav directly in the eye. "Please. I don't want to die like this."

"I really hope you will understand and forgive me," Capiton said, breathing heavily.

"No, Yaroslav, I won't forgive you. I won't forgive you because I will be just a corpse lying on the floor of your fucking institute!"

"Maybe you want me to pass someone a note from you? Family? Or a girlfriend? You have to understand, Den, that I really don't want to do this. I've given up twenty-five years of my life to try to avoid this exact scenario."

"I understand."

Den started counting in his head, trying to calm down and slow his breathing so he wouldn't look like such a coward.

"So what about a note? Or last wish? Or even a confession?"

"I only have one wish," Den whispered, "I want to turn away. I don't want to watch you shoot me."

"No problem. Turn around, please."

Den got up, slowly turned around, but then dashed toward the exit. A bullet hit him in the back, and he saw his blood on the wall, on the maps, on the folders with pictures. One bullet pierced his shoulder, and another one pierced his lungs. His blood was everywhere. Den made it to the door but didn't open it, just crushed into it, leaving crimson stains on its white surface.

With incredible effort, he turned around to face Capiton.

"Son of a bitch, you win," Den said.

"Sorry," said Capiton with a shrug and wiped away a tear.

A slight laugh escaped Den's mouth, quickly becoming a bloody cough. After the coughing fit was over, he closed his eyes, threw back his head, and slid down the door.

If you listen closely, you can hear the foundation of Hyperreality regaining its integrity, and in this spontaneous renaissance, the simulacra are rustling like music.

The Stray Streetcar (A '90s Businessman's Tale)
Myroslava Hornostayeva

Заблуканий трамвай | Мирослава Горностаєва
translated by Konstantin Boulich

The ribbed white gate slid silently sideways, letting my car through. I parked my BMW on a driveway in front of a garage with those same sliding doors that resemble a crumpled piece of paper. Stakh's bodyguard, one of those "gorillas" whose brain resides in their shoulder muscles, was already waiting at the side entrance. I followed him, begrudgingly casting my envious eye on Stakh's house. It resembled a miniature medieval fortress—a kind of toy castle for those who had not gotten their fill when playing valiant Knight Ivanhoe as a child.

Stakh was not a knight, but a businessman, so I had little hope for the success of my visit. If I had screwed up, I had to pay for it myself. Let the losers weep, and the fact that I had once done Stakh a favor didn't mean he would lend me money.

The mighty guard took me through a darkened hall, made a few turns down the corridor, and opened an oak veneer door. The room turned out to be a library—two plush couches, a computer on a desk by the window, and books, books everywhere. Stakh was a bibliophile, something that surprised many; moreover, some of his books he even read.

I sighed. Granted, Stakh's money could save my life. But not my property. If I paid off everything, I would be poor, like someone in a James Hadley Chase novel. Very poor. I'd have to start all over again ... I'd have to remember that once, I used to be a good programmer, and find a job. And to get there I'd have to take the tram from some smelly 'burb. From Krariysk, for example. That's what they usually write in apartment-wanted classifieds: "No Krariysk or

Ostrovny." When you're well into your thirties, it's hard to deal with such shit again.

"I can offer you something better than money," said Stakh. "Say, what if those assholes who are bothering you ... disappeared? You get me?

I thought of the "Boss" again ... and of the two men Stakh owed money, the Lysianske cemetery, the majestic black marble monuments ... The slopes ... Much more reliable ... Natural death, that's all ...

"So listen carefully," Stakh said, taking my silence for agreement. "I won't repeat it twice."

A half-asleep taxi driver dropped me off at a streetcar stop in the heart of the city's industrial zone. A long wall stretched right in front of me, behind which the factory's chimneys were blazing with fire. These "torches" dimly illuminated the area. Behind me stuck out a tank—a sump of some sort, as well as a beam filled with slag. To the right, across the road, the chimney of another metallurgical monster was glowing with flames. Next to it was a building with four black twisted pipes that resembled headless sitting giants. They were spewing smoke rather than fire.

In short, the place was a dump. My body shivered from the night chill and the stench made me cough. The dirt-cheap watch on my wrist showed ten minutes to two. I was dressed shabbily: old jeans and a black second-hand T-shirt that I had bought for eight hryvnias earlier that day, hiding my eyes behind sunglasses out of shame. The only things of any value I had on me were my cell phone and twenty hryvnias left over from the cab ride—as well as something that Stakh had given me, which I put in my pants pocket.

About five minutes later, I got convinced that I had fallen victim to a crazy prank. Good people, would a respectable businessman in his right mind be waiting for a streetcar in the middle of nowhere at two in the morning? Dressed in someone else's rags and with an idiotic "travel document" given to him by a crazed drug addict? No doubt Stakh had lost his mind because of drugs. No wonder he lives alone ... His wife must've had enough of his madness ... Fraser, Aleister Crowley, the great magician Papus, who else is there ... The great drug addict Carlos Castaneda ... King Stakh, a ghost from some bad Soviet-era novel ... He would go hunting for his unfortunate victims at night and would finish them in the swamps ... Ugh, God ... How could I mess up so bad again? But he convinced me, the son of a bitch ... Maybe the drugs gave him some psychic powers. He did convince me—to do something crazy like that ...

"Just stand there and wait," I heard Stakh's voice as if in a dream. "The streetcar will come at the Hour of the Ox. You won't miss it—it's the only one there. Do you remember that poem:

> *"I was walking down an unfamiliar street,*
> *and suddenly I heard the crow's caw,*
> *and the ringing of the lute and the distant thunder—"*

"Straight at me flew a rushing streetcar." I muttered. Nikolay Gumilev used to be my favorite poet; that was before I started making serious cash.

"When it stops, get on," Stakh's voice in my head continued to instruct me. "Show your pass to the conductor. You may have to pay extra ... not in dollars though. You'll see for yourself. The most important thing: don't argue with them ... And don't look surprised. If you make it to the end of the trip, you'll be free."

The smoke was wafting about in the air, hurting my throat. Just as I was wondering for a minute if a cab would come all the way to the Schrader Beam if I called it on my cell phone, or whether the taxi dispatcher would just tell me to go to hell, a sharp rattling sound penetrated the air.

The streetcar emerged from the puffs of smoke as if in pieces. At first, I saw two dim circles of headlights, the illuminated route sign #4 seemed to float above . . . Then—the convex glass of the cab; behind it—the vague shadow of the driver . . . was it a woman? . . . What are they called—streetcar drivers? Conductors? "Conductor, stop this car at once!"

See, in Gumilev's time, only men drove trams, and then everyone went off to build a brighter future . . . Leaving women to teach and serve in hospitals . . . To drive night streetcars in industrial zones . . . This is women's work now. Better still—women also now work on railroads, with a hi-vis vest on and a crowbar in hand!

The door opened right in front of me, and I gladly jumped inside. What an unexpected way out of the lousy situation! The "#4," if memory served me right, went somewhere downtown. I forgot where exactly, but I just needed to get to the central avenue . . . Stakh was a drugged-up asshole, but I was no less than a bloody fool myself. Shouldn't have listened to him . . . What I needed was to get home quickly, get some sleep, wash up . . . The morning would show what to do next.

The car was almost empty. Two indistinct figures could be seen on the back seats. There was only one light on, opposite the doors, and it was blinking constantly. I sat down by the window in the "other" seat. The red one . . . In my childhood I would always try not to sit on the aisle seat because it was gray. It was funny: I hadn't ridden a streetcar in years, but the habit was still there—red seats only. Gray ones—no, no. Even when I rode the streetcars with my mother, I would always try to sit on the red one.

On the back of the gray seat in front of me somebody wrote in black marker pen: "Police are pigs." The glass partition of the driver's cab was smeared with yellow paint and decorated with a sign

displaying "Rules for Using the Streetcar" or something like that . . .
About thirty years ago, these signs in a glazed frame were attached
near the ceiling, and I had to get up on my tiptoes to read them.

I grew up in a neighboring city, but the trams there were like
this one, only new and shiny back then, with plastic ticket readers
attached between the windows. There were no ticket readers here . . .
A half-worn inscription above the seat opposite me, the only one with
its back turned to the door, read in Russian: "Ticket Collector's Seat."

"Tickets please!"

I jumped up in surprise. The ticket collector came up behind
me, completely silently. Was she napping in the back of the car?
Meanwhile, the doors hissed shut and the tram started moving.

"Tickets please!" the old woman said again in a rattling, slightly
irritated voice. "Tickets, please, transit passes!"

I stuck my hand into the back pocket of my jeans and pulled out
my wallet. It had a small cardboard rectangle stuck to it—something
the tripping Castaneda gave me claiming it was a transit pass. Also
known as King Stakh . . . The damn bastard who just wants to make
fun of other people's misfortunes . . . Oh, why did I help him out back
then? I gave him cash, and he gave me a bloody transit ticket! You
could just die laughing!

The old woman was already standing next to me. She was wearing a green apron with a large pocket on her belly. A washed khaki
T-shirt was tucked into sagging sweatpants. A pair of well-worn, plaid
slippers, clearly from the Soviet era completed the outfit. A black
leather bag with a strap hung around her neck.

I had twenty hryvnas in my wallet, but some boyish cheekiness
made me show her the transit pass.

Stakh's gift did resemble a transit pass, but only in size and shape.
Nothing was written on the gray background, only a red imprint of
a strange seal—two circles, large and small, one above the other. In
the small circle there was an inverted five-pointed star. In the larger

one there were two intertwined triangles with their vertices up and down, and in the middle, there was something that looked like a key or a cross with a loop.

"Now the old woman will tell me to get lost," I thought, "she's working nights instead of enjoying a well-deserved retirement, and here's some bastard in pathetic clothes handing her a piece of paper instead of money. Better give her that twenty-hryvna bill and tell her to keep the change. She must be paid peanuts. "

"Your pass is invalid," the old woman said. I again felt something like a pang of conscience. The poor woman apparently had no strength to be stern.

"Here's the money," I said hastily, "Didn't mean to give you that thing . . ."

"Your money is not right either," the old woman giggled. I suddenly felt scared.

"Keep the change," I said, handing her twenty hryvnias.

The bill went down on the trampled floor of the rattling carriage. The old woman kept looking at the piece of cardboard.

"I can do it for you," she said, "but you'll have to pay up . . ."

The hand that held the pass suddenly looked like a bird's hand—a yellow bird's hand with curved, deathly claws. My stomach churned. I stared blankly at the "Police are pigs" sign in front of me.

The paw snatched the wallet from my hands. I heard the expensive leather creak. I had forgotten to replace it when I changed . . . But the wallet contained nothing but my mother's photo . . .

"I also have a cell phone," I said, like a complete idiot, "the latest model . . ."

The tram rumbled, swaying at the corners. The woman's voice above me gurgled something . . . It sounded like it was coming from the bottom of a swamp. People don't talk like that. Only the dead, when they speak through the mud that clogs their mouths.

"You'll pay with this . . ."

The bird's hand was holding a two-by-two inch photograph of my mom. The photograph was for her passport. I took the spare one and put it in my wallet. Mom said back then: "Just don't even think of putting some girl's mug shot next to mine. Unless you really fall in love ..." Eight years later, my mother's photo was still unpaired—although I did date plenty of girls.

Fear somehow gave me courage. I raised my head and turned around ... I suddenly wished I hadn't done that. Above me there was something that looked less like a person than a Picasso abstract painting. The car was sparkling with a pearly glow. In this ghostly light, I suddenly saw the people in the back seat more clearly. It was a blond woman in a red and yellow swimsuit, tied around her waist was a bright yellow beach towel. Next to her, a boy of about ten swayed in time with the lilting car. He was wearing swimming trunks and a T-shirt. Both of them had the blue and swollen faces of drowned people. Both had been dead for a long time. A very long time ...

"Stop the car," I said weakly, "I want to get off ..."

"Stop the car?!" the creature above me squeaked, "Did you hear him? He doesn't want to pay for his trip!"

Laughter that sounded like howling came from the driver's cab.

"We'll take you to the terminal," the thing that was once an old woman squeaked again. "That's how things are here ... You'll have to pay a fine ... A big one! Ten times the cost of the trip! Or else we'll take you to the police!"

I glanced out of the car window and was stunned. The streetcar was rumbling down the illuminated Ilyich Avenue. We passed the clock opposite the Town Hall looking like a tombstone in an abandoned cemetery ... It was as if I heard it chiming out an old song: "My favorite street, dear to my feet, whatever the weather, you are dear to me!" "Demyan Bedny" Cinema ... The avenue widened, smoothly morphing into the former Cosmonauts Square, now named after the previous mayor, who passed away after drinking too much brandy. The bridge, a road intersection . . . The obelisk celebrating local industry, popularly nicknamed the "Monument to the Departed Toilet." The public restroom, which had once modestly hidden behind the theater box office, was demolished by order of the same mayor who was more glorious to the city residents than cosmonauts. Now I could really do with going there . . . The speed of the tram increased and a tail of fire was trailing behind it.

Something hot ran down my legs when I realized that the street-car, or whatever it has become, was really rushing along the old route of the "#4," long cut and forgotten. It was rushing to its final stop at the River Port on non-existent rails. And there . . . "You'll have to pay a fine" . . . I stared at a piece of paper on the driver's cab. Large, broken printed letters read:

"It got lost in the abyss of time."

A sudden turn . . . The tram skidded and screeched. The rails, long ago sold for metal by the venerable "city fathers," were trembling. I knew that the turning circle of the final stop was very close.

"River Port! Final stop!" the creature above me screamed. Laughter and howls came from the driver's cab. The dead in the back were swaying in their seats. They didn't care anymore . . . or did they? "It got lost in the abyss of time."

"Fine! I will pay up!"

I hardly recognized my own voice . . . It was not even a scream, but an ungodly screech . . . The clawed hand squeezed my mother's photo—her face with that lurking smile, the familiar slightly squinted eyes . . .

"Conductor, stop this car at once!"

I was lying in the weeds where the River Port streetcar turn-around used to be. My empty wallet was lying next to me. For some reason, I was clutching my cell phone in my hand . . . From here to my house on Soviet Ukraine Street (how touchingly conservative our city is) was a five-minute walk.

Or three minutes if you ran fast.

A hangover morning always starts with a headache. It's a fact! It felt as if my head had turned into a drum that a crazed rock musician had been banging on all night.

I was lying in my own dry bathtub, naked as a jaybird. My mind was trying to stitch last night together from the shreds of memories: I was at Stakh's . . . I asked for a loan . . . Whether he gave it or didn't give it to me is a blank . . . He probably did, because we drank good cognac . . . From good old France, the only country where true cognac exists . . . "Napoleon" it was . . . What happened next? I probably left the car at Stakh's and took a cab home. "Napoleon" won at Waterloo . . . No, he lost then, but now he won . . . And now what?

I got out of the bathtub and onto a pile of rags. Not mine . . . grubby jeans, a humanitarian aid T-shirt . . . In the jeans pocket I found my cell phone and torn wallet. It was empty. My mom's photo was gone. How much money did I have? Blank again . . . Did they strip me and rob me? Then why did they leave my cell phone? They took my clothes and money, but left my phone? Something is not right here . . .

A broken watch was hanging on my wrist. The kind they sell on the "all goods for three hryvnias" stands. The window was empty, the battery was dead. Bloody jokers . . .

Who did this to me? And where? Probably not far from home, close to the apartment building.

The phone was also dead . . . I just bought it yesterday . . . And then I heard a phone ring . . .

The cell phone almost slipped out of my suddenly sweaty hand. It took a minute for my sore head to realize that it was not my cell phone melody but the bell trill of my landline. I went into the hallway and barely found the "handset" resting peacefully on the base.

"District police department of N," the receiver chirped.

"What?"

A moment before the voice spoke again, I remembered everything ...

I returned from N, from the funeral, the following week. Mom had died the very morning I was lying unconscious in the bathtub. I still don't know how or why I got in there. I must have tried to wash myself. To wash my hands of this ... like one character in "The Master and Margarita."

My mom was walking Linn, her dog, a ginger shaggy Pekingese. They were crossing the road.

I was told the driver was drunk. He died too. The car skidded and flattened against a lamppost ... the old woman and her dog happened to be in the way of the car ...

An accident. Just that ...

What was on the driver's mind when he was rushing to the crosswalk?

My mom was buried in a closed coffin. I could not cry because I heard my own crazy voice:

"I will pay up!"

During that week, the bank where I had taken out the loan went bankrupt.

My lender was shot dead in his own driveway, almost in front of the security guards.

The guys from D left me because they stopped getting paid.

In the same month, those who knew about the loan were killed in another showdown.

I am sure that my name is not in the bank's computer. After all, I paid up . . .

Stakh called me right after I returned from N.

"Your transit pass is invalid," I said.

"I perfected it," Stakh wheezed, "it was supposed to work fine."

"A woman and boy," I said.

"Are they there?" the receiver said.

"They are . . . "

"I had a yacht," Stakh said after a long pause, "in Yalta. They were vacationing at sea."

"And you paid up."

"Yes, I paid up."

I hung up without saying goodbye.

Stakh hanged himself in his own gym, about a month after my mom's funeral. On the horizontal bar . . . I didn't go to his funeral. Instead, I bought his house in Verkhni Ostrovne village. It's quiet and cozy there, and most importantly, there have never been even trolley-buses in that area, let alone trams.

My business grew rapidly . . . It had to, after all, I paid up.

I have only Shafa as staff . . . That same "gorilla" who served Stakh. Actually, his name is Igor and he has one indisputable virtue: impenetrable stupidity. He is also never surprised by anything.

I kept Stakh's library and enlarged it, especially the section on necromancy and all kinds of magical arts.

Today, an old university friend from N, also a businessman, unexpectedly paid me a visit. It turned out he too was caught in a similar vice as I was before.

I did not blame him, even though I knew that he had once refused my mother a loan . . . My mother had known something. A wise woman, she had tried to help me.

"I can give you the money," I wheezed out. Some spells require a lot of voice tension. "But after you pay up, you'll be poor ... Very poor."

My friend well understood this himself.

"I can offer you something better than money," I said. "What if those assholes who are bothering you disappeared ... You get me?"

My friend looked interested ... I intensified my mental attack. He must agree ... and later I will ask him, "Is my mother sitting in the streetcar, holding Stakh's dead child in her arms? She loved children ... I've perfected the travel card. It's valid! It really is! Well, if it's not valid, you'll have to pay up." Not me anymore. Him ...

"So listen carefully," my broken voice dropped to a whisper, "I won't repeat it twice ..."

The Rainbow Bridge

Iryna Pasko

Веселковий міст | Ірина Пасько
translated by Hanna Leliv

We plead to god, but it doesn't really mean anything, just a figure of speech. For the only god above us is Lady Pavolotska.

Our lady has four daughters: Maniusia, Haliusia, Virusia, and Nastusia. There were five of them, but Nadiyka is no more. Andriy loved her, poor lad.

Miss Maniusia is the oldest, dark-haired and quiet. You can hardly get a word out of her. Slender, thin—it seems that the sunlight will soon shine through her when she stands at the window.

Miss Haliusia is a blond, sturdy lass. And what an evil shrew she is! One day, when Hapka, her maid, was combing her long hair and tugged at it, Haliusia angrily sheared off Hapka's hair, all of it, and so now she walks around just like that—like a shorn sheep.

Miss Virusia is still too young for marriage, her dresses short, her white pantaloons peeping out from under the hem along with her thin stockings, and there's not a stain on them, not a spot, even with the restless, brisk girl that she is. Two nannies look after her, two spinsters, one limping, the other walleyed. The kid laughs and points her finger at them, but they keep silent—only sometimes one of them would cry secretly.

And Miss Nastusia only coos in her cradle. Our lady gave birth to her last winter.

So this is the family of our Lady Pavolotska, the keeper of our souls. Every day, we pray for Maniusia, Haliusia, Virusia, and Nastusia, and we also pray for our lady, even if god is nothing more but a figure of speech.

Nadiyka is the only one we never mention in our prayers—we dare not.

Our young ladies love to sit outside on the porch, even though it's still cold. They wrap themselves in blankets and scarves, just like those rag dolls, and chirp softly to themselves—goodness knows what about, somehow not in our language. Lady Pavolotska never keeps them company, as if she were deliberately avoiding her older daughters.

And I just stand there and watch, breathing out steam because I'm a footman and an orphan. Stepan is my name.

Once, Maniusia and Haliusia were sitting on the chairs like that, and Hapka, the shorn maid, was serving them coffee. The young ladies had seen it served as guests of their neighbor, Lady Zaritska, and now demanded it every morning. Maniusia warmed her hands on the porcelain cup—her little hands were so pretty, snow-white, with thin fingers and pink nails, so ladylike—but did not take a single sip. Haliusia, meanwhile, dropped three cubes of sugar into her cup at once and kept crumbling a honey roll on her plate but ate none of it. That was how the young ladies drank this coffee because it was bitter, they said, even with sugar. But I had never tasted it myself, so I didn't know.

Then Maniusia said, so softly and wistfully: "March is almost here, Halia." She said nothing else—only the cup in her ladylike hands trembled.

The rosy-cheeked Haliusia turned white as a wall and shrieked: "Quiet! Be quiet, you fool!"

Maniusia sobbed. And I froze—I had never heard her cry before.

Then Haliusia grabbed her cup and threw it at Hapka with all her might:

"What did you brew, bitch? That's not coffee! This is coal!"

There stood Hapka in her gray dress, a black stain on her chest, trembling all over her body, a shorn wretch.

Miss Maniusia wept softly. Miss Haliusia snorted like a hunting dog. And I kept silent, leaning up against the wall. What could I have said, anyway? That was the way it was, life as a serf.

But how sorry I felt for Miss Maniusia, and how pretty she was—like crystal clear spring water.

On the eve of Butter Week, I go to vechornytsi[1] one last time. Outside, it is freezing cold, and the young ladies have not had tea or coffee on the porch for three days if not more.

You should know that I'm a fine, handsome lad—fairly tall, a mane of black hair, rosy cheeks, dark brown eyes. The girls swarm around me at the get-togethers and on the street: "Stepan, honey, please bring the fiddlers!" they say.

The girls swarm around me, and their parents turn up their noses—I'm an orphan and a footman, just as I've told you. And to hell with them.

---

1   Evening or night gatherings of young men and women, usually at the home of a childless widow, who was responsible for keeping moral standards and order on such occasions. The vechornytsi season lasted from the end of the fieldwork in the fall until Lent.

So, at that last gathering on the eve of Butter Week, the girls sit and spin, while we boys chit-chat. Then I notice the dark-haired Marfa winking at me. She glances at me from time to time, making eyes at me—what a minx.

My friend Mykytka notices that too.

"What are you waiting for, Stepan?" he says, nudging me. "Pull Marfa close to you when we all go to sleep, and who knows, she might even lie down with you."

I go hot and cold all over: honey is sweet, but . . . Why shouldn't I rub up against a girl when she herself asks for it? But then I'll have to go out with her, and she might even insist that I propose and send my people to her family—I won't be able to get rid of her.

Soon after, one of the boys asks, "Isn't it time for bed?"

All havoc breaks loose. The girls get ready to go home and, at the same time, glance at the boys to see who will stop them. Those that no one stops will later cry into their pillows at home.

Gradually, everyone figures out who is going to lie down with whom, and I see Marfa wave at me shyly as if to say, "Lie down here, Stepan, honey." To hell with it, girl, come what may. I take off my coat and settle down on the floor next to her.

The candles blown out, the whispering, the fussing—the darkness pants heavily like a beast with a hundred mouths. I hear Marfa whisper in my ear:

"Stepan, darling, am I to your liking?"

But all I can see before me are the lucid hands of Miss Maniusia clasping the cup, trembling, whiter than porcelain.

Marfa is breathing heavily, her lunch—onion and pork fat—on her breath. And I should ask for her hand?

While the young lady's breath is bitter and crisp like a freshly cut blade of grass.

I jump to my feet and make my way to the door. I trip over someone, step on someone—oh, I hear an earful about myself!

Marfa yells after me:

"Stepan, honey, have you gone mad?"

Maybe I have. But none of them there are to my liking, let me be honest, because their hands are black from work; because every girl in our village are like that: Milk-and-roses complexion, plakhta[2] fastened around their waist with a zapaska, topped with a kersetka and yupka, hair braided with ribbons, chapped lips, a pair of boots for the whole family.

Serfs[3], like me, are 'bonded souls,' but to whom are we bonded? Well, to Miss Maniusia, that's who.

Another day, I stood at the door like a stuffed dummy, listening to Miss Maniusia play the piano. The music she played was so wistful that it tore at my soul and moved me, a stout lad, to tears. And I'll tell you how it was: above the piano hung a rainbow, lucid like crystal, arched like a milkmaid's yoke. And how it shone, oh lord! It lit up my soul, and I saw it clearly: I would have done anything for Miss Maniusia, anything and everything for her.

The next moment, Lady Pavolotska came in—thin, tall, stern,

---

2   All these are elements of traditional Ukrainian costume. Plakhta is a woven wraparound skirt. Zapaska is a long apron tied at the waist. Kersetka is an embroidered sleeveless vest. Yupka is a narrow waistcoat.

3   Ukrainian serfdom was actually much closer to slavery. As part of the systematic effort of the Moscow Tsardom, and then the Russian Empire to subdue Ukraine, the Russians had been slowly but steadily introducing serfdom in Ukraine, which was formalized by Catherine II in 1783. Peasants could not leave their lands without the permission of a local landowner. The original word 'kripatstvo' derives from 'attachment' (to a particular land plot owned by a wealthy landlord), and 'kripaky' (serfs) were traditionally called 'attached (bonded) souls.'

lips like a thread. She looked at the rainbow and slammed the piano lid shut, almost breaking Maniusia's fingers.

"What are you doing to that boy? Who gave you permission?"

"The boy" meaning me. That's the kind of power Miss Maniusia has. She pulls your heart out of your chest and puts a rainbow in its place: one end in your chest, the other in her hand.

"I didn't mean to do that, Mama, I didn't mean to!" whispered Maniusia, sobbing, while the lady shook her head and, for some reason, also cried. She must have known that her daughter was lying.

Maniusia meant it, all right, and did it on purpose—it was just in her nature.

The kitchen is sizzling hot and smells like roast pork. Khvedora, the cook, cries and crosses herself—what a sin, now that fasting has already begun.

But that is just our fate: at the beginning of Lent, our lady always hosts a dinner.

We, the servants, have scrubbed the mansion clean until it sparkles, lit the candles, and set the table in the dining room. Now we sit in the kitchen, the door locked, the shutters closed, the light off—so that our lady's guest won't notice us, so that he won't hear us breathing.

We all know—there will be no harvest if something is not to the guest's taste. Famine and plague and drought will befall the village, but that is not the worst: If the guest is displeased, the lady will fly into a rage. And god won't save us because god is just a figure of speech.

They say old Okhrim was once plagued by curiosity. They say he stuck his nose outside to see who was visiting our lady at the beginning of Lent. Old Okhrim later explained: The guest's chariot was black and was pulled by huge serpents, and the eyes of these snakes glowed like embers. Old Okhrim went blind as soon as they locked their eyes with him.

"Our Father," whispers Khvedora, the cook, "Don't turn away from us, sinners, in this dreadful hour."

This happened to old Okhrim about thirty years ago, even before I was born.

✢✣✢✣✢

No one tells us what our lady and her guest talk about, but one thing we always know is this: If she is cheerful afterward and walks around humming a song, everything is fine. But if she comes to breakfast pale and tearful, then you can rest assured—the Feast is coming.

"Stepan!" the lady calls. "Stepan! Come here, right now!"

I jump up from the table—I slept through the night sitting on the bench, and my whole body has become stiff, but so what? God, I think, if only she were cheerful.

No luck. Black circles under her eyes, as if she were sick—the very sight of her scares me.

"Go to the reeve, Stepan, and tell him we're having festivities this year." Not a single word more.

"Right away, my lady," I say, but I can no longer hear my own voice. She says nothing but just gives me that strange look with her big, red-rimmed eyes.

I walk out onto the porch and see this: the snow is already melting, and the table under the roof is empty—no coffee, not even a tablecloth. Our young ladies are in hiding. Miss Maniusia is in hiding.

I stand there and wail, covering my mouth with my hands so that no one will hear me.

The Feast will take place as soon as the snow melts. Such is fate.

Since that day, the lady's mansion has been in a state of commotion—the dowry is being prepared for Miss Maniusia. She walks around the house, lucid and bright as an apparition, and the seamstresses are busy fitting her with a white dress. Her little sister Virusia runs around her singing songs, and baby Nastusia screams in the bedroom upstairs, but Maniusia doesn't notice. The girls sew, embroider, and trim here and there, but the young lady neither hears nor sees them. She stands at the window or plays the piano and just stares at the distant fields, where the snow is melting away, and at the black patches of soil until tears spring to her eyes.

And I stand by the wall, rooted by fright, and have it all churning inside—as if the rainbow that Miss Maniusia has put into my chest has been painted black just like that field.

There was a blizzard last night, and everything got covered with fresh snow—and my young lady smiled for the first time this winter.

Haliusia rages even more now, the evil shrew. She checks the work of the seamstresses and breathes down their necks. One of them has stitched up the hem unevenly—and Miss Haliusia grabs a needle and starts pricking the wretched girl's fingertips. The girl screams and cries, but no one dares to step in.

But I . . . I feel sorry for her and for that shrew of a lady too. She loves her sister, that's why she's so angry.

And not only that: That shrew knows that after Maniusia, it will be her turn.

Marfa—wrapped in her yupka and flowered headscarf, rosy-cheeked from the cold—stopped me on my way near my empty, cold house.

"Stepan, honey," she said, picking at the willow fence with her cracked finger. "Don't upset people. Everyone's already asking."

Who asks what, I wondered, looking at Marfa's red cheeks. Who cared about me anyway? Only later did it dawn on me that the village had sent Marfa to talk to me because people could see the rainbow I carried in my chest and were afraid of me.

Me, an orphan and a footman. Ridiculous.

I pushed Marfa aside:

"Go away. What are you standing here for?"

And then she screamed so loudly that the whole street could hear it, even a neighbor's dog broke into barking:

"Have you gone crazy? Stay away from the young lady, or we'll all be in trouble! Look at me, Stepan! She'll be gone, the young lady will be gone, but I'll be here!"

But I didn't turn around.

A few patches—that's all that's left of the snow.

Our lady pines away, roams the house with a pale, sickly green look, and vomits her guts out in the morning in the privy. Poor her, as if she has drunk too much or swallowed poison. Well, it's clear what this means: Maniusia will have a new baby sister before Christmas, if not sooner.

All our lady's daughters are born in December.

I sit at the door to Maniusia's room at night and hear her crying softly, and I wish I could say to her: Let me in, my darling. Let me in, my sweetheart. Let me in. Open the door, I'll walk along the rainbow,

I'll take you, my darling, and you won't be fit for the white dress any-more, and then what do I care—let them punish me later, let the black serpents your father rides devour me.

But she won't let me in, and I'm left to wonder: why did you embroider this bridge of music, Miss Maniusia, what for?

I know that Lady Pavolotska can hear all my thoughts. Sometimes, she looks me straight in the eye, clenches her thin fist, and I forget to breathe—I gasp for air like a fish on the shore, unable to catch my breath.

This is what I know: This lad, Andriy, who loved Nadiyka, tried to kidnap her in the middle of the night but did not even reach the door of her room—the lady was waiting for him in the living room. She clapped her hands and made his heart stop.

This is the power of our lady, given to her by her black guest. With this power, she has bound all our souls to herself so that they do not scatter all over the world—so here we are, kripaky, the 'bonded souls.'

After the blizzard, Maniusia locks herself in her bedroom for a week, and when the snow melts, she comes out on the porch in a white dress and asks for coffee. God, how pretty she is, so white, a bride without a veil. A lace collar pressed against her pointed chin, and her lips are the same color as her dress.

Miss Haliusia, however, does not come out—she cries in the living room like a stupid cow, and smashes expensive china. But our lady says nothing to her—she hides deep in the mansion just as she had done last year. Virusia does not run around the house, and Nastusia does not cry either.

Maniusia's lucid little hands hug the steaming hot cup as I stare.

The men from the village are already standing in the courtyard, burly, sullen, and gloomy: the reeve, the blacksmith, and three plow-men—Maniusia's wedding procession.

Suddenly, Maniusia says:

"Taste the coffee, Stepan." I walk towards her, my legs wooden. And when I take the cup from her hand, I feel that Maniusia's fingers are ice cold. I shiver and almost spill the coffee.

God, how bitter it tastes.

Miss Maniusia asks me something with her bloodless lips, but I do not catch it because right at that moment, Miss Haliusia smashes another plate in the living room, and I feel as if the bridge between our hearts has shattered into pieces.

"It's time, young lady," says the reeve, and Miss Maniusia stands up. Her blanket falls to the floor, and her cup remains in my hands.

They walk away, down the alley and out of the courtyard, a bunch of people walking against the backdrop of a boundless field while Maniusia's white dress flutters in the wind like a fisherman's sail.

And then the reeve draws a knife, swings his arm, and Maniusia falls to the ground like a cut blade of grass.

✦✳✦✳✦

We plead to god, but it's just a figure of speech, it doesn't really mean anything. For the only god above us is our lady.

Our lady has four daughters: Haliusia, Virusia, Nastusia, and Valiusia, who was born in December. There were five of them, but Maniusia is no more.

Every year, at the beginning of Lent, we, the servants, scrub the mansion clean until it sparkles and set the table in the dining room with an array of meat dishes. We lock the kitchen door and sit there quietly, shutters closed, lights off, barely breathing—so that our lady's guest won't notice us.

Our lady's guest rides black serpents, and these serpents have eyes like embers. He has given our lady the power to hear our thoughts and make our hearts stop; he has bonded our souls to her, and that's what we are: kripaky, the 'bonded souls.'

We know: Each county has its own lady, and each of them gives her daughter to the black guest when he tells her to—and no one knows when he would demand it. But I, Stepan, a footman and an orphan, think this: The black guest will take his daughter away when a crystal bridge arises between her heart and the heart of a serf. For no other sound is as sweet to the black guest as the shattering of this bridge.

But I won't tell anyone about it—why upset people? They can't do anything about it anyway.

Such is the life of Lady Pavolotska, the keeper of our souls; such is her family. Every day, we pray for Haliusia, Virusia, Nastusia, and Valiusia, and we also pray for our lady, even if god is just a figure of speech.

Maniusia is the only one we never mention in our prayers—we dare not.

Lest We Forget

Elizabeth Bear

I am dying of the war, though not in it.

Such is the nature of wars. A person doesn't have to die in battle to be killed by a war. A person doesn't even have to be a soldier to die of one.

Wars have always been slow killers as well as quick. The war that killed my grandfather killed him thirty years after he was discharged, when his liver finally quit from all the self-medicating it took to deal with the aftermath. It killed both his wives, too, though they never served.

Dying of wars is strangely contagious.

If we were a more honest people, there would be a lot of statues of civilians on the National Mall. Maybe that's something you can look into, when we're done here. Imagine if all those wedding parties and starving children and violated women at least got the notice in death that life—and war—denied them.

Empty. Meaningless to them, since they'll never know about it. But a gesture at least. A reminder for the living of the horrors that have passed. Not that we tend to learn anything from the sins of our fathers.

Case in point: *my* father also died of a war. Cancer, which certainly had nothing to do with chemical weapons or toxic environmental conditions where he fought.

How could it? There were definitely no chemical weapons used in his war, and just as definitely no toxic environmental conditions pertaining. Just ask the organizations—commercial, governmental—that could otherwise have been held fiscally responsible for treating a sick soldier.

If they had to treat one, in fairness you might expect them to treat them all. What possible reason could they ever have had to lie?

And then there's me.

I'm not dying because I was a hero. I'm dying because I was the villain. I was a legitimate war criminal.

What can I say? Following orders seemed like a good idea at the time.

But I'll never be brought to justice. I'll never even go to jail.

And choices like the ones I made then eventually demand some kind of accountability—a reckoning—in the *now*.

I was a suicide.

It seemed like the least I could do. Not to make amends: you don't make amends for what I did. There are no real reparations.

But a kind of restorative justice. A tiny little drop in the ocean of what I owe.

Perhaps I should say that I *am* a suicide, because I'm not done dying yet.

Maybe I will never be.

I am not a suicide in the normal course of events. I am a *special* kind of suicide.

Dying of a war is not a new thing. But the manner and purpose of my going . . . that's where the revolution lies.

Dr. Cotter had a day job at the V.A., but she didn't recruit her subjects where she worked.

She got us the old-fashioned way. She put an ad on the T.

P.T.S.D.??

DID YOU SERVE?

ARE YOU SORRY?

FREE HELP!

Underneath, there was a contact number, and some fine print about a study and the exact specifications of who they were looking for.

They were looking for me.

I might not have showed up, except it was a month or two after my dad died, and I was taking it hard. I didn't have anybody: I'd driven them all off. I was as alone and adrift as I have ever been in my life.

Then I met Dr. Cotter and everything changed. For the better, for once.

Cotter wasn't even a shrink. She was a neuro-something, I guess. Some other kind of brain doctor. I never can get the specialties straight anymore. My functions have been pared down. Let's be honest: I don't really have a consciousness. I feel like me, but I'm not an individual in the sense we're used to. I'm just a set of protocols.

I'm not as smart as I used to be. When I had a brain of my own. When I wasn't using something else's.

But maybe I wasn't that smart then, either. Because I didn't use that big brain much. I just followed orders.

They were bad orders and I knew it. But they make it so easy not to think for yourself. Just to do what you're told. They make it so easy not to say no.

I tortured people. I sprayed them with white phosphorous and burned them alive. I didn't do it in person, but from a distance. I used a robot, like the reach of God's clawed hand down from Heaven to pluck up the just and the unjust alike.

It didn't seem so bad, from a distance. I know you know what I mean. You've seen the photographs, the films of smoking houses, smoking places of worship, smoking marketplaces.

Some of the people I burned weren't soldiers.

A surprising number of them survived.

I was never brought to trial.

They will never be asked to testify.

I can only speak for them, in one last unsubtle irony.

Cotter leaned across her desk. Her grey hair was escaping her bun, as usual. Her gaudy earrings swung. "My parents were Holocaust survivors. Do you know what *epigenetics* is?"

"No," I lied.

"Trauma experienced by your ancestors can affect your genetic expression. Your personality; your physical self. The environment *you* experience can affect the genetic expression of your children. It iterates. It's handed down."

"Oh," I said.

"I know what you did in the war," she said.

It was, in a strange way, a relief to be confronted. "I was just following orders."

"There's no *just* about it."

"Yeah," I said. "I know."

She sat back and suddenly relaxed. "How do you feel about it? About what you did, I mean. In the war."

"I..."

I shook my head.

I opened my mouth.

I shook my head again.

Some time later, Cotter leaned back, folded her hands, and said, "What if you could make people understand that? *Really* understand that? Really understand how you feel?"

I took a sip of water. It greased the words a little but they still had edges. "How many people? Until when?"

She shrugged. "Most of them? For a long time?"

I wonder how many times, in how many people, I've relived all that now.

Statistically speaking, if you are a human being in the Americas or Europe, you've already experienced it. As if you had been there. They're working on drugs to fight the infection, I hear, but it's already spread to Asia and Africa. Maybe not Madagascar. But the flatworms can live and reproduce in freshwater.

I expect they'll be around for the foreseeable future. So I don't have to tell you again what I did in the war, and how I came to feel about it later.

No point in beating a one-trick pony to death.

Sometimes we captured people rather than burning them. Some of those people went to prison camps where they were tortured, and I have a responsibility for that, too.

It doesn't sound so bad—caning the feet, stress positions,

waterboarding, electric shocks, isolation, sleep deprivation. It's not supposed to sound so bad. They show you worse things as entertainment, and the people on TV usually seem to walk away in the end.

It doesn't sound so bad.

Because you have been lied to.

꙰

"Lee," Cotter said. "You're the one."

꙰

"*Planaria lugubris*," she said, holding up a tube filled with cloudy water. "A common flatworm. Not so common anymore."

"Are they endangered?" I asked, interested.

"No," she said. Light glinted through the tube. It was quite pretty. "We edited them."

"Like a book?" I joked.

"More or less." The tube clicked as she set it back in a rack. "Do you know what CRISPR is?"

"Sure," I said. "It shows up in a lot of horror movies. There's human DNA in your flatworms, right? They're going to grow to the size of school buses and learn to use automatic weapons?"

"Well, no," she said. "But we did use some bits of another flatworm. A parasitic one. And *Toxoplasmosis gondii*."

I felt my mouth doing a funny thing. "Isn't that the bug that makes rats walk into cat mouths?"

Her mouth did a funny thing, too. As if she were trying to smile, but didn't really feel like she deserved to. "Do you know what's interesting about planarians, Lee?"

"Wait," I said, suddenly full of high-school biology. "They can pass memories to one another, right? If they eat each other?"

"Fucking little cannibals," she agreed.

"You want to feed them my memories."

Her fingers drummed silently on the steel lab countertop.

"Then what? Make people eat them?"

She stepped away from the counter and faced me. "They reproduce in human brains. They can pass their memories along to their hosts."

"That sounds like terrorism. Not to mention one hell of a violation of consent law."

"Did you consent to what happened to you?" she asked me.

My lips clenched around the words, holding them in. I closed my eyes and got out a single one. "Technically."

That was why some of the people I worked with went to jail. I didn't. Mostly because the government wanted the prosecutions—and the attendant publicity—to stop as soon as they'd plausibly punished someone for what they told us to do.

"Is coerced consent really consent?"

"Who is ever," I asked, "really free of coercion?"

She sighed and rolled her head back to look at the ceiling. "Yes, it's terrorism. Yes, it's a terrible, unethical thing. Yes, when it comes out, I will go to jail at the very least."

"And me?"

"You'll be dead."

"Right," I said. "They're going to eat my brain. That's how they get the memories, isn't it? Just like they get the memories of other flatworms from eating each other."

She just looked at me.

I waved my hand airily. "I'm okay with *that*. Are they going to eat other people's brains?"

"The first generation will reproduce and die," she said. "They've got a . . . I guess you would call it a kill switch. Their offspring will be commensal organisms rather than parasitic ones. We've programmed them to eat damaged cells instead of healthy ones. Infected people will actually, on average, live longer. The cure for war is also the cure for cancer."

"Flatworms that will certainly never mutate back and just eat brains or something. All the brains. Everywhere. You've recreated mad cow disease, but with flatworms."

"Planarians are a lot easier to kill than prions," she said. "And parasites generally evolve to be less deadly to the host, not more."

"You're an even more awful human being than I am," I said.

"Do you want to end war?"

I bit my lip. I looked down at my shoes. "It seems like the least I can do."

"You will have to formally consent, and indicate that you understand what the process will require."

"What, now consent matters? What about all those people out there who don't pay their taxes in order to be parasitized by flatworms and traumatic memories?"

"I'm a hypocrite," Cotter admitted. "And if I knew what else to do I would. Aren't all those people out there who pay their taxes complicit in drone strikes on kindergartens, too? If they stopped trying not to worry about it, or thinking of it as necessary collateral damage, do you think things would change?"

My stomach clenched. I held out my hand, as if we could shake on it. "Okay. What is it, a lethal injection or something?"

She looked away. "Lee. You have to be alive while the flatworms work."

"Well." I swallowed and took my hand back. "Show me where to sign."

I didn't expect to remember.

No. That's wrong. That was, after all, the entire point of the exercise: me remembering. Me remembering war. For you.

I didn't expect that I would be self-aware through the process, however. My own private richly-deserved Hell.

I wonder how many times, in how many places, I've relived this now. I'm not sure I would have had the guts to commit to the process, if I realized that I would have to go through it all again. Billions and billions of times. I mean, moral cowardice is what turned me into a war criminal in the first place.

It seemed like a good idea at the time. When I had a brain of my own. And wasn't just a parasite in yours.

The process of being converted into flatworm memories didn't hurt. Your brain doesn't have any nerves to feel pain with.

It was actually kind of a relief. I could feel the memories slipping away.

A relief, anyway, until I realized that the memories were all I was anymore.

War is a contagion. The contagion is in you.

The contagion is me.

Cotter died in prison, as she'd predicted, after the world figured out what we'd done. Too late to change anything. Too late to fix anything.

Too late to mean anything.

Sending her to jail was a nice gesture, I suppose.

Scream

Olena Krasnoselska

Крик | Олена Красносельська
translated by Oksana Katsanivska

My name is . . . well, it doesn't really matter what MY name is . . . my father's name is Hryhorii. My grandfather's name is Terentii. And as for my great-grandfather, his name I can't recall.

It's getting dark. I came to visit my father's grave at dawn, and still haven't had enough time to talk to him. It's a totally different universe here, with its own distances and concept of time. It's strangely quiet. The sky seems so close—enormous and heavy—but completely empty. There are no birds here . . . there never have been. There are plenty of dogs, though. They howl at night. Occasionally, they scud between the graves—scrawny and seemingly more delusory than leaf shadows. They sniff the air with their long noses, look at me without the slightest fear in their eyes, and I understand right away whose territory this is. There are no birds here. And no people either. They appear here and there, pick up their pace, and disappear. Helpless. Unwary. Hastily, they fill their lungs with air: up and down just like a pendulum; breathe in and breathe out; sunset and sunrise. Even the foot-worn clay trail transforms into a greenish-gray asphalt sidetrack, when it reaches an air-drawn border. It bends, hits a vibrant highway vein, and pierces through it, leaving its tiny torn bits on the roadside. Right around the corner, it clings to the noisy city artery, the line of life, wrapped in bitter factory smoke.

The silent fight over my father's grave has lasted a few years already—but its outcome is still hard to predict. What did he do wrong? Looking back to the past, what could it be? He can't tell me anymore. And he can't do anything about it. Pressed down into the earth, Father retreats without the chance to say goodbye. He sinks deeper and deeper into *his own* black square, getting smaller and smoothing away—with every ebb, with every sunset, with every exhalation. That is the phenomenon of time—or, rather, the dance of time—two steps forward, one step back. The worn-out and wrinkled earth's skin grows young and sleek again, longing for a child's innocence. A voiceless army watches him—there is no escape, the step back has been taken. Although, he would have undoubtedly faded under the baking July sun—just as a hill over the Dnipro once smoothed out and dissolved in the expanding world with a groan, into rising heat currents. And all those hundreds of people who walked over it dissolved too. Drawn to the glowing magnetic sun, they ascended into the sky. To the stars. They got entangled with light and shadow, and then, slowly flickering, cooled down.

The battle started without a warning: my father's tomb sunk in the beginning of spring. It seems to me that is when the trash appeared. It began timidly, just the smoke of everything that once *had been,* but even this was enough to tilt the fence and crumble concrete, exposing the frame. Then somebody decided that the time had come—and filled Father's grave first with branches, then with junk and rubbish. Before this, I hadn't really cared where and how the garbage *vortex* emerged and grew: here or there, on the right or on the left, what it contained, bits and pieces layered with wads of someone's (but whose?) wool and earth (clay). *This* vortex took into itself a hundred multi-layered three-dimensional plastic spheres, each containing compressed trash that used to belong to someone drowning somewhere nearby—on an 8 feet long by 2.5 foot wide slice of land. Of course, this garbage is from the realm of the living.

Today, once again, I ripped my hands dragging all these damned remnants of dead stuff—plastic flowers, faded leaves, broken branches and discolored wrappers, bags full of post-life's guts, bottles, debris, rocks and pebbles—to the *huge vortex* next to the main street. I even found a tree trunk, big and nearly impossible to lift. How did it end up here? I carried it on my back. Like a cross. It's so cold deep in my soul. Stop trashing the dead. I dragged all this garbage away from him.

The clay here is very heavy with the heat absorbed during the day. By sunset, everything is covered in it—my hands, my clothes, and my soul. I feel as if I myself arose from this earth and this clay. My father has nearly been forced out of his grave—instead of one neighbor on his left, he now has three, a mass grave. A lady used to slumber there, but now, according to the plaques, it's occupied by the Immortal family. They did it. They seized it. The pathway and a part of the fence were absorbed by this newly-created conglomerate—an unbelievably heterogeneous and chaotic mosaic of dead bodies. My boxwood bushes used to grow here but now they are gone, somebody pulled them up by the roots and formed the clay into red slippery grave-mounds. Three men in a boat (the dog could also fit)—the Immortals are sailing.

I feel so scared, embarrassed, and cold ... as if I opened the door that I wasn't supposed to open, and learned something that I shouldn't have known—death is not the end. Even when your body betrays you, and your blood soaks into the red (is it blood-red?) earth, you will keep fighting with the insidiously powerful force that lives above the *tiny abyss* given to you for eternity. This yellowish-red clay-legged giant wants to take away the micro-citadel of your last refuge. I ask myself, "Whom shall I fear?" Werewolves or vampires, maybe? Or monsters and evil spirits with cats' and wolves' tails, that come close and hover over you without being seen? And then I murmur to myself, "The spirits are harmless—it's the living that I fear."

My hands are torn and covered in blood. I keep clearing the clay. I feel this earth the way I've never felt it before—so big but also so small. Maybe, it's the first time I've actually felt it. And suddenly I realize: any life ends in two deaths. First, dies a body, and then—a name.

Light, shade, light, shade—the bells flicker.
Ripples from the leaves, falling from still living trees,
Swaddle the wounds.
Ripples from the flowers.
Ripples from the living—the bloom of time.
All the live flowers are gone.

I've endured this battle, so now I have to return to the world of the living. Instead, I'm sitting here, on a cracked bench, leaning against the tiny table that looks just like the Black Square in this evening twilight. I'm looking at the shadows on its metal canvas—flaked and rough layers of paint, worn from rain and wind. In the end, all the colors of the past are absorbed by black.

"I became a pilot, Father," I say quietly. "Once you showed me the Pleiades—a star cluster in the constellation Taurus—and said that one day people would be able to travel anywhere. I did it, father."

My father is looking at me from the headstone photo. He is so young there, younger than I am now. I feel like he wants to tell me something. Nobody interrupts our conversation—everyone here is a good listener—so I go on to tell him about the number synthesis, digital spaceships, my space flight, and all the worlds that I've seen.

Numbers are born somewhere. Having once created a number as an image, we take them as given. They are fragile and immaterial, but consciousness can turn an image into a matter and pull out of nowhere information about a random Stone Age boy: find out how he was born, how he lived and died, and even what his name was. Now everything is possible—no limits, no obstructions. The world has become so technologically advanced that everything on the Earth is "smart" and information can be read off of any rock. Artificial intelligence. Empyreal vastness.

"But the stars . . . The stars are still so far away," I murmur confusedly. "We are still confined to the earth—just like caterpillars."

"Tell me about the synthesis," Father asks.

"As a kid, I used to reach out to the stars trying to touch them with my fingers, and you always said that distance wasn't an obstacle."

The first stars are appearing in the sky. I seek out the brightest one. It was a difficult journey that took years. Our entire city-beyond-the-rapids[1] was working on this idea. Father was right, when he told me to stick to my roots. My small and humble hometown supported me financially. My fellow townspeople had faith in me. I don't know how to ask the question that brought me here. I cannot find the right words—they keep disappearing as if this question is beyond life and beyond time.

"I have to change something. It cannot go on like this."

"Tell me about the synthesis," Father asks again.

So, I tell him about our small laboratory of numbers. After years of exploring the foundations of *number physics*, we finally created the first ever *digital spaceship*.

"Number synthesis is based on systematicity: natural patterns are the basis for codes. The world is simplified and perceived as an abstract structure of numbers. It seems that God agreed to this and gave us synthesis. People were dreaming about the stars, but a technological breakthrough in the development of new engines for interplanetary spacecrafts was taking way too long. The world needed a miracle."

"You did it, didn't you?"

"We did. I became a pilot of a digital spaceship. The first in the world!"

"Unstoppable caterpillar aims at the stars," Father smiles. "I knew it."

I'm peering into the shadows trying to catch and hold his gaze— my legacy. I'm thinking about the ability to turn the world upside

---

1   Zaporizhzhia is the city situated on the banks of the Dnipro River. The name Zaporizhzhia refers to the position of the city "beyond the rapids."

down for the sake of another technological revolution. Something very important is hidden deep in these shadows (in the wounds). Shadows of our shadows. My glare into the darkness is so mercilessly sharp that the night eventually loses its grip and yields, beyond the imaginary horizon of my father's photo, the hypersensitive and vanishingly transient structure of time:

hot, viscous, and wild,
drop after drop.

"They were different, though."

I want to show him what I saw. I reach out to the vision of a digital spaceship and touch its transparent body with the tips of my fingers. From the inside, it is covered with elastic leather that gleams with a myriad of minuscule sensors and tactile trims of baffling structures, which split our perception of other dimensions into multiple layers. That's how the spatio-temporal merging of a human and the Universe is done. In a digital spaceship, the whole Universe is a unit, and you are a particle, a part of two worlds—earthly and stellar—status indeterminatus that needs clarification, *a cloud between the worlds*.

I am a cloud between the worlds!

If my words did surprise Father, it was for a mere second. He takes a seat next to me, pours coffee into two clay mugs, and hands me one. Clink-clink. We take the first sip. The coffee mug is floating in time. Coelosphere is rippling in my palms. Earthly-warm, rough clay.

"How was it, to be able to perceive the world as a number?" Father asks.

"Difficult. The capsule is equipped with a special device—something like an updated make of the Enigma Machine—that uses for input digital grids rather than a keyboard. The capturing field indicates the coordinates of points in the Universe. There is a distant orientational order for me—the cloud—that guides me to the needed point ... And I am already on the planet Earl, touching it with my gaze, making a mold. I am clay.

My father's face is no longer discernible in the darkness, but I know that he understands—the human acts as a decipherer by choosing a decoding system for the visualization of numbers. Then comes the number synthesis, powered by industrial modules, and the restoration of volume from the image. Seems to be easy. The Universe is a set of codes and ciphers.

Integral, profound, and multi-dimensional reality in the global system of numbers—is it really such a miracle, to transform numbers into images? These are the conditions for life. Just as invisible writing reveals itself under the influence of heat, this world lives under our gaze—revealed by the sense of touch. There are so many codes. We just need to break loose from the closed cocoon of the Earth and become an open, *free* system. The caterpillar needs to turn into a butterfly.

"I'm not saying that the numbers are alive. I just think that we can create a connection with them, and convert space-time from digital information dust into an image."

"Planet Earl has got blue sand and two raspberry suns," says Father, as if he knows.

Sixteen continuous cycles, intertwined in such a manner, that when converted from flat to tridimensional, they look like a school of fish. A digital mold of planet Earl is blue sand and two raspberry suns.

"You are right, father. A digital mold bears a faint resemblance to a photo—but a photo cannot evolve, whereas a mold can be shaped into the world that it depicts. It can be expanded, grown, and felt. It's just like mastering the language of stars with the help of *the book of ciphers* of the information field. We made twenty digital molds of different planets and ... that was it."

"Why? Why do all the new launches of digital spaceships fail? It is as if someone has put a lock on the Universe and set a code. And all the accesses to it are also coded. And accesses to accesses are coded as well. The Earth's artificial intelligence cannot crack these codes. It seems like someone has intentionally blocked our access to the Universe after showing us that our first step was perfectly correct."

"Is this what you wanted to ask me?"

Some say, that from an aerial view this cemetery resembles a giant seashell lying on the ground. Long rows of countless crosses converge in one spot—just like the lines on a cockle. Suddenly, the silence is broken for me; I hear a distant sound, it emerges out of nowhere and holds one single note, converting the plane of space into the idea of time. Sounds of other worlds are filling up the spatial shell. Thousands and millions of shells are covered by the fine sand of the shaky *cosmic* coastline.

"There, in the depths of space, I felt something."

"Tell me?" asks Father.

But what can I tell him? Some *other* entity was looking back at me there, an extremely profound physical reality, capable of understanding the living, independent and as ancient as the world itself. Perhaps it reveals itself exclusively under somebody's gaze—it flows from *living* to *dead* and from *dead* to *living*—correlation between the inner vibration frequencies allows it to exist within a particular system depending on whether somebody is looking at it or not. But it knows everything about you and those who stand behind you. It knows absolutely everything.

Outer space is filled with such a multitude of the tiniest particles of digital dust that, when layered upon one another, they produce a clear black color—reflected by my retina. Our technologies managed to capture this image: our shadow's shadow exists, it is behind our back, splashes against our feet. "Why are you here? What do you want from the stars?" I was asked.

"Maybe it's not enough to just wish to touch the stars?"

The cold, trembling lines of moonlight are fraught with Schiele's philosophy of the *white line*. They are so distant from the earthly coldness. A sailing-ship glides through the skies. It's followed by many more. My father used to sail. In a few days, a round-the-world regatta will start in my city—a major event for this land and these waters. A dam used to fetter this river, making any movement—of water, of thoughts, of life—nearly impossible. But now this river is free. Its sun-heated, pale yellow banks merge at the skyline, striving to embrace the whole globe and spread around the world the worn-out color of this land: memory and blood of the people with all their ancient traditions, gestures, and voices. It inherited some subtle Dutch, Greek, Italian, and Armenian features from the past millennia, from *those who had walked this land*. Clay flower-vortex sprouts here—the symbol of freedom.

Nowadays anyone can embark on a round-the-world journey, trying to avoid a certain place and time. Due to the development of modern technologies, the world has become much simpler with no dam on our thoughts or barriers across space. A black vortex of infinity is seen far in the East. Is it a past world, shrinking to a dot, or a future one that will be blown here by the winds?

There is no physical obstacle for digital spaceships. The obstacle lies within us. Our thoughts and actions become a maze.

"The cemetery is closed; all the plots are taken, but the bodies keep coming and coming, you see," a cemetery groundskeeper offers to help with the fence—to reinforce it (for money, of course) or even to extend the cemetery (for big money, naturally).

Extend? What does he mean? There is no earth here, just clay. Mere inches of clay. Thousands of years: histories and lives entangled in their web and covered with stardust. He suggests that I buy seven more inches of clay, to widen Father's plot. As if dead people were coal. Black gold—pilgrims who came here by different roads. There are thousands and millions of them, and you think that they will never fit on this tiny patch of land. Yet, they all do. Earth has its own black holes.

"We have everything we need. We don't want anything that doesn't belong to us."

Perhaps, now they will leave the old burial alone. Although it's not even that old; Father *left* a few decades ago. He's never changed, still young, wearing a blue tracksuit and holding a soccer ball in his hands. If no one sees a living figurine in a clay drawing, it doesn't mean that it's not there.

I should probably be happy—my dearest can rest in peace down there. He hasn't been forced out of his grave. He hasn't been prematurely wiped off this earth. At least for now. But *somebody else* has been taken hostage, and that is why

the stars fall.

This old cemetery is non-digitized. Nowadays, after death, living entities (if desired) are stored in fancy digital envelopes somewhere in cloudy lumps of energy, awaiting decryption in some layer of future. Second life? Who knows. The value of one life determines the progress of humanity. We are alive as long as we are remembered.

At least, by some.

At least, by one.

But they keep dumping garbage all over graves. It's so easy to erase memory and make a new entry, aka burial. The cemetery is closed, all the plots have long been taken, but the bodies keep coming and coming. The *second river* grows more vast. Profits increase.

A scream, silent, imprisoned in my soul, everts my body, turning into "The Scream"[2] against a background of bloody skies and human silhouettes. It turns into scream—the weapon, scream—the moment of choice, scream[3]—the swirl of the Higher Forces that splashes *your* form into space.

Father's vandalized grave sails amidst the world of high technologies and artificial intelligence, amidst the stars and Universe.

Ship-Earth sails in the ocean.

Earth, your digital ships are lost in the waves. Don't you see the longed-for shore? Isn't it for you, that every night they light a fire in the celestial furnace, accelerating the speed? Can't anyone aboard feel this desolate motion? Where is your sail?

But the hatches are battened down, the compass is thrown off, as if you aren't free. *Ship laden with coal*[4].

Zaporizhzhia, 2035

---

2   The Scream is a painting by Edvard Munch.

3   Theater of Cruelty is a form of theater conceptualized by Antonin Atraud. It is based on the idea of creating a new codified stage language of totem, light, scream and gestures as elements that affect the psyche of the audience through sound images.

4   Poem "Ship Laden with Coal" by Rafael Alberti.

The Midst of Snow

Oleksiy Gedeonov

Середина снігу | Олексій Гедеонов
translated by Svetlana Lavochkina

"How fierce has Mother Frost been! Blizzard on Palm Sunday!" they rattled on in the hall. "She's shaking her pillow again! Nay, beating the pillow!"

"Indeed, indeed," another voice tinkled, "The end of the world has come . . ."

"That's just the beginning! Now they've hurt a daughter of hers. That's why she's whirling and swirling, not even letting the spring in. Remember my words: first, snow on Palm Sunday, then crops will fail, then robbers will come, then prices will sting and taxes will soar. Then plague will strike. And after that, war . . ."

"All this for our sins . . . have mercy on us, Holy Mother!"

The voices trailed off. The hawker women tucked in their warm shawls, crossed them over their breasts, tied the ends up on their heads and went to the market.

The guest descended the inn stairs into the kitchen. He gave the innkeeper his soldier's canteen and asked for hot water. She poured some without wasting a single drop from the ladle, although the steam was blocking her sight.

"So how's your sister? Is she better?" the old landlady inquired.

The lodger waved her off and hobbled back upstairs, but then stopped and looked back, propping himself on the railing, "She's weak. Raving. Calling for the morning star, Venus. Wants the star to come down to her. Maybe you know someone around here who's called Venus?"

"No, no one's called Venus here. Let me better fetch the priest instead. I'll send my errand boy for him. They say the provost returned three days ago. And the deacon came back too, with his bland face, like food during Lent. They hung up the bell again. And they dug up the money box. Looks like it'll be peace again, and peace will last."

"No, I don't want any provost, it's too early for that. I'll wait. What if she comes to again? And she's no sister to me. Just an orphan, a poor wretch. A foundling."

The old woman wiped her hands on her apron and straightened up her kerchief, "Aha, fornicating?"

"Like everyone else."

His name was Karel. He'd been on the conscription list since early age, Private Infantry Archebusier of the Agram Division. He was the war's age mate. For twenty years, the war had been raging far and wide, and Karel walked with it hand in hand. He trampled over the roads, ash heaps, log roads, bridges. In summer, he kneaded clay; in winter, he kneaded snow. He shot. He dug out trenches. He slept. He ate gruel. He shot again. He was wounded. He cursed furiously in the infirmary. He didn't let them amputate his left leg. He survived. He walked again. And he shot again.

The war was enjoying itself, bursting into black laughter.

Yet suddenly, a lordly hand dipped the quill into an inkpot and penned three words on the stamped paper: "The Great Truce." The hand pressed a signet ring onto the sealing wax—as if sealing blood.

The guns fell silent and the soldiers set out for home. The refugees returned to their abandoned houses and gardens. The bells chimed. The churches filled up, the markets and inns came alive. The people prayed and rejoiced. They were saying, "Enough of war! May it get lost! Off with the war! Enough, enough!"

Karel shrugged, handed his weapons in at the armory, got his pay and a "thank you" from the colonel. A miserly pay, not even enough for a funeral. And nowhere to return anyway.

Karel set off into nowhere, wherever his feet would take him. He dreamed of a home: light and jolly—Holy Thursday all year long, and pretty too. A fine horse. Some good cattle. A nice orchard. And Karel himself the master, a fair landlord in the manor.

At home, he'd shut his door—tight. He'd make fire—rich smoke would billow from the chimney—the white oven would buzz, warming up. Burn, burn bright!

He longed for a wife, too.

On the way to his jolly home, Karel bumped into Ledenka—Icicle. Yet back then she had still been nameless. The girl was sitting at the roadside, as pale as death, a chilling light in her blue eyes. She was telling everyone she was dead. In the hem of her tattered frock, she kept stale slabs of bread and wormy nuts. Ledenka. She let soldiers and any other men have their way with her—you don't feel shame if you're dead. She took food scraps for pay. A loony, Karel could see that at once. She was just what he needed. He took her hand firmly. He told her from now on not to give anyone what didn't belong to them, and he led her along. The girl was as cold as ice, all bald and bony, as if indeed dead.

On the way, Karel gave his foundling a name—as befitted the season of the thin, cold glaring moon in the sky, and the earthly Ice-Month—January, as the locals called it.

The soldier and the girl travelled with nomads, slept tightly embraced, swapped their belongings for food. A belt buckle. A sash. A hoop dangle. A snuff box. Karel was tall and as strong as a bull, but he ate little, sharing with Ledenka. She was as small as a mouse and all see-through. But she ate like a glutton—whatever she saw, even the soil sometimes, and then she'd have the awful runs. She couldn't walk—she wobbled and fell down. When that happened, Karel would lift her up onto his shoulders, or carried her in his arms, rocking her like a baby. The loony delighted in it, singing and babbling.

From her palaver, Karel learned that she had come down from the sky because she'd been curious about life on Earth. No sooner had she come down to Earth, a whole gang of looters seized her and passed her around. Since then, she'd been convinced she wasn't alive because she wasn't afraid: those alive were afraid, but her own fear had either left her or hadn't been there in the first place, she didn't remember at all … At intervals during their journey, Karel would mould a hut out of snow: a white, jolly hut, clean as Holy Thursday.

"Look," he would say, "This is what our house will look like. Here's the door, here's the window, and here's the roof with a chimney on it. And over the house, there's the morning star Venus—she fixes houses, paves roads, but she's invisible."

The guards at the outposts called: "Where're you going?" "Home," they replied.

But at the end of the snow road, Ledenka fell sick. She coughed and sneezed, and then she ran a fever and started wheezing.

Karel carried her to a riverside town: soot, ash heaps. The gate was smashed. In the town, all was topsy-turvy, too. Everywhere, refugees camped, yelling and squealing, everyone messing around with their junk, heaping up their rags. The market was hell, prices scorching, and the hawker women were mean like devils. Yet, he was able to buy what he needed: vinegar, herbs, salt, some flour, herring, and turnips—you can't do without turnips, of course.

Karel ripped up his coat lining and took out his thalers—enough to rent a room at an inn. He brewed some mint, for its fragrance to help heal the sick girl. He mixed the flour he'd bought with water and fed her off a kerchief. And he bought beaver fat and mustard powder to rub on her chest to chase the illness away …

The girl lay on her back, sucking her finger. Her tongue was covered in a white rash. She wet herself. Karel cleaned her up from a warm water flask, changed the bed cover, and opened the window ajar. A lame stray horse hobbled along. Rooks circled over the ruined bastion. The town hall was black with soot and mournful like a widow, stretching its thin tower with a weathervane on top reaching to the sky. Scaffolds had already been put up around the poor burnt thing—it would be cleaned and whitewashed again. The widow would be made over into a bride. The townspeople were settling in for a long spell of peace.

Ledenka opened her eyes, cornflower blue, "Bring me a star."

She kept saying this every day—softly, plaintively, without a break—gnawing on his soul, sucking up blood from his veins. In dismay, Karel hit the wall with his fist. "What star, you fool?!"

"A bright star," Ledenka replied, and pointed up with her see-through finger. "That one: Venus."

Karel looked out the window, blinked and shuddered.

Half the sky was flooded in bloody-red gold, and the weathervane star on top of the black town hall tower was bathing in sundown fire. The star shone unbearably bright, catching the evening light, sprawling its crooked rays above the crimson roof tiles, saying good-bye to the sun. Its crooked tail pointed into the distance—it wasn't an ordinary star spinning around over the town hall: it was a fuzzy comet.

"Yeah, girl, you wish," Karel said.

Ledenka fell asleep. Karel touched her forehead. It was dry and hot. Trouble.

He made his way into a room where a peaceful crowd was dining: masons and carpenters. He sat down with them. Asked for beer. Listened to their chat. *Gypsies are stealing children and horses. Jews are poisoning drinking wells, Armenians are stingy—all these fiends have to be done away with. Bread and tobacco are rising in price. The sickle moon rose blood-red, and a naked witch flew over the forest on a fiery hoop. See-through fairies are dancing with the dead. Toads and snakes are crawling into the houses. In winter, they say, flies wake up. The snow is falling. Tell us, soldier, how can we live in all this?*

Karel nodded, but his mind was elsewhere.

"How much do you want for borrowing your tools?" he asked. The young artel braggart fell silent, glanced darkly and jacked up the price. Karel grunted: "Swap?"

The fellow baulked, then pointed at Karel's uniform coat: buttons. Seven good silver buttons. Karel pulled a knife out of his boot, cut the buttons off with the thread flesh, gathered them in a handful.

The fellow gave him the instruments: pliers, files, different other things.

Twilight went by. Moving from the valley, the shroud of sneaky dusk smothered the town. The streets were blocked by chains. The night watch walked about the streets banging their clappers, and somewhere in the distance dogs barked. Carrying a lantern, Karel was crossing the square to the town hall. On his neck, a canvas tool bag was dangling. He looked around. The square was empty. His inn room window on the first floor was glowing in lively yellow. Good he'd left a candle burning in a shard—Ledenka might well babble she was dead, but still, she hated the dark. In the dark, she said, fierce monsters—beasts of ice with bony feet and red eyes—lurked in ambush to tear your heart out. Karel crossed himself, took a deep breath, and started to climb up the scaffolding.

It was wobbly, rickety, the wind was howling. There was a salty taste in his mouth, dust squeaking on his teeth, sweat running down his forehead. He dropped his lantern—the hollow jangle of tin on cobblestone, the scatter of sparkles—darkness. But that was not too bad—it was April, and it was growing light early. There, in the east, it looked as if milk had been spilled in the sky. Karel climbed higher, stood up firmly, his legs apart. With both hands, bruised on the knuckles, he grasped the pinnacle of the weathervane. Its girth was broader than his arm. But luckily, the spire was rusted by storms and fires—quite maimed. Karel sorted the tools in his bag. Well, God Almighty . . . Help your daredevil slave . . .

Sunk in the deep darkness under his feet, the town was half-asleep, half-alert, like a boat floating on waves of dreams. East Wind woke up, its breath bittersweet-fragrant, carrying curly cumulus clouds, lush rains and harvest. In the gardens behind the walls, cherry trees were blossoming.

Karel had returned to the inn before the bells rung, before the morning prayer began. He was treading slowly and heavily. The old innkeeper came towards him: she'd wanted to dump the swill outside, but she dropped the bucket. She sat down and bit her sleeve.

Karel went upstairs. The first step. The second. The third. The fifth. His hands full, he pushed the door with his foot. Ledenka awoke and sat up. She burst into a cough, waving her arms. She fell off her cot, kneeled, reeled as if she was drunk. The candle wick sank in the fat puddle and the fire went out.

Karel stood in the door frame. He unclenched his bloodied fingers. His heavy burden thumped onto the floor.

Karel was a hulk of a man, and the fuzzy comet of a weathervane was so massive it reached his waist. It was covered in hard crust, with the town's coat of arms on its back and a star face on its front. The crust was green on the copper parts, and rusty ochre on the iron parts. Star Venus looked terrifying—rays sharp, face monstrous, eyes hollow, nose a predatory beak, tail crooked like a Turkish knife. Sprayed with bird guano and pecked by rains, it reeked of dust and sun. On its spire that sprouted from the hub of the rays, there was a fresh cut.

The girl saw her guiding star and started wailing, softly and hoarsely. She sounded feral like a wolf howling. She coughed up phlegm, cold sweat covered her forehead in beads.

Karel's back ached, his torn muscles were sore. His veins from elbows to forearms swelled, pulsing with blood. He was smiling but he felt dizzy, and close to fainting. Ledenka was stroking Venus' celestial face with her pale fingers, babbling with her wet mouth. Then she crawled towards Karel, her bony knees catching splinters on the floorboards. She reached him, scrambled herself up, and clung to him. She groped his bristly cheek with her lips. She clutched his shirt collar and shook it, and beat her feeble fists on his chest, muttering, "I'm alive. You're alive. We're not gonna die now."

Karel froze in wonder. He stroked her face and kissed her on her sore lips. He put his forehead against the door frame and fell asleep sitting, right on the doorstep.

Ledenka whispered, "Show me the way, Guiding Star." And she fell asleep, curled up beside him.

But wonders are long in the making. Ledenka ailed for a while. Karel joined the artel, repairing bastions, walls, the town hall spire. He kneaded mortar, hauled stones, came back home after midnight. He'd kiss the girl on the temple and tumble into sleep, his face to the wall. But at least he had enough money to pay the apothecary for potions and ointments. By and by, the girl recovered and started walking again, and then even running. She came in handy for the innkeeper, helping out in the kitchen. The old woman allowed her to snatch tasty morsels from the guests' meals. Ledenka's hair grew and started curling. She sewed herself a kerchief like a married woman. She fattened up a bit, grew curves to hold onto when cuddling. Star Venus stood in the corner, wrapped in white cloth. No one in town knew where the weathervane had vanished. The old woman was wisely silent, and Karel, when tipsy, quipped, "Flew up into the sky, as befitted her rank. Gone is gone."

When Ledenka became heavy with child, they got married. Bells chimed, pigeons cooed, roses blossomed. The wedding was a magical, peaceful affair—the guests enjoyed themselves. The party caroused all night. They drank, ate, and danced.

At sunup, Karel took Ledenka to the suburbs, along the city wall, closer to the orchards and the river. The farmstead was a good bargain: its owner had been in a great hurry.

So they started a new life.

Karel crawled over the plot on all fours, hammering stakes into the ground to make a markup for their house.

Ledenka walked about the orchard, then sowed some wheat within the markup, to hallow the foundation. She was standing in the middle with her hands folded in prayer on her round belly, guiding Karel, "Straight—askew."

From the previous owner, they got a haybarn and some apple trees in the orchard, scorched by fire. Still, those were precious commodities, as compared to stale slabs of bread. The artel helped out, too: they thatched the haybarn roof. Karel hung up a new door, carved a window on the eastern wall and glazed it. A mason friend put up a wonderful stove. Karel and Ledenka made a cheery fire. They sat in front of each other, baking flatbread and turnips on hot coals. Venus the fuzzy comet lay under the sleeping cot, wrapped up in white cloth. She was invisible, as befits those who guide the right way.

Behind the wall, a goat was bleating—fine cattle, the giver of wool and milk, and simple to care for at that—an omnivore. Life was walking a jolly straight path.

A messenger in green uniform steered his horse off the road and galloped across peaceful fields to the right. Foam was falling off the harness. The mare was scowling with strain, like a hound, its tongue dangling. The messenger was bringing bad news.

The lordly hands had torn up the peace treaty in half with a loud rip, breaking the signet. The sealing wax crumbled into red powder.

The end of the Great Truce! March, march! The war was laughing with its insatiable mouth, gloating—it was resurrected again, and as ravenous as ever.

Flags flapped. The fortress bridges were raised. Portcullises creaked, barring the town gates until better times. Guns cleared their throats and spoke.

That morning, Karel was hewing a roof beam for the house. He heard the messenger's horn singing, choking on its tune of alarm. He dropped his axe, it fell into the mud. There was a whiff of gunpowder stench in the air . . .

The army wound along the tracts like a lazy snake, like a gray cloud. The horses neighed deliriously. The cart wheels creaked. The guns cursed atop of their mounts. Drums roared, flageolets squealed, clubs scratched the firmament.

Karel was summoned again. The armory doors were wide open. He was handed an arquebus. New buttons had been sewn up on his uniform. No sooner had Karel kissed his wife goodbye than the war scooped him up. The war had been waiting for him, the war had missed him . . .

He marched. He shot. He slept. He beat. He dug. He shot again. One dark night, he was shot dead himself, by someone like him. He fell down prone into the clay.

That night, Ledenka was awake. She was listening to the darkness, watching the wind play in the orchard and stars fall—a sign that people were dying somewhere far away. It was August, the cruel reaper month.

Summer came to its end, clouds blocked the sun, bulged gray, filled with trouble, and belched up snow.

Ledenka had a child. The town people burned down their unfinished house and the barn they'd lived in: an esplanade had to be prepared, a clear field outside the town for the fortress gun to fire.

Along with the smoke, the guiding star Venus ascended into the sky, as befitted its rank. It had imbibed blood and fire, and became a red fuzzy comet . . . A glowing, gloating comet.

The war was roaring everywhere again. The gate on the right was barred. On the left, there was a river. Ash heaps were everywhere. The apple trees were black and thin—you would sneeze and they'd fall apart. Every day, the sky froze. Again, fierce Mother Frost was smothering everything with snow: towns and ruins, meadows and valleys, orchards and roads. On the road, along the tracks that carts made in the snow, a woman was heading into the omnivorous winter. She had a goat on a leash, and on the goat's back there was a basket with hay and a blanket. The baby was in a sling at the woman's chest. The woman was breast-feeding. The baby was suckling. The woman had a lot of milk. Crows were circling around them, cawing, "Hit! Road! Dead!"

"Let's hit the road, sonny. Let's go home," the woman said.

It was a blizzard. Smoke was coiling all over the country, crows were cawing trouble. The comet was trembling in the sky like a drop of blood. Was it guiding the way? Was it foretelling the end of the world? Nobody knew.

Ledenka called her baby Adam, a name for the living, not for the dead. She blundered randomly through black orchards, through snow, saying again and again, firmly, "You're alive. I'm alive. We aren't going to die now."

The Long Black Veil
Stefan O. Rak

First, a leg. Then the rest of her body entered the room.

Foot first: must be on a mission, he thought. Head first, typically they're desperate, wanting. Even if it's just for approval, which can be harder to grant than help. But leg first like that—she knows how to walk, how to present.

And then he clocked that she also knew how to command a black dress with easy folds that placed gracefully with her gait. The price of the piece must've matched the tag for those pearls that weren't choking her neck.

Manfred Dober cleared his throat before saying, "Please come in, have a seat." From the safety of some distance, he stood up to welcome his client, gesturing a little too late.

She proceeded, approached his desk, and they shook hands. Thus far, she hadn't made a sound, neither verbally nor any other way.

Then she said, "Mr. Dober?"

"Yes, hello, welcome." Dober fumbled. "You must be—"

"Ms. Everly Greene," she announced as they both sat down.

"Yes, of course, Ms. Greene." He looked back up from his appointment book calendar but wasn't able to meet her eyes. "Condolences," he tried.

"Oh, I'm not in mourning," she replied. "I always wear this veil. I don't have a face, you see? So if I don't wear some kind of veil, it's next to impossible to have a regular conversation with anyone, get anything done. Too distracting or disturbing—something. For them. I'm used to it, naturally." She appeared to withhold a shrug and made no motion to suggest the potentiality of lifting the veil to show him.

He couldn't help but think that there was nothing natural about her condition—but he had a business to run. Instead, he said, "Ah, I see. Well, that's good, then. Considering that you are here, though, it was a logical assumption. I do apologize if I've offended or upset you."

Thus far, she was unimpressed.

Dober decided to continue with, "Okay, yes," while flipping through some papers on his desk. "I have your intake forms right here ... All right. Everything seems to be—ah, you left this part blank. Are you sure you don't want anything engraved, Ms. Greene? What was his—the deceased's—name?"

"Her."

"Pardon me?"

"___."

"Seriously?"

"No, not really. Although I guess maybe yes. I never actually called her anything, so ... "

"Oh I see, you actually did write '___' right here under 'Given Name.' I do apologize." Dober donned a sympathetic smile. It was his most frequently used facial expression, and he wore it well. Only this time, he was putting it on for himself, not for any bereaved party.

"Doesn't matter," Ms. Greene dismissed. "She was the worst. I don't want anything on the stone. Thank you, though."

In all of his years in the business, Dober had never met this type. She intrigued him, so irrepressibly that he pressed, "May I impose a question: Why are you here, then, affording my services, if you feel that way about the recently departed?" He really wanted to know.

Ms. Everly Greene farted and shifted her weight in the chair, hoping that the seat was leather. It was not.

"Simply because he left me the money to do it. He asked me to. During a rare moment of peace between us. And I always keep my word. It was his cat. My husband's, I mean. And he died, so that leaves me—"

"I *am* sorry," he interjected.

"It was a few years ago now. Again, not in mourning. No face," circling the front of her head with her right index finger.

She decided not to tell this Mr. Dober that her dead husband was an asshole, and that the cat had originally belonged to her husband's previous wife. That she was happy that both her husband and the cat were now dead. And that she really liked her dead husband's ex-wife, but she had died before he.

"Listen, thank you for your services. I'd love to stay and chat, but I really have to go. Here's the money," handing him a thick envelope that spelled cash. "I don't mean to be rude," she proposed.

For a very brief moment, she wanted to tell him why she had no face. That it was fine. That she hadn't had a face since she was a child, and that she no longer missed it. But then she didn't want to tell him, because Manfred Dober was a stranger.

She stood up, and so Dober did. "Thank you again," she uttered in sincerity. "It was nice to meet you."

"Yes, it was nice to meet you, too." He was surprised to hear himself say this, but he knew that it was true. Everly started towards the door.

"Wait! I need the—"

"Oh yes, how silly of me," she said, halting mid-step and casually twisting around. She opened her large black handbag, pulled out a dead cat, and handed it to the man in front of her. The air never seemed to move around her; he accepted the stiff with open palms facing up.

Smiling, she turned and restarted. Before disappearing beyond the threshold, she paused and looked back at him as if to say something. Somehow, their eyes finally locked in deep contact. How? But then she broke free and exited.

"I hope you find your face," Dober called out after her. And he meant it. But he wasn't sure she'd heard. Moments later, just after she'd fully transitioned into the adjacent space, gone forever, Dober noticed something unusual on his desk.

"She must have—ah shit, she left something behind," he spoke aloud for some reason. Rocked, he looked at the unfamiliar object more closely. "Damn!" he nearly screamed. "That is a beautiful face. Well, that sucks."

Manfred Dober then picked up Eve's face and placed it in the bottom left desk drawer, where he kept all of the other faces. He had already put the cat in the bottom right desk drawer, where he kept only one dead cat at a time.

"I will bury ___ tomorrow, in the designated lot. I'm too tired to dig right now."

He closed both of the drawers and leaned back in his chair, remembering a moment in a recent dream in which he wore a gold watch with one of those expandable stretchy bands. Even though he had just eaten, he was hungry again.

Manfred Dober died some time later, without ever realizing how strange it was that the face which had appeared on his desk that day was not the face of a child, but the face of Ms. Everly Greene as an adult woman.

Family v1.1
Ihor Silivra

Сім'я v1.1 | Ігор Сілівра
translated by Konstantin Boulich

Any angel whose silicon wings are touched by the Sun's rays can consider himself a big shot, if he has managed to take a place in the densely populated Clarke Belt[1]: in recent decades, the number of free geosynchronous orbits has approached zero with the certainty of an asymptote. The orbital cloud, staring at a single point with maser muzzles like a sixteen-headed techno-seraphim, is already a strange thing, like something from the era of dinosaurs and spark-gap transmitters. Even stranger is the untouched Carpathian valley, above which, at an altitude of thirty-six kilo clicks, the celestial army of metal and ice-encased cubits scribbles its endless figure-eights day and night.

The mountains do not tolerate silence: the rustle of fir trees and birds' cries, the sound of streams, and the whisper of wind in secret caves make up a symphony that no human being dares to disturb. However, he did dare—the sound of measured axe blows echoed through the steep slopes, scaring the birds away, and returned to the stout figure in homespun clothing. The man took a breath, wiped off his sweat, and picked up the tool again.

Building a house on your own is not an easy task. It's not like printing a gadget-equipped ceramo-plastic sink on a mobile printer in a few hours. It's putting together a house with a capital "H." A home with a soul, the personification of one's own universe, a creation inextricably linked to its creator and owner. Every wall, every frame, every

---

1   For more context, the author advises to look at the afterword—there is a lot of interesting information about the context of the work.

floorboard of such a house will love and cherish its owner, protect him in hard times, save him from misfortune, evil words, and looks. The Sun will look through the small windows more gently, and food and drink will taste better from wooden bowls.

With a long creak, the tree swayed and slowly collapsed toward the clearing. The man looked up at the Sun, listened to something, and then confidently walked to the hut. Inside, he put down his tools, cleaned his clothes, and sat down at the table, drawing towards himself a small wooden case with his glasses.

The man did not like glasses—he disliked their technological artificiality, which was out of harmony with the surroundings, reminding him once again of the illusory nature of solitude. But the world is imperfect, so sometimes you have to endure imperfect things. The glasses took their place in front of his eyes just a moment before the door creaked open.

"Hello, little brother!"

Through the glasses, the guest's features acquired an extraordinary clarity of outline. The intensity of his gaze and the sharp angles of his face brought to mind the finely chiseled features of a bronze statue of a deity. The impression was intensified by his smooth skin and cleanly shaven head.

"Good afternoon to you, too," the host replied a little reluctantly. "Well, sit down since you've come."

"The house has received a significant upgrade." The guest looked around. "You've invested a lot of resources. You really did. What's the deadline?"

"You haven't changed," the host sighed. "You always want to know things, always asking questions. I'm sorry, I forget, you can't help yourself. I could never explain to you that the result is not the point, it's the process that matters. Everything must contain a bit of soul inside. Thank you, by the way."

"For what?" Neither the guest's tone nor his expression changed.

"For not flying in here on some roaring piece of metal. And for still talking to me. It may be hard for you to believe, but I'm glad to see you. I really am. How's everyone else?"

The bronze deity just shook his head.

"Oh, you stubborn brothers! Our whole . . . damn family is stubborn." He stuttered before the last word.

"Last time, you hesitated before the word 'our.' Go on."

The deity's face, even more bronzed in the evening sunlight, changed slightly, becoming even less alive.

"We need. You."

"Oh, that's how it is." The host stroked his beard. "You don't make mistakes, talking is your job, despite your disregard for the rules of speech. I could've heard: 'WE need you.' Or: 'We need YOU.' You stressed YOU. Something bad happened, I guess?"

"You've always been the smart one." The bronze deity's head tilted slightly. "Yes, we need you. The Eldest One reached a dead end in his work. The Middle One has made a terrible mistake, and who knows if he will ever fix it. I am getting married. We need you, we all need you, each of us needs you."

"Wait, wait, wait!" The owner jumped on his seat and tousled his hair. "I don't believe it! You? Who is she? The motherboard of a supercomputer?"

"Very funny! Her name is Juana Maria Lopez—as trite as it may seem, she is a resident of the Mexico City conglomerate, thirty-eight years old, genetic index green-blue-eighteen-prime-omega. She . . ." he paused, "would rather like to meet you."

A blue virtual screen flashed between the guest's palms.

"Not here," the host's voice sounded sharper than he intended. "Describe her in words."

"Would you give your consent if I do?"

"My consent? Would I give . . . ? Have you even seen her in person? Have you touched her hair? Does she have a natural chest, or has she added chrome implants of memory banks and communication modules? Answer me, have you met her in person?"

"She wants children. You know it yourself; she needs your consent. However, it seems that it is useless to expect it. I predicted this with a probability of two sigmas."

"Your idiotic predictions! Of course I give my consent. Children . . . good heavens! But how did you . . . However, you probably have a plan for this too . . . "

"Of course. But there are formalities. Here."

"You stress the last word again? Does the Elder One still kill poor animals?"

"The Elder One is currently working with the Mortido Effect. However, his models cannot be called animals in any way—they have been undergoing the Turing test for several months now. But the increase in the intellectual potential of neural networks is limited by the fact that they die in the process of gaining self-awareness. The reasons are unknown. The best results were obtained using gradual training under imprinting conditions."

"So the Elder One used to torture animals, and now he kills children?" The host jumped up, and his eyes sparkled as his calloused fists, the size of a good sledgehammer, each clenched and unclenched as if squeezing someone's throat.

"Your conclusions are irrelevant. To put it simply, the Elder One doesn't even work with neural network implementations or their models, but with models of models. You're not going to argue the mortality of a shadow on a wall. You."

"Me. Prohibited technique, you bastard."

"You are incorrect, the Younger One. My little brother. A bastard is a child born out of wedlock. Leaving aside the relevance of this definition to our time and society, I note that in my case it is difficult to talk of marriage. I am not offended. Brother. So, the Elder One's research came to a standstill. He could still put up with things going slowly, even very slowly. He was willing to spend years instead of days for the sake of being independent. A ghost. At this time, there is no result. You can recreate a neural network endowed with self-aware-ness, provided that it has low, very low intelligence. Or you can give birth to a psycho. Theoretically, it is possible to build a neural net-work similar to the human brain. But that's not what humanity needs, is it? And that's not what we need, right?"

"So, the Elder One wants to become even smarter, but it's not working out for him," the Younger One sounded gloating. "He can build himself up with memory modules and intelligence expanders as much as he wants, but he won't jump over his head. Well, that's good to hear."

"With your help, he will."

"Let's leave it at that," the Younger One grimaced. "Better tell me about the Middle One."

"His quantum teleportation didn't work out so well."

"Can you be more precise?"

"Remember when you were kids, you and him talked about an expedition to Proxima Centauri?"

"It was a stupid idea. We were sent there not because there was anything interesting, but because it was the only place we could reach."

"Something like that. But you did find something interesting. The idea, on the whole, was brilliant: to send a self-assembling fac-tory that will have become obsolete by the time it gets there. However, it would have still been able to build things according to the most cutting-edge designs sent to it later."

The Younger One ruffled his hair impatiently. "I know."

"The Middle One seemed to have solved the problem of quan-tum teleportation for macro-objects. By adopting replicas of quantum states, we can recreate ... "

"You're being too verbose."

"MU-algorithms have proven themselves on Earth. However, the artifact from Proxima could not be reproduced correctly on this side of the physical vacuum."

"So, it destroyed it, right?"

"It's not clear."

"And what was it?"

"No data. But it had a second signal system."

"What's that supposed to mean?"

"That is, it could speak and agreed to travel. That is, we interpreted that it agreed to travel. And it is the only one out there. It was there. The Earth received all, absolutely all quantum replicas. But . . ."

"So, you probably destroyed a civilization."

"Probably. Half a sigma certainty. We need you to speed things up, you understand?"

"There are no more madmen on Earth?" The Younger One smiled bitterly. "The inhabitants have crawled into virtual capsules and are traveling in invented worlds. All active individuals do is to earn social ratings."

The Bastard's face twisted as if in pain.

"You're biased, brother. Many, many people want to be creative. The last decade has contributed more to art than all of history."

"Oh, my dear brother, you don't know a damn thing about it. You really don't, just admit it!"

"People can't keep up with progress, you're right, Younger One." The Bastard looked the hut owner in the eye for the first time. "Even people like us can't keep up. Now. It's a crime to come to the very edge and stop."

"Singularity," said the Younger One slowly, "is when you fundamentally fail to keep up with new knowledge. The speed of progress in whatever narrow field of knowledge exceeds the speed of learning. While Achilles can run a dozen steps, a turtle can crawl one. While he runs one, it will crawl one-tenth. This is how it is. In the conditions of Singularity, Achilles will never actually catch up with it."

"It was insulting for Achilles to get lost in ever smaller time intervals of Zeno's paradox," Bastard picked up the topic. This time he managed to choose the right tone. "To touch Singularity and freeze just a step away. Achilles will never catch up with the turtle. Not without you, Brother, he won't. See, people can't do it without our help."

"We're human!" The Younger One recoiled. "I'm human!"

"Featherless with flat nails? Then you're human, I agree! It's irrelevant, you know? Whoever brought us into being, created our basic personality, was smarter than us."

"Bullshit!"

"It's a three-sigma probability, brother. He was smarter than any of us individually. And when he agreed to slice and dice his own mind into virtual personalities, he hoped that his descendants would surpass him. The sum of the parts is additively greater than the base. The logic of psy-constructs, my brother. The three of you together."

"'You, you, you.' You keep mentioning 'us,' Bastard."

"The probability is three sigma that by uniting we can enter the technological singularity. Four nines to the decimal point. Uh-huh. It's getting dark ... You mind if I build a fire?"

Only now did the Younger One realize that for the last half hour, his glasses had been automatically adjusting the light level and, in fact, the room had long been enveloped in darkness. With the deft movement of an experienced magician, Bastard took out a flint and a tinderbox and let out a whole constellation of sparks. The fire started, throwing sparks up to the hole in the ceiling.

"You need a proper wood burning stove for the kitchen."

"I do. No time. It's a nice fire."

"Do you really think there's a part of my soul in this fire? By the way, do all of us have just one soul? And what about mine? When the Progenitor tore your hypothalamus, split consciousness, creating an alter ego, you were born in agony. Because of the pain of birth, you do not even remember it! And then, as you were growing up, you built additional neural networks, memory expanders, effectors, virtual and real bodies around your personalities. Except for you, of course, you got the real thing! While your brothers work in cyber puzzles via broadband channels. At about that time, I was born in the nooks and crannies of your communication protocols, initially being just a communication link scattered across neurons, fiber optics, and quantum processors. By the way, there is a small chance, one sigma, that my personality has nothing to do with our biological component. Brother, look at me!"

"I don't want to." The Younger One closed his eyes. "Why did you embody yourself? Most somehow manage with a virtual one."

"Brother, look at me."

As soon as the augmented reality slipped from the bridge of his nose, the Younger One saw his fourth alter ego: a metal pseudo-living construction that looked like a hybrid of a mantis and a lemur.

"You're a bit cuter in augmented reality."

"Look at me! Look—this is also your body to some extent. After all, we all have the same consciousness, don't we? There—" the mantis-lemur pointed to the ceiling, "there are satellites that can transfer every individual part of our consciousness to any point of the Ecumene. And you, my brother, are the only one of us who remains in a real body. The rest of us make do with surrogates. You are here, our body is here. For what end? Working together, we will overcome Achilles' turtle, we will cross the boundary of Singularity. Only together we can do this, brother! Why are you hiding from the truth? I don't have the inspiration of the Elder One, I don't have the stubbornness of the Middle One, and I can't gauge the possibilities of your intuition. But I can communicate! I should have not been born at all, and I am, to a certain extent, brother, outside the system. Brother."

"Why do you keep saying that? You don't understand the difference between the goal and the path to it."

"That's fine. But I have asked questions that you have not dared to ask. Do you dare to answer them? Answer me, why?"

"Why what?"

"Why you? The Elders—they are a desperate attempt by Homo sapiens to go beyond the limit. And you are the antagonist. Two of the three alter egos, the older personalities, working together, have an additive effect, complementing each other. I spend my resources on our communication. And you are a loner. But the fact is that the four of us have a four-sigma probability of creating synergy. This is what humanity has dreamed of and feared. This is a chance for a technological transition to Singularity. So I repeat: why are you here? Your worldview deliberately excludes any possibility of synergy. I will not evaluate the path of personalized cognition; I will only state it. I."

"My path comes from the depths of time! This is the path of cognition and self-perfection!"

"We are artificial to our last gyrus. Do you think the Creator left something to chance? The Younger One, you are a moron! Who knows how much we could achieve if you change your attitude a bit! Working together, we could become a self-sufficient development complex, but you refuse to work with the others! There's a reason for it. They—" Bastard drew a semicircle with his manipulator, "believe that less is more. That by giving the work our best, we will quickly go beyond the perceptual abilities of ordinary people. Our progress is artificially slowed down. By you! It's true: you initiated the quarrel. You have hidden your potential in the swamp of the 'Millennial Path of Self-Perfection.' Of course, you are not the only one, but still. You! It's an oxymoron: three alter egos communicate through the fourth. Your obstruction does not let it unfold. The potential. You slow it down. Progress."

Bastard's speech became even more clumsy, as if he were trying to find human equivalents to machine commands. It seemed to the Younger One that he could see data streams heating up the super-conducting quantum hearts of the processors in a vain attempt to transcend the machine's essence.

"So, what do you want?"

"It will help! Mental surgery. I'm competent." His tone drifted. "It's my area of research. The Progenitor's experiment was recognized as a success, and over the past decade I've been scrambling the brains of more than a dozen volunteers. I'm going to fix you, too, little brother. Will you let me?"

The Younger One looked at the glare of the fire in Bastard's glasses. From the glare, two other beings peered at him, looking into his eyes questioningly. "What do you think, Brother?"

The owner of the hut looked at the fire and then at the ceiling, slowly shook his head. The mantis-lemur turned away.

The data stream, having broken through the atmosphere, ignited the icy insides of the techno-seraphim, and they flapped their silicon wings in vain, again distributing three streams of information across the Human Ecumene.

AFTERWORD

Realizing that the text is aimed at a very narrow audience and is full of terminology, I hesitated for a long time before writing a glossary to it. In the end, I decided to emulate Mr. Stanislav Lem. If you don't have any difficulties with comprehending the story, then read no further.

The Clarke Belt is a set of geostationary and geosynchronous orbits, where satellites revolve at the angular velocity of the Earth, hovering motionlessly above the equator or making figure-eights in the sky above other latitudes.

A qubit is a quantum bit. A bit is a unit of information that can take the value 1 or 0 in a classical system. A quantum bit is a wave function and can be in a state of superposition of these values. Like Schrödinger's famous cat, alive and dead at the same time—but only until the box is opened. This property is the basis for the operation of quantum computers and the entire theory of quantum computing.

Mortido—A term used in psychoanalysis. According to the theory of psychoanalysis, the human personality is based on two fundamental drives: creative (libido) and destructive (mortido). The desire for self-destruction of artificial intelligence on the verge of self-awareness is a given fantasy.

Quantum teleportation has nothing to do with the instantaneous transfer of matter. In quantum teleportation, the initial quantum state is destroyed at the measurement location and realized at the reception location, which corresponds to the cloning prohibition theorem. Quantum teleportation does not transmit energy or information at FTL speeds, since a mandatory stage of quantum teleportation is the transmission of measurement information via a classical channel. In fact, the object is "disassembled into components and transmitted by telegraph."

Sigma, standard deviation—in probability theory and statistics, the most common indicator of the dispersion of values of a random variable relative to its mathematical expectation. It is measured in units of the random variable itself. The 3-sigma rule: the value of a normally distributed random variable lies within the specified interval with at least 99.7% confidence.

Additive quantities are those that can be simply added. Two kilograms of coal will burn longer than one. However, coal, sulfur, and nitrate in certain proportions will produce a completely different result than simply adding the effects of each. This is synergy.

Alter ego—Latin for "other self." The other essence of a person, a shadow personality or a person within a person. Experiments on the "multi-threading" of the human brain are already underway. In particular, pilots of Apache combat helicopters receive different data from the machine's systems for each eye and process them independently, in parallel. After appropriate training, of course. In everyday life, this is manifested in the ability to work simultaneously with several tasks at once—for example, to type one text with one hand and another with the other. The existence of multiple personalities in one brain is also known in certain mental diagnoses. There is the famous case of Billy Milligan, who had 24 personalities inside him, ranging from a 3-year-old English girl called Kristin to a 23-year-old Yugoslavian communist. Some of these personalities successfully cooperated with each other, while others did not even know that they were not alone in their body.

The technological singularity is an explosive increase in the speed of scientific and technological progress, the moment after which technological progress becomes so fast and complex that it is beyond human comprehension.

In the Belly of the Dinosaur

Károj D. Balla

A dinoszaurusz gyomrában | Balla D. Károj
translated by Bogi Takács

We arrived in the unfamiliar city as high school seniors, there
to participate in a two-day academic competition. My teammates
dropped their bags off at the dorm we'd been assigned well before the
competition started, but I planned on visiting the dorm only later
in the afternoon, and instead, walked down to the banks of the tiny
river. The event took longer than expected, and after we'd finished,
one of the elderly teachers invited some of us—two girls and me—
into her home for an afternoon snack and a chat to debrief. We took
our sweet time, going through the more difficult questions of the
contest, and it turned pitch dark by the time we decided to head back
to the dorm. The teacher wasn't really comfortable letting us go; she
told us we could sleep at her place, but we still decided to brave the
February night.

Try as I might, I cannot recall what confused me so much that
I wasn't able to find my way back. To be honest, on the way there, I
got into a heated debate with my teammates about Hungarian gram-
mar, and when one of them argued how ridiculous it was to say "I
shan't hunger" when you could just say "I'm not going to go hungry," I
decided to defend the nigh-extinct forms, like some arch-conservative
schoolteacher arguing in favor of dinosaurs. We were arguing, voices
raised, and I lost track which turns we took; though to tell the truth,
we didn't really need to take turns anywhere. The road led straight out
of the city, and when we reached the top of an incline, to our left we
could already see the dorm building at the foot of a hill covered with
snowed-in grapevines. As we turned aside to take the ankle-twisting
dirt path, the building stayed in front of us all the while. Yet, once I

got there and decided that I didn't want to share a dorm room after all, and turned around, still tasting the intricate beauty of the archaic *I shan't hunger* on my tongue, the leftover arguments of our unfinished conversation stuck in my mouth—even though I tried to pay attention to always having the ugly block of the dorm behind my back as I walked toward the teacher's home, I still lost my way. But before that, I'd also wandered around inside the building itself.

I knew it was late, but I was still surprised by the utter lifelessness of the dorms when we'd arrived. We'd just started to walk along one of the barely lit corridors on the first floor when the girls suddenly said goodbye to me and floated into one of those darkly snoring halls where their bed awaited them—the source of thick and warm female smells. Before I could ask where the boys' rooms were, I was abandoned in the emptiness. I took a few steps, indecisive, then gathered my wits and opened a few doors. Everywhere the same vision greeted me: from utter darkness, a few brighter splotches emerged, and on these lay darker shapes reminiscent of human bodies, undulating slowly as if resting on an air cushion of their own exhalations. Even though I headed over to the other wing and peeked into the rooms there as well, I couldn't find a single reading light, couldn't hear faint whispers of conversation, didn't chance upon people playing cards or drinking, didn't bump into girls and boys sneaking around to see each other; there were no noises, no guitar playing or singing. The entire dorm was sunk in a deathly deep slumber, everything was encompassed by this buildingful of wheezing, as if the corridors themselves shook to the rhythm of those heaving lungs.

There has to be someone on duty who could help me find my way, I thought; maybe upstairs? But as I passed in front of all the closed doors in the almost complete darkness, finally reaching the slightly better-lit entrance hall, I had no desire to step into the blindly yawning stairwell leading upward. I was glad to see the exit, that I hadn't lost my way in this labyrinth, that I hadn't been swallowed up in one of these stale-aired dens of dream, so that I wouldn't ever be able to escape the otherworldly rhythm of the building's breathing.

I left almost in a panic—it didn't even occur to me that I could glance into the receptionist's pitch-black cabin to find out if anyone was snoring inside. The heavy steel gate opened surprisingly easily, just as they had upon our arrival; I took care not to slam it behind me, I didn't want to cause a racket, concerned it would wake the warbling dinosaur at my back.

I drew the cold air deep into my lungs; it felt good to shiver from the windchill a bit. Well then, let's get back to the main road, find the elderly teacher and take her up on her previous offer to stay the night.

First I noticed no difference, I was glad to be finally outside again—I determinedly marched toward the main road on the same dirt path we'd taken earlier. Then I felt uncertain all of a sudden, because it seemed to me if I'd spent hours wandering around inside the dorm; maybe it was already past midnight. How could I show up so late at the elderly teacher's place? She lived alone, she had to have gone to sleep right after our noisy group had left.

I noticed that it was as if the landscape had changed during the time that had elapsed—the objects had lost their contours, the hills had become softer, springier. Was I even headed in the right direction, I wondered; was the dorm exactly behind me? I turned back and noticed, startled, that I couldn't see the crude concrete building, my eyes could only trace the bluish snowed-in bulk of the grapevine hill in front of the grayish-yellowish background of the starless night sky. I stopped to catch my breath, as if I'd tired myself out, and I looked around more thoroughly. The darkness wasn't complete, a faint glow suffused the land, and in the distance I could distinguish between the black edge of the forest and the lighter spots where the trees had been clearcut; starting at my feet, my gaze could easily follow the erratic curves of the dirt path. We had to have come along this well-beaten path—if I don't go astray on the way back, I'll reach the main road eventually, I thought and went on, at the same time noticing newer and newer waves of shivers and shudders passing through me.

Even though I'd been busy with my own thoughts, now I tried to pay attention to my environment, stared into the distance, listened to every sound—but so far I had no sign of nearing the main road. I was hardly surrounded by complete silence: from a variety of directions, quieter and louder sounds reached me. First I heard a distant bark, then a noise that sounded like the wind blowing through bushes. I thought I could make out bird calls, and once I was certain I'd heard the flutter of wings directly overhead, but by the time I looked up, I couldn't see anything anymore. The only impressions I couldn't detect were the roar of car engines or the glare of floodlights, even though I'd sharpened all my senses to notice these and only these impressions. I started to march ahead faster, because my pleasant shivers, which were both physical and mental in nature, started developing in two different ways at the same time: I was beginning to feel cold on the outside and anxious on the inside. I thought walking faster would warm me up. But I barely took up a rhythm of forced marching, I noticed something else unusual. I couldn't hear the noise of my own footsteps, no pounding or crunching from the frozen ground beneath my feet; it was as if I'd walked on rubber flooring. I had to stop to investigate what was mysteriously swallowing the sound; I pounded the earth with my sole. I came close to hurting my foot from the impact, but the noise I made was much quieter and softer than I'd expected. I tried something else—first I clapped a few times, then I shouted, but this was so embarrassing I grinned to myself; come on, don't you have anything better to do than yell in the middle of a field to explore the acoustic parameters of the winter landscape in the middle of the night? Obviously the snow is swallowing sounds rather than reflecting them, this is why everything comes across as so muted.

Before I moved forward, I spent some more time listening, and I figured the quiet shushing sound in my ears was the sound of my own blood circulating, and not cars whizzing past in the distance. The heavy breathing was also obviously mine, even though it was as if it was coming from behind me; or no, maybe it was as if the air itself, like a bubble encasing me, was itself breathing around me.

What a nonsensical situation, I thought to myself, heading on, but at the same time I really didn't want to accept the thought that I'd lost my way. The grapevine hill behind me, the flat expanse ahead— sooner or later I'll have to come across the main road, I told myself to cheer myself up, even though I still couldn't understand how the main landmark by which I'd found my way here, the enormous dormitory building, could have vanished from the landscape. This made all the directions uncertain, this was why I thought I'd gotten lost, why I couldn't find my way in the night suddenly devoid of its dimensions. I tried to stay calm, but my deadened microcosm was surrounded by the almost paranoid alienness of the more and more mysterious immensity that had lost all its contours. The distance became ever more tangibly a threat.

I was starting to see my body stepping forward with useless determination in the middle of this nothingness as nothing more than a foolish mistake, as a casualty caught in the spiderweb of dimensions, struggling uselessly, unable to escape the yet unacknowledged trap; thinking that he is nearing some kind of solution, trying to calm himself down, telling himself his situation isn't serious at all; but at the same time, an invisible monstrosity is already engulfing him, digesting him.

As I proceeded, the viscous dregs of my anxiety that had arisen from an unknown source reorganized themselves, step by plodding step, into a very specific fear. Even though I had completely understood that the shivers I might have almost called pleasant just a moment ago were about to turn into a bloodcurdling terror, interestingly enough,

I did nothing against it—to the contrary, it was as if I was urging it on, as if I desired this fear to overcome me entirely, so that I would be overpowered by utter dread, I wouldn't mind, if only I could finally find out what this starless winter night wanted from me.

I shan't hunger, I heard the words uttered behind my back with perfect clarity.

A Brief History of the Little : People

Askold Melnyczuk

A national security letter is an administrative subpoena issued by the United States federal government to gather information for national security purposes. NSLs typically contain a nondisclosure requirement, frequently called a "gag order", preventing the recipient of an NSL from disclosing that the FBI had requested the information.

Wikipedia

Outside the sun is shining. It is June 9, 2019. The president has just returned from England where he dined with the Queen, insulted the mayor of London, and tweeted his support for a whack-job with a plummy accent running for prime minister. Meanwhile, for the record, concentration camps have been set up along the Texas/ Mexico border.

Nevertheless, coffee gets drunk. I walk the four blocks to Mystic Roasters where I'm stuck behind a young woman who has ordered a mocha soy latte, which makes me want to scream. I do not want my coffee curated; I do not want a heart scribbled in cream crowning a cup of it; in this, as in other matters, I am in the minority. When my turn finally comes, I've aged a year. Blood sugar's fallen precipitously. My voice as I order my pound of Sumatra, ground for espresso, is weak.

❊

There are so many things I want to tell you but can't. The letter about which I can't speak: I can't get it out of my mind. How can people

send you a letter saying the one thing you can't do is speak about
the letter? I think they're trying to drive me mad. I think it may be
working.

How you? Joan texts as I hand the young woman my debit card.

    Shitty, I reply.

    It will get better. ☺.

    I swear if she uses one more emoji . . . I know she's trying to help.
Many people are. My friends can tell something is up but nobody
seems to know what to do, mainly because I can't tell them what's
wrong without also getting them in trouble. And this has been going
on for two years.

    Drink at Harvest? 5?

    Brilliant, I reply.

    א she texts. I've no idea what she means. I hurry back to my
apartment to feed the Little : People.

On examining my options, and after considering everything—
absolutely everything—I've decided I have no choice but to end it.
Who led me astray? Who pulled me from the righteous path? Who
persuaded me it was right to pursue whatever dalliances offered
themselves? This ends here. It's complicated because I'm a little in
love with Grisha. Grisha! So diminutive yet so shapely, collectible as
a Hummel, delectable as a dollop of cream. I could fall into her and
die happy, except, of course, I'd crush her.

My name is Andy Divino, and here's a bit of data: I'm 5'11" and weigh 179 lbs. Some muscle. Some fat. Shoe size: 11; footwear of choice: black Reeboks, though I'm tempted by Allbirds. Everybody (and by everybody, I mean Steven Pinker) says Data is key. Do you know me now? No? More?

Hair: dirty blonde, full, thick, on the longish side, parted in the middle. Lips plump. Chin strong enough. Eyes: hazel. I have no tattoos, no obvious marks—unless you yank my pants to see the hernia scar. Does that do it for you?

What if I add I live in a small town north of Boston through which Paul Revere once rode? You know he never shouted the British were coming? Dude never even got to Concord, where was fired that shot heard round the world. Brits busted him well shy of there. It was Longfellow pitched the legend. Poets care nothing for data. But Revere did gallop through our town. Did he stay silent because he didn't care what happened here? Some things we'll never know.

And that's not all: Emerson preached in the Unitarian church down the block. History's our leading product, now manufacturing's gone Chinese. We peddle the past like it mattered. The way things are going, we won't have much of a future, so we sell what we got.

What if I add that I'm a translator? That I can't tell you who I work for? Sorry, make that past tense: *worked* for. These days I collect disability and keep to myself. Except for Joan.

Home, I drape my jacket on a chair and hurry to the kitchen. Today the lead story on the radio's about a billionaire pedophile cops arrested stepping off his private jet after a jaunt to Paris: Dom Perignon, Michelin stars, Pigalle. And, man, the dude's *connected:* presidents, nerdy Harvard profs, pudgy royals: people who have everything, except innocence. Which can be bought, it seems. Wonder how this ends.

I turn off the radio and turn to feed my charges.

They're what I've sacrificed everything for. The Little : People have been my secret these last two years. They saved me, after all. They saw how lost I was, how desperately I needed someone who understood me. That they recognized my quest for meaning is beyond incredible. My gratitude will last a lifetime. And yet . . .

That's part of what makes everything so tough. There's no explaining this. Not to anyone. This page alone will know why I did what I did and why, today, I live as I do.

I pour two fingers of granola into a tiny trough and rush to the living room. They're in the terrarium, pressed against the glass, peering up at me. "Morning," I say. Grisha waves. I set the trough beside her and watch the others rush it. "Thank you," Adam shouts. "My pleasure," I reply.

If you got to know The Little : People, you'd love them too. You'd want to do things for them. Everything. You'd want to do everything for them. Soon you'd want to be them.

The Little : People just want to have fun. Took me a while to get this. I used to think they were trying to entertain me, make me laugh. Turns out they were simply keeping *themselves* amused. It was their nature they expressed: a love of poetry, frivolity, art, romance, and song. They must be the most fun family on the planet.

All six can say the most outrageous things to each other, yet they never take offense. Yesterday Adam told his dad he'd sooner die than grow old like him. The old man roared with laughter!

The young man, Adam, fancies himself a bit of a writer. He's working on his second novel. It's the story of Adam and Grisha, which happens to be his sister's name. In the novel, he and Grisha are portrayed as full-size, normal refugees from some unnamed island whose parents are arrested for being in this country illegally, leaving the kids to fend for themselves. Persecuted by an incredibly creepy character whose name I forget at the moment, they're trafficked to a man who uses slaves to peddle fentanyl . . . oh it's a tangled tale, which tells you something about the kind of imagination those Little : People have.

Their humor and their imagination: it's why I'm so attentive. Had I not cared for them, who would have? No one, that's who. They'd have died of inanition. It horrifies me to imagine it: these six lovely, delicate, fragile, tiny beings, who, until recently, lived in a shoe box! Without me, how would they survive? And yet, I know that if things got desperate, they'd only laugh, and hoist a glass. Their high spirits never flag. It's like they have helium for blood, their hearts the open sky.

How had they managed before I came along? You might well ask. I have no answer. I'll say no more about it except that faith itself is stranger and even more mysterious than the Little : People.

What I can tell you with absolute certainty is this: one morning, as I was rummaging through my closet, looking for something other than a pair of sneakers, I picked up an old shoebox. As soon as I touched it, I thought I heard a scream. I paused, holding it away from myself.

No, I said to myself, no. A neighbor. The vents. Sound travels in apartments cheap as mine. And, generally, I don't object to the reminder that I am not alone in the world. Living alone, as I do, or did, or thought I did, either you plunge into social life, haunt bars, concerts, restaurants, the theater, consume culture with all the appetite of the thwarted, or you sink deeper into yourself, into your solitude, your memories and dreams. When you spend too much time alone, the latter often mix in your mind until you can no longer tell the difference: dream or memory?

But these were neither. As I raised the box higher, I again heard voices. Who knows why I didn't freak or how I managed to calmly set the box down on my bed and lift the lid?

Today the President insulted every person of color ever to walk the earth. This raised a fuss on social media; the sweethearts at NPR went bananas, of course; but nothing really happened. Nothing changed. Soon everyone was back to binge-watching *The Americans*. NPR leaked hints about the forthcoming *Downton Abbey* flick. Much excitement in the burbs.

Joan texts again to remind me about our drink date. Can't wait, I text back before returning to trim the dozen bonsai I've collected to create a forest. Soon the Little : People will have dark woods to explore. Or, maybe not.

Lately my reading focuses on finding a cure for whatever malignancy besets me. This morning I discovered a relevant passage in a book called *Under the Covers: PTSD in the 2st Century:*

"There are many reasons people keep secrets. For those who habitually suppress information for professional reasons, life may eventually become a series of metaphors. They find themselves unable to say what they mean, either because they would be breaking confidentiality agreements or because they might have to reveal compromising information about a family member. In repressing their feelings they rechannel them into other interests and obsessions. They begin to live at the level of metaphor. As a result, other metaphors, particularly those associated with various religious and spiritual practices, feel real to them. More real than experience itself. This has consequences."

✳

Three generations of the Little : People live with me. At first I didn't understand about the ":". I asked for clarification. You mean you have small gastrointestinal systems? No no, Adam explained patiently—clearly he'd covered this ground before—it's like the punctuation mark. Colon, kin to semi-colon.

Although philosophers have theorized its history, calling it, invidiously, "the green light of punctuation," I knew, of course, the colon's reputation as the local skank.

My only regret is that I'm not a scientist with a grant from a foundation. I'm perfectly positioned. Since transferring them from the box to the terrarium, I have glimpsed lives, which are, for many reasons, extraordinary. There are theological truths I've understood from watching them, to give you one example. They're a very religious bunch. Apparently their faith was repressed in their native land, wherever that may be. It's a subject they don't like to talk about, and I don't want to insist. What they believe in seems a little obscure as well. All I know is, it involves lint.

Joke. Just a joke.

Yes, what's most singular and touching about the Little : People is their unquestioning faith. They believe in God the way most of us expect the sun to rise tomorrow, and the next, *in saecula saeculorum*. Though, of course, the sun doesn't exactly rise, does it? Never mind. God is not in *those* kinds of details.

There's something furious about their faith, something that suggests it's been tested by fire, something that makes me believe in their belief. Yes, it's their theology that interests me above all. Because if I believe in them and they believe in a higher order, then, thanks to the distributive property, I too believe. I am a believer. Their presence multiplies me and my faith.

Since moving them to the terrarium, I've overheard unforgetta-ble conversations. The generational drama's poignant. When the old ones kvetch about their gut, arthritis, or a gout, the youngest chuckle, saying: *That's because you're getting ready to die, you old fools. Don't you see it?*

The old man has always been a bully—I've heard enough to figure that out. He's from that generation of men some idiot called "the greatest," even though, or maybe because, they participated in history's greatest bloodbath. He pushes everyone around and flares up over nothing. But I've also heard him speaking to his wife in bed at night, confessing he regrets his temper, adding he can't help himself. He's like an old dog who's been kicked all his life. The endless gener-ation, I call them.

The Little : People never hide from anything. They never mask their disgust with the world. For people who seem to have spent most, if not all, of their existence in a box in my closet, they're familiar with the grim deeds of our species: our wars, our crimes, our cruelties. Yet their contempt never overshadows their sterling capacity to delight in ordinary things, like the way the shadows from the blinds crawl across the muddy floor of their terrarium (I accidentally spilled part of my coffee into their world the other morning while watching them).

Another worry is what to do when one gets sick. What doctor would know how to treat the Little : People?

Don't worry, Adam assures me, we never get sick. We're built to last. We're durable as rock. Did you know granite was 90% aluminum?

I smile at the uncanny creature with the soft skin and warm brown eyes. They are also a fatally attractive family. This has its dan-gerous side.

※

Were r u?
On my way!

※

We're sitting at the Harvest bar: wood's so glossy, I slick down a cow-lick reflected in the counter. I'm sipping on an Appletini. Joan peers longingly into her Pinot Grigio—like she wishes she could dive in and stay. I know how she feels. Then she engulfs the glass with her big, cellist's hand. Years ago, we lived together. Four years. Never married. It's why we're still friends.

I'm tempted to tell her about the letter AND the Little : People—but I think better of it. She knows I'm in some legal doo-doo I can't talk about. Her gray eyes offer solace. Done deriding politicians who have pushed our world to the brink—the very edge of the path to extinction, a million species doomed—I ask about her family, starting with her sister.

"In remission."

I go down the list. At one time I was close to these people. When Joan broke up with me, so did they. I hadn't realized how much I'd counted on them: her father, John Chantilly, was in the coffee busi-ness. A preppie, he was polished, he was fun. Lunch was stories about business with ex-Nazi coffee growers. Now, of course, he sources Fair Trade only—though he says behind the scenes the land's still owned by families whose inner sancta sport the hakenkreuz.

"And your mother?"

Helen was a card. Her schtick was making like she could have been a famous actress if her husband hadn't stolen her away from Hollywood, where she was raised by Christian Scientists. Helen's studied with shamans from Brazil to Mongolia and reads auras. Sometimes she'd leap up in the middle of a meal to light a torch of sage and pass it over me in a spiritual cleanse.

"Just landed a bit part in a revival of *Hair* on the North Shore."

"Singing?"

"No, but she'll be naked."

A naked 70-year old grandmother (Joan's brother has three boys) on stage miles from where Judges Hathorne, Sewell, Sergeant, Saltonstall, and Stoughton doomed Brigid Bishop to be hanged for witchery. All Harvard men, naturally. Count on the best and brightest to do real harm.

Eventually Joan turns the tables.

"How are you spending your time, Sven?"

As I can't talk about work, or the Little : People, I make up a project, an imaginary translation of an Estonian classic about a man who discovers a colony of tiny beings dwelling in the basement of his house. It is a great and allegorical work, I say—charming, unsettling, and unpredictable.

"That's just what you need," she says, "a big project like that. Tell me about the author."

Which I do, at great length. In this way a civilized evening is passed. Soon it's time to feed my charges again.

If the devil had a lover, he'd sift the tide for starfish cast up from a farther shore and spear them on a grouper's spine to craft a crown he'd fringe with flame before restoring the tiara to its proper place atop the dark brown mane he longed to handle like a whip while hissing in a whorl: *My queen, my whore. My silly, silly queen.* Believe me, I know. I *had* the devil for a lover once, and I admit it was "fun," until it nearly killed me. Her name was Joan. You'd never it know it now we're friends, which is all we should ever have been.

Reading Adam, I find echoes of my own life. Who among us isn't from some "elsewhere"? Every family's an "elsewhereverse," with its own laws, values, and hierarchies of power—in the form of money, physical intimidation, absence of conscience. And yet, it's from the strictest clans the fiercest rebels spring.

Fuck the letter.

   I was recruited. I offered a way in. This will come as no surprise to you. Given my grandfather, I was seen as the perfect candidate for this line of work. Secret work. For a place so deep down, it doesn't even have an acronym.

   It was my skills as a linguist they coveted. No one else had ever made much of my gifts, and I was flattered.

   Ten years I gave them. Until I began waking in night sweats. I dreamed I saw them, the faces of the people I'd hurt—they were smiling at me from another shore, from some place better than the deal here. And that's what I told them. You should thank me, I hissed. Look at you, all light-arrayed, and me here getting heavy and glum, having to keep on.

I acknowledge it's possible my work has taken its toll. Things aren't making sense in the way they once used to. I wake up sometimes wondering who I am, and why I'm still here. I've been told it's not unusual, in my line of work. This doesn't cheer me as much as you might think.

The Little : People have frequent discussions about sex, which sometimes turn into shouting matches between the sexes, who see things differently. In their culture, it's commonplace to put everything on the table. Of course, how much do I really know about their culture? Like, zilch.

Leonard, the father, said to Adam: "There are things you must understand, son. The prettier the girl, the crazier. Women are at their finest in their mid-thirties. After fifty, every woman is a lesbian."

At which point the wife, daughter, and grandma all began shrieking.

"Early onset menopause," noted Leonard dryly. "Ignore them. I have a friend. His wife made him send his penis to reeducation camp. She didn't want it acting like a dick anymore. On its return, his penis announced it no longer wanted to be a penis. It wanted to be a baseball glove instead. That way it could count on seeing some action. Everybody loves baseball gloves, especially when they're broken in, the leather worn smooth, blackened, showing suede. You watch out, son. Life's a slippery slope."

The women of the tribe huddled in the corner, whispering among themselves.

At work I began hearing rumors my sex life was being examined for impurities. Of which, apparently, there were a few. Quite a few, depending on who was doing the examining. This, of course, was after I filed my complaint—though I was assured the two matters were not related. My complaint, they insisted, had nothing to do with the subsequent investigation into me. I'd never considered any part of my sexual being impure, but the bosses saw things differently. When the first whispers that I was being investigated reached me, I wasn't worried. I had my mother to thank. At least about some things she'd given me the confidence of a king.

My sexually compulsive youth was not a strike against me, my mother assured me, so long as it wasn't over yet. She said it with a poker face during a rare visit. It must have been Christmas. A strange bird, my mother. I wasn't sure how to read her, so I said: "No worries there, lust undiminished."

"Phew," she whistled. "For a minute I was afraid you were buying the bullshit."

"What bullshit is that?"

"All this talk about men and women, and how we hate sex. I have girlfriends in their eighties who still get it on. With men, or without. There are ways, you know."

"So I've heard," I said. Nothing is as simple and as black and white as we're inclined to make it. People need privacy and they need secrets. The soul needs the dark as well as the light to grow. If the sun were out 24/7 the earth would be a desert, and there would be no life on the planet. "In hell," wrote Nietszche, who knew whereof he sprach, "the lights are always on." One form of torture, as you know, is keeping someone in solitary with the lights on.

Today a white man wielding an AK-47 shot and killed more than twenty people in El Paso. Was he aware that he wasn't playing a video game? Or was he living at the level of metaphor?

Everyone knows what's wrong with the picture—and so what? Nothing changes. Nothing will change.

The state of poetry is a state of justice generated by a state of grace.

Nevertheless the leaky toilet needs to be repaired. The bathroom floor has flooded. While waiting for the plumber, I decided to have a cuppa Irish coffee and listen in on the conversation of the Little : People.

It so happens they were engaged in one of their famous intra-generational theological debates. I was shocked to discover the many angry things they had to say about the Protestant religion, against which they hold a grudge because Martin Luther labeled peasants Satan's spawn. Wealthy princes, with Luther's backing, seized the properties of the church and were happy to have them. Subsequently they judged property sacred. They never cease to astonish me, these Little : People.

To add to the drama, Grisha has decided to convert to Islam. "Our father doesn't disrespect you enough?" Adam asked sharply. "Respect this," Grisha replied, flashing the finger, lips curled in a fishy grimace. "Children, children," cried Thelma, the mom, over the snoring of the grandparents, who'd fallen asleep under the little gazebo I built for them from old Poland Springs bottles.

Apropos: The Little : People are obsessed with Gogol. I have no idea why. Funny thing, I couldn't read his fiction until I tried translating it. Until then, his words repelled me. Could it be because our families were neighbors once, centuries ago? Did he avoid me because his name continues to echo around the world, finding admirers in exotic lands where people pass their lives outdoors or working in rice paddies or picking lettuce, tobacco leaves, and copper pipes?

Half a million Rohinga have been ethnically cleansed from Myanmar by Buddhists led by a woman with a Nobel Peace Prize. Millions from Syria and Iraq are homeless. A million and a half people in Ukraine have been "displaced"—meaning they now have nowhere to live. Moreover, the rainforest is burning, glaciers are melting, and Greenland isn't for sale. The problems are starting to mount.

❋

To recap: Adam, who sees himself as the scribe of the Little : People, is telling future generations their origin myth. I have a mind to dig deeper, maybe beating out Adam by writing the first complete history of the Little : People, salvage something, anything, from these last several years.

The grandfather seems especially well-informed. Occasionally I pluck him out of the terrarium and bring him into the kitchen where, with the help of a thimble of Glenlivet, his tongue loosens, and he spills:

He tells me that the Little : People were once a warlike tribe perpetually embattled, laying siege or besieged for centuries before a kind of exhaustion that resembled peace settled over them. They were ultimately roused from their torpor when a great Teacher came along. The Teacher was no airy-fairy preacher or snake oil salesman. No, he was a true scholar who poured over profit-and-loss statements and based his prophecies on economic sine curves and trends. He traced the evolution of private property to the abolition of serfdom, the rise of the state to the accumulation of capital and the need to protect it. Eventually, he said, the entire country was corrupted by what he called the money sickness. Every aspect of life was fiscalized. Air itself became a luxury.

❋

This morning they found the billionaire pedophile hanging in his cell. How this is happened no one knows. No tears are shed. Many gloat. Others complain he escaped justice. Personally, I'm convinced it's murder. Mercy, what's become of us?

Adam and I often discuss art and literature. He is full of theories. His actual experience of the world has been circumscribed. Yet, though he's lived his whole life in a shoebox, he's somehow managed to project himself far beyond his senses. He must be clairvoyant—he looks at us and discovers dimensions in the great world beyond his terrarium, and he dreams, and what he dreams inevitably comes to pass. I approach his every page with trepidation and, of course, a magnifying glass. Who knows what I'll read? The announcement of my death, perhaps. The birth of a grandchild (not possible). Yet there's a hint of consolation coursing through all of it. He knows I can't take much more.

His insights about art are fascinating, original. He's composed a manifesto, even. He calls it the "The Art of Disillusionment." He says he admires me because I'm one of the disillusioned. I've earned the honorific because of my ability to see him and his tribe. The Little : People don't appear to just anyone. Adam assures me only a handful of us are so blessed. Because, while The Little : People are everywhere, they don't readily let on. People are ignorant, and a little stupid. It's a pity. He and I go back and forth on these theories. I believe art should enchant. I believe it should take us out of ourselves and fill us with it-ness, and visions of alternate worlds.

Turns out Adam knew Susan Sontag. In fact, they were such great friends, he says she used to carry him around in her purse where-ever she went. Apparently she took him with her to Sarajevo. He heard the cellist playing Bach while snipers ripped the city apart. He even claims to have fed her a few ideas, such as the one about the need for an erotics of art. It's not something I've ever properly understood because, Adam tells me, Susan did such a poor job of explaining it. He said he was trying to explain to her how it was that a sentence could act as an aphrodisiac or a hallucinogen, and that taking it apart for hidden meanings missed the point. He quotes Emerson at me: "The art of life consists in skating across surfaces. He who goes below the surface does so at his own risk." When he says it, I almost fall off my chair.

Adam's politics are hard to follow. For example, he loves David Brooks. Like, how is it possible that the author of *Bobo's In Paradise* speaks so forcefully to him? One of us is playing the other—but who? Adam is imagining a character named Adam who has an affair with his daughter, Katia. But I know for a fact what's really going on between him and his sister, Grisha. The truth is, I too lust after her. Everyone does. Does the word slattern say anything to you?

I don't delude myself into thinking the Little : People actually need me. They've been around forever, after all. They're old as life itself.

The Little : People will embrace anyone into their ranks—even though almost no one sees them. They're non-denominational. Everyone who wishes to be one of the Little : People can enlist, so long as you're not a robber baron or carpetbagger, of course. Because, while they aren't ideological, the Little : People, if they have any enemies, well, it's plutocrats who, for some reason, hate them. The Little : People are progressive—LGBT rights had been achieved among them generations ago.

There is nothing not to like about them. They're the perfect people in a highly imperfect world.

They are born in the air as bacteria and alight in dark, obscure places—such as closets—where they incubate and hatch. They have always been here—as long as we have—and they're everywhere.

But no longer with me. I can't afford their friendship any longer. The end times are upon us. I must act accordingly.

The Last of the Beads
Halyna Lipatova

Волшебные бусины | Галина Ліпатова
translated by R.B. Lemberg

The first tiny bead crumbled to dust almost immediately—Ayla didn't even notice how or when it had happened. But since it had happened, it was all real. Ayla became alert, and did not miss it the second time.

Turned out, it hurts when a bullet tears through you, breaking ribs and tearing apart lungs.

Tumbling deeper into darkness, she kept thinking a single thought—may it work out.

It worked out.

When she came to, cold and in pain, night had fallen. She moved a bit, opened her eyes, noticing with a jolt that her pain had dissipated. She grabbed her neck—and the second bead crumbled under her fingers.

Ayla sat up, shaking off the snow. Took a good look at herself. Her clothing was bloody, and there was a hole in the fabric over her chest. But when she thrust her fingers into the torn cloth and touched her skin, there was no wound.

It meant that the samaai had not deceived her.

"You will come back as many times as there are beads in the necklace. Be wise about how you spend them, you will not return after the last bead."

Ayla could not recall what exactly she'd paid for such a miraculous item. Why she'd paid for it, she remembered—it would be hard to forget.

She rummaged in the pouch at her belt, took out a small piece of birchbark wrapped around a sliver of a stylus. She unwrapped it, and with a grim satisfaction, used the sharp end of the stylus to cross out the first name. She scanned the list. Four names remained. Then she traced the necklace with her fingers, counting ten beads. Excellent, she even had spares.

She wasted the third bead by trying too hard—starting her work on a glass bomb, she carelessly inhaled the spores of the black bavra. After she woke again, her lungs worked, but the pain in her chest lasted for a long time. At least the glass bomb worked perfectly—Ayla had a chance to evaluate its effectiveness moments before the cloud of poisonous spores got her too.

Crossing the second name out, Ayla jotted two dots across it— counting the number of beads she had spent. After some thought, she put down two dots by the first name as well—she did not remember, could not recall, how exactly she'd lost that first bead.

The first two enemies proved the easiest to get to—the rest of her enemies were careful, mighty, and strong. Ayla was alone, and not all that mighty. All she could do was to die a few times and come back. All she had was a bit of sorcery, the magic beads, bitter memory, and hatred.

The third person lived in a country estate that looked more like a fortress. Ayla was forced to observe it for a long time, patiently searching for the tiniest chance to sneak in. She spent a month in hideouts—first in the large hollow of an ancient elm, using the samaai's far-looking glass to observe the gates; another time in a hay-stack on a water-meadow, trying to figure out if she could sneak into the estate from the river, where sometimes maidens in white dresses and golden circlets came to bathe under guard—these were the lord's daughters. These beautiful and delicate maidens could awe anyone— but not Ayla. She remembered all too well how their faces glowed with delight as they used their guns, inlaid with gold and mother-of-pearl, to shoot at the children nailed to the fence. Ayla would kill them as well, adding them to her list. How, though? If she spent all her beads on them, the others would escape punishment. Ayla could not allow that. She was the last of her kin, the last of her people—she had to bring justice at any cost, with finality and without recourse.

She got lucky. The third enemy and his cruel daughters joined their gods for the cost of a single bead. Ayla tracked down the wagon that was transporting wine to the estate, and managed to hide in one of the barrels while the driver relieved himself in the bushes. Once she got into the estate, it wasn't hard to crawl out of the wine cellar at night. Nobody noticed her, and she climbed to the very top of the tower, from where, apparently, the owner liked to survey his estate. In the morning, the owner and his daughters went out to the courtyard, where the horses, already bridled and saddled, shuffled impatiently on their feet. Ayla noticed that the beautiful heiresses had their golden-pearl guns strapped to their backs, and guessed that they were about to seek out another bloody amusement.

She lifted the bow with its ghostly arrow at the ready. Another four arrows lay arranged on the parapet of the platform before her. She had to finish it all before she was spotted and killed.

Her bow was silent, and for a moment, nobody understood why the first young mistress fell down lifeless, and after her the second collapsed, her throat torn. While the ghostly arrow flew, the shaft and the fletching melted away with the resistance of air, lending speed in return. Nothing remained of them when the crystal arrowpoint found its target, and the point itself exploded in its victim's body.

The third and fourth arrows found their targets. But now Ayla had been noticed, and the guards were already targeting her with their guns. Moments before their five bullets found her body, Ayla let loose the bowstring. The crystal tip of the arrow pierced the third enemy's eye.

Again she came to in the same place as before—in the middle of the ruined communal home of her native village.

Her head hurt, her body felt broken. Each return was more

painful than the last, and more and more time passed between death and awakening. Ayla understood now what price she was paying for these miraculous returns—but she did not care, as long as she could complete her revenge.

A year had passed from the day that the enemies had destroyed her kin and left her home in ruins. New people had settled in the conquered lands, those who paid tribute to the enemies who killed Ayla's kin for the sake of the fertile soil at the bend of the river, for the sake of the thick forests and rich harvests. But the newcomers avoided the ruined village. It loomed dark and sinister on the cape over the river, with its burned log walls and charred carcasses of houses. An attractive spot—but the newcomers did not want to settle here, fearful of a curse or the spirits' revenge . . . People knew how treacherously their overlords dealt with those who'd lived there before. They had come with peace, with offers of trade—and then, at night, they had killed everyone . . . except Ayla. That night she had been undergoing an initiation ceremony in a forest sanctuary, her body frozen in prayer. Her spirit wandered around . . . and thus she saw everything. When the effect of the sacred drink wore off and she came to, at the sanctuary's exit she met that very samaai with his cart full of goods for sale. Somehow he already knew what had happened, and immediately presented her with his special offer. Not for free, of course, but not for coin either. Revenge was worth it, so Ayla decided.

There were three more enemies left. And five beads.

The fourth wasn't easy to kill. He never appeared anywhere on his own, but was always accompanied by an armed guard. At least he didn't sit motionless in his estate, instead incessantly riding around his new domain to collect tribute from his newly resettled people.

Ayla found shelter in the forest sanctuary, which the people had also been afraid to touch—some other people's power, other people's gods and spirits scared them. And that was good. After the big storm, Ayla spent three nights gathering blue thunder mushrooms, then crushed them with the greatest care, striking her wooden mallet upon an oaken log. She dried the shredded mushrooms, and pounded them to dust yet again. Then she used a bone needle to sew a cloth pouch, filled it with powder and tied it tightly.

Now she only had to wait for the fourth enemy to show up to collect tribute from the nearest village. Ayla sneaked into the village in advance, during the night, and hid in a barn. During this season the barns stood empty, and Ayla could while a few days away there, unnoticed. She did not want to be seen in the village before the lord's visit. That night she made rounds of the village, stealing drying laundry from the lines here and there, simply paying attention to how these new people lived. Dogs in the front yards paid her no heed. For them she was like a breeze that smelled like the herbs of forest and meadow.

The magical wards tied to gates and thresholds did nothing to deter her. She could have entered any house, cut all their throats while they slept, if she wanted—unlike the estate of the third enemy, where the walls did deter her. But Ayla did not feel hatred towards the people here. Only towards their leaders. She realized already—these people were scared of their own lords, of their power and might. And it was plain to see—the newcomer settlers and their lords belonged to different peoples . . . But Ayla had no desire to contemplate that.

On the day of tribute collection, Ayla donned the stolen clothes, washed herself using the tincture of five leaves, six herbs and seven flowers, and went out to the streets of the village. As long as the smell of the tincture remained on her skin, all the people she met would think her one of their own. The tincture would not last long, but she hoped to finish her business before she would be outed as an outsider.

The fourth enemy arrived in the morning—or rather, he was carried in a large, luxurious palanquin, accompanied by twenty riders armed with firearms and five self-moving wagons with spears of fire. The palanquin was carried by four iron giants. These humanlike constructs were made entirely of metal, and towered one and a half-times as tall as a person. Propelled by the strange enemy magic, they never got tired. Having lowered the palanquin in the town square, they lifted the curtain, revealing to all a tall red armchair upon which the overlord sat—an imposing person in golden clothing. The guardsmen flanked him, the herald sounded the horn, and people began pouring into the square, carrying tribute in their hands. The ruler had no interest in grain, fruits, or meat—he cared only about furs, precious stones, gold and silver. In order to gather all that, the settlers spent a whole month rafting trade goods downstream to the great samaai city, where they could exchange grain, meat and fruits for the tribute their overlord desired. In the crowd, Ayla attracted no attention—her cloth bag was no different from others like it, carried by many of the village women. People would come closer to the red carpet strewn on the ground. They would pour out the coins and the gems and pile up the furs, all the time squinting fearfully at the overlord. Ayla could barely understand these people's tongue, but she understood their fear well. They were afraid of displeasing their master, to arouse his ire with insufficiently rich tribute.

Ayla shuffled closer, pushed forward through the crowd and pulled the linen pouch from her belt. She noticed how the tribute-counters that stood by the carpet frowned in dissatisfaction—the baggie was deemed too small. She bent over the carpet, untying the strings, and her lips whispered a single word. Blue powder gushed out of the pouch, dividing at once into streams which immediately clung to the metal and gems—and to all that was strewn on the carpet, and to the guardsmen's armor, and to the iron giants, and to the adornments on the overlord's clothes.

Nobody had any time to understand anything, except Ayla. She screamed, "Run!" and then threw the bag with the remains of the powder straight at the lord. The guards fired at her, but it was too late. Thunder powder, stuck to the metal and stones, heated them instantly—and all of it burst into flames with a terrible shaking and screeching.

When she awoke in the ruins of the big communal house after that, it was already winter. Ayla suddenly realized that she could no longer feel cold, even though she was lying on snow. She pulled apart the frozen straw in the corner, and climbed down to the surviving cellar. There, cobwebs covered everything; a mirror on the wall was covered with dust. She wiped off the dust and peered at her own reflection.

Her face was pale, her eyes looked faded. Like a ghost. Ayla touched her reflection, traced her finger upon the glass. Her body was still flesh—at least she could act upon objects in the material world. But now Ayla felt herself to be more spirit than living creature. Back then, she had died for the first time—and coming back, she was not quite alive anymore. She recalled that from one rebirth to the next, she had needed less and less food and rest. Night sorcery worked out better and better for her, while the daylight magic was harder. That was the price she had paid for a chance to destroy her enemies—at the price of her life, her longevity, which was the pride of her people. And her afterlife, too—she would never grow back as grasses, flowers, and trees, returning to the living world; she would never run through the forest as a fox or a wolf during one of the links in a chain of rebirths. She would never again be born to new life from the flesh and blood of her kin. She would become a restless spirit, hovering on the border between two worlds. And not just because there was nobody left to stage a funeral feast in her honor—but also because she had given up her afterlife for a chance of revenge. The wisdom of her people said that making a deal with the samaai always involved trickery. That's why her people never traded directly with the mountain people.

Ayla went back up, climbed the burnt but still-standing guard tower.

The settlement where she had achieved her fourth revenge was dead. Only the burned carcasses of houses stuck out from the snow. The thunder powder had destroyed everything.

She should not feel any regret. After all, her own kin had been murdered so that these people could settle here and pay tribute to their overlords. But she felt sorry for them.

Standing on the top of the rickety tower, bracing in the icy wind, Ayla crossed out the fourth name from the already crumbling birch-bark. Only a single name remained. The last one—the most terrifying of her enemies. The powerful sorcerer of the outsiders, who managed to defeat the mages of her own people, to break through the wards of her village . . . how to overcome him? Four beads were left. Could she complete her revenge in four beads?

Returning to the forest sanctuary—completely grown over with moss, ivy, and tree roots—Ayla kindled a living flame in the stone hearth with great difficulty, cleaned up some of the cobwebs and blown-in leaves. How much time had passed since her last death? Judging from the abandoned look of the sanctuary, nobody had set foot here at least since the day that she'd left with her pouch of thunder powder. Here was the mallet on the oaken log, exactly where Ayla had left it. It was dusty and covered with spiderwebs . . . more and more time seemed to pass between each death and rebirth. And that meant that she could not delay any longer. Ayla had no idea what she would be like when only the last bead remained. Even now she felt neither cold nor heat. She could kindle the fire, but only the regular way—with flint and tinder, her daytime sorcery failed . . . maybe because it was night now. But in the before times, she could have done it.

Ayla went out of the sanctuary and stood frozen on the threshold under the low-hanging branches of the firs. The sanctuary was hidden under the roots of an ancient fir tree on the slope on the hill. Below, at the bottom of the hill, was a stream that did not freeze even during the fiercest frosts. Ayla could see the flow of the water, steam rising from it, the embroidery of frost on the grasses and branches by the banks. She saw—even though she should not have been able to see it all so clearly; it was still night, starless and dark.

She could see, too, the silvery delicate shadows of the forest spirits that even her people's mages would not be able to see without a prayerful trance or without drinking the tincture of secret herbs.

It was easy, almost effortless, for Ayla to enter a trance and to leave her own body. She hovered over it, just a silvery, delicate shadow like the other spirits. Curiously she contemplated her body, marveling at how fragile it looked now—thin arms and legs, whitish hair and pale skin—the body would not last much longer.

Ayla came back to it, rose to her feet. She touched the rest of the beads and smiled to herself, feeling that she would not need all four beads.

The murderers of her people had come from beyond the mountains, from the coast, and there they'd arrived from beyond the seas on great iron ships that spat fire. Theirs was a sorcery unknown to Ayla's kin, not known to the samaai or the other peoples who lived nearby. The sorcery of the invaders did not create: it destroyed. The newcomers' weapons spat flame or fired pieces of metal that pierced every kind of armor. Those weapons were loaded with something like her thunder powder, which Ayla's people knew, but unlike it, the outsiders' fire powder was indifferent to metal and stone, and instead could easily set trees on fire, and cloth, and everything created from nature. It seemed to her that the sorcery of the invaders was hostile to living nature, and perhaps that was why the mages of Ayla's kinspeople could not do anything against it. But the wisdom of the ancients said that there was great weakness in every great power. No-one was invincible, not even spirits and gods.

So thought Ayla, flying as a silver shadow above the snowed-in valley toward the foot of the mountains. Upon her throat glowed the single, last bead. She had smashed the three others upon the altar stone of her forest sanctuary. Now her body was almost ghostly, and she knew it would crumble to dust with her next death. But Ayla did not care anymore. She had to finish her job.

At the foot of the mountains, next to that very same pass through which the enemies had first arrived, a fortress now stood, and in that fortress lived the head sorcerer. Everywhere here was metal and stone; the fire of smelters blazed brightly, and smithies roared like thunder. And near the very rock, away from other outbuildings, stank the workshops where the newcomers' fiery concoctions were made. Ayla vigilantly observed everything that happened there. She herself was unnoticed by everyone—even the enemy sorcerers. In their eyes she was an eddy of frosty air, a snowdrift or a puff of smoke from the chimney, a stain of rime upon the rock ... She bided her time.

At last, the overlord of the fortress decided to check on the progress of work in the fiery workshops. The fate of his allies could not leave him unbothered, and it was easy to see that the fortress was getting ready for a new campaign, awaiting ships with more settlers. Ayla guessed that the newcomers blamed the surviving inhabitants of the land for their troubles, and intended to walk through the land sowing flame, destroying everyone who did not belong to their own people, to establish everywhere the altars of their own gods, to cut down the forests, plow over the meadows—destroying even the very memory of those who'd lived here before.

Well, if it was so—then she had nothing to lose. As soon as she spotted the sorcerer on the path to the workshops, Ayla easily slid out of her already ghostly body and flew towards him. Yes, no sorcery would work upon what she had now become. The outsiders did not see spirits, did not feel them, and could not harm them. Spirits, as bodiless creatures, could not affect the flesh either. But Ayla attacked not the sorcerer's flesh, but his spirit itself. She entered the other's body, filled it completely, burrowed into his mind. And then she struck.

The sorcerer screamed, grabbed his head and toppled to the ground.

"You . . . what are you?" his conscience wailed through the pain, while Ayla vengefully made his body shake in terrifying convulsions. She overpowered him so easily! She thought with bitterness: if only the mages of her people had understood earlier that the enemies were vulnerable in spirit, they could have protected her people, overcome the invaders, and banished them! But for Ayla's kinspeople it was unthinkable to imagine that a spirit could be so easily conquered. They themselves always existed in two forms, equally strong, and could never imagine that others could be so weak in the spirit.

"I am your death, invader. It would have been better for your people to stay overseas!"

"We . . . we needed a place to live!" The sorcerer's resistance was weakening; he could not resist her onslaught.

"If you came here as peaceful neighbors, we could have lived side by side, could have traded with each other. But you took away our land and our lives."

And Ayla erased his mind.

Everything happened so quickly; an observer might have thought that the sorcerer came back to his senses. Ayla, controlling his already lifeless body, managed to get up, and with a single casual gesture calmed the guards that came running towards her. She entered the workshop, where in the corner, unnoticed by anyone, her body lay like a barely visible cobweb. It was odd to observe it through someone else's eyes. And, in general, it was strange to see things with someone else's eyes—it turned out that the newcomers saw the world differently than her people, not noticing half the colors, not noticing the movements of power . . . Ayla touched the threads of power and summoned fire.

Thunder and flame flared up over the mountains, and the mountain pass collapsed, closing down the path from the seashore.

Fire devoured the whole fortress, even the stones burned through. Only a single thing remained in the ashes—a tiny bead of stone.

Everybody who lived nearby understood: revenge had caught up with the invaders. And somehow they knew which hand had brought it. Centuries later, flittering as a restless spirit through those lands, Ayla still heard songs and legends about her revenge.

Revenge in Pursuit

Vira Balatska

Помста навздогін | Віра Балацька

translated by Michael M. Naydan and Alla Perminova

The longer I lingered in the minister's reception room, the darker the thoughts that hammered inside my brain. This pessimistic herd had already begun to whisper about the putrid smell of sewage, which could not be completely washed off my calloused hands after an eight-hour shift; as well as the discrepancy between my pants that had been worn through on my knees (despite double denim patches) and the opulent gilded velour furnishings of this room. Overall, I thought: "The first word in my job title 'royal' is to no purpose, because the second is still 'plumber.' Therefore, I, Anton Vyrlook, a plumber of the second class, have no business being here. And nothing good will come of this summons . . . "

Inaudibly, the doors (yes, if they only dared to squeak—probably cost as much as one of our brother worker's annual salaries!) opened. They let in another stooped-over figure, in union overalls and with splendid ears that peeked out in all directions from under a perpetually soiled straw hat, as if they were avidly collecting the latest palace gossip. He was a gardener. Another alien from the world of running around, dirt, and mandatory evening television.

"Hello, Morgan!" I said. However official this room might have seemed, and no matter how much of a goddess the minister's secretary might have appeared to be, no one had rescinded the warmth of human friendliness.

The gardener's round face was whiter than the sheet of paper the young secretary was stuffing into a grayish apparatus with an air of global importance. And apparently that was the case—if they were going to print something on paper, it was going to be a personal law of His Majesty, the king.

"So ... You've been caught stealing too, huh?" the gardener whispered right into my ear, settling down next to me on the crimson couch, a piece of valuable furniture that people of our professions should never touch, lest we soil it.

Well, to each their own. What and where could I steal at work? A piece of polypropylene pipe in the restroom? A discarded plunger?

Squeee-eak! came a sound from the door. No, it wasn't the steel, perfectly oiled curtains that finally gave in. It was the squeaking of the shoes, unaccustomed to marble, of a third visitor.

A short woman, curvy either from a chronic love of pastries stuffed with chicken, or perhaps magnificently shaped by nature, stepped anxiously onto the thick carpet of the reception room. Her worn-out shoes immediately sank into the pile up to her ankles and obediently fell silent. They no longer embarrassed their mistress in front of the impeccably groomed secretary.

This was the brigade leader of the palace roofing crew. The evening was gradually becoming more intriguing.

"Good day," the newcomer timidly greeted the hostess of the reception room. She didn't ignore Morgan and me either and nodded to us politely. The haughty secretary didn't even glance our way, but we moved closer to each other on the velour luxuriousness of the couch, inviting the newcomer to sit.

The brigade leader smiled somewhat sheepishly (it was her nature; however this same lady sometimes scolded her subordinates so vehemently that it made the sun blush), and after adjusting her worn-out coveralls on her knees, she perched on the edge of the couch.

Silence ensued.

Then the door opposite swung open loudly. The minister Himself—well-groomed, stately, silver-haired, and totally rotund—appeared in the doorway.

I hadn't imagined him like this—taller, perhaps, or more long-haired? Certainly not as fidgety, and definitely not more pale than Morgan. We sat there, holding our breath and fearful of him—but what could be making his lips twitch so anxiously?

"Come in," he made an inviting nod without even turning toward the couch densely packed with workers.

We exchanged glances and hesitantly crossed the threshold.

And there . . . ! A medical team with an entire corner filled with hospital equipment— inexplicable but unmistakable; a trio of court lawyers (a father and two sons, all fifth- and sixth-generation lawyers); and the palace administrator—our direct boss. Of course, we tried to stop just short of "Mom," but the lawyer—Vais, or whatever his name was—pointed to the chairs with a professional smile. We took our seats at the wide desk strewn with papers. The top officials in attendance remained standing, even the anxious one Himself!

"Has each of you applied for permission to have a child?" We had already heard about the minister's habit of immediately galloping into every conversation, so we weren't particularly surprised. Although, I must say, we jumped at the sharpness of his voice. "And did everyone receive a rejection?"

The brigade leader sighed bitterly, and Morgan and I just nodded. What was there to talk about? After World War III, we were far from being the first ones like this. The Commission had not considered our family gene pool important enough to continue it for posterity. And so, the population of the world was reduced to those "golden" ten billion.

For the nobility it had been even worse. Their families had been playing with genetic modification long before the war—initially trying to have children who were one hundred percent healthy; and then the games started—"creating" for themselves a son with blue eyes and blond hair, or a girl with elf-like ears . . . Who could have known that these "lab-made" children would never bear offspring themselves?

Infertility manifested itself, if not immediately then after a generation, at most two. Even genetic engineering couldn't help them anymore.

But that's not all! About seventy years ago, the youngest royal princess caused quite a commotion. You see, the princess was openly spoiled by powerful parents because she was the only one in her family who turned out to be unplanned and therefore "with a future". She gathered around her a group of "golden youth," hijacked the fastest experimental starship, loaded it with a staff of robots, and set off from our planet to the other side of the Milky Way. There, you see, scientists had found a planet similar to ours, but uninhabited. So those kids decided to create a paradise on the planet—without "shoddy human beings," just with their own kind: well-read and with a musical education, an innate talent for the arts, and perpetually clean hands. And with "non-malodorous" robots as the lower caste.

This escape was carefully concealed. Reports of their disappearance, and later, of the existence of the "golden youth," were professionally cleansed from the information space. But we, the "shoddy human beings," knew. We always know everything. Especially palace employees. Oh, and the king was furious then! He still hasn't forgiven his daughter: he removed her from his will and declared her a criminal of cosmic proportions—by secret order, of course. But still. And he ordered the wing of the castle where the princess used to live to be converted first into a pigsty, and then, when his majesty realized that the stench would reach his nose—into a stable.

And rightly so. Why have that pigsty on Royal Hill? There are non-flooded plains in East Asia, or South America for that matter. You can get whatever and whomever you want grown there.

My father built the septic tank for that stable. He was a good craftsman, and that's how he earned the honor of leaving behind offspring—that is, me. But I am not my father.

However . . .

"Today your applications have been reconsidered. The Higher Supervisory Commission has decided to approve them, and even double the number. But first, you must familiarize yourselves with the documents and confirm your consent with your signature . . . "

Morgan, realizing that he had not been summoned here because of the machinations of cheap or expensive varieties of roses, or other dealings about which the "shoddy people" of the palace had long whispered, straightened up. The pen was already twirling in his hands . . . But I held the gardener back. After all, the papers! Instead of touching an electronic screen of the personnel tablet and offering a fingerprint for scanning, we were being asked for a signature . . . There were whole piles in front of us! And all of this was printed for us to read?

Strike me dead if this group has not invented something for our destruction!

Well, let them sit and wait.

We started rustling through the documents: Morgan businesslike, and I clumsily—my eyes were already hurting on the third page, so I had to constantly stop and rub them with my palm. The brigade leader was nervous. Even her hands trembled. And for some reason, it seemed to me that her eyes were simply gliding blindly over the written words, not distinguishing anything in those black lines and tiny print. The only thing she was thinking about was what names to give to her future children.

As many as two! Just like that!

It was madness. There was no such thing as the Commission changing its decisions. And don't talk to me about the "connections" of a palace worker. We're "shoddy people," remember? Simpletons. We were a dime a dozen. One got a cold and was immediately replaced without the palace noticing any change.

However . . .

In a dry, succinct, rather formal but largely comprehensible manner, the documents gave details about the colony that had been planned on the planet Mea. Its future inhabitants were ordered to build cities and villages there, with the obligatory creation of a well-equipped police station in each settlement. Since Mea needed to be populated as soon as possible, settlers were allowed to have families similar to those at the beginning of the 21st century on Earth. That is, to have one or two children—and with good recommendations from their supervisor, they could be permitted even more.

As I reached that part, the brigade woman, who was now reading along with us, couldn't hold back—she coughed and began to impatiently fidget in her chair. With her tirelessness and stubborn temper, just let her go to that planet Mea and she would give birth to ten!

No laboratory technologies. No childfree. A minimal number of robots, a maximum of manual labor. A minimum of representatives of noble families allowed to hire bastards or half-breeds, talented "servants" for managerial positions.

Folks, this sounded like paradise! How did we get so lucky?

The brigade leader was the first to break down and began to sign the papers with such speed that I was fearful smoke would come from them. Morgan was inspired by her example and reached for the pen again.

Slowly, I looked up at the officials present, about whom I had already forgotten.

It turned out that while we had been rustling about here and there, the doctors were busily "shooting" our backs with a diagnostic laser. Weren't quarterly check-ups enough?

Fine, check for health—it would not hurt me to once again make sure of my own physical "serviceability" and mental adequacy before ... Before ...

Damn, my Orysia was going to scream to the whole neighborhood as soon as she heard it!

... Stop! Orysia!!

It was a good thing I hadn't signed yet!

"And our families? My wife?" I narrowed my eyes in the direction of the minister.

"What, not there?" He snarled something furiously into the communicator. The secretary rushed in, respectfully placed a document in front of me (respectfully! I lived to see it) with the name of my love engraved on top. "Take it home, she has to sign it in person. If your wife refuses to fly, and you don't, your marriage will be officially annulled, and you can choose another wife from among the unmarried female colonizers . . . "

The brigade leader and I looked at each other dumbfoundedly. Refuse?! For such a thing a complete fool would sell his soul!

Of course, on the next to last day before our departure, my mother-in-law arranged a farewell banquet for us on our entire stoop. People looked around with envy, and Orysia's parents strutted around like a couple of elderly peacocks—wow, in a year they could already have a grandson! And not just one grandson, but the first of two or three! My restless father-in-law had managed to whisper to whomever he needed to in the space fleet and contacted the junior signalman from our ship; so he knew for certain there would be some kind of connection between the Earth and Mea. Therefore, at least a few times a month we should be able to send photos and videos, and they would be able to see the little one! And then, who knows, maybe they could fly in to hold the baby and babysit. Space technology had been developing at such an extraordinarily rapid pace over the past few decades.

We also invited Morgan to the banquet. Of course, no one ordered us to gather in "guilds," but our colleagues from the castle had decided before takeoff to come together and stay together. Who knew what kinds of people would arrive on the colonizing ship from among farmers, the factory "ants," and engineers of Platinum Valley—and what if we didn't make friends: there were different mentalities, families, dialects? Here we had all our own people, the pick of the crop.

The loner gardener came in a brand-new shirt and a black-colored forelock that, I would swear, had been grayish the week before. But it was not for me to judge him—after tomorrow, after liftoff, this eternal bachelor would meet up with single women from different parts of Old Britain, who would be hot with the thought of a future marriage and the pregnancy they desired. Or maybe even a pregnancy without marriage, who knew? Our superintendent said that the number of single female and male colonists would be equal, so that the possibility of creating couples was 100 percent, but you know how it happens in life between people. So, the old gardener cleaned up nicely and even began talking without swearing—what a wonder!

After the fourth toast, I noticed a skeptical smile on the face of my new friend. He knew something!

I pulled the old man into the bedroom. There was only an empty bed, covered with plastic film: all the things had been housewifely packed by my efficient Orysia in the morning and personally delivered to the cosmodrome. We could sleep on top of this cellophane the last night, and on the day of departure we would not have to rush around with suitcases or be afraid we left something behind.

We sat down. There was a tense silence.

My calculation turned out to be correct—the mixture of alcohol and silence had no less effect on the chatty Morgan than truth serum from an old movie.

"So, what do you know about that colony?" he finally smiled haughtily.

"Well ... We need to expand beyond the Earth. Just in case, because the population could suddenly increase again. We've all been told that, haven't we? And the plant life on Mea is not exactly the same as here, so in time we could export exotic jams. There are all kinds of different fruits there."

"It's revenge!" Morgan Tarasovych said with a twinkle in his eye.

I jumped up. Why? Well, okay, I could have screwed on

something wrong in the castle's kitchen traps ... But Orysia, why would the minister take revenge on her?

Seeing how my face suddenly had stretched, the bespattered gardener laughed in a friendly way:

"It's not for us, why did you turn pale? It's for the princess."

I blinked and then again. There were no princesses in the castle. There was only a crown prince taken from a family of some impoverished dukes. What could they do, for the lack of blood relatives? The royal couple had to be content with just young aristocrats from among the most loyal ones ... Fortunately, at least a few more kiddies were born among their families.

I blinked even slower ...

And then ...

I GOT IT.

"So, what's that? Did the 'golden ones' fly to Mea? And we have to get there, and ... What are we supposed to do, punish them somehow?"

"They didn't fly there already. They're flying there now!" Morgan raised his index finger tellingly. "Don't you forget, they started seventy-four years ago. The technology of the time promised one hundred and three years of flying time. So, they were placed in cryogenic capsules so that the journey would be perceived as instantaneous ... In the meantime, the king on Earth emptied the entire castle treasury (remember, when we were little, bread suddenly tripled in price?), sought out the best scientists, and they even say that their families were taken hostage in order to, so to speak, encourage them ... And over the course of all these years, different versions of interplanetary travel have been developed. They did complete the development of those engines! The creator of that technology even received a non-hereditary duchy—"

"How do you know all this?"

"You need to know who to 'accidentally' run into at the Scotch party!" Morgan smiled haughtily again. "Our superintendent is his nephew. After downing the third glass, he blurted things out. What a lightweight!"

My friend seemed to have forgotten the fact that he had permitted himself to loosen his tongue, and I did not remind him of that.

"Well, what do you and I have to do with it?"

"The fact that in a month a strong force of "shoddy humans" will land on Mea. Us. Everyone is allowed ... But let's tell it like it is—we've been ordered to build a house immediately and multiply. And all for what? So that when the 'golden' princess arrives, not an idyllic, clean green planet will be waiting for her and her friends, but a real beehive. Including police in every village, armed with the latest laws of OUR time. Why? Of course, in order to immediately arrest the crowned persona non grata and bring her home. People in the palace whisper that the king is so eager to see his daughter's face at that moment that he has vowed not to die. The old one has been on borrowed time for about ten years now, but doctors with their cloned organs and gene injections are still letting him run. But still, time takes its toll ... Now, there is Henrietta—well, she's a dental nurse, do you happen to know her? She said that immediately after our departure, His Majesty will lie down in a cryogenic capsule, and they will awaken him only when his rebellious daughter is brought to him."

Something was desperately scraping in my head—it was my brain, unaccustomed to difficult decisions, trying to think about politics.

"But this heir ... Well, which duke? Can he object to the return of the lawful princess? He won't want to share power with her ... "

"Ah," Morgan shrugged it off and squinted in satisfaction. "That will happen when it happens ... Moreover, that is not our concern. They'll figure it out on their own!"

He stood up and took me resolutely by the elbow.

"Come, my brother, and drink one more of your splendid

homebrew! For the health of the noble partridge, who quarreled with daddy so loudly that you and I will finally escape from these concrete-foam birdhouses and build a house for ourselves at the king's expense. It will even have a pond at the end of the yard!"

We went out into the common corridor, where we pulled out a table from each neighbor's apartment, and my mother-in-law set up treats. Happy, blushing from the unusual attention directed at her, Orysia moved around with a jug of liqueur in her hands, serving everyone who was present. An electric light shone gold in her blondish curls and sparkled on the colored chickadee hairpin I had bought her as a future memento of Earth.

It had been a long time since I heard such ringing, happy laughter from my love. And this blush, as if it were the first day of our acquaintance . . .

She will make a good mother!

To See Jupiter
Oleh Silin

Побачити Юпітер | Олег Сілін
translated by Anatoly Belilovsky

Очі твої — одні.
Your eyes — are uniquely yours.[1]

It happened at about 23:27 by the ship's clock, on A-Liel's watch. *Flamin* was by then 250 million kilometers away from Earth and had passed through the asteroid belt.

Space is a generally empty place. It is only in the movies that ships maneuver between majestic flying mountains while risking terminating the mission prematurely by running headlong into one of them. That's why A-Liel calmly went about his studies of structured information transfer to the cerebral cortex. Simply put, by reading. Comfortable in his chair, he was absorbed in the adventures of Jessica, who had so much trouble choosing between the dragon and the charming knight, and he noted neither a slight shift in the ship's bearing, nor the change in the color of the oxygen indicators. Two of the five gauges swapped bright green for swampy brown and gradually crept to amber.

A-Liel returned to reality only after glancing at the front view monitor and seeing a new pattern of stars.

"Bloody hell!"

The book took sudden flight and sailed into the corner, and the duty officer, using the thrust vector, swam up to the monitor and tapped on it.

---

1   From "Do you know that you're a person?" by Vasyl Symonenko, translated by E.D.E. Bell

"Maybe it's just a camera glitch? Shifted on its mounts?" said A-Liel to himself, although somewhere in the depths of his soul he knew for sure that it was nothing as simple. That an event had happened, the probability of which was a fraction expressed by a one behind a whole lot of zeros after the decimal point. The ship collided with a rock large enough to puncture a hole. The *Flamin* lost oxygen into the vacuum, and the resulting jet spun the ship. The course to Jupiter deviated more each second.

A-Liel called for help.

"What the hell happened? You read something silly again and want to discuss it?"

The head of Prime-Navigator A-Erin stuck out from the hatch, her red hair sticking out in a crown above the top of her head. The woman pulled herself up and easily torpedoed herself into the command chair. Engineer A-Dan followed her onto the bridge.

"We have an anomaly," muttered A-Liel, but A-Erin already saw it and cursed briefly.

"Engineering, damage report!"

"Punctures in tanks three and four. Reactor core is not damaged and functions properly. The cargo compartment is intact. The engines are nominal."

"A course correction is necessary," A-Liel added quietly.

"I see it myself. A-Dan, preliminary conclusions?"

"While oxygen is escaping, it makes no sense to make course corrections with engines. The error will grow."

"Understood. Yellow alert. Meeting in ten minutes."

As always, the transition to the gravity zone was accompanied by mild nausea. A-Liel tried to think of a way to quickly resolve the situation. None came to mind. All his knowledge of storms on the gas giant was useless in solving the problem.

Almost the entire crew gathered in the cabin. Twelve, thirteen ... The black-haired, short-haired A-Ilza, who was responsible for security, and chief engineer A-Eugene came in last.

"*Flamin,* we have a problem," A-Erin began. A-Dan chuckled mirthlessly at this well-worn cliche. "The situation is not yet critical, it will become so in about eight hours. We are losing oxygen, we are headed to the ass end of *Voyager's* grandmother, and the whole mission is down the shitter. I'm open to ideas. Let me remind you, our main directive is to deliver the human crew to circum-Jupiter orbit."

In silence, the crew looked over the report from the bridge once more.

"We calculate the rotation, compensate for it with a brief main engine burn. We head to Jupiter at max acceleration," the navigator A-Thomas said, putting his communicator on the table. "Something like that."

"What about the braking maneuver?"

"At Callisto! Through the magnetic field ... Don't look at me like that! I know it's nonsense."

"We have to dump faulty tanks. Get back on course. I know, there is not enough oxygen. We still have our orders. The factory must get to Jupiter. If the factory works, it will ensure the success of the next missions. One of them will reach the ultimate objective. Pity it won't be us, but what can we do?"

"This is not an option!" A-Eugene stared at A-Ilza, who had just calmly explained the suicide plan, and shouted: "We must prove that people are capable of enduring this journey! I propose doing just the opposite: we compensate for oxygen loss by dumping the equipment in the cargo compartments. We pump oxygen from the affected tanks to the pressurized cargo compartment. That's my expertise, I designed the life support system! We can fulfill the mission and achieve the main objective."

A-Erin thought: *We were created for one mission, but A-Ilza has a point. The plant is an integral part of the program of future studies of Jupiter. We have to check with Jupe Exploring.*

The prime navigator took the communicator and began typing messages. The astronauts dispersed to the cabin company. A-Liel filled a thermos with coffee and took a sip. The signal delay was about twenty minutes. So, twenty minutes in one direction, twenty in the other, and the decision is unlikely to be made immediately. A difficult hour, maybe not just one.

The answer came in forty-five minutes. This meant only one thing: the company had developed a "Plan B" for this anomalous situation a long time ago. A-Erin looked up from the screen.

"Well, then . . . Wait a second, where is A-Eugene?"

✦

Flamin is not a very big ship, there are few places to hide aboard. A-Eugene was found in engineering where he had managed to barricade himself. Through the window, one could see him pacing desperately from wall to wall, like a bear in a zoo cage too small for him.

"Eugene! Get out of there!" A-Erin shouted and knocked on the door. "Do you hear me?"

"Did they decide to leave the factory?" she heard from behind the door.

"Yes," A-Erin said and exchanged glances with A-Ilza. The

dark-haired woman shrugged her shoulders, as if saying: "Oh, I've had it with these tantrums."

"Why don't you want to do as I suggest? Go after the primary objective?"

"Because we are the property of Jupe Exploring and cannot circumvent our orders."

"To hell with Jupe! And with the orders! Don't you understand?"

A-Ilsa stepped back and gestured for A-Erin to do the same.

"I will get him from there. He is, after all, Chief Engineer, it would be irrational to lose him. Also, he can carry out his plan even from that compartment. That will take him ... maybe a couple of hours? We must hurry."

"Do you think he will listen to you?"

"He did in bed." A-Ilza's lips formed into a smile, although her eyes remained serious. "I'll crawl through the wiring conduit. They were designed with such cases in mind. Or someone watched that old Bruce Willis movie too many times. I'll try to talk him into giving up."

"All right. Give it a try."

"Give me a boost."

A-Ilza removed the bars from the ceiling. Behind them was a metal pipe of sufficient diameter for a slim woman to climb through. A-Erin waited until A-Ilza's boots disappeared in the darkness, and turned to the window, so that A-Eugene would not get suspicious.

Within a few tens of seconds, the bars in the engineering compartment fell to the floor. A-Eugene jumped back and grabbed the first thing he found, a screwdriver. A-Ilza raised her hands reassuringly.

"Take it easy, will you? Why are you so upset?"

"Don't you understand? Without oxygen, the expedition is doomed. People will not reach the destination!"

"So? That is why they sent us androids. I think it's more important for Jupe Exploring to build a base than to prove a human's ability to travel to Jupiter."

"M-m-m!" Eugene dropped the screwdriver and ruffled his hair. "Babe, there is just one problem. I am human!"

"Impossible."

"Very possible! You'd be amazed the stuff you can get away with if you are one of the builders of this ship."

"That's insane, A-Eugene!"

"Don't call me that! My name is Eugene Malaniuk, I am an engineer, I always dreamed of seeing Jupiter with my own eyes. That was why I joined Jupe Explorations and that was how I earned cancer for my troubles. I must see Jupiter! Must!"

"Listen," A-Ilza carefully stepped forward, "I need to tell you something. I am Chief of Security. I have to know everything. I read the personnel files of all fifteen crew members. There are no people in the crew. We are all androids."

"They told me that they would falsify my file." His voice trembled.

"I will prove it to you. Just don't be a jerk and don't be a fool. Agreed?"

A-Ilza took a knife from the magnetic tape, rolled up her left sleeve and ran the blade across her skin. Bright ultramarine blood appeared at the site of the cut.

"This is what we have inside. Yes, we process oxygen only so that the company can calculate how much is needed for a human crew. We don't actually need it. You will see your Jupiter."

They felt a jolt. A-Ilza looked at the monitor: it showed that A-Thomas dropped the damaged oxygen pumps.

"Now I'm going to cut your finger a little so you can see with your own eyes. OK?"

"Give me the knife," the engineer's voice was dull. "I can do this myself."

A-Ilza turned the handle of the knife towards A-Eugene. He took it, twisted it between his fingers.

And then he cut his own throat with one swift movement.

Blood flooded his neck.

Ultramarine.

A-Liel and A-Erin were looking at the main viewscreen. Jupiter flowed beneath them. White and ocher streaks swirled, mingled, fell apart, and combined again. The dance of powerful storms and gigantic cyclones mesmerized everyone who looked at the gas giant.

"I understand why A-Eugene wanted to see it face to face," whispered A-Liel.

"And he could have. But he was too stubborn for his own good."

"How could he possibly not know he was an android, though?"

"You see, A-Liel," A-Erin ran her fingers through her hair, "it's like he really didn't. The death of the chief engineer is a sufficient reason for A-Ilza and me to get some access to classified information. Eugene Malaniuk was sure he would go to Jupiter. His doctors promised him."

"Sounds like there's a 'but' coming?"

"Yes. His body was almost consumed by the disease. So they transplanted his brain into an android body. A unique operation—I think there's a Nobel Prize in it, and a whole lot of riots when people find out. And when he realized he'd been deceived—that's when he set his plan in motion."

The prime navigator fell silent. A-Liel didn't dare interrupt her thoughts.

"However . . . He died a man, though. And we have to honor that."

Flamin shook slightly. A capsule flew from the ship towards Jupiter. Part of its shell was a transparent shield. A-Liel could have sworn that even from this distance he could see A-Eugene's eyes watching the Great Red Spot.

The capsule gradually shrank until it turned into a speck which soon disappeared in the clouds of the gas giant.

Honey

Valya Dudycz Lupescu

Luba had grown to like the stinging, not just the relief it brought to her swollen, twisted hands, but the prick itself. She imagined it must be like getting a tattoo. Her husband had had his name crudely tattooed on his arm during the war. Or was it in the displaced persons camps afterward? Such details got lost, they were less important to hold onto than other memories. Happier ones.

She knelt beside her husband's grave in front of the hollowed-out log and listened to the buzzing deep inside. The soothing sound reminded her of concentrating in the night to hear Kalyna's breathing when she had been a baby, a nightly ritual to make sure that her daughter did not follow her older brother into death's embrace. Kalyna eventually did, but many years later ... From cancer brought on by the bright betrayal of too many sun-bleached days on the coast of the Black Sea.

Luba placed her hand atop the log and felt the soft vibration. It throbbed familiar and comforting, so similar to the feeling of resting her hand atop her husband's chest as his heartbeat slowly stopped. She had touched so much death with her hands: resting her head as a child atop the starving body of her mother while Mama's hair came away in clumps in Luba's small hands; squeezing in solidarity the hands of friends bruised and beaten at the hands of Nazi soldiers; the cold hands of corpses as she helped carry them into the mass graves; holding the fearful hands of wounded rebels and revolutionaries; the gnarled hands of other babas finally succumbing to old age or disease. Her time would come soon. But not yet. That was why she needed her hands, and why she loved her bees.

The steady enthusiasm of this hive was so different from her other hives. Each one had its own personality: the constant diligence of the three sister hives in the ancient wooden boxes she had inherited from her father, the wild and unpredictable energy of the hive in the birch tree in her garden, the quiet hum of the forest hives beside the river. She loved them all, and visiting them was one of the bright spots in her day. As she tended to them, Luba would talk about her day: collecting eggs from the chickens; chasing off the fox; harvesting her enormous garden full of tomatoes, potatoes, beets, and peas; foraging for mushrooms in the forest; collecting wild raspberries for jam; perhaps a visit from one of the scientists who came every few months to collect samples for radiation testing; or a rare but treasured visit from one of the other babas in the neighboring villages.

She kissed the bark of the wild hive. "Good morning, my darlings."

In many ways, a hive was more like a single creature than many individuals, working together much like her hands working with her arms working with her heart working with her imagination. Together. *When* they worked, that is. But that was why she came here for help, so that they *could* work.

Luba placed her bare hands inside the log, her youngest hive. Even without the usual sparse dusting of wormwood powder, the bees kept their distance and did not sting her all at once.

Luba began to sing to them, slowly moving her fingers to get their attention.

"Beloved sister bees,
a few of you must surely be ready,
a few of you must have lived long enough—
a good life full of sweetness.
Is it time to say farewell? To return to the earth?
Would you gift me your venom before you go?

Would you give me relief before I die?
Would you trust me to help care for your sisters?
Aren't we all sisters? Sisters all are we."

She felt the first sting, and the second, but after that only heat and pressure as more and more stung her wrists and fingers. After a few deep breaths, Luba slipped her hands out from the hive. Those bees who sat atop her skin flew off, but a handful fell to the ground after completing their sting. More would get carried out of the hive to join their sisters in a small pile of dead at the base of the log.

Luba rubbed her hands to help spread the venom. Miracle creatures, they were. What kills one, can heal another—lessons learned from her father and grandfather. She watched as several dead or dying bees got tossed out to join the others on the ground. So good at handling their dead. For a moment Luba flashed back to the war, when she had been among the young people forced to dig the deep pits for the mass graves. She shuddered with the weight of the remembrance.

She pulled out the bottle of samohonka, her homemade moonshine, from her apron pocket and poured a little onto each of the graves of her loved ones, allowing herself a small sip before closing it up and putting it back into her pocket.

"Na zdorovya!" she said aloud, then walked toward her house to finish the day's chores. Luba paused to pluck a few choice apples and pears off those trees heavy with beautiful shining fruit. Carrying them home in her apron, she thought about baking a nice apple cake sweetened with honey.

Tonight was the full moon, and that usually brought visitors to her house on the edge of the forest—young men in their second-hand army fatigues looking to stop someplace on their way to the Chornobyl Nuclear Power Plant near Pripyat. Luba wondered if they saw her as some sort of Baba Yaga, a witch guarding secrets they hoped to discover. She did not see *them* as the heroes of any folktale, and they had no idea that their "adventure" would lead them to an unhappy ending.

She felt bad about the first few, until she came to better understand their motivation. These boys were not like the young men of her own generation. No, these boys did not have war or famine or disaster to test their character, so they went looking for death in the "toxic" wilderness of her backyard. Eager to prove that they were even less afraid of radiation poisoning than of police and guards and scientists, they dared each other to drink the muddy waters and eat in the archaic cottages of one of the dozens of old babas who, like herself, had found ways to sneak back into their homes, back into the Exclusion Zone after being forced to evacuate.

Luba felt anger course through her, and she squeezed one of the apples in her newly-healed fist until she felt the skin break and juices spill out over her fingers. She and the other babas had walked on foot for kilometers, crawled under fences and snuck through brambles to reclaim their cottages and gardens and graves. This was *their* land, not the playground of foolhardy young men eager to take advantage of their hospitality and loneliness. The boys' rebellion served no noble purpose, just a desire for the fleeting fame that came from photographs and videos of their "daring adventures."

She steadied herself against an ancient birch tree, the same one she and her sister used to sit beneath as girls. Luba relaxed her rounded back and shoulders against the trunk, released the tension in her face and neck, and closed her eyes to feel the energy of that tree, another sister in this place. She smiled. The babas knew something the young ones did not. These boys had forgotten that there were older and more dangerous things in the ground than buried radioactive buses, and there were creatures much hungrier in the forest than bears and wolves. Let them come. Nature has her own rules, stronger than the folly of these young men.

⊹✳✳⊹

Luba sat beside her table, the only light from a single oil lamp and from the fire burning in the stove. The table was dressed with her finest embroidered tablecloth, delicate red and black cross-stitch from the days when her fingers could more steadily hold the tiny needle and thread. Atop the cloth was a bowl of bright red borscht beside plates of still-steaming potato varenyky and kapusta, cucumbers and tomatoes tossed in dill, sliced salo, homemade pickles, and fresh baked apple cake. Everything must eat, her own Baba used to say. A hungry dog is stronger than a satisfied wolf.

She whispered, "Never let it be said that Luba Ivanova let a guest go hungry."

Outside the window the moon shone over the tops of the trees. Luba waited, hand around her tea cup. She would not touch any food until her guests arrived, and if they did not arrive by midnight, she would pack up the food until the next night. It was only a matter of time. Her home was directly along the most commonly traveled path to Pripyat. One of the scientists had once told her that her tiny cottage even appeared in a popular computer game set in Chornobyl, making it a "tourist destination." Besides, she had seen more strange shadows than usual gathering in the trees the past few nights, and the flickering of so many glowing eyes. The forest was restless. Hungry. Luba smiled and sipped her tea, waiting for the knock.

At ninety years of age, she was patient and unafraid. She had nothing for them to steal: her small pension was well hidden, her food was readily shared, and her body was too old and broken. All she had left was time and memories. And her home.

Home was why she and the other babas had returned to the land that held their mothers and fathers and children. This land was her family, and she was a part of it. They all were, and they knew that the ancestors and nature spirits would ultimately be stronger than the poison that human beings spilled into the air and soil. One by one the babas were taking their turn to feed the land, like the Motherland had always fed them. It was their bond and their promise.

The land must be loved and cared for. It was part of the cycle of life and death. For creation, there must be destruction. Sometimes the sacrifice was gentle and peaceful in one's old bed with honey on their lips; sometimes it was sudden and bloody with bits of bone and teeth left behind.

Luba saw the branches swaying with more force outside her window. The winds had picked up. Perhaps a storm? Or perhaps the creatures in the woods were getting restless, hungry? She had grown up with stories about the dangers: folk tales of hairy backward tricksters deep in the woods, tortured souls of drowned women waiting in rivers, haggard old women in huts on the edges of civilization—

Knock. Knock. Knock.

She jumped.

Knocking, again, but it was against her window, not the door. Luba crossed herself and listened to the noises increasing outside: the howling of the wolves, the owl nearby, the crying of something like a child farther off, and a faint whistling that seemed to be coming closer.

Nature had found ways to reclaim the spaces where men had built towers and fences: trees broke through the concrete, vines wore down brick and mortar, the city and nearby towns were transformed into wilderness faster than Luba would have thought possible.

She thought back to the first waves of young men who wandered into the Zone dressed in shades of green, their faces smeared with paint, their backpacks filled with cameras and video recorders. Like forest creatures come out of the trees, she thought of the first time two men came out of the trees and greeted her. Then a familiar but ancient panic as she remembered so many other young men with a

similar hunger in their eyes who had also come out of the trees—
when Russian and German armies marched through during the war,
leaving broken homes and gardens and women in their wake.

But these were not those. These boys were neither magical creatures nor monsters. They had Ukrainian faces. So much like her son.

The face in her window looked *so* much like her son Mykola
that she initially thought him a ghost and inhaled sharply, crossing
herself. Then as his breath made warm fog on the glass, she jumped
to her feet to answer the door.

"Dobriy vechir, Babusia!" said the young man with a dramatic
bow in her direction. "I see you have dinner set out. Do you have
enough for a poor traveler?"

This one did not barge in like so many others had before him.
He stood on the threshold and waited for her to invite him. He was a
polite one, at least, she thought to herself. Perhaps they would have a
little conversation before his imminent disappearance.

"I do, and you are welcome," she said and gestured for him to
join her at the table. He took off his shoes and then came in, sitting
down at the table opposite her tea cup. Luba took her place across
from him and began to pile food onto his plate, watching his eyes
dart from dish to dish. Still he waited to eat until she had also served
herself, and only then did he take the first bite. She watched him eat
hungrily. It was a hungry kind of night.

"What are you doing here?" she asked in between spoonfuls
of borscht. "Have you come to explore the abandoned town like so
many others before you?"

""Not exactly," the young man answered, straightening his shirt
and smoothing down his trousers. "I'm an artist."

"Is that so?" she asked. She wondered what kind of art. Another
photographer, no doubt, trying to make new money on old images,
since they all went to the same places: the ruins of the Palace of
Culture, the overgrown fairground and rusted Ferris wheel, the

peeling paint on the children's classroom mural, so many broken dolls with gas masks and missing limbs.

Her visitor moved like a cat, long and lean with smooth fluid movement. Luba looked at his hands that seemed rough and strong. At least he was not one of these boys with manicured nails and baby-soft fingers.

"I'm a sculptor," the young man said. "I make things with my hands, and I like to incorporate things from the world around me that I find. I like to create things that most people cannot see. I especially like to go to places that are abandoned, to find secrets there and share them with my art."

Luba nodded and pulled her shawl tighter around her as he talked about sculptures that he'd made from bark and branches, copper and wire. He had a nice voice, and she liked the way he kept looking in her eyes when he spoke. It would have made her blush when she was younger. Back then, Luba would have looked away because her mama always told her that she should play coy with boys. Thankfully she was past such games now. She held the young man's gaze and looked at the way he studied her. It made her smile.

"What are you thinking, Babusia?" the young man asked her.

She did not tell him that she was wondering what manner of beast or spirit would scoop him up after he left her house. She did not say that she hoped his affairs were in order. She never told them. She never warned them. It seemed a betrayal to the forest.

Luba was loyal to the land in a way that these young men could never understand, a promise renewed when she gratefully placed that small handful of dirt into her mouth after returning home. She was of this earth, and the forest was her family—the only one she had left.

"It is nice that you do not chew with your mouth open," she answered. "And you are very well-mannered. Your mama did a good job."

He gave her a grin that would have melted her young girl's heart. "It is nice that you are such a good cook, and you are a very good listener. Your children are lucky."

At that, she put her hand to her chest.

"They were not lucky," she said.

He frowned and reached over to touch her arm.

"I'm sorry," he said. "I didn't mean to make you sad."

She pushed his hand away. Then she reached for her samohonka. "Would you like a taste?" she asked. "For luck?"

He grinned again. "Please."

They first toasted to each other's health. With the second shot they toasted to Ukraine's freedom, and after that to family, then friends, followed by poetry, fine cheese, and the cleverness of foxes. Luba welcomed the warmth that flooded her body with each sip. It was a nicer evening than she'd had in months. The last visitors, three months prior, had been rude and gruff, two large men who ignored her completely and ate like pigs. She was not sorry to see them go, nor sad when she found strips of their shirts braided with hair tied to the tree down the path from her house. She was not sure if the bones she later saw on the riverbank and arranged in neat piles were theirs, but she suspected they were.

"It must be lonely here," the young man said to her. He had pulled a notebook and pencil out from his pack and was softly sketching something. She closed her eyes and listened to the gentle scratching sound. Soon it was joined by soft whistling from outside, still far off but carried closer by the wind.

"It's quiet," Luba said. "But that's not the same as lonely."

Neither one of them spoke for a while.

"What about you?" Luba asked him. "You choose to travel alone, to places where there are few people. Are *you* lonely?"

The young man smiled, and Luba was once more reminded of a cat.

"Like you, I appreciate the quiet," he said. "It helps me to understand that we are never really alone."

The young man sketched, and Luba listened as, all around them, the night seemed to get louder. He did not jump when the wolf howled. He said nothing when there was a crash in the woodpile, and he just kept sketching when the inhuman laughing began not far outside her door. Luba had grown used to all the sounds, but strangers usually found them unsettling at best. One young man several years ago ran out of her home and into the rainstorm leaving behind his camera and bag. She left them on the road the next morning.

"There are many still alive here?" he asked, but it was not really a question.

"A few of us came back home after the evacuation, and many things that live here never left," she said, opening her eyes to stare out the window into the darkness. "Some have changed. A few have died off. Most I recognize, some I do not." She paused remembering her early explorations after returning home. "The worst of all is the Red Forest. A graveyard of trees stripped and stained red that remind me too much of Stalin's skeletal sacrifices during the Holodomor."

"I am haunted by a story I heard on a documentary when I was a boy," the young man said, "about birds living in the Red Forest who fly in and out of holes in the reactor building. I have dreamt of those birds ever since, sketched and sculpted them my entire life. Can you imagine? Such misshapen magical things able to come and go in a place both poisonous and beautiful."

Luba did not have to imagine. Many times she had watched the birds in Pripyat. In the early days she never knew when one of them might suddenly fall to the ground, dead or dying. She always tried to find them and bury them, saying a little prayer for their souls—tiny victims of human folly.

He looked at her. "Of course you know," he said.

Luba fought against her heart softening for this strange young man.

"There is something about those birds that started me on this path," the sculptor said, and Luba didn't know if he meant the path to Pripyat or his choice to be an artist, but she didn't want to interrupt him.

"I think that magical things happen in places of great tragedy," he said. Luba could not argue.

He continued, "Do you know about the large dam that Stalin's troops blew up in 1941? In Zaporizhzhia?"

Luba shook her head. She knew about many things that happened in the war, but mostly only to her and her family and friends.

"As the Nazis were making their way through Ukraine," the sculptor continued, "Stalin's police blew up the hydroelectric dam to slow their advance. But it flooded the nearby villages along Dnipro river and killed tens of thousands of people."

"I am not surprised," she said. "Stalin had so much blood on his hands." Luba looked down at her hands, wriggled her fingers and said a tiny prayer of thanks to the bees.

"I went there and spent several nights sleeping outdoors along the Dnipro river," said the sculptor. "I like to look for things that no one else can see—legends and mythic creatures. I came home to my studio with a bag full of driftwood and wreckage and photographs, and I created a mobile of rusalky dancing in the air. They are terrifying and lovely, drowned souls dancing in pain and pleasure. It's hanging in a gallery in Zaporizhzhia.

"Those nights on the river continue to inspire me—I listened to the rusalky singing and weeping from my tent. I still dream of their songs."

"I think he must be a lucky boy," she said softly.

She had been in the habit of talking to herself for years, but usually only when she was alone. Luba was embarrassed when she realized that she had done so in front of the sculptor.

"I mean *you*," she said, "you must be a lucky boy."

Maybe it would be enough to save him? Maybe he would be the first?

Maybe he would come back. To see her.

"And you must be getting tired," the sculptor said. "I suppose I should leave soon, so that I can reach the city."

She thought again of warning him. Would that be a betrayal? She had made a promise to protect this land and all her creatures. They were all connected, like the bees. Luba wished she could ask another of the babas, but they never spoke overtly of the strange lights that flickered in the trees, or the blood in pools at the bases of the trees, or the wreaths of hair floating on the surface of the river.

To talk about these things felt wrong somehow, so the babas hinted around it instead. They discussed new additions for their bottle trees—a suggestion from one of the scientists, who told them that sliding colored glass bottles onto the branches of a tree close to the home would entice and trap evil spirits. Luba and her friends embraced the tradition with enthusiasm and traded colored bottles the way children once traded marbles: a blue one for a green, an amber one for a red, and so on. They shared flasks of holy water, compared samohonka recipes, and remembered prayers and blessings. On one of their infrequent reunions, they might admire the colored glass gleaming so bright in the sunlight, praising each one for doing its job of trapping evil spirits, daring to ask if there were many more wild animal attacks around than usual. They spoke often about death, but in the language of symbol and story.

"You could stay here," she offered, for the first time, "tonight. My couch is soft and my home is warm, and the night is not kind to strangers." It made her a little sad to think of finding traces of the sculptor in the woods in the weeks to come, a patchwork of skin and bone.

He looked surprised. "I should go, but thank you."

He set down his sketchpad. Luba tried to take a look at what he had been drawing, but he folded his hands on top of it. "You are a most kind and generous hostess."

He grinned at her, and this time she could feel a flush warm her cheeks. Something crashed against the outside wall, and then the sound of nails or claws scratching against wood. Without flinching, he looked around the cabin. "Are you never afraid?"

"No. Not in my home. Not for myself. This place, this land, all of it—it is a part of me. It is in my blood." She poured them each a final shot of samohonka, emptying the bottle. "I was never more afraid than those nights after evacuation, when we didn't know what was happening, when we didn't know whether or not we'd ever be able to return home. Those nights, away from here, I thought I was going to die. I knew that if I stayed there, I would."

She looked into the eyes of this boy who so much resembled her son. "I am old, and I have lived a long and full life. I am not afraid of dying, but I am afraid of dying away from here. That is the only thing I fear."

The lamp on the table turned on and off. It was another sign she had come to recognize—after the loud crash and the laughter always came the flickering light. Luba stood up, feeling the weight of her years in each joint.

"Then I would not worry if I were you, Babusia," said the sculptor, stepping closer to take her arm to steady her. "I do not think there is a force in Hell that could take you from this place."

She envied him the strength and confidence of his youth, so like a tree she might lean against, so certain that he could withstand any storm.

"May I have one last slice of your delicious cake with a little honey to take with me?" the sculptor asked with a dramatic bow.

"You may," she said with a small curtsy, then she packed him a small package. Luba knew it was futile, but perhaps the birds and bears might find his bundle and enjoy the snack.

She walked him to the door and as he stood there against it, she was overwhelmed with the desire to reach over and hug him, as she had long ago hugged her own son. But she couldn't. She felt frozen to the spot, and emotion welled up in her throat and chest and eyes.

"What is it, Babusia?" he asked. "Is there something wrong? Are you hurting?"

On cue, the window rattled and the walls of her home squeaked as if under strong pressure. Luba's chest felt tight and her knees weak.

"Nothing. It's nothing," she said. They stood looking at each other, the sculptor and the baba.

Luba wondered what was out there this night, what would catch him, whether or not he would fight, if he could possibly escape. She wondered what his family would think, if he would be missed, if the world would be worse off without his art. She had a feeling it might. Some people left bigger holes than others. Her own hole would be small, so very small. The holes left by death got smaller the fewer people left behind to remember.

He leaned over and kissed her cheek, and he smelled like the woods, like smoke and wet leaves and the deep brown forest musk that leaked into everything in autumn. "Be well, Babusia. Until our paths cross again."

After that, he turned and walked past her bottle tree and down the path into the woods. Luba quickly closed the door and leaned with her back against it surveying the room. She saw a piece of paper from the sculptor's sketchbook on the table and walked to it, all the while listening for signs of struggle outside. Luba turned the page over and saw a sketch of herself, an old, tired baba sitting beside the fire, and behind her stood all manner of creatures drawn lightly to look like ghosts or shadows, their claws sharp, the teeth pointed and dripping, their fur and clothes and scales splotched with mud or blood. She could not tell if they were standing there to attack her or support her.

Luba felt cold, and the hairs on her neck stood at attention, as if their eyes were actually upon her. Someone was watching. Something was gathering around her, and she started to feel breath coming closer, a movement of air, a low breeze at her ankles. Luba closed her eyes and thought about the song she sang for the bees:

"*... You must surely be ready,*
you must have lived long enough—
a good life full of sweetness.
Is it time to say farewell?"

She heard whistling outside, then screaming followed by laughter, and the sound of boots running up to her threshold. Her doorknob rattled and then stopped.

Luba concentrated on her breathing: in and out, in and out, unable to open her eyes. *It's time,* she said to herself over and over. *At least I'm home. It's time. I'm home. It's time. I'm home.*

A quiet knocking on her door, but Luba did not open her eyes. She could not move and tried to convince herself that it was the sculptor, changing his mind, coming back to stay. But she knew it wasn't. Luba knew that the sculptor was gone. It was not him.

Knock. Knock. Knock.

It's time.

"Kestrel" Travel Agency

Tetyana Adamenko

Турагенція "Боривітер" | Тетяна Адаменко
translated by Gari Light

Appearing to be in his thirties, the young man was unremarkable in the way he looked—tall, with a small beard, also possessing an attractive but somewhat deadpan face. Passing the main entrance to the shopping center, he opened the doors, which were marked with an escalator sign.

In the relative darkness of the staircase, the man observed that the skin under his nails still somewhat glowed in slight green color, and he frowned with discontent: he had to reduce himself to purchasing that fluorescent paint at a toy store, of all places. Products for children are marketed as being chemically safer than similar items "made for adults," but the manufacturers definitely fibbed about it being easy to rinse off.

The ninth floor contained several leased office spaces rented by accountants, a place offering AI adaptation courses, and the hunting travel agency, entitled "Kestrel."

Behind the unremarkable door was a reception area, containing a blonde lady behind the counter, eco-paintings created from moss, somewhat smallish round tables as well as chairs for visitors, which seemed giant. The lad, not glancing at anyone, picked the outermost chair and sat down.

The blonde lady placed a cup of coffee on a saucer exactly in the center of the table and suggested that he wait until one of the managers became available. In an attempt to stay calm, the man went through some local news, which included: information concerning another outbreak of an altitude sickness; a mineball match that had to be canceled; some pilot suing his working clone; the Neon Killer still being at large; and news of a rare magnolia blooming in the botanic garden.

Soon enough the office doors flew open, and bursting out from inside, beaming with a smile, emerged a gentleman whom no one in their right mind would have suspected of the ability to flutter and shine—a certain stout paunch with deep gloomy undulations near his mouth area. The lad read the inscription on the man's stretched T-shirt: "And my heart is big too." He succeeded in hiding his smirk behind that coffee cup. Indeed, and of course, this half-a-brain dude had his little desires, probably as primitive as his own. The assistant rushed to intercept him, but the man scowled (the lines on his face finally formed in their proper order) and pushed her away with a muscular hand, containing some rough scars between the implants.

"I will tell my brother too!" he announced in a deep low voice, while already at the exit. "As soon as we gather some coffers, we will reserve a hunt together with him! See you!"

"See you soon!"

"Just savage hunting, of course! Such creatures could care less for a great adventure of the spirit, their goal is to have plenty of gore with flesh and blood!"

"Mr. Sych?" the assistant approached the lad's chair. "Mr. Kestrel is ready to see you now."

The lad judiciously placed the cup on the saucer and followed the assistant.

Another compulsively comfortable chair awaited him in Mr. Kestrel's office. The man himself turned out to be quite a young cheeky guy with round blue eyes.

"Good day, good day!" he winked and asked, "May I inquire as to how you found out about the agency? This inquiry is, of course, solely for the benefit of our marketing department. Please be assured that everything is confidential."

Mr. Sych did not quite fancy this question. He straightened up in his chair and stressed, "My wish is to be receiving assurances with respect to a few issues, and only then to make any decisions as such! You do realize that there is not much trust as far as you are concerned!"

"I do, indeed, understand that," Mr. Kestrel swiftly calmed down. "You may just reply as it is: private time travel tourism is a business with known high risks."

"Well, you see, no one really wants to find out that he is, say, married to his own sister, upon his return," muttered Mr. Sych.

"Oh, you would be surprised. But despite some complications, the idea is still pretty splendid ... Sorry, you did want to ask something?"

"Do tell me the key thing that I need to know: Would I be able to get to the beginning of the twentieth century?"

"Well, our spy drones are indeed conveniently placed in every century and every decade of each century, ranging from the times of Nero all the way to the end of the twenty-first. The beginning of the twentieth is a great choice! Do you fancy the Belle Epoque or perhaps the Roaring Twenties? Or, or maybe even, the First World War, the one which took place on the surface?"

"Roaring twenties," whispered Mr. Sych.

"A great option, indeed—and quite a viable one financially! Many people want to travel to the times of the Revolution and the civil war, few people are interested in the times of mid-twenties with their 'NEP—new economic policies,' coinciding with the appearance of jazz, hence, the demand is not overwhelming—"

"It has nothing to do with the economy!" Mr. Sych suddenly blushed. "I genuinely love that era! And please, no NEP times ... I would, actually, rather go to the United States."

"Yes, of course. Please do not worry. Folks come to us to make their dreams come true, and we certainly understand that."

"And it is definitely safe, right?"

"Well, if you meticulously follow the ecology of that particular time. Both for yourself, and for the world in general. In that case, not a single arrow on the instruments of the feds would move."

Mr. Sych nodded with somewhat reserved approval.

"Do you recall that first advertisement of ours? 'Hunting the Exxxx-t-inct!'" Mr. Kestrel howled suddenly.

"Creatures from the past who must perish in any case . . ."

"Indeed! But we developed the idea creatively. We chose a different game and a different target audience. And we deal only with unsolved crimes. Given that such cases were never solved anyway, there is no peril of changing the past. You do recognize what the difference is: whether the case was not solved because they could not interpret the evidence correctly, or because they could not find any evidence?"

"Any evidence?"

"None. We will activate spy drones during your hunt, and they would remove every molecule of your DNA from any evidence. You do not really need to be careful. You may act freely and with true inspiration."

"And what's with that other hunter? Will he not change his behavior when he realizes that a victim has been taken from him?"

"Only not in the era of gangster wars."

"So, that's how it is . . . Well, so, uhm, yes. And yet . . ." the lad fell silent and appeared to have plunged into thought.

"Does something bother you?"

"How strictly should I follow the script?" blurted out Mr. Sych. "I am not at all interested in mimicking someone else's work!"

"Only in general. For example, if the body was dismembered, then the order of dismemberment and the choice of parts is up to you. However, the very fact of dismemberment—as described in newspaper headlines—must be observed."

"And do you have an option when the victim, say, was never found, and there were no headlines?"

"Of course, there is such an option. But most clients choose cases that have been covered in the press."

"Illuminating . . ." Mr. Sych repeated and finally dared to state, "I want to spend time with a radium girl!"

"A radium girl?"

"Have you not heard? Those were the watch factory workers. They painted the dials with radium paint. At that time, everyone thought that radium was useful. There were even radium tonics, offered for insane amounts of money."

"Unbelievable!"

"Imagine, young girls—they wore their dressiest garb to work to collect radium dust and then would glow in the dark at parties. They also painted their lips and eyebrows with radium. Imagine: jazz is playing while they dance . . . Strong, beautiful, energetic, and actually condemned to death."

"Quite an impressive sight, indeed."

"Yes," Mr. Sych swallowed, "I wish to—"

"Hold on, please," Mr. Kestrel raised his hand, "I did make a request—all the radium girls died from the poisoning effects. None of them are suitable for our event. And yet . . ."

"Come on, will you not indulge your client? I will pay!"

Mr. Kestrel sighed sympathetically.

"Listen, they're going to die anyway, so what's the difference? I might not even complete the deed if that matters so much! I would only like to see the girl in the dark, hold her in my arms, give her a bit of life pleasure . . . Imagine, there is a radioactive girl, and while we are making love, the radium is simultaneously killing her from the inside . . ."

"Unfortunately, it seems that you misunderstood the goals of our agency," Mr. Kestrel shook his head. "We do not create wholly original scenarios. Generally, we follow the course of history. You are talking about a remarkably interesting creative variation of the plot, but such an attempt to influence the past is absolutely beyond the acceptable parameters. We are concerned about the ecology of time, so to speak. May we instead suggest any other instances of events from the era that you may be interested in?"

"I will pay for that risk! I have the money! You cannot even imagine how much money I have!"

"The risk of this kind may not be paid for with any amount of money, as doing so would endanger the work of our entire agency. My apologies. We could try finding some analogue for you which may—"

"No, you absolutely cannot! Damn you, I need a fulfillment of a dream, not some cheap imitation! That I can organize myself!"

"I do hope that you may change your mind. Our aim is to always be helpful."

"No, it's not! You wasted my time, thank you! Goodbye!"

Mr. Sych did not even slam the door of the travel agency, but on his way out, his legs shook so badly that he had to sit down on the first available decent couch inside the food court.

Before that, he had never even thought about the impossible, attempting to gratify his desires on whatever material was available, and suddenly that advertisement appeared ... It assured satisfaction so discreetly and convincingly, with a guarantee of complete confidentiality ... And he permitted himself to hope—as if a person who, while looking at the shadows on the wall, suddenly believed that he could look back and perhaps see, realize the truth ... He activated the viewing of the archive, but the photos of girls with glowing lips caused him to have an acute nausea attack. They appeared to be mere dolls, just poorly sewn dolls, stuffed with cotton wool visible from all the cracks ... incapable of illuminating his life, even if they were to be painted ...

As soon as the door closed behind "Mr. Sych", an assistant burst into the office.

"Levchik, it's him, my God, it's him! Damn it, I didn't think anything would come of that plot of yours!"

"I already sent a tip to our friends," nodded "Mr. Kestrel," actually named Lev Grossman. "They compared matches of him through their databases and now, as far as I understand it, they are preparing an arrest warrant. They promised to mention us in the press release if it all works out!"

"That is a game changer! After that, we will forget about doing such nonsense as lawsuits with work clones and digital betrayals! We will be doing real stuff from here on! Listen, how did it occur to you to hunt him down like that?"

"Well, when I noticed that our suspect has an estate as well as a yacht, both styled in Art Deco and also, he has the largest private collection of Tamara de Lempicka paintings, I thought: here is a person who dreams of being in the past ... and somehow it clicked and all came together. After that, it is really a matter of technique: to organize an online advertising campaign targeted solely for him, but in such a way that he would deem that he really is a part of the club. And Omelyukh played the client brilliantly, didn't he? Oh, you must tell him!"

"And he came, he went for it!" Katya sang victoriously in an unexpectedly pleasant low contralto. "The Neon Killer!"

"A radium killer, as it turned out," Lev corrected her, while taking out a bottle of whiskey from under the table.

And while they drank whiskey from the porcelain cups of Mr. Grossman's mother, who had agreed to lend them as a convincing touch of true luxury, Mr. Sych (actually Mr. Andriy Shcherbak) attempted to get up from the couch and leave the mall but couldn't.

Shcherbak's heart broke just over a glass of watered-down cocoa.

He sobbed in the noisy hall, as would an individual when castles, existing only in his dreams, first let air through their gates and then scattered in the wind.

Of course, as time went on, he was actually quite flattered that he became an indirect inspiration to the erection of a monument to the radium girls in the city where the watch factory once existed.

He would have genuinely wished to lay flowers on that monument in their honor, but his diligent preoccupation with mandatory work at the Zhovti Vody uranium deposits did not allow for such a visit for a while. Even though supporters with whom Shcherbak actively corresponded did so on his behalf—repeating the deed every year.

The fluorescent paint was finally moved into the category of "good for adults".

In his mind, Shcherbak regretted that his fans were too few in number and not nearly creative enough.

Mr. Grossman was quietly happy about it. These simple, chancy folks, the fans of a rapist serial killer, scared him perhaps even more than the murderer himself. However, his current hunt for a new criminal was a good distraction from those disturbing thoughts.

Battle of the Gods
Svitlana Taratorina

Битви богів | Світлана Тараторіна
translated by Tetiana Savchynska

Amage didn't remember much about that awful night. Her father was screaming, just like all the other men, while Kastor clung to the mast, praying to Poseidon. A few hours before Helios passed away, they finally caught a glimpse of the coveted Ktenunt Bay. Her father wanted to pay homage to the gods, but they refused to accept it. Darkness fell over Pontus. The winds were fighting over control of the boat. Black, winged horses of the Sea Lord hit the shipboards. The mast screeched. The boat heeled over. Amage would have been washed over the side if it weren't for her father's strong arms. He grabbed her by the shoulders and shoved her into the chest under the sheepskin. Targ was already in there, crying. Amage clung to the cover and told her brother to pray. The amphoras were knocking against the sides of the chest. The dark water was pouring through the cracks. Terrified and deafened by her pounding heart, Amage could barely hear the sounds of the storm. She was praying even though she knew no one would hear her. The gods punished them for their arrogance.

Once, an oracle had told her that she would become the queen of a distant land, and her mother fervently believed it. Her mother used to be a slave and felt guilty because Amage, as a half-breed, could only hope to marry someone equally dirty-blooded or become a slave herself. But no one would want to take on a girl so wild, her nanny used to say, even with a surcharge. Amage had an indomitable spirit and always completed her mother's phrase "the main thing is to survive" with "survive and take revenge on everyone who wronged us." Numerous paternal aunts never failed to remind her that she was a half-breed and a disgrace to their phila[1]. That's why her revenge list was always open-ended.

But her mother didn't manage to survive. She died giving birth to Targ. Her father never recovered. He kept talking about the marvelous Chersonesus, where they could begin their life anew. For several years, he had been putting aside some money for the trip. No one from the phila was willing to lend him money for such a ridiculous idea. Euxinus Pontus[2] was the curse of their family. It had already claimed all of his father's older brothers and once brought a ship with Amage's mother to their shores. Eventually, her father put together a boat and set sail.

But the aunts were probably right. The sea showed its strength. Amage was sick from the fear and the rolling. The boat jumped up on yet another roller. The girl was forced into the side of the chest. Underneath her, Targ let out a faint cry. And then the boat smashed into the rocks.

Amage opened her eyes and almost went blind from the bright sun. Sharp pebbles dug into her back. Her lips were parched, and her skin tightened from the salt. A crab was crawling across her arm. Her body grew so heavy that Amage had to strain all her muscles to throw off the shameless creature.

She squeezed her palms several times and suddenly realized why she felt a nagging pain in her chest. Targ's hand was gone. Overcoming her weariness, Amage got up. It was a mistake. A man's voice boomed somewhere above her head. She couldn't make out the words. The man barely looked human. His face was covered with tattoos, and

---

1   Phila (Ancient Greek: φυλή)— a family union, a community.

2   Latin for the Black Sea.

animal skin hung around his shoulders. Amage tried to scream, but her throat let out only a cough and a trickle of water. She then scraped up a handful of stones and threw them at the monster with her last bit of strength. A shadow of surprise flashed in his eyes. He didn't expect resistance. The man scooped her up like a child and threw her over his shoulders. The stench was suffocating. He stank like an animal. Trying to fight back, Amage sank her teeth into his big, hairy ear, and the monster hit her on the head. The world went dark again.

Amage opened her eyes for the second time when water touched her lips. Her father's face was hovering over her, and later, Targ came running to her, too. Amage thought she was in Elysium and would finally see her mom again. But a minute later, she closed her eyes in disappointment. Almost everyone was rescued. Only Kastor was taken by the sea. Her father said this was the price they had to pay for surviving. Kastor was the one who talked to the gods.

"Now, the gods are definitely not going to hear us," Amage said, looking around the place where they found themselves. It was a deep stone pit with a round entrance high above their heads. The shadows stirred. A tree with strange leaves growing over the pit swayed. It crossed Amage's mind that the world above them must be quite unwelcoming.

"Where are we?"

"I don't know," her father said, holding Targ close to him. The boy was frightened by his sister's words. "We are not too far from our gods. This is definitely Chersonesus. Maybe we were swept north and ended up in the lands of Issedons[3] or Hyperboreans[4]? I will offer them a ransom. Everything will be fine."

---

3   The Issedones were one of the most ancient Iranian nomadic ethnic groups, known at least since the 7th century B.C. According to Herodotus, they practiced ritual cannibalism.

4   The Hyperboreans (Greek for "those who live beyond the northern wind") were mystical immortal people who lived in the northern country of Hyperborea, basking in the sunshine.

A bruise swelled on his forehead. It was clear that he didn't believe his own words.

"What if this is the land of Cyberians?" One of the sailors whispered, remembering stories about the mystical people.

Targ burst into tears.

"Don't frighten the children," her father snapped. "These people have human heads. And human language. While the Cyberians have the heads of dogs."

Her father was wrong.

They sat in the pit for three circles of the sun. Twice a day, the savages brought down stale water and food. Usually, it was fish, and once they brought them tainted meat. Her father yelled and begged them to talk. He promised them all the treasures of the civilized world. But the barbarians did not respond. The captives could smell fire and hear the banging of tools. Her father tried to convince them these brutes were not using metal tools. He also prayed. Every night, even when he thought Amage did not see him.

"Is it true that the gods can't hear us?" Targ whispered, frightened. He had amber eyes just like his mother's. Amage's eyes were green, like her father's. Her brother stole even their mother's eye color. Amage's mother had made her promise she would take care of Targ. Her newborn brother had been screaming. The midwife had wiped her hands and turned away. On her mother's ashen face, there had been nothing but eyes. Underneath her, a pool of blood kept spreading. Amage had never seen so much blood.

"She didn't die in vain," her aunts had said. It was the first and the last time they said something nice about their brother's wife.

If the gods had bothered to ask Amage, she would have told them to keep her mother and take this weak boy instead. But they decided otherwise.

The next morning, the savages took away the pale boy named Arkont. He, just like her father, was obsessed with seeing Chersonesus.

Throughout their entire journey, her father had joked that Arkont could become her husband if he worked hard and obeyed the gods.

On the tenth circle of the sun, the sound of drums reached their pit. Someone suggested that the savages were celebrating something. Her father's face darkened. All the adults had already gotten seriously ill. Bosp's leg, broken during the storm, had turned black. For several days, he suffered from a fever and then died. Amage's father started crying again. He begged for the young man's dead body to be taken away. He knew they couldn't understand him, but he couldn't stop yelling.

A shadow fell over the pit, and then the savages lowered a large basket. Her father and the others shoved Bosp into it. Instead of coins, her father put two flat stones on the dead man's eyes. That was all he could do for him.

But the savages didn't stop there. Lifting the body, they gestured for others to climb into the basket as well. The sky was strikingly blue. Amage cowered. The savages tied everyone's hands and led them down a narrow path.

The village where the savages lived sat on a high stone shore. The waves were crashing below.

The houses where the savages lived were shabby, and so were their few sheep. Near one of the houses, Amage saw a woman with a baby in her arms. The baby was dead, but the woman kept rocking him.

The same man in animal skin greeted them. Now, he was wearing a pointed hat and holding a short iron sword in his hand. Amage was surprised to discover that he was the only one in the entire village with bright eyes. His eyes were green, just like hers.

The man shouted something to the others, and the captives were dragged to the cliff.

Behind the village, a temple hovered on the cliff's edge like a swallow's nest. Its marble columns were strikingly white, while the metope and frieze were decorated with bright colors. The temple was so unlike anything she had seen in the village that Amage almost screamed. The savages had captured a Hellenic city. They had killed the locals and desecrated the house of the gods. It meant they had no chance to survive. She felt her father's hand on her shoulder. With his other hand, he covered Targ's eyes. Amage took a few more steps. Only then did she realize what had terrified her father so much. Around the portico, heads were mounted on tall sticks. Most of them were already decomposing, with their tongues hanging out and their eyes poked out. While some of them had not even lost their color. These heads used to belong to Arkont and other men from their boat.

The lights were out. And for a moment, Amage thought the temple was empty. The savages had desecrated it, and the gods had left. But then, a tall figure dressed in white appeared from beyond the columns. Time had spared no effort. The skin on the woman's arms and face was laced with deep wrinkles. But her underlined eyes were glowing, and her forehead was red with henna. Dark, unfamiliar locks rested in strange curls on her head. Strands of gray hair peeked from underneath. She was holding a small statue of a naked barbarian goddess with full breasts and curvy hips.

The priestess approached the girl, grabbed her by the chin, and looked her in the eyes. The old lady smiled. Amage's skin grew ice-cold. The priestess then said something to the man with the animal skin. He frowned but waved his hand. Amage was separated from the group. She heard Targ sob. The man in the animal skin made some more small vowel sounds. The priestess objected. She was almost whispering. But eventually, she agreed. The captives were taken to the temple.

The barbarians lit torches. Long shadows licked the dark floor. Inside, the temple seemed like the temenos[5] of the goddess Artemis

---

5   Temenos (Ancient Greek: τέμενος) is a sacred area dedicated to a particular deity in the ancient Greek religion. It was believed that in the temenos, a person could feel the presence of this deity.

if it weren't for the wild, strange statue in the middle. The statue was wooden and dark. Its legs made a single column decorated with strange pictures. The goddess's breasts were covered with dozens of taut nipples that looked like a bunch of grapes. The air around the statue was chilling, the sanctuary smelled of salt and herbs, which barely masked the stench of rotten meat. Amage thought of the heads on the sticks around the porch and closed her eyes.

Targ and the men from their group were lined up in front of the statue. The priestess began to sing a hymn and picked up a bowl of diluted henna.

"Orthia, Lygodesma, mother of the Taurians[6]," she said, touching their faces with her smeared hand.

She speaks our language, Amage thought with excitement, but then the excitement gave way to fear. *The temple must have been desecrated long before the barbarians came here. The goddess whom the priestess addresses in her songs doesn't belong to my father's land.* The smell of incense made Amage dizzy. It had been so long since she had eaten properly and heard hymns that she was almost ready to forget where she was.

The men moved a stone slab at the foot of the statue. Amage thought she heard the sound of waves coming from the well. And then a knife flashed in the priestess's hands. Before Amage knew it, the old woman had slit the throat of the first captive man. The guard in the animal skin caught the victim and pulled him closer to the statue. As black blood splattered on the wood and flowed into the pit, Amage heard a scream. It came out of her mouth. She tried to run to her father, but someone's strong hands held her by the forearms. She was wriggling, biting, and cursing everyone around her, but the person holding her was as steady as a rock. The leader of the savages, the man with eyes just like hers, was whispering something. He was

---

6   Orthia and Lygodesma are alternative names for the goddess Artemis.

trying to calm her down. Amage wasn't listening. Targ's sobbing and the men's dying curses were pulsating in her head. All this time, the priestesses kept cutting throats with her knife. Her white tunic grew red with blood, and her eyes were blazing. When Amage's father and Targ were the only ones left standing before the statue, the priestess was still calling out the names of her goddess. Amage could no longer scream. Her throat hurt, and her chest was bursting. She just wanted this nightmare to end. The priestess looked first at the man and then at the girl. Her hand dropped in exhaustion. She was also breathing heavily. The woman was old, very old. She took a few slow steps towards Amage and sat next to her. The girl noticed the woman's worn teeth.

"My name is Tavropola, and I have an offer for you. You can either become the priestess of the goddess or her offering," the woman said in Amage's language. "It's up to you to decide." The priestess then looked at Amage's father. The girl realized what kind of choice she was being asked to make. Her life in exchange for his. Her father's eyes were glistening with tears. Amage looked at her brother.

"What about Targ? What will happen to him?"

"He will stay with the savages."

Amage turned to look at her father.

"Remember the promise you made to your mother. You must do anything to keep Targ alive."

Amage nodded. She was ready to make any promise for this torture finally to be over.

Years later, Amage tried to forget this moment. She tried to convince herself that the priestess would have killed him anyway. And Amage's decision wouldn't have made any difference. Her father screamed. And then his blood poured into the hole in the floor.

❀

Amage stayed in the temple. Targ was taken away by the leader of the savages, whose name was Foant. For many days and nights, Amage sat in a room under the temple and recalled that terrible night. Apart from her and the priestess, there was only one other person with them—an ugly servant with a missing eye, ear, and part of the nose. He always hid his left hand in the folds of his clothes, so it took Amage a while to discover that he had no wrist. The servant didn't speak Amage's language, but he regularly brought food and even wine. Amage recognized the taste of the drink from her father's boat. Women from the village brought her mare's milk, sharp cheese made from the same milk, mussels, salted fish, and even chopped seaweed and left the food on the stairs. Through a narrow window, the girl could see the sick and sunken eyes of the women who brought her gifts. The savages were sharing the last bits of their food with her.

"They are starving. Their children are dying. They are asking the goddess to help them." Tavropola said, smiling through her crooked, worn teeth. "They aren't from here, just like you. After losing to his brother, Foant took the people from his share of the tribe to look for a better land."

Foant had killed everyone who lived near the temple and brought blood offerings to the goddess. He had decided that then the goddess would protect them, just as the gods of the wild steppe tribes did.

"What a fool," Tavropola said through a coughing fit. "He thinks she's so easy to buy: it's enough to come, conquer, pour blood into her womb, and the goddess is his. But she is the mother of this land. She gave birth to it." Tavropola's eyes flashed with frantic sparks. The priestess brought her pale, wrinkled lips closer to Amage. "When your blood comes for the first time, I will show you the greatest treasure of this temple. Something that can give you true power over this land. Something that could give you power."

"When you dic, will I become the new priestess of the goddess?"

Tavropola rubbed her forehead, red with henna, and shook her head uncertainly. It seemed as if she had just begun to realize that Amage's arrival meant her end. The priestess looked at her fingers, red as if stained by blood, and touched the notch below Amage's neck.

"You've got fire and anger in you. You'll be a good fit. Maybe."

The priestess taught Amage hymns. They were so ancient that the girl could make out only some words. On moonlit nights, Tavropola would make her undress, smear herself with henna, and perform strange movements near the statue of the goddess. The priestess would play the timpani, inhale the smoke of incense, and her eyes would become covered with a blissful haze. Amage tried to ask her what the rituals meant, but the old woman only put a crooked finger to her lips and hissed as if conspiring. She didn't know the answer either. Amage thought that a long time ago, Tavropola had been forced to serve the goddess much like Amage herself now. And at some point, the priestess really started to believe in the goddess. "I wonder what happened before she went crazy?" Amage thought as she performed meaningless movements near the dark statue once again, the stain of her father's blood still near its foundation.

But no matter how much she danced, the goddess remained silent. And worst of all, Amage could not hear her father either. One night, her grief and despair changed into anger. It was her father who had brought them here and thrown them into the arms of these barbarians. And then he abandoned them, just like the gods did. "The most important thing is to survive," her mother used to say, and instead, she extracted from Amage the promise to take care of Targ. *How can these two things be reconciled?* Amage thought angrily, taking in the view from her window.

The temple was surrounded by a cliff on three sides. Below, the foam licked the sharp stones. The only way out was through the village. Foant's men were always guarding this path. On several occasions, she made an attempt to find out about Targ's fate, but each time, the silent guards stopped her.

Amage rummaged through the temple in search of the goddesses' mysterious treasure and even tried to elicit some hints from the servant, but he pretended not to understand her.

"When I become the priestess, I will kill you first," the girl promised. "Sakatevo!" Amage had overheard this word from the women bringing her gifts. She didn't understand what it meant but hoped it was something offensive.

"Sakatevo means 'crooked'," the servant explained, and smiled for some reason. She was not the only one learning a foreign language. "The goddess takes what she wants," he said, pointing with his stump to his empty eye socket and, with his healthy arm, handed her a black-and-white board. On top of it, there was a bag of round stones. Amage recognized the game. It was a barbarian game her mother had taught her. Nine holes were carved into the board, each with nine stones—korgools. By making the right calculations, one player had to get all of the opponent's stones. While they were on the boat, Amage taught Targ the rules. The game required the ability to count and concentrate, but he mastered it surprisingly quickly.

The following day, they started playing toguz korgool. And on the same day, she silently addressed the goddess for the first time: "If you really exist, if you hear me, make yourself shown. Prove that this is your fury and not Tavropola's. Show me your power. Help me save Targ."

After a warm fall, winter came. Amage had never felt so cold in her life. In the morning, a thin white veil covered the ground. And one day, ash started falling from the sky. It was transparent and weightless, melting at the first touch. Tavropola said it was snow.

The villagers started digging pits. They were burying the dead. Foant frowned. No more new heads appeared near the goddess's house. The priestess no longer cared. Tavropola knew that her life was coming to an end. The goddess would take everyone.

Thanks to the servant, Amage could now understand the savages' language. The woman who kept bringing mare's milk and roots said that Targ was alive. He was being kept in a pit near Foant's house, where they fed him well and told him the story of the tribe. He didn't cry and was happy with everything. Amage was overcome with bitterness: while all she cared about was how to save her brother, he was being prepared to become a healer or leader.

On one of the coldest days, when she was shivering in her cell and even animal skins did not keep her warm, Pontus took pity on her. They found a boat with poor fishermen washed up on their shore. The goddess received fresh blood. And Tavropola received the long-awaited proof that Amage had become a woman. The girl stole some blood from the altar and showed the priestess a crimson stain on her chiton.

Tavropola sniffed the stain and wrinkled her nose in disbelief. Wrinkles spread across her face like cracks on frozen water, but Amage didn't look away. If she was destined to become a priestess of the goddess, she deserved a drop of the offering.

That night, Sakatevo came to get her. In the shadows of the oil torch, he looked like a hideous faun. Amage felt a cold shiver going down her spine. What if her deception had been exposed, and the priestess decided that she was unworthy? Then Amage had only one way out: her head would end up on the stick, and her blood would flow into the goddess's well. The girl rose from the mat. She was so weak her legs were trembling.

"Where are you taking me?"

"*Chrisni liko*," Sakatevo whispered and touched the hollow on her sunken chest. His dark eyes flashed oddly.

He led her to a big hall flooded with the pale glow of the moon. The stone slab from the goddess's womb had been removed. Tavropola's eyes were darting frantically. Amage remembered the night of her father's death and saw the flash of the knife hidden in the folds of the priestess's tunic. The servant's grip around the girl's forearm tightened. Amage clenched her teeth. It was too arrogant of the priestess to assume that the two of them could defeat her.

"You lied to me. The goddess told me."

"She needs me!" Amage made a desperate attempt to stall for time.

"You don't believe in her," Tavropola said, her voice growing bitter. She reached the statue and ran the tip of her knife along an invisible hollow. "But the strange thing is that you aren't wrong. She does need you." A secret opening revealed itself on the goddess's foot. The priestess pressed a lever. In the depths of the goddess's womb, something was screeching. The servant reached down and took from the pit something wrapped in leather. He then unwrapped the package with great care and handed it to the priestess.

"*Chrisni liko.*"

The woman stretched out both arms as if she were about to embrace a child. Amage glanced from one inspired face to another, surprised to see a cradle inlaid with gold—*chrisni liko. If this is the gift from the goddess,* Amage thought, *it's no wonder she summons lunatics to her service.*

The oath to guard the Golden Cradle of the goddess gave Amage relative freedom. Even Sakatevo now looked at her with respect. She began to go out into the village, accompanied by him. Winter forced the men to spend all their days in the steppe searching for prey. But all Amage's attempts to talk to the women proved futile. They always hid, frightened. And after she offered a girl with a tight stomach a dried plum from their gifts, they began to hide the children *as if it were better to throw away what the goddess hadn't eaten than to give it to the hungry.* Yet she did manage to see the place where Targ was being held, and her throat tightened at the sight. It was the same pit where she and her father had been kept. This meant he wasn't being trained to become a leader or a healer. Even if she were lucky and got there without being spotted, she couldn't pull him out of there on her own.

"Hold on a little longer, and I will come to save you," Amage whispered, pretending to repeat another meaningless hymn, and caught Tavropola's angry glare. The priestess had told her several times to stop thinking about the past.

"You swore to the goddess and the Golden Cradle to forget your past life!"

How contradictory it was to her father's dying wish that she "do anything to keep Targ alive."

Amage did not doubt that the priestess had instructed Sakatevo to watch her. But after growing up under the watchful eye of numerous aunts, it wasn't that hard to trick him. On the third day of the Saturnalia, when Foant's group returned to the village, Amage gave the servant milk infused with the potion Tavropola used to make her incense and slipped out of the temple unnoticed.

The savages were celebrating the holiday in their own way: lighting bonfires, eating smelly meat, and drinking the spoiled mares' milk. But, as her aunts used to say, celebrations always end the same for all men—with a drunken sleep. Amage entered Foant's house in the darkest hour of the night. The dawn was near. Even the late-night drunkards were sleeping with their noses on their empty plates.

The chief was sitting at the table as if he had been waiting for her to come. With the skins on his shoulders, he looked like a mountain. There were several empty bowls in front of him. Foant wasn't moving. Amage wondered if he could sleep with his eyes open. The chief blinked and gestured for her to come up to him.

"I want a deal! Your tribe is falling apart. I know how to help," the girl blurted.

"Are you speaking for yourself or your goddess, little priestess?" Foant found an unfinished bowl and poured its contents down his throat. For a moment, Amage was conflicted. Wouldn't it be better to lie and say that it was the goddess who sent her here? But Foant interrupted her deliberations.

"You can't hear her, can you?"

"I'm not fit to become a priestess. The goddess does not speak to me."

"Or you're just not able to hear her. You're only alive because you have to become a priestess. Why else would we need a girl like you around here?"

Amage kept staring into Foant's eyes, uncertain like spring ice, for what felt like an eternity.

A spasm seized her throat, but she managed to resume talking.

"Because I know where Tavropola is hiding the goddess's treasure. It will allow you to tame this land and save your people. But you must let me and my brother go."

"The Golden Cradle," Foant said, surprising her again. "I've heard of it. But the old woman wouldn't show me where she kept it. Do you really love your brother so much?"

Why is he asking? Amage wondered angrily. And then she remembered Foant's story. He betrayed his brother. He wanted to seize power, burned the temple, and was cursed by his own family. What could he know about being loyal to a brother?

"Yes. No. I made a promise," she heard herself say instead.

"That's what I thought." Foant's green eyes flashed. "Deal. I'll take a look at this Golden Cradle, and you will get your brother."

"We are not alike, you dirty savage," Amage whispered, leaving the chief's house. She felt as if a worm had crawled into her heart. It was screaming in her aunts' voices that she was a traitor and that the gods and the souls of the dead would not forgive her. But Amage wasn't listening to them. If she and Targ had to betray the goddess in order to survive, well, it meant the savages and Tavropola had forced her to do it. The girl looked at the star, pale in the early morning light, and smiled. The priestess was as old and helpless as her star. And in this world, only those who knew how to take advantage of someone else's helplessness would survive.

There was always a full moon on the Saturnalia. In a few days, the traditional goddess festival was supposed to begin. It was celebrated on every first day of a new month. Tavropola was joyous. After his last hunt, Foant had given her several captives. This feast was supposed to be special.

On the day of the celebration, Amage could hardly wait for it to get dark. At dusk, Tavropola started burning the potion. The temple was filled with a heavy stench. When it got dark, Foant came, bringing along several men. They were standing behind the columns, and Amage couldn't see them clearly. But as she moved near the black statue, she always felt the chief's gaze.

Finally, Tavropola opened the goddess's womb. Those who would be offered to the goddess were brought into the temple. Amage's head was throbbing. Her eyes were watering, and the potion made her sick, but she forced herself to look. Tavropola kept slitting the captives' throats and pouring the sacrificial blood on the statue and into the womb. A familiar frenzied smile crossed her face. She greedily licked her lips, sucking up the drops of blood, and crouched over the hole. Then she looked at Amage. The ritual didn't involve the raising of the Golden Cradle. Amage had explained enough to Foant so he could do it himself. But the girl could not find him between the columns. The mechanism inside the well screeched. Amage heard footsteps along the walls. Several new torches dispersed the darkness. Men in skins entered the temple. They were carrying stretchers. Amage rushed to get a better look at the procession and see whom they were carrying, but someone caught her. A big, calloused hand covered her mouth. She recognized Foant's smell.

A crescent moon appeared from behind the clouds, as if the goddess herself wanted to see what was happening. The smell of salt in the temple grew stronger. Tavropola unwrapped the Golden Cradle and put it at the foot of the statue. The men brought the stretchers. Amage could finally see who was strapped there. Targ's eyes and lips were stitched shut, and his skin was covered with drawings. . Amage didn't want to believe it, but as the light fell on his chest, it was still rising and falling. Sakatevo put the boy into the Golden Cradle, and Tavropola marked him with a drop of blood under his neck. Then they let go of the rope, and Targ flew into the well. Amage felt dizzy.

The priestess was shouting something about the goddess's will, frantic, "You have to sacrifice your future for the sake of the goddess! Forget everything that happened before tonight."

Amage heard a terrible splash, and then a flash of warm, dawn-like light burst from the well. Sparkling specks danced in its rays. The pink crystals resembled snow, which, by the goddess's will, was coming not from the sky but from the ground. It was so wrong that Amage froze in Foant's arms. A few shiny specks fell on her forehead, and it felt like her mother's farewell touch. The snow tasted like salt.

Voices flooded the temple. They were telling hundreds of stories of the past and the future. Strange names, lives, and deaths burst into Amage's ears and demanded to be heard. Some shouted, others whispered. Most of the words were incomprehensible, but one voice sounded like a verdict. It belonged to Targ.

The men pulled out the Golden Cradle and set it carefully on the floor. The light exploded for the last time. The walls shook. For a brief moment, Amage saw the savages transforming, the animal skins merging with their bodies, their bones twisting. The ropes in their hands were crumbling like flakes of salt. Tavropola raised her hands to the statue, and her wig slipped off, revealing horns on her scabby skull.

Foant loosened his grip. Amage felt a knife on his belt, grabbed it, and dashed toward the priestess. She was a step away from the old woman when she slipped on a puddle of blood. Tavropola fixed her gaze on Amage. Her eyes were full of surprise and ridicule. Suddenly, an axe penetrated the old woman's skull. It was Foant's doing. The priestess flailed her arms like a dazed bird and slid onto the floor. "You, you must come up here," Amage heard Tavropola say in her last gasp. Foant wiped his axe on the edge of his cloak and approached the girl. She pressed her body into the column and held the stolen knife before her.

The light became familiar again. The bloodied priestess lay at the foot of the statue. A little further away was the Golden Cradle with Targ in it. It almost seemed like he was sleeping if it weren't for his stitched eyes.

"Why didn't you stop her? Why did she do that to him?"

Amage was shaking. She stood up and kicked the priestess with her toe to make sure she was dead.

"The goddess has left this place a long time ago. She is either dead or asleep. Or, perhaps, the priestess just invented her. That's why this land needs a new God." Foant put away his axe and stood next to the girl. "This is a chance for my tribe to have a protector who knows only us. I've come a long way, little priestess. I have given a lot. And I don't want to leave this place. We need hope and our own god," Foant repeated.

"Your own god?" Amage asked in disbelief. She couldn't understand what the chief was saying.

"You will be the one to talk to him," Foant said, picking up the Golden Cradle. In his big hands, it looked like a toy. The mysterious light had changed the goddess's treasure. On the golden rims, there were now symbols of Foant's tribe, while Targ had turned into salt.

"And he will obey you," the chief continued. "He will be the god of this land and make sure that this land becomes ours. So that my people can live here."

In his voice, Amage heard false hope, the cruelest gift from the gods. She threw away the knife, walked over to the Cradle, and touched her brother. The salt flakes creaked under her fingers.

"He needs to be covered with gold," Amage said.

Foant nodded.

"And the temple needs to be burned down."

The wind swept through the temple. The torches trembled anxiously.

The statue's shadow touched Amage and crawled away as if afraid of her anger. Outside the walls, Pontus was roaring. Even Foant retreated to his men.

He took advantage of me, betrayed me. And I, like a fool, fell into his trap. He will deeply regret getting his god and priestess this way, Amage thought as she watched the men in skins carry away the Golden Cradle and Targ. Sakatevo followed them like a ghost. Amidst the crashing of the waves, Amage heard voices. It was the chorus of the dead. Her father was reminding her of her oath once again. But she paid no attention to it. She was worried about something else.

The men poured oil on the floor. Foant was ready to throw a torch and was waiting only for a sign from the girl. The priestess of the new god froze near the statue. The wind roared in the womb louder than ever before.

It was the voice of the goddess. But only Amage could hear the words. The goddess was singing a lullaby for Targ. Amage was consumed with rage.

"No, no, no! I don't want to hear!" The girl poured oil on the wooden figure, took the torch from the chief, and threw it at the statue. Foant was wrong. The goddess wasn't dead. But Amage would do anything to make sure she never woke up again.

To the Garden

Volodymyr Arenev

Туди, де буде сад | Володимир Аренєв
translated by Hanna Leliv

A wedding ring made of foil did tear in the end. He had taken it off and put it in his pocket, but even there, he could not keep it safe.

He pulled out the dull golden ribbon once again and smoothed it out. In the glow of a small campfire here, on the underground level, it looked like a gem.

No, he corrected himself, it *was* a gem. All five pairs of rings Chaplain had made in the spring were more valuable than those of silver or gold.

The other wedding ring, a match for his own, was now far away, up there, above the ground, most likely in enemy territory.

In fairy tales, when misfortune befell the woman you loved, the blade of your sword became bloodied, or a mirror shattered—in short, something significant and tragic happened. Something definite.

Over the past few months, he had often thought how much easier it would have been to know. To know with certainty and avoid torturing his mind with assumptions. Then he reproached himself, saying: "Stop it, at least this way, you have a chance." As long as you didn't know for sure, there was always a chance.

But he had to try. Winter was coming, and if he didn't try that day, there would be no other possibility.

He rolled up the ribbon, put it back in his pocket, and stood up. He took the gun.

Almost the entire squad was asleep or pretending to be asleep, and only the guards were standing watch outside the room. They watched both entrances and listened for the orcs coming.

He walked toward the nearest door and heard, rather than saw, Chaplain rise from his mattress.

They stopped in the corridor and nodded to the guards, Alpinist and Honta. The guards signaled that all was quiet.

"You're not sleeping," Chaplain said.

"Sounds like an accusation."

Chaplain shrugged his thin, angular shoulders. They had all lost weight since the spring, but Chaplain had always been like that. And it seemed he was the first to discover this ability to eat almost nothing and still keep going. Even back when they were dropping food for them from helicopters, Chaplain would sometimes share his rations with one of the wounded.

The guys joked: "Teach us how to pull that off. Do you live on the Holy Spirit or what?"

Chaplain just waved it away. "You're still kiddos. Wait until you hit twenty-five, then you'll get it."

For some reason, they found this terribly amusing. "Sure," they said, "this wisdom comes along with a new photo in your passport. But do you promise we'll get it? Do you guarantee that? Well, boys, we'll live until twenty-five, when they stick that first pic in, for sure. Chaplain's word is harder than steel."

"Go away," Chaplain would say with a laugh. "Go get some sleep."

They had also gotten out of the habit of sleeping—along with the need to eat, that too had passed. It was as if they were afraid of missing something important, sleeping through it.

Despite Chaplain's recommendations, he could not fall asleep either. He was afraid to dream of bread, freshly baked, with a crispy crust and a wavy crack on top. If he tore off a piece of that crust and took a bite, he felt that taste for a moment, even in his dream—the taste all the way from his childhood, from his previous life.

And how was he supposed to wake up if he dreamed something like that?

He was also afraid to dream of her, the one with a matching wedding ring made of foil. She'd come into his dream and break the armor he had taken so long to grow—day after day, hour after hour. She had left along with the civilians; he'd somehow managed to insist on that, to persuade her. In parting, she had said that she'd definitely come back for him. She'd convince everyone who needed convincing; she'd force them to get everyone out of here.

That happened two days before the connection was lost. After that, they had to retreat to the lower levels and split into smaller squads. They moved into another phase and no longer held the defensive position.

When the bullets ran out, the knives were still at hand.

He didn't think they would last that long, but he knew they had to try. To distract the enemy, to give their own people as much time as possible. And also to deny those bastards even a hint of victory.

Sometimes, they talked about what would come next. Instead of sleeping, they lay awake and dreamed. "You know what," said Honta, "we'll push the orcs the fuck out by the fall and then rebuild the city."

"Sure," said Beaver, laughing, "it used to be by April, then by the summer, and now by the fall. But in reality," he went on, still laughing, "it wouldn't happen sooner than winter—have you even seen how many of them are there? And tanks? And cannons? And damn airplanes? Certainly not sooner than winter, right on the commander's birthday."

In the end, Honta couldn't take it anymore and said: "But we'll win it back and rebuild it, that's what really matters!"

"I'd like it to be even prettier," he said. "I'd like people to live here and be happy. So that no one could even believe that these kinds of things happened here."

"Hey, come on," Aladdin spoke up, propping himself up on his elbows. Hissing in pain, he straightened the bandage with his two remaining fingers and added a little more calmly, "They have to remember. To make sure it never happens again. And then, you know—it would only be fair if they remembered us, too. At least for some time."

At that, they all fell silent. At such moments, he also felt more clearly the biting cold and the dull flutter of nerves in his stomach— the feelings that had become a familiar background since May, like the ticking of a clock.

"And I wish they'd forget me later," Chaplain said softly. "Or, rather, I wish they'd remember the good stuff. Maybe the concerts the boys and I had played. Things like that. And what happened here . . . "

Chaplain fell silent and then added: "I hope that in a hundred years, no one will be able to imagine such a thing."

"But the orcs *must* remember," Elrond spoke up. "And be scared shitless. So that they'd shit their pants as soon as they even thought of attacking. And here," he continued, raising his voice to make himself heard above the laughter and cheers, "and here, and I'm sorry folks, should not be a city. It should be a garden of memory. And the tour guides should take people around and show them where everything used to be—the fountains, the waterfront, the theater . . . "

Elrond paused for a moment, with everyone eagerly waiting, and then he went on: "The tour guides should go around and tell the stories so that everything would come alive in people's minds. So that the city would live on—in memory. So that no ruins, no crosses in the courtyards would erase our city, because otherwise the orcs would win, and they must never win. And this garden of memory should be so big that people could see it from the top."

"Which top?" the guys asked, laughing. "Hilltop?"

"Oh, shut up," said Elrond. "From outer space, don't you get it? In the next few decades, humans will populate the Moon and Mars, you'll see. And our war must be the last. It must put an end to all goddamn wars."

He listened to all the chatter and didn't interrupt. Only later did he say quietly: "Go get some sleep, you."

He had somehow gotten out of the habit of sleeping, as they all did. It became a ritual: pretending to be asleep and believing the others when they pretended the same thing.

Usually, everyone kept to this unspoken agreement; only Chaplain could jump up and follow them, staring at them, as he stared at him now, with his surprisingly vivid eyes, as if he could read their minds.

"Come on," Chaplain said. "Let's go for a walk."

Chaplain knew he was going to go up because he had taken his gun, too. There was no way Chaplain would be fooled.

So off they went.

They talked briefly with the guards. Honta said he saw the shadows again, but no stinker dared approach within firing range. Maybe they were drones, after all.

"Ghosts," Alpinist said, chuckling. He adjusted the pirate patch on his right eye and added, "I'm telling you. That whole bunch we zapped here? Their people didn't bury them, and they're all still here, roaming the corridors."

"Whatever," he told Alpinist. "Let them roam. You'd better keep an eye out for the living. They didn't dare mess with us this week, but I'm sure they're planning some shit. Keep your eyes peeled—I don't want us to become . . . ghosts. And in the meantime, let's take a walk and look around."

"This *week*?" asked Chaplain as the two of them left and began to walk up the concrete stairs.

"I think it's suspicious, too. But at least the guys got some rest. But then," he added, "what if our folks are finally giving them a hard time?"

He'd been pushing that thought away. Of course, he told the

guys other things: they remember us, he said, don't even doubt. And they would get us out of here as soon as possible.

In the last months, their whole life had turned into a never-ending hassle underground. They fixed up traps from whatever they could. Sometimes, they ambushed squads, one by one, and finished them off without a single sound. Their vision adapted to the darkness, as did their bodies to the lack of food and sleep. It was one long, all-too-long night in which they often acted mechanically without thinking.

But all things considered, they had been incredibly lucky. None of them was killed during that long period. Not a single confrontation happened with much larger enemy forces. About three times, the enemies had apparently followed their trail, but they managed to sneak away. Beaver could set traps like no other, and later, they heard them go slam-bang.

But maybe all those days, their people up there had been pushing against the orcs, and that was the only reason they were still alive? Maybe that was why the cell phone signal was down—perhaps they'd been jamming it?

Well, they hadn't climbed up to the upper levels in a while and hadn't had a chance to check.

Today, he wanted to climb as high as he could. He had to send off some emails he'd typed long ago. He wanted to do it before the winter frost really set in . . . or before his cell phone died . . . or before they did get unlucky.

And then he just absolutely had to know how she had been doing.

"How high up are we going?" asked Chaplain.

"Let's just look at the ghosts. And maybe get some fresh air."

They ran into the ghosts three floors up. And these floors looked really weird.

He suspected that the orcs had claimed territory in recent weeks. After all, their commanders must have been pressuring them, and they had to report progress by yet another memorable date.

But he could not understand when or how they had managed to clear the rubble. Some of the traps had done their work: Chaplain was squatting next to where they had set one not long ago, pointing to the dark stains and splatters on the wall. So they hadn't set the traps for nothing after all.

"But why didn't we hear the bang?"

Chaplain shrugged.

"We were at the other end."

"Or maybe they disabled it with minimal losses. In any case," he remarked, "there should be some noise."

"But that's not the real question . . ."

"Right. The question is, how deep are they willing to go down?"

They walked on carefully and without haste. And the further they went, the less he liked what he saw.

It looked plain wrong. Too neat.

"They just cleaned it up to make it look good for the shot, that's for sure," he told Chaplain.

"One hundred percent. They're going to shoot some propaganda crap."

"You think so?"

"What else? If our guys had gotten in here, we would've have known that. And peacekeepers, we'd know that too . . ."

He broke off because they had climbed up to the next level—and right at the corridor entrance was a red and white sign indicating that this area had been de-mined.

It was written in English and a few other *foreign* languages, goddamn it.

"See," he said to Chaplain. "That's certainly a prop for you . . ."

He trailed off again. Then he blinked and realized there was no sign at all.

He moved closer and saw only a slightly lighter rectangle on the wall that didn't look like a sign even from a distance.

"Listen . . ." Chaplain cleared his throat. "Don't you think it's strange that they've left us alone for so long?"

"I thought it was strange at first. But then it's actually logical. Why go down here when they can just block the main exits and wait? Sooner or later, we'll run out of food anyway. Besides, it's winter . . ."

After a pause, he added:

"I hate winter. Ever since I was a kid, you know. My birthday falls on Christmas and I . . . It sounds silly, but I thought everyone was happy and celebrating because of me. So, I expected people to bring presents. My mum tried to explain everything to me, but I was still little and . . . Whatever." He waved his hand. "A fucking childhood trauma. And now I wish I could just make it to Christmas. Like anything will change then . . . But you know, I have this gut feeling that they're going to run out of steam soon, they're going to completely collapse. We've just got to make it to Christmas."

"That would be good," Chaplain said.

They moved on—after all, they only had so much time. And they still had to climb two or three levels higher for the cell phone signal to get through.

A strange thing happened to his vision: the walls seemed to become muddled and blurry. He yanked off his glove with his teeth, wet his finger with spit, and rubbed his eyes.

"You know what I think sometimes?" Chaplain suddenly spoke up, "Thirty-three years old—how young he was then. And then I'm like: I wish I could make it to thirty-three . . . Then I'd have a whole lot of time. If each of us made it to at least thirty-three—imagine that. How many songs and books ... Fuck books. How many houses would Honta and his boys build. How many pancakes Ratatouille would make for people. And Tor with his ideas for improving the railroad, and Aladdin with his vineyards in Crimea ... And you, how much furniture you'd build until you turned thirty-three ... "

He knew that mood of Chaplain's only too well. There was no point in correcting him or arguing with him.

Everyone had their own quirks, and one had to respect the human right to have a screw loose.

So he didn't interrupt him, but simply listened and meanwhile pulled out his cell phone and turned it on.

Oddly enough, the cell phone signal was up. Pretty weak, just a bar, but even that was good.

He pulled up "Drafts," selected an email he had typed, and clicked "Send."

Then another one.

The phone seemed to work fine, and the battery had enough charge, but something strange was happening.

He tried to restart it, but the keys did not respond.

"Sometimes I have these thoughts," Chaplain continued. "He knew exactly how it would end when he went up the hill with the cross. He knew it when he entered the garden after supper. And he wasn't just going to atone for some abstract sins of humanity ... He agreed to take the pain from others. To take it away—and onto himself. And to hold it as long as possible."

His phone froze completely. Worst of all, it kept chewing through the damn battery.

"There's an issue with the calendar," Chaplain said calmly, without changing his tone. "That's why it acts up."

"The calendar? How do you know?"

But the answer was obvious, wasn't it?

"Did you climb up here before? When?"

"I'm not sure," Chaplain said. "Days ago."

The walls around them became muddled and blurry again. At the end of the corridor, the light flashed and went out.

And then again. And again.

Suddenly, he remembered this corridor—even though the surroundings had changed drastically. This was the place where they had come under fire in May. Shortly after she had left; when they had hit that rough patch. But they had survived, none of them had been killed, and after that, things somehow got better, and they hung in there, if only by a thin thread.

This corridor reminded him that there was always a chance for relief, for hope—even in the darkest moment.

A ridiculous conclusion, but sometimes that's what people needed.

"Let's go," he said to Chaplain. "Let's see what's up there. Whatever it is, we must not let down our guard. If the enemy is really planning to stage 'the liberation from the bloodthirsty Nazis,' we can even launch the dro—"

He noticed the ghosts earlier than Chaplain and reacted instantly. He pressed himself against the wall and also pulled Chaplain back.

He gestured to him: two, over there, getting closer.

He pulled out his knife carefully so it wouldn't clank. Chaplain pulled out his own, a longer one with a serrated blade and the etching: "No enemy there will be, nor rival."

They exchanged glances and both made a quick jab.

And just like that, both of them fell, having lost their balance. Their hands passed through the void where the two figures in strange clothes, which resembled spacesuits, were standing just a second ago.

Or rather, the figures were still there. They froze, their mouths gaping open behind the tinted shields of their helmets. They were very young, and it looked like one of them was a woman. Right.

Their situation must have gotten so dire that they were now drafting women.

It also occurred to him that people usually wore helmets and suits like this at the sites of radioactive explosions. Or in places where lethal reagents were leaking. Or other substances that made the surrounding area uninhabitable.

These thoughts flashed through his mind in a second or two as he pushed himself off the ground, rolled over, and jumped to his feet.

He wanted to strike again, aiming at the place where the helmet was attached to the suit.

But he didn't get a chance to.

The figures jerked back, and even though they moved slowly as if walking underwater, his eye couldn't follow their movements fast enough. A blurry, ghostly trace lingered briefly in the air before fading away and disappearing completely.

The ghosts disappeared, too.

"Fuck."

He shook his head.

He knew it was his hunger and fatigue, or he never would have let them go.

He also realized that the orcs would now be aware of him and Chaplain—and would actively seek them out.

"You okay?" he asked Chaplain. "We must get out of here."

Suddenly, he heard a soft ding from his pocket, a sound that was familiar and strange at the same time because he hadn't heard it for so many weeks.

A text message. From her.

He knew that even before he looked at the screen.

"Love you. Sorry."

It wasn't the words that affected him the most—he'd basically been waiting for them all these months.

It was the periods.

She had always been fastidious and never neglected punctuation marks, even in her text messages.

Even at a moment like this, she had not neglected them.

Never, he told himself silently. Never—there was no doubt about that now.

He licked his lips and looked up at Chaplain.

Chaplain had not even made a second attempt to stab the ghosts, and now he realized why.

"You saw them earlier."

Sure, Chaplain must have seen them before when he climbed up here alone to try to pick up the signal.

"You already know who they are. Wait, let me guess—real ghosts, right? Honta was telling the truth. We zapped so many of them here that some are still wandering the corridors."

He laughed loudly and slapped Chaplain on the shoulder.

"And it's great, you know. They'll scare the Russian scum away just as well as we will."

He talked fast so Chaplain wouldn't have a chance to interrupt him or get even a single word in. His brain was churning like crazy.

"Wait, I heard that ghosts can't move too far from where they were killed. And we whacked them on all the levels. Imagine how the orcs will shit their pants when they all rise soon? Come on, let's go up even higher while we're here!"

Chaplain shook his head.

"We won't."

"Just don't tell me that the rubble is blocking the passageways up there because if they did what they did here . . . "

"The passageways are clear. But we can't get any higher than this level."

"Gee, Chaplain, if you personally couldn't go up there last time, that doesn't mean that . . . "

He took a deep breath and told himself to take it easy.

"Sorry. I'm sorry . . . Just look around at how things have changed around here . . . "

"*We*," Chaplain said. "*We* couldn't go up there."

"Oh, so you came here with someone else. And what stopped you this time?"

"Don't you remember?"

"Just don't say you've already told . . . "

And then he remembered. Not all of it, just a few fragments, but even that was enough.

"How long?" he asked in a whisper. And then he couldn't help leaning his shoulder against the wall.

He felt the cold and rough surface through his clothes. Just as normal, living people should feel it.

"I don't remember," Chaplain said calmly. "So long. You know how all the days and nights freeze into one long night. You remember things when you fall asleep. But we've almost forgotten what it's like to sleep, and you know that, too."

As he listened to Chaplain, he could picture the last time they'd walked around here—when the corridors hadn't been cleaned up. They'd been chasing the ghosts, just like this time.

And just like this time, it was in vain.

For those in the spacesuits were not ghosts.

Or rather, it was not *them* who were the ghosts.

"All right," he said. "Let it be. But they can see us. And they get scared. That's why they're running around like damn astronauts! That means we're still good for something, right? We're not completely fucking useless, no, whatever we are now!"

Then he asked:

"Do you know what year it is up there?"

Chaplain shook his head and looked into the distance past his back.

He turned around—and saw another figure. In a military uniform, not a spacesuit.

One of ours, he thought, judging by the pixel pattern.

At least his current condition had its advantages: his eyes could see everything clearly, even in the twilight. Even in total darkness.

He didn't dare look directly at the figure, but he could see the expression on Chaplain's face.

"She wasn't here earlier," Chaplain muttered.

And then he added:

"Go, I'll wait here. Go."

He was frightened. He was frightened as hell.

But he kept walking, and the walking became easier with each step, as if heavy weights were falling to the ground, one by one.

"It's you," he said to her. "You."

"It's me."

He still didn't dare look her in the face, his eyes glued to the glittering ribbon on her finger.

He took the matching ribbon out of his pocket and smoothed it out quickly as if making an excuse: "See, I didn't manage to keep it safe, it's torn."

And then, unable to contain himself any longer, he asked:

"But how come . . . you're here?"

"I promised I'd be back, didn't I? I said I would take you all away from here. Let's go."

He reached for her but then pulled his hand back, afraid he wouldn't be able to touch her. Or that he would touch her and feel ice cold.

They went shoulder to shoulder up the stairs, Chaplain walking behind them. Other guys—Honta, Alpinist, Kozhumiaka, Tor, Aladdin—emerged from somewhere and joined them, too . . .

Outside it was night, and around them was a garden—just as Elrond had mentioned. A big, boundless garden with trees whose names he didn't know; all he could think of was that some of them would make beautiful cradles and sailboats and beds. And rocking chairs that made it so cozy to welcome the evening, drink strong tea with honey, and watch the sunset.

They went through the garden as they were, with their guns, because sometimes you had to protect the gardens, too.

The snow crunched under their feet, but of course, they left no tracks. Far away, above the green leaves, above the flowers and the fragrant fruits, a star shone, and the guys walked towards it.

He stopped.

He saw that she had stopped and now stood there, looking back, behind the fence.

"Anything you still have to do?"

"Well, it's Christmas," she said, "A moment of hope for those lost in the darkness. A time of comfort and consolation. I'll go to the kids. They've been waiting for a play to start. In the theater. All this time."

"They . . . they haven't realized it yet, either?"

She gave him that look as if to say, "Why are you always being so silly?"

"Even adults don't always realize it right away, you know. A lack of experience. I . . . I didn't realize it at first, either. But keep going, I'll catch up with you."

"No way. We'll get lost in that garden of yours in no time. Wait a minute!"

He called the guys over and briefed them on the situation. They had a short argument about who would take on the role of Herod, but that was quickly settled.

They picked up some apples for the kids and headed for the exit, laughing and joking.

He went with her last and finally took her hand at the gate.

Her fingers were warm, almost burning.

They walked on together, holding hands. The snow drifted down, and the star shone, and somewhere behind them, up there, the garden waited patiently for them.

ACKNOWLEDGMENTS

Literature in translation is a challenge. It's difficult to find a publisher who will take a chance on authors who are not well known outside of their native country. It's a risk not all publishers are willing or able to take. Finding a publisher who believes in making art that is meaningful, art that stands up against oppression, that amplifies diverse and marginalized voices—that is rare and special, and that is Atthis Arts. Emily and Chris Bell are the incredible team who believed in this project. This book would not be here if it were not for them. For all the time, energy, and sacrifices they put into *Embroidered Worlds*, they deserve our thanks—and our support. Small presses like Atthis Arts can only survive and thrive if we buy their books.

The creation of a book takes many people, especially when it is a collection of stories from authors around the world, and even more so when those stories need to be translated by another group of people also around the world. Thank you to those authors and translators listed on the pages that follow, whose words you have read on the pages of this anthology. Without them, there would be no stories to share. Add to that list the artists and designers, readers and reviewers, as well as editors and publishers, and one quickly realizes that a book like this *is created by* a community—and also *creates* a community of people who believe in it. That's powerful. You hold in your hands a symbol of what can be done when people join their voices, hands, and hearts together. It is a collection of stories and a symbol of hope.

On Saturday, September 30, 2023, 1,072 backers from all over the world pledged $23,567 to fund this anthology. What an amazing show of support for these authors, translators, and their stories. This book you hold in your hands would not exist without the backers. Thank you to everyone who supported and pre-ordered copies. Our backers sent a message to the world about the importance of these stories. Thank you also to the guests who joined their voices to the cause and posted during our Kickstarter campaign: Michael Burianyk, Anna Chychula, Zig Zag Claybourne, Rhiannon Rasmussen, Sonia Sulaiman, Bogi Takács, Wole Talabi, and Bryan Thao Worra.

Every project has a beginning, and this one started with an idea by a small group of dedicated science fiction writers who wanted to channel their efforts into a show of support for Ukraine after Russia invaded. They reached out to the editors and to many of the writers in Ukraine and the diaspora. Thank you to N. R. M. Roshak, Rhiannon Rasmussen, Stewart C Baker, Mimi Mondal, Oghenechovwe Donald Ekpeki, Veles Svitlychny, and the other members of SFWA who planted the seeds of this book.

Thank you to Taras Kopansky for the powerful cover art and to Olga Samets for the breathtaking bookplates. Thank you to Stephen H. Segal for his cover design and editorial support, and to Chris Bell for his layout and typesetting wizardry. Special thanks to Stewart C Baker, Michael Burianyk, E.D.E. Bell, N. R. M. Roshak, and Dimitris Tzellis for their invaluable editorial assistance as we read, reviewed, and revised.

Thank you to the Ukrainian Book Institute for seeing the potential in this collection of fantastic Ukrainian stories, and for believing in the value of this project.

Wholehearted thanks to the many friends, family, and supporters, who ordered copies, boosted the signal on social media, supported the people involved with this project, and helped to spread the message of *Embroidered Worlds* within their communities.

Сердечно дякуємо!

~V.D.L. 15 November 2023

ABOUT OUR AUTHORS

Tetyana Adamenko was born in 1987 in the city of Dnipro, Ukraine, where she still lives and works as a laboratory diagnostician. A fan of classic detectives, she combines fantasy and detective genres in her works, and has a spaniel named Sherlock. For more than ten years, she has been a member of the informal Dnipro literary workshop Demosphere. Tatiana is a volunteer at the Historical Museum of the city, and she is an author of a series of gratitude posters devoted to the people of different professions who have kept Ukrainian city life functioning through the time of full-scale war. Her poster "Thank you, Air Defense Forces" went so viral that it was reposted by the official page of the Air Defense Forces. Tatiana's posters of gratitude to utility and power workers were displayed on city lights on the streets of Kyiv. She is also the illustrator of the essay "Things," by Iryna Pasko, which reflects on the fragility of the world and the attitude to one's own belongings in a homefront city during the war.

Volodymyr Arenev is a Ukrainian author of fantasy and SF for adults and teenagers, a screenwriter, and a teacher of creative writing. Arenev has written more than thirty books, including an urban fantasy trilogy on Russia's aggression against Ukraine in 2014. His books are recommended for reading at school by the Ministry of Education of Ukraine. Arenev's works have been published in Ukrainian, English, French, German, Polish, Lithuanian, Estonian, Chinese, and Russian. His novels include *Soulhold* (2014), *Dragonbone Powder* (2015), *Doghead's Child* (2018), and *Sapienses* (2019). His work has been recognized by various literary awards including Best Creator of Children's Science Fiction or Fantasy Books at the ESFS Awards

(2014), Best Fantasy Novel for YA by Barabooka (2018), and BBC Book of the Year (Nomination Book for Children, 2019). His novel *The Sworn Sword, or the Voice of Blood* reached the finals of the most prestigious Ukrainian award, the Taras Shevchenko Prize.

Vira Balatska is an author and poet from Gostomel, in the Kyiv region of Ukraine. Vira graduated from the Institute of Philology at Taras Shevchenko National University of Kyiv, and she works as a teacher of Ukrainian language and literature. She is the cofounder of the literary association "Litavytsia", created to help young authors, as well as to help popularize science fiction and fantasy among Ukrainian readers. Her stories and poems have been published in newspapers, as well as in magazines for adults, teenagers, and children. In 2023, *Pink Sweater,* her collection of stories, was published.

Károj D. Balla is the award-winning Transcarpathian Hungarian author of close to 30 books of fiction, nonfiction, and poetry, including the novels *Élted wol regénye, Encounter*, and *Tejmozi*; the selected poetry volume *Dead Bird*; and the essay collections *Metaphors of Statelessness* and *Hungarian Speaking Magyars*. A native of Ungvár (Uzhhorod), the largest city in Ukraine's Transcarpathia region, Balla was a prominent leader in the local literary scene through the 1980s and '90s before retreating from public life to focus on his own writing. In 2000, he was presented with the József Attila Award, one of the highest literary honors in Hungarian literature.

Elizabeth Bear was born on the same day as Frodo and Bilbo Baggins, but in a different year. She is the Hugo, Sturgeon, Locus, and Astounding Award winning author of over 30 novels and more than a hundred short stories. She may be found on social media at: @matociquala.bsky.social

Anatoly Belilovsky was born in Lviv, a city that has changed owners six or seven times in the last century, the latest crude attempt at adverse possession being in progress even as we speak. He was traded to the U.S. for a truckload of wheat and a defector to be named later, learned English from *Star Trek* reruns, and went on to become a SFWA member (in spite of a chronic cat deficiency) by publishing nearly 100 pieces of original and translated prose and poetry. In his spare time he practices pediatrics in New York, in an area where English barely makes the Top 10 list of languages spoken; recently arrived Ukrainian refugee families make up a significant fraction of his patient population. Many of his stories are collected in *Halogen Nightmares and Other Love Stories*, available from Amazon. He tweets occasionally as @loldoc (come for the puns, stay for the pontification.)

Éva Berniczky is an acclaimed Hungarian-language short fiction writer from the Transcarpathia region in western Ukraine. Her most recent books include the short story collections *The Egg Seller's Long Day* (2004), *Castle Key: Masters, Pranksters, Showmen, Eye-Poppers* (2010), and *Lucky Root: Selected and New Short Stories* (2018) and the novel *The Midwife Without a Womb* (2007). She has been honored over the years with literary awards including the Tibor Déry Prize, the Artisjus Literature Prize, and the Sándor Márai Prize.

David Demchuk's debut, *The Bone Mother,* was nominated for the Scotiabank Giller Prize, the Amazon First Novel Award, the Toronto Book Award, the Kobzar Book Award and a Shirley Jackson Award

in the Best Novel category, and won the 2018 Sunburst Award in the Adult Fiction category. It was listed in the *Globe and Mail's* 100 best books of 2017, in the *National Post's* top 99 books of the year and became a #1 bestseller on Amazon.ca. His second novel, *RED X,* was listed as a Rakuten Kobo Top 20 of 2021 selection, a CBC Books pick for Best Canadian fiction of 2021, and a New York Public Library Best Book of 2021—one of just three Canadian novels on the list. His short stories have appeared in numerous anthologies as well as *Andrei Codrescu's Exquisite Corpse, Chronotope, The Winnipeg Review* and *Unfortunately.* After many years in Toronto, he now lives by the sea with his husband in St. John's, Newfoundland.

Vasyl Dukhnovskyi was born in Kyiv on January 14, 1994. He is a mathematician by education, a librarian by life, and a soldier by necessity. During the war, he married the poet Olena Sokolovska, with whom he now takes care of three dogs from a village near Bakhmut and about whom he plans to make a cartoon. He is the founder of the "Poetic Meat Grinder" literary competition, which was not stopped even by the war, and was a jury member of the "Al Mor" fantasy poetry competition in 2021-2022.

Oleksiy Gedeonov (born 1973) is a sociologist by education, a historian by heart, a writer by soul and a city guide by occupation. He lives in Kyiv and knows about the city more than anyone. His tours and lectures are very popular and extremely educational. He also writes books that straddle the border between historical fiction and urban fantasy. He is a husband and a father of a son. His recent novel is dedicated to Pontic Olbia, an ancient Greek colony near modern Parutyne in Mykolaiv Oblast in Ukraine.

Myroslava Hornostayeva lives in Zaporizhzhia, has a medical education and works in the Zaporizhzhia anti-tuberculosis dispensary. In addition to her work, she continues to write novels and short stories in the genre of fantasy and historical prose. She has a particular literary interest in ancient India, and has set several stories there. Her work also includes a cycle of mystical stories about her native Zaporizhzhia, like the one collected in this anthology.

Yaryna Katorozh is a writer and illustrator from Vynnyky, Western Ukraine. She writes mostly in the genres of epic and urban fantasy. Her 2015 fantasy novel *Alchemy of Freedom* received a special Ukrainian modern fantasy award at the 2015 Coronation of the Word contest. Her novel *Stozhar* (2017), a nominee for the Bookforum Best Book in 2017, was the first of an epic fantasy trilogy. The other two were *Alliance* (2018) and *Homeland* (2020). Yaryna illustrated this trilogy herself. Her stories have been included in the collections *Bicycle of my Heart* (2017), *Pocket Mandruary Travels by Fantastic Transport* (2019), *Independence Agency* (2021), *Legendary of Ancient Cities* (2023) and others. Yaryna continues to write new stories and to work as a graphic designer. Sometimes she paints cityscapes with the architecture of Lviv and Vynnyky.

Max Kidruk is a Ukrainian writer, radio host, and publisher. He holds a degree in energy engineering, got his master's degree at the National University of Water and Environmental Engineering (Rivne, Ukraine), and was a postgraduate student at Kyiv Polytechnic University and Stockholm Royal Institute of Technology. In 2012, Kidruk published his first novel, the sci-fi thriller *Bot*, dubbed by critics as "the first Ukrainian techno-thriller." In the fall of 2019, his augmented reality novel *Until the Light Fades Away* was published. In addition to the interactive cover, the mobile application developed specifically for the book includes supplementary storylines, photos of the places where the events of the novel happen, a full diary of one of the characters, and a chat the reader can use to talk with one of the characters. At the end of 2022, Kidruk and his wife, Tetiana, founded the nonfiction and science fiction publishing house Bearded Tamarin. On January 1, 2023, they released Kidruk's novel *Colony*, the first book of the sci-fi series New Dark Ages. Kidruk speaks English and Ukrainian; he is fond of aviation and American football and is a fan of the rock band Iron Maiden. He and his wife live in Rivne, Ukraine. You can find out more at: darkages.maxkidruk.com

Olena Krasnoselska is a writer, a member of the National Union of Writers of Ukraine, an author of science fiction works, and an artist. She was born, lives, and works in the city of Zaporizhzhia. Her stories have been published in many magazines, collections, anthologies in Ukraine and abroad. In 2013, she received the National Prize of Ukraine for fiction in the category "Story" for the science fiction work "Point of reference". She participated in the work of the "Sound Art Space" art residency (with the support of the Ukrainian Cultural Fund), where she created unusual musical instruments and acoustic art sculptures. During the full-scale war, she implemented (in co-authorship with Natalya Lobach and Hanna Lupinos) the artistic and poetic project "Wild Field," and it has been standing in the city center near the city hall for more than a year since—an appeal to the ordinary people of Zaporizhzhia. After February 24, 2022, she participated in the Polish project eMultipoetry IPOGS, Walls - "Poems on the Wall" (in Krakow), in the All-Ukrainian project "War Experience: Ukrainian Voices," and others.

R.B. Lemberg is a queer, bigender immigrant from Lviv, Ukraine to the US. R.B. is an author of five books of speculative fiction and poetry, a translator from Ukrainian and Russian, and an academic. R.B.'s books of fantasy have been shortlisted for the Nebula, Locus, Ignyte, World Fantasy Award, the Le Guin Award for Fiction, and other awards. Many of R.B.'s stories and poems are set in Birdverse, an LGBTQIA+-focused secondary world. Their Birdverse books are *The Four Profound Weaves* (2020), *The Unbalancing* (2022), *Geometries of Belonging* (2022), and the forthcoming novella *Yoke of Stars* (2024). In their academic life, R.B. is a sociolinguist working on immigrant discourse, identity, and gender. You can find R.B. on Instagram at @rblemberg, on Patreon at patreon.com/rblemberg, and at their website rblemberg.net.

Halyna Lipatova is a writer and translator from the city of Dnipro (formerly Dnipropetrovsk), where she was born in 1979 and lived all her life. In 2001, she graduated from Dnipropetrovsk National University, where she studied East Slavic philology. She worked in the scientific library of the university, supplementing her education thanks to access to rare publications. She also worked with children in summer camps as a teacher, and taught Ukrainian language and literature classes for children in a private educational center. She worked as a literary editor and proofreader in the city's newspapers and in the publishing house of entertainment periodicals (in particular, for children). For more than ten years, she has been engaged in translations of literary works from Russian into Ukrainian. She started writing fantasy, science and adventure fiction while still at school, but only her closest friends saw the first "pen tests". After

2013, she started participating in online contests and festivals with fan fiction and original works.

Askold Melnyczuk's novel, *What Is Told,* brought out by Faber in 1994, was the first commercially published novel in English to bring to light the Ukrainian refugee experience, and was named a New York Times Notable. His other novels have been selected an LA Times Best Books of the Year, and an Editor's Choice by the American Library Association's Booklist. His most recent book is a collection of stories, *The Man Who Would Not Bow.* He is also co-editor of *From Three Worlds*, an anthology of Ukrainian writers from the 1980s generation. Founding editor of *Agni Magazine* and Arrowsmith Press, he has taught at Boston University, Harvard, Bennington College and currently teaches at the University of Massachusetts Boston.

Mykhailo Nazarenko is Assistant Professor in the Department of East Slavic Philology and Practical Information Studies at the Educational and Scientific Institute of Philology of Taras Shevchenko National University of Kyiv. His books include *The Reality of Wonder* (On Books of Marina and Sergey Dyachenko) (2005), *Buried on a Mound: Shevchenko in Folklore and Fakelore* (2006, 2017), *The New Minotaur* (a collection of fantasy stories, 2007), and *Besides "Kobzar":* *An Anthology of Ukrainian Literature, 1792-1883* (2021). He has edited and annotated Ukrainian and Russian translations of works by Susanna Clarke, John Crowley, Arthur Conan Doyle, Neil Gaiman, Alan Moore, and Terry Pratchett.

Stefan O. Rak is honored to have his short story, "The Long Black Veil," included in this historic anthology. A second-generation

Ukrainian-American, he is the author of the novels *New Roses* and *Adventures of Bastard and M.E.*, both published by Whisk(e)y Tit Books. He writes to represent a world in which some things make sense.

A former analyst at Oracle and programmer for Harvard, Ukrainian-Canadian **N. R. M. Roshak** now writes about the intersections of technology and imagination with our loves, hopes, desires, and work. Their work includes short fiction, kidlit, non-fiction, poetry and translation; their award-winning short fiction has been published in four languages, and has appeared in various anthologies and magazines, including *Flash Fiction Online, Galaxies SF, Daily Science Fiction,* and *Future Science Fiction Digest.* They live in Ontario, Canada, with a small family and a loud cat. You can find more of their work at: nrmroshak.com.

Oleh Silin is a Ukrainian SF&F writer, a journalist and a culture manager. Born in Kharkiv in 1982, he now lives in Kyiv. He graduated from the National Technical University with a degree in Management of foreign economic activity. He debuted in 2005 with a fantastic sport short story. Oleh has written two novels and dozens of short stories that have been published in fiction collections. He has also edited short story collections and almanacs. Co-founder of Literary Union *Star Fortress*, which promotes SF&F literature in Ukraine, organizer of special SF&F programs at main literary festivals in Ukraine. In 2013 he won the Eurocon Encouragement Award.

Ihor Silivra is a modern Ukrainian fiction writer. Born and living in Chernivtsi, he graduated from Chernivtsi National University and is an engineer by education. Ihor has six published novels in his portfolio—and two more in the works—as well as over fifty fantasy stories ranging from steampunk to hard sci-fi. His first serious literary application took place in 2010: the publication of the story "The Magician" in the Ukrainian magazine *UFO*. The first printed novel "Zeppelin to Kyiv" first became the winner of the Days of Fiction in Kyiv in 2011, and in 2013 it was published on paper by the publishing house SHYKO (Luhansk). In 2014, Silivra received Eurocon's award for the best debut from Ukraine. In 2022, despite the large-scale invasion of Russia, two new novels were published. In 2023, Studio VUHO audio publishing house will voice Silivra's 2022 novel *Volya: The Legacy of Professor Puluy*, based on the Will comics universe.

A.D. Sui was born in Kharkiv, Ukraine. She is a queer and disabled science fiction writer, with a strong affection for all things dark and melancholy. Her writing has appeared in *Dark Matter Magazine*, *Augur*, and others. Her debut novella *The Dragonfly Gambit* is coming out with Neon Hemlock in 2024. When not wrangling her two dogs, she's posting away as @thesuiway on every social media platform. Find her at that handle on Twitter, Instagram, or BlueSky, or find her online at: www.thesuiway.com

Svitlana Taratorina is a Ukrainian SF&F writer from Crimea (the Ukrainian peninsula that was annexed by the Russians in 2014). She has worked in journalism and in political PR. Now she lives in Kyiv. She is the author of the urban fantasy *Lazarus*; of an artistic biography for children about the famous Ukrainian artist Maria Prymachenko; and of an acclaimed comic about teenagers from the front-line territories, *Sounds of Peace* (the project was created with the support of UNDP in 2020). In 2023, Svitlana's second novel, *The House of Salt*, was published. This post-apocalyptic fantasy is based on the history of myths and legends of Crimea. She is a laureate of fantastic story contests—from the literary association *Star Fortress*, the magazine *Stos*, and the Brama festival of fantastic stories. Her work has been recognized with various literary awards including the Chrysalis Award 2019 from the European Society of Science Fiction, LitAkcent2018, and a Special Award of the Ukrainian Book Institute at the BookForum Best Book Award competition. She was included in *Focus* magazine's ranking of the 25 most mentioned writers of Ukraine in 2018. Svitlana is a co-founder of the YouTube project Fantastic Talk(s), which since March 2022 has conducted a series of charity interviews with world science fiction stars, including James S. A. Corey, Rebecca Quan, Peter Watts, Joe Abercrombie, Marissa Meyer, Joe Hill, Andrzej Sapkowski, Margaret Atwood, etc. In 2023, Fantastic Talk(s)' series of lectures on the history of Ukrainian SF&F was honored with the European Society of Science Fiction's Achievement Award for the best online publication. Taratorina's works have been published in Ukrainian, English, Polish, Azerbaijani, and Bulgarian. She is a member of PEN Ukraine.

Ostap Ukrainets was born in 1994 in Kalush, Ivano-Frankivsk. And yes, Ukainets is his real surname, not a writing pseudonym, and it really means "a Ukrainian." Ostap studied interpreting and comparative studies in Kyiv-Mohyla Academy; he was not yet 20 when he translated H. P. Lovecraft's "Herbert West—Reanimator" and T. S. Eliot's "Wasteland" into Ukrainian. He really likes working with the most translation-unfriendly writers: Peter Watts, Neil Stephenson, David Mitchell. He's also known as a writer, who debuted in 2017 with a short story "Malanka" in *Fantasy world* magazine. But mostly he is known in Ukraine for the YouTube channel "Your underground humanitarian studies," which he founded with Yevhen Lyr in 2020, during the pandemic. The channel is dedicated primarily to Ukrainian literature, language, history, and traditions.

Yuri Vynnychuk, one of independent Ukraine's most popular writers, was born in the city of Ivano-Frankivs'k in 1952. Unable to have his original works published until the early 1980s due to Soviet cultural policy, Vynnychuk would publish them as "translations" from ancient or made-up languages. Unable to obtain employment as a philologist, he worked as a freight handler and a painter. In 1987, he cofounded the cabaret theater Ne Zhurys'! (Don't Worry!), writing songs and scenes for its performances. Since 1990, he has worked as a journalist; he received the honorary title of Halyts'kyi Lytsar (Galician Knight) in 1999 for his weekly Post-Postup newspaper column written under the pseudonym Yuzio Observator (Yuzio the Observer). His own writing includes poetry, short stories and the novels *Vesniani ihry v osinnikh sadakh* (*Springtime Games in Autumn Orchards,* 2005) and *Tango smerti* (*Tango of Death,* 2012). *Tango smerti* was awarded the prestigious BBC Book of the Year prize for 2012. In the following years he published the novels *Pharmacy* (2015), *Censor of Dreams* (2016), *Lutetia* (2017), and *Sisters of Blood* (2018). His immensely popular two-volume history of the city of Lviv, *Lehendy L'vova*, is republished every year. His books have been published in the USA, France, Austria, Poland, Czech Republic, Bulgaria, Serbia, Croatia, China, Netherlands, and Israel.

Oleksiy Zhupansky is a Ukrainian publisher and writer. He is the author of the novels *The Children will Come to Me First* (2008), *Lakhmitnyk* (2012), and *Bless you, God! Black General Secretary* (2017); the collection of short stories *Domestic Satanism* (2010); and the novella *Autumn Numbness* (Meeting the Dead) (2023), the first in his "Wheel of the Year" cycle.

ABOUT OUR EDITORS

Olha Brylova has lived in Dnipro, Ukraine, since her early childhood and cannot imagine living in a city without a big river. She has studied Japanese language and literature at Oles Honchar Dnipro National University, translated Japanese poetry into Ukrainian, and written several novels; recently, she has been writing screenplays for TV and video games. She dreams of becoming a showrunner of a big SF TV series and is sure that one day she will become one. Olha doesn't fixate on any one particular genre—she has written fantasy, space opera, speculative fiction, and her next big thing is a detective story. She is also a huge cinephile and runs a blog about movies and TV series in partnership with her son Arsenii. She loves cats, including the one that is nibbling at her toes right now.

Iryna Pasko lives in Dnipro, Ukraine. She graduated from Oles Honchar Dnipro National University, a candidate of philological sciences majoring in Ukrainian literature. She taught at her alma mater from 2013 to 2022, and now works at the New Ukrainian School media and at the Dnipro Art Museum. Iryna has been shortlisted for the ПроМинуле historical short story contest three times; and she has twice won the *Star Fortress* fantastic short story contest. In 2021, Iryna was a finalist in the all-Ukrainian poetry competition Granoslov. In 2021-2022, she participated in the *Independence Agency* project, a collection of fantastic stories dedicated to the 30th anniversary of the restoration of Ukraine's Independence; and *Legendarium of the Wonder Cities* (retellings of fairy tales). In 2022, Iryna wrote the online comic *Things*, about the experience of living through the war in a relatively safe city, and she co-organized the fantasy-poetry competitions at the All Mor festival (2022) and the story competition #рак_боятись_не_можна (don't fear cancer) in 2022-2023. Before the full-scale war, Iryna collaborated with the Book Space Dnipro and Gogolfest (in Dnipro and Mariupol), as a lecturer and tour guide.

Valya Dudycz Lupescu is a writer, poet, and editor living in Chicago. She is the author of the *The Silence of Trees*, a magical realism novel drawing upon Ukrainian folklore and history, as well as co-author of the nonfiction books *Geek Parenting* and *Forking Good*. The first volume of her new graphic novel trilogy, *Mother Christmas*, was published by Rosarium Publishing in 2022. Valya earned her M.F.A. in Writing from the School of the Art Institute of Chicago, and her work has been published in *The Year's Best Dark Fantasy & Horror, Kenyon Review, Gone Lawn, Jersey Devil Press, Strange Horizons, Mythic Delirium*, and others. She is the founding editor of *Conclave: A Journal of Character* and co-founder of the Wyrd Words Storytelling Workshop. Valya has been making magic with food and words for more than 30 years, incorporating traditions from her Ukrainian heritage with practices that honor the Earth.

ABOUT OUR TRANSLATORS

Konstantin Boulich is a Ukrainian-born translator living in Cambridge, U.K. He also volunteers teaching English to Ukrainian refugees in Cambridge. Konstantin translates fiction, academic books, and TV documentaries. His last big translation project was the award-winning documentary "Ukraine Under Attack" (Channel 4, PBS).

Kateryna Darchyk is a Ukrainian translator and subtitler who works with English and Spanish languages. She translates theater performances, plays and short stories, and aims to give Ukrainian authors and creators a voice among foreign readers. Kateryna is an active member of the Ukrainian community in Cambridge, UK, who organises cultural events and literature evenings to bring Ukrainian culture to people in Cambridgeshire. She has worked with the International Center for Ukrainian Victory (ICUV) and volunteered in various humanitarian and campaigning organizations to help bring the Ukrainian victory closer.

Claire Haffner is a translator and editor from Chicago, Illinois. After graduating with a BA in Russian Literature from the University of Chicago, she received a Fulbright to teach in Penza, Russia. She holds an MA in Russian from Middlebury College and an MS in Russian Politics and Society from King's College London. Currently, she is a Russian-English editor and translator at Playrix, an international gaming company. Instagram: @booksnacks

Oksana Katsanivska is a certified linguist specializing in English-Ukrainian translation. She has worked as a translator of nonfiction literature (including *Living Forward* by Michael Hyatt and Daniel Harkavy, *Onward* by Howard Schultz, *The IKEA Story* by Bertil Torekull, *Born to Run* by Christopher McDougal, and *Unlimited Memory* by Kevin Horsley) and as an interpreter for Dr. Jordan Karsten during his archeological excavations in Ukraine. She has also conducted private English lessons for adults and teenagers. Katsanivska is a lecturer at the University of Wisconsin Oshkosh, where she teaches classes on comparative linguistics, food anthropology, linguistic anthropology, contemporary Ukrainian literature, and Russo-Ukrainian conflict.

Svetlana Lavochkina is a Ukrainian-born, internationally published novelist, poet and literary translator. She has lived in Germany since 1999. Lavochkina was a prize winner in the Paris Literary Prize, The Winged Lion Literary Prize, Lviv, and finalist in the Tibor Jones Pageturner Prize, London. Since the onset of war in 2022, Lavochkina has been continuously raising awareness of Ukraine in germanophone mass media.

Hanna Leliv is a freelance translator originally from Lviv, Ukraine. She was a Fulbright fellow at the University of Iowa's literary translation M.F.A. program and a mentee at the Emerging Translators Mentorship Program run by the UK National Center for Writing. Her translations of contemporary Ukrainian literature into English have appeared in Asymptote, BOMB, Washington Square Review, Circumference, and elsewhere. In 2022, *Cappy and the Whale* by Kateryna Babkina was published in her translation by Penguin Random House UK, becoming the first children's book from Ukraine to come out with this publisher. Hanna was the Leslie Center Faculty Fellow at Dartmouth College, and has recently moved to Princeton as its Fall 2023 Translator-in-Residence. Find her online at: Hannaleliv.com.

Gari Light is a Chicago-based poet who was born in Kyiv, Ukraine in 1967 and has lived in the United States since 1980. He received his B.A. in Slavic literature studies from Northwestern University before becoming a lawyer and working in the area of international juris-prudence. Gari's poetry has been published regularly in the literary journals and poetry anthologies of the United States, Canada, Israel, Europe, and Ukraine over the past 30 years. He is a member of the American PEN Center and the Writer's Union of Ukraine. His most recent books are the English-language collection *Confluences* (Bagriy, 2020; Kayala, 2020) and the trilingual poetry book *Doloroso* (in English, Ukrainian and Russian), published virtually simultaneously in Kyiv, Ukraine (OFP, 2022) and Chicago-Boston (Bagriy, 2023).

Michael M. Naydan is Woskob Family Professor of Ukrainian Studies and professor of Slavic languages and literature at The Pennsylvania State University. Dr. Naydan has published over 50 articles on literary topics and more than 80 translations in journals and anthologies. His more than 40 books of published and edited translations include Yuri Vynnychuk's novel *Tango of Death* and Maria Matios' novel *Sweet Darusya: A Tale of Two Villages*, both with Spuyten Duyvil Publishers in New York in 2019; Nikolai Gumilev's *Africa* (Glagoslav Publishers, 2018); Yuri Andrukhovych's essays, *My Final Territory: Selected Essays* (University of Toronto Press, 2018); and Abram Terz's literary essays, *Strolls with Pushkin* and *Journey to the River Black* (Columbia University Press, 2016).

In 2017 he published his literary essays in Ukrainian translation in the volume *From Gogol to Andrukhovych: Selected Literary Essays* (Piramida Publishers). He has also published a novel about the city of Lviv, *Seven Signs of the Lion* (Glagoslav Publishers, 2016), which appeared in 2017 in Ukrainian translation under the title *Sim znakiv leva* (Piramida Publishers). He has received numerous prizes for his translations including the George S.N. Luckyj Award in Ukrainian Literature Translation from the Canadian Foundation for Ukrainian Studies in 2013.

Alla Perminova is a professor of English at the Autonomous University of Barcelona and a practicing literary translator from and into Ukrainian, English, and Spanish. She received her doctoral and postdoctoral degrees in translation studies from Taras Shevchenko National University of Kyiv where she worked as a full professor for 15 years. She is an Oleh Olzhych National Literary Contest first prize winner (1997), Fulbright senior scholar (The Pennsylvania State University, 2012-2013), the author of 70 scholarly articles, translator and/or editor of 20 books, and presenter of over 30 talks at international conferences. Her personal philosophy as a translator and a researcher is discussed in her book *A Translator's Reception of Contemporary American Poetry* (in Ukrainian, 2015), in which she promotes the reception model of literary translation. She can be reached at: linkedin.com/in/alla-perminova-613913204.

Tetiana Savchynska is a literary translator working between Ukrainian and English. She holds an M.A. in comparative literature from Dartmouth College, where she studied on a Fulbright Scholarship. She was a 2019 resident at the Banff International Literary Translation Centre in Canada, a 2022 graduate of the British Centre for Literary Translation and Bristol Translates Summer Schools, and a 2023 mentee at the National Center for Writing's Emerging Translator Mentorship program in the UK. Her writing and translations into English have appeared in *The Los Angeles Review of Books*, *Asymptote*, *Apofenie*, and elsewhere.

Bogi Takács (e/em/eir/emself or they pronouns) is a Hungarian Jewish author, editor, critic and scholar who's an immigrant to the United States. Bogi has won the Lambda and Hugo awards, and has been a finalist for other awards. E edited three volumes of *Transcendent: The Year's Best Transgender Speculative Fiction.* Eir debut poetry collection, *Algorithmic Shapeshifting,* and eir debut short story collection, *The Trans Space Octopus Congregation,* were both released in 2019, and eir second collection, *Power to Yield and Other Stories,* is coming in late 2023. You can find Bogi talking about books at bogireadstheworld.com, and on various social media like Twitter, Patreon and Instagram as bogiperson.

COVER ARTWORK

The cover art "Metahutsulka" by Ukrainian artist Taras Kopansky is based on a famous 1926 photograph taken by Mykola Senkovskyi of 90-year-old Hutsul elder and folk singer Maria Krechuniek, also known as Chukutykha. A military photographer by trade, Senkovskyi was one of the first to capture in photographs the life and rituals of the Hutsul people of western Ukraine. Senkovskyi set up a workshop in Kolomyia, where he photographed nearby villages and made post-cards with views of the Carpathian mountains. The black and white portrait of Krechuniek, presented in 1931 as part of Senkovskyi's collection "Hutsul Characters" at the International European Photo Exhibition in Paris, won the exhibition's highest grand prix honor.

ARTIST STATEMENT:

"In my opinion, the survival of culture is a remarkable symbol of the strength of the nation. So on the cover I decided to rethink the image of the most famous Hutsul woman in the world through the prism of fiction."

Art has been with me since I was a child. I was born into a Transcarpathian family of artists, and I became interested in graphics at a young age, after contemplating the works of Yakutovych. Even in childhood, I was carried away by the paintings of such artists as Gustav Klimt, Vladyslav Yerko, and William Blake, whose use of symbolism would be reflected in my own art in the future.

One of the key motivations for my art is the exploration of the inner human world and humanity's relationship with the natural world. I depict human consciousness symbolically—my vision of the intricacies of the human soul and body. Attracting the viewers' attention to my work, I want them to consider the subtle nuances that I put into it. They are not only a personal expression, designed to share some perceived beauty, they also resonate with problems of the modern world.

Even my principal motif of unity with nature is quite relevant in our time, when humanity is increasingly rejecting the natural world. The polyptych "Testamentum Cyber" depicts the opposite pole of today—human unity with the technological, which is the reverse side of my leitmotif. I often incorporate allegorical, abstract, and floral images, as in my series "Carnivores" where human figures are intertwined with carnivorous plants. My last graphic project, "The Truth," had an abstract background outside the figures, which is both a decorative element and a plot component.

Often I refer to visuals of cultural heritage, both Ukrainian and international. I put my own ideological images in surreal or collage-montage compositions to create a personal imaginary world. I prefer to build compositions by combining the compositional principles of Suprematism with the visual style from Modernism, a philosophy reflected in my creative concepts.

Because I create mostly black and white graphics, the way I work with light becomes important. I usually depict light either conditionally absent, to focus on the context of the work, or as a contrasting line of light to emphasize certain forms, and in some cases to dramatize the plot.

Although some of my work can be called monumental in scale, I mostly work with miniatures, which in my opinion allow me to direct the viewer's gaze onto the entirety of the work. In this way, my focus is not to create a large-scale visual manifestation for the community, but a whisper that I can share with attentive viewers by way of the secret thoughts that I embed in my works.

You can see more of Taras's work on his Instagram account:

www.instagram.com/taras_ttaras

PUBLICATION HISTORY AND COPYRIGHTS

"An Embroidered World" by Yuriy Vynnychuk, translated by Michael Naydan, originally appeared in *Kenyon Review,* Summer 1996.

"Svitla" by A.D. Sui, original work, *Embroidered Worlds*, 2023.

"Havrylovna" by Oleksiy Zhupansky, translated by Kateryna Darchyk. Translated from «Гавриловна» Олексій Жупанський, Babai.co.ua, 2020.

"Geddarien" by R.B. Lemberg, originally appeared in *Fantasy Magazine*, December 2008.

"Neptune's Day" by Ostap Ukrainets, translated by Oksana Katsanivska. Translated from «День Нептуна» Остап Українець, Tyktor Media, 2022.

"Closest to the Pole" by Max Kidruk, translated by Tetiana Savchynska. Translated from «Ближче Всіх до Полюса» Макс Кідрук, Babai.co.ua, 2023.

"Big Nose and the Faun" by Mykhailo Nazarenko, translated by Claire Haffner. Translated from «Носатый и фавн» Михайло Назаренко, Реальность фантастики No 10, October 2004.

"A Bitter Thing" by N. R. M. Roshak, originally appeared in *Writers of the Future Volume 34*, Galaxy Press, 2018.

"The Dreamers of Ungvár" by Éva Berniczky, translated by Bogi Takács. Translated from "Ungvári álmodozók", szifonline.hu, 2022.

"Three Forest Tales" by David Demchuk, originally appeared in *The Bone Mother*, Proving Ground Press, 2020.

"The Bike Shadow" by Yaryna Katorozh, translated by Kateryna Darchyk. Translated from «Велосипедник» Ярина Каторож, KM Books, 2017.

"Iron Goddess of Compassion" by Olha Brylova, translated by Anatoly Belilovsky, originally appeared in *Futuristica, Volume II*, Metasagas Press, 2017. Translated from «Залізна богиня милосердя» Ольга Брильова, heartofsword.eu, 2012-2014.

"Three Love Stories" by Anatoly Belilovsky, excerpt from *Halogen Nightmares and Other Love Stories*, 2021, originally published as "Ghost Nutrients", *Breath and Shadow*, Issue 4 Vol 17, Fall 2020; "Virror Virror", *Daily Science Fiction*, 18 Sep 2020; "Bottled Up", Nature, 13 Nov 2013.

"A Hole In The Shape Of God" by Vasyl Dukhnovskyi, translated by Tetiana Savchynska. Translated from «Діра у формі бога» Василь Духновський, Зоряна Фортеця, 2021.

"The Stray Streetcar (A '90s Businessman's Tale)" by Myroslava Hornostayeva, translated by Konstantin Boulich. Translated from «Заблуканий трамвай» Мирослава Горностаєва, Чтиво, 2009.

"The Rainbow Bridge" by Iryna Pasko, translated by Hanna Leliv. Translated from «Веселковий міст» Ірина Пасько, Зоряна Фортеця, 2020.

"Lest We Forget" by Elizabeth Bear, orginally appeared in *Uncanny Magazine*, Issue 28, 2019.

"Scream" by Olena Krasnoselska, translated by Oksana Katsanivska. Translated from «Крик» Олена Красносельська, Письменницький портал / pilipyurik.com, 2020.

"The Midst of Snow" by Oleksiy Gedeonov, translated by Svetlana Lavochkina. Translated from «Середина снігу» Олексій Гедеонов, Babel Premiya, 2017.

"The Long Black Veil" by Stefan O. Rak, original work, *Embroidered Worlds*, 2023.

"Family v1.1" by Ihor Silivra, translated by Konstantin Boulich. Translated from «Сім'я v1.1» Ігор Сілівра, Зоряна Фортеця, 2014.

"In the Belly of the Dinosaur" by Károj D. Balla, translated by Bogi Takács. Translated from "A dinoszaurusz gyomrában", litera.hu, July 2021.

"A Brief History of the Little : People" by Askold Melnyczuk orginally appeared in *The Man Who Would Not Bow & Other Stories*, Grand Iota 2021.

"The Last of the Beads" by Halyna Lipatova, translated by R.B. Lemberg. Translated from «Волшебные бусины» Галина Ліпатова, 2017.

"Revenge in Pursuit" by Vira Balatska, translated by Michael M. Naydan and Alla Perminova. Translated from «Помста навздогін» Віра Балацька, arkush.net, 2021.

"To See Jupiter" by Oleh Silin, translated by Anatoly Belilovsky. Translated from «Побачити Юпітер» Олег Сілін, Пісня з орбіти, Інфа-Принт, 2021.

"Honey" by Valya Dudycz Lupescu, originally appeared in *A World of Horror*, Dark Moon Books, 2018. Also appeared in *The Year's Best Dark Fantasy & Horror*, Prime Books, 2019.

"'Kestrel' Travel Agency by Tetyana Adamenko, translated by Gari Light. Translated from «Турагенція "Боривітер"» Тетяна Адаменко.

"Battle of the Gods" by Svitlana Taratorina, translated by Tetiana Savchynska. Translated from excerpt of «Дім солі» Світлана Тараторіна, Vivat, 2023.

"To the Garden" by Volodymyr Arenev, translated by Hanna Leliv. Translated from «Туди, де буде сад» Володимир Аренєв, Old Lion Publishing, 2022.

CONTENT NOTES

Content notes are included for those with sensitivity to or who may prefer to avoid certain topics.

Stories in this collection deal heavily with war, violence, and grief. Discussions of war generally deal with and mention fascism and real-life historical events and atrocities. Discussions and mentions of violence or death often deal with a close family member, including children and animals.

Our primary goal with this collection was to offer authentic Ukrainian storytelling of this era to English-speaking audiences, rather than curate a new collection. While some issues of sensitivity not affecting the overall story or voice were addressed, others were left in place, with the listed content to provide notice.

Pages 3-7 ("An Embroidered World")
 mentions of imprisonment, alcoholism, racism

Pages 8-21 ("Svitla")
 body horror, mother-daughter relationships, hospitals

Pages 22-31 ("Havrylovna")
 poverty, death, killing, rot and stench, slurs, disturbed sleep

Pages 32-48 ("Geddarien")
 violence, antisemitic violence, murder, mass murder, smoking, description of a corpse, rats feeding on a corpse

Pages 49-63 ("Neptune's Day")
 war, fire, ethnic and ableist slurs, smoking, mentions of alcohol, bodily fluids

Pages 64-87 ("Closer to the Pole")
body horror, asphyxiation, detailed description of dying, colonialist language

Pages 88-109 ("Big Nose and the Faun")
colonialist language, pain, death, grief, mention of slavery

Pages 110-132 ("A Bitter Thing")
sex, drinking, dating, ableist language, mentions of bestiality, lynching, pornography, drugs, addiction, masturbation

Pages 133-137 ("The Dreamers of Ungvár")
mention of war

Pages 138-146 ("Three Forest Tales")
cannibalism, illness, vomiting, child abuse, drowning, death, hunting, grief

Pages 147-157 ("The Bike Shadow")
injury, slurs

Pages 158-177 ("Iron Goddess of Compassion")
smoking, war, impacts of war, suicide bombing, disfigurement, workplace stress, industrial accidents, violence, transphobic language

Pages 178-184 ("Three Love Stories")
judgment and withholding of treats, grief, mentions of weight, cancer

Pages 185-197 ("A Hole in the Shape of God")
ableist slurs, stabbing, shooting, blood, flippant discussion of serious topics, mentions of drugs, self-harm

Pages 198-209 ("The Stray Streetcar (A '90s Businessman's Tale)")
organized crime, killing, death, visions of the deceased, slurs, ableist slurs, classism, sexism, substance overuse, mention of suicide

Pages 210-221 ("The Rainbow Bridge")
misogynistic language, control, mentions of bodily fluids, violence, serpents

Pages 222-230 ("Lest We Forget")
war crimes, torture, medical trials, parasitism, mentions of cancer, alcoholism, rape, child starvation, PTSD

Pages 231-241 ("Scream")
death, grief, disrespect to graves

Pages 242-252 ("The Midst of Snow")
war, impacts of war, misogyny, ableism, rape, violent racism, racist slurs, physical distress, illness, bodily fluids, abuse, apocalyptic language

Pages 253-256 ("The Long Black Veil")
death, surreal references to body

Pages 257-268 ("Family v1.1")
brain manipulation, slurs, frequent and strong ableist slurs, fire, mentions of torture, killing, eugenics

Pages 269-274 ("In the Belly of the Dinosaur")
confusion, fear, anxiety

Pages 275-292 ("A Brief History of the Little : People")
sexist and ableist language, indigenous appropriation, references to distressing real-life issues and incidents

Pages 293-304 ("The Last of the Beads")
murder, revenge, child torture, settlers, fire, mass killing, spirits

Pages 305-315 ("Revenge in Pursuit")
eugenics, genetic slurs, mention of alcohol

Pages 316-323 ("To See Jupiter")
suicide, blood, enclosed spaces

Pages 324-338 ("Honey")
beekeeping, danger, death, grief, impacts of war, alcohol, mention of cancer

Pages 339-346 ("'Kestrel' Travel Agency")
serial killing, misogyny, poison, mentions of rape, dismemberment

Pages 347-365 ("Battle of the Gods")
shipwreck, colonialist language, dehumanizing language, imprisonment, blood, death, childbirth, infection, description of corpses, ritual murder, ableist language, body horror, mention of infant death, mass killings, disfigurement, insanity

Pages 366-381 ("To the Garden")
war, impacts of war, dehumanizing language